All the Finer Things

A Novel ~

All the Finer Things

A Novel ~

Stephanie Connelley WORLTON

Spring Canyon
MEDIA

ISBN-13: 978-0991458905

Published by Spring Canyon Media.
Herriman, Utah

Library of Congress Control Number: 2014903950

To Ryan. My life is full of the very finest things because you choose each day to love me!

Acknowledgements

There are many people who make it possible for me to share my stories. First and foremost, my children. It must be tough to share your mom with a keyboard. More than one dinner has been made at the hand of my capable, amazing children. More than one load of laundry has gone stale in the washing machine. And certainly more than one conversation has been tolerated about my "imaginary friends." Thank you for putting up with this Krazy Mama of yours! I hope I haven't damaged you too much.

To my awesome Beta readers: Jaynan, Kathy, Tiffanie, Raelin, Cindy, Laura, and Sally. Thanks to your keen eye, brutal critique, and honest feedback, I have a few new gray hairs, but I also have a book that I am proud of. You guys are rock stars!

And a special thanks to the man with the ruthless red pen and the not-so-gentle but ever insightful evaluations of my drafts. Thanks for finding the holes in my story and the magic solutions for filling them. It takes a special man to love me despite my many, many make-up free, frumpy hair, pj's and t-shirts kind of days. You are my biggest strength… and my greatest weakness. I love you, Ryan. Thanks for believing in me!

Chapter One

The front door closed almost as abruptly as it opened, rattling the framed photos on the wall. A rippling chill coursed through the dark foyer and into the parlor at the clank of car keys tossed onto the glass entry table. There was a brief, hopeful moment of silence before the hard soles of Matt's patent leather shoes thumped their way heavily over the polished mahogany floor. Megan sat motionless on the low-backed sofa, watching his labored movement across the obsessively organized room. Pursing her lips so tightly they'd become numb, she waited for his recognition.

"What are you still doing up?" He pulled his already loosened tie off his neck and tossed it - along with his suit coat - over the back of a sleek-lined black leather chair.

Wrapping her fingers around a brightly hued throw pillow, Megan swallowed back the anger threatening to burst out of her. "I was waiting for you." The words slid out across her quivering lips.

Shrugging off her comment, Matt worked his fingers down the front of his tailored dress-shirt, fumbling with each button as he did so.

Megan positioned the pillow intently into its place on the sofa before she stood. "I..." she curled her toes into the white shag throw rug, clenching back her frustration as she rephrased her thought. "Next time you're going to be late, can I please get a phone call?" She thought it was a reasonable request, considering, he expected to have dinner on the table precisely at seven o'clock.

Her bare feet left the plush warmth of the throw rug and padded their way across the cold wood floor towards the dining room. She gathered his unused utensils from the head of the glass dining table and placed them on top of his untouched, now five-hour-cold, chicken parmesan.

"Sorry," he said, non-apologetically, giving up on the third button. "I had some stuff to do at the office."

"I'll bet," Megan mumbled to herself. She gathered his dishes into her hands and, stopping just long enough to blow out the flickering stub of a candle on the center of the table, paced heavily into the kitchen. Guided only by the illumination of the city lights pressing through the floor-to-ceiling windows, her feet made the distinction between the smooth finish of the hardwood that interlaced most of their two bedroom penthouse and the rough, unforgiving texture of the eighteen inch slate on the kitchen floor. Making her way around the sizable island, she dumped Matt's warm drink into the sink. Focused on controlling her frustration, she pulled at the lip on the cabinet face, opening a well-disguised trash compactor.

"You got something you want to talk about?" Matt's voice echoed from the doorway.

Flinching at his tone, she dumped his dinner – plate and all - into the trash. "No," she offered softly, hoping to diffuse her husband's flippancy. The gate of his long-legged stance and the shiftiness of his tilted stagger were indication enough that he'd had more than a few drinks. Now was not the time to pick a fight.

Reaching her hand into the trash she retrieved the dropped plate. The cold slime of pasta and tomato sauce slopped over her skin and under her manicured nails causing her to cringe.

"Do you think ignoring me will solve your problem?"

Her problem. It was always *her* problem.

He didn't wait for an answer. "This is absolutely ridiculous – you stomping around this house like you're so hard done by. I give you everything..." he swung his arms out from his torso indicating the exquisiteness of their home and pricey possessions. "And just because I'm a little late coming home you think you have the right to get all huffy?"

Huffy? She set the tomato coated plate into the sink basin then stuck her hands under the tap, allowing the warm water to rinse over them. "I'm not huffy," she smiled over her shoulder, hoping he wouldn't catch the quiver in her voice or, worse yet, read unintentional indignation into it.

He moved across the room in three easy steps. "Then what are you?" He pressed his chest against her shoulders. His hot breath stung at her neck.

"I..." she shrugged. "I'm just tired and..." She didn't want to finish the thought. She didn't want to make him mad. She couldn't tell him that he'd hurt her. Today, of all days, he'd forgotten her. Surely he'd jotted the date down at least once while at the office. *Had he failed to make the connection or did he simply not care?* She shut the water off then wrapped her hands into a dishtowel.

"And what?" he grabbed her arms roughly, spinning her around to face him. His eyes, like weather worn battleships, were hard and grey. She'd already triggered something - a trace of the rage within him. "And what?" he demanded again.

Megan had to force herself to swallow. She had to stay calm. "And... and I was worried." Her heart was racing. She forced another smile. "I left a half a dozen messages on your cell phone," she explained, "and when you didn't call back... I... I started to get worried."

"Well here I am," he spat the words at her, "safe and sound like the big boy that I am!"

She flinched at the pungency of alcohol that lurched through Matt's lips and into her face. "What?" He gripped her arm even tighter, cocking his head as the last hint of softness drained from his face. "Am I not allowed to have a little drink after a hard day at work?"

She blinked back the fear in her eyes, afraid to speak. Afraid to cry.

"Huh?" he yelled, unnecessarily loud. "Answer me woman!"

"No, Matt... you know it's not like that," she tried to wiggle her arms free of his hurtful grasp, but that only made him constrict his fists tighter. "I'm sorry you had a bad day," a tear dropped down her cheek. Despite her sincerity, his demeanor held as tightly as his hands. The dishtowel fell limply to the floor.

"Did you make it to the gym today?" His glare was so intense she considered lying just to make him happy. He raised his eyebrows - an invitation to cross him.

"No," she dropped her head dejectedly. "Jacob was running a fever so I thought it'd be better for me to stay with him." She hoped he'd appreciate her truth but doubted the existence of any tender mercy. Even before she'd given birth to their son, Matt's disgust with her had begun to boil into fury. In the ten short months of Jake's life, Matt's discontent had become outright terrifying.

Every perfectly sculpted muscle in his face contorted as he tightened his jaw. "Why can't you understand that I have an image to maintain? I have

3

one of the most successful practices in the city. Do you think that comes without a price?" He lashed out and in a sudden movement her body flew across the room. Her hands, still tingling with the numbness from his grip, smacked onto the slate floor, cushioning the blow to her knees. Her forehead, however, was spared nothing as it struck the refrigerator door. Anchoring herself for another blow, she rolled into a ball and closed her eyes against the blurring spots in her vision.

"I should've never agreed to let you have *that baby*! I should've known that you'd be too lazy to take care of yourself." He shook his head. "Look at you. You're disgusting! The last thing a plastic surgeon can afford is a fat wife!"

What about a mangled one? The irony of his accusation seemed lost in the fire of his rage. Megan swiped at the warm stream on her forehead, preventing the trickle of blood from reaching her eye.

"I only weigh three pounds more than I did before I had him," she whispered. She thought of their sleeping son down the hallway as she gripped the edge of the countertop and pulled herself to her feet. Three pounds seemed like a small price to pay for such a sweet angel.

"Three pounds? Are you sure that's all?" Matt lunged at her, gripping the soft skin under her belly button. "Maybe I need to schedule a little nip-tuck for you. This..." he pinched roughly, leaving the indents of his fingertips in a bruise, "is unacceptable."

"Is that why you're having an affair?" As soon as the words slipped over her lips she wished she could suck them back in. This wasn't the time to bring up his new twenty-year old, bleach blonde, legs-to-the-moon receptionist.

"You think I'm having an affair?" He raised his brow over fury blazon eyes. "I have dinner with one of my assistants and all of a sudden I'm having an affair?" He knotted the neck of her blouse in his fist and twisted it powerfully into the base of her chin. She strained to keep her toes in contact with the tiles as her heels left the floor.

"I thought you said you had a bad day at work, not that you'd been out with Ashlee." Megan fired back before she could stifle the remark. She knew better than to egg him on. *Bite your tongue,* she warned herself. But it was already too late.

The tip of Matt's nose touched hers as he leaned in. "I *did* have a rough day," he barked. "And if I decide to go out to get some drinks or have some dinner, that's none of your business, is it?" It wasn't a question. He lifted her up by the tuft of her shirt and slammed her backwards into the pantry door before releasing his hold. Her bare feet closed the distance to the floor in record time and crashed brutally into the rough tile. A shock thrust from her ankles to her hips. Her knees buckled. Arms flailing, she tried hopelessly to gain control of her falling body. Blindly, she reached for the counter top. Her hand slid across the slick granite, pushing a glass sugar bowl in its path. Her body tumbled helplessly to the floor but not before sugar and glass were scattered from one corner of the kitchen to another.

"Now look what you've done," Matt's voice shook the glasses in the cupboard. "I'd suggest you clean up your mess before you come to bed." He kicked the broken jar out of his way. "I'd hate for Alessandra to have to deal with it in the morning."

He dusted his shoe over the sugar, spreading the pile even further across the floor. Rubbing his hand through his golden locks, he released another intoxicated breath as he squatted down to her level. "Why do you insist on making me so angry, Megan?" His voice was suddenly calm. "I wish you wouldn't push me so far." He tilted her chin up with the tip of his finger, forcing her to look at his smug face as his voice softened even more. "You know how much I hate fighting, and..." he touched the wound on her forehead gently, "I'm really sorry about this." He ran his eyes over the wound, expertly assessing the damage. "It's pretty superficial," he nodded. "Just a tiny little cut. Head wounds are always bleeders but it'll heal pretty fast. You'll be as good as new in couple of days. Just like it never happened." He stood up, slid his hands into the pockets of his slacks and turned to leave.

"Hurry and get this mess cleaned up," he added on his way out the door. "I'm tired." He ambled out of the room, kicking arrogantly at the sugar dust as he went.

Megan slumped back into the floor, her body shaking uncontrollably. She buried her face into her hands, grateful Matt's anger had dissolved as quickly as it had. She'd lost count of all the times before when it hadn't.

Her head throbbed and swirled with pain. The tops of her arms were throbbing too, pressurizing tighter and tighter with each beat of her heart, as if his hands were still wrapped fiercely around them. Slowly, she gained her composure then crawled away from the pantry door and methodically pulled her way off the floor.

He was right about at least one thing, she admitted: the wounds were just superficial. Her heart, however, had suffered a near fatal blow. "Happy anniversary," she whispered as she reached for the broom. "Happy anniversary, Matt."

Chapter Two

Megan hugged the down comforter to her chest waiting for the front door to close before she dare move. Matt had surgeries scheduled in the morning but that wouldn't change his routine. If he was anything, he was predictable. By nine-thirty there would be a delivery man at her door with a ridiculously pompous bouquet of flowers, followed by a smooth-talking phone call apology around noon, topped off with an expensive bottle of wine, suave compliments, and overt affection when he got home this evening.

She drew a deep breath as the door clicked closed. He was gone. She tossed the blankets aside and headed straight for the shower. Tracing the small porcelain tiles with her eyes, Megan set the water temperature then climbed in and let the heat wash over her. Every inch of their penthouse was a testimony to the ideals that Matt held important. Image was everything... from the fine, designer clothes that filled their closet to their trendy modern furnishings. Their former kitchen and bathrooms - which Megan loved - weren't contemporary enough to satisfy Matt's taste, so he'd hired a designer to transform their home into a show room. The penthouse now sported clean lines, crisp colors, and sharp angles. It was elegant, to be sure, but it lacked the warmth of a home.

Megan was afraid to live... afraid that the baby might hit his head on the corner of one of the glass tables or scrape his knees on the slate floor. She was afraid that he might get Matt's precious white rug dirty or leave his fingerprints on the shiny surface of the stainless steel appliances. She was afraid... afraid that one day Matt might turn on Jacob the same way he'd turned on her.

Steam filled the room as she shampooed dry chunks of blood from her scalp. They swirled into brown streaks before disappearing down the drain. This was a routine becoming all too familiar. She stepped from the shower and cleared the fog from the bathroom mirror, second-guessing her resolve before noticing the dark bruises on each of her biceps. Perfectly delineated black and blue hand imprints screamed back from her reflection. Nobody would ever believe that they'd been left by the skilled, precise hands of a surgeon. Nobody would ever believe that Matt – debonair, charming, perfect Dr. Hamilton – would hurt a fly, let alone his own wife.

Retrieving her cell phone from her handbag, she stretched her arms in front of her body and snapped a camera shot of the incriminating marks. For good measure, she took a couple more, zooming in to get a close up of the angry gash radiating from her forehead. Hearing Jacob's morning whimper, she drafted an email to her lawyer, attached the photos, then powered off her phone and tossed it in her purse.

"Hey baby!" she smiled, responding to Jacob's outstretched arms. He'd been crawling for quite some time now and had just begun to pull himself up to a stand. "Before long," she giggled as he lifted his foot up onto one of the crib rails only to have it slip down again, "you're going to figure out how to get out of here, aren't you?" He was an ever-bouncing ball of energy. Mischievous and determined in his mobility, she was sure he'd be walking soon.

She lifted him out of his crib and he responded by snuggling his head tightly into her chest. Losing herself in his tiny embrace, she stroked the soft, blonde whisps of hair on his head. He'd inherited all of his father's best features... his striking blue eyes, his long, agile fingers, his dimpled grin, and his flaxen, curly hair. She kissed the top of his head, savoring his sweet, baby smell. This was love - unadulterated, unconditional, and unceasing. *What more did she need?*

After feeding and bathing Jacob, Megan stationed him on her bedroom floor with a box of building blocks and a collection of chunky little plastic people, animals, and vehicles. The toys, however, provided little entertainment. He was much more interested in emptying the bathroom drawers.

"Thank you, buddy," she reached around him, retrieving Matt's electric razor from his curious little hand and replacing it with one of her plastic handled brushes. He looked at it oddly, inquisitively touching the tips of his fingers to the ball-tipped bristles before roughly smacking it towards his head.

"Soft." She encompassed his hand in hers and gently guided the bristles through his tender curls. "Just like this," she kissed his head then stepped over him and into the closet.

Standing on a stool to reach, Megan pulled her largest suitcase off of the top shelf, unintentionally bringing Matt's carry-on bag down with it. The carry-on hit the floor with a bounce, sending a stream of post cards fanning out of it. Jacob heard the disturbance and was quickly on his way to investigate. Megan set her suitcase down and moved quickly to the floor, gathering the mess before his curious little hands had a chance to get a hold of it. She admired the collection – Venice, Paris, London, Hamburg, Saint Lucia, Hawaii, Miami, Puerto Rico, Cancun - post cards from everywhere that she and Matt had been together. She cradled the memories to her chest with the realization of all that she'd lost. Those happy, carefree days would never be hers again.

Systematically moving her way around the huge closet, she filled a small suitcase with all of her most treasured shoes. Thoughtfully she opened her larger suitcase and gathered some clothes. With spring in early bloom, she grabbed only a couple lightweight sweaters, anxious for warmer weather to roll in. Nothing too ostentatious, she decided... except... well... *she really couldn't leave it hanging there in all its ruby splendor, could she?* Matt couldn't wear it and he certainly couldn't take it back. It'd been custom tailored to her; a gift for Christmas that she'd yet to wear. She added the crimson Vera-Wang gown to her suitcase and pushed things around until there was room for her coordinating Jimmy Choo's. She zipped the overstuffed luggage closed and dragged it to the front door before returning to the bathroom to fill Matt's carry-on bag with a few more essentials.

"Almost ready, Jake." She scooped his cuddly little body off the bathroom floor and playfully kissed his ear as they made their way into his bedroom. Two bulging Gucci diaper bags and a small satchel full of toys later, she worked through her mental checklist. "Clothes, blankets, diapers... and," she rummaged through the laundry room cabinet, retrieving a stack of legal-sized envelopes.

Two of the three manila envelopes got tucked immediately into the front pocket of her suitcase. The third she placed at the head of the dining table where Matt would surely be expecting to find his dinner tonight. She ran her fingers over the neatly printed letters on the front of the packet. "*Dr. Matthew R. Hamilton,*" they read.

The doorbell chimed, reminding her of the time. Just as she'd predicted a smiling young delivery boy greeted her across the threshold. "Someone must really love you!" he snapped his gum behind the massive bouquet of roses.

"You'd think so, wouldn't you?" She sighed, wishing it was true. She pushed the pile of luggage to the side with her foot and opened the door wide enough for him to bring the monstrous display inside.

He settled the crystal vase onto the center of the dining table. "Nice place." His eyes darted around the room. "Is your husband a lawyer or something?" he innocently inquired.

"Plastic surgeon," Megan answered as she signed the delivery slip and politely ushered the boy out the door. "Thank you," she smiled, sliding a hundred dollar bill into his hand.

His face flushed. She guessed that it was the biggest tip he'd ever gotten. "Are... you... sure?" he stuttered, offering the bill back.

"Yep," she smirked, "the good doctor's got plenty more where that came from."

"Th... thanks." He turned on his heel, moving quickly down the hall. He rubbed the bill between his fingers for a moment then tucked it into his pocket.

"Have a nice day," Megan called after him before closing the door.

She moved across the room toward the gigantic flower arrangement. Pretentious as it was, the sparks of colorful blossoms were breathtaking. She touched a rose bud to her nose, deeply sucking in its rich aroma. Her heart fluttered. He'd really outdone himself this time. Maybe it was a sign. Maybe things really would be different from now on.

She glanced at the pile of luggage by the front door, then out the penthouse window at the majestic Los Angeles skyline before pulling the attached card out of its envelope. She fumbled with a moment of hesitation then read the handwritten message out loud. "I'm sorry. It will never happen again."

She set the card down on the table and stared blankly at the beautiful possessions that filled her home. A single tear escaped her eye as she wrung her hands tightly together. "*Is it really that bad?*" she asked herself. The crisp, sleek lines of furniture blurred together through her moist eyes.

"He really is a good man most of the time," she reasoned, her momentum defusing.

Wiping the moisture from her eyes, she smiled down at Jacob's chunky form sitting on her toes as he admired his reflection in the lustrous, black table base. Watching her son innocently explore his world, her resolve returned. She could endure for herself, but for Jacob... there was nothing that could stop her from preserving his safety.

After scribbling her own message furiously onto the bottom of Matt's pseudo-apologetic card, she slid the extravagant gold band off of her left hand and placed it at the base of the floral arrangement.

"Let's go, buddy!" She swooped Jacob off the floor and hugged him tenderly. Reaching her hand into her purse, she dug through the mess for her car keys. "Won't be needing this anymore," she grunted, pulling her country club membership out of her wallet. She looked over the plastic card one time then tossed it carelessly onto the entry table. She sent a text to Alessandra, allowing her to take the day off, called the doorman for assistance with her bags, hitched Jacob to her hip, and walked out the penthouse door.

Chapter Three

Doctor Matt Hamilton slid his silver Jaguar XKR convertible into his reserved spot of the parking garage and popped the transmission into park. There weren't many things he loved more than his car... in fact, off the top of his head he couldn't think of any. It was a Jag, of course, need he say more? He'd custom ordered it from the factory, and even the dealership had been impressed by the sheer beauty of its every detail. It was a work of art; crisp, clean, curvaceous... as perfect as if he'd sculpted it with his own hand.

"I'm sure they'd love it, Kat," he spoke into his blue-tooth with mock enthusiasm as he polished the fingerprints off his steering wheel with a handkerchief. "I'll have to reschedule my last couple of appointments on Friday, but that should be do-able," he said, feigning excitement for his mother-in-law's benefit. He was more enthusiastic about breaking in his new golf clubs than the actual invitation of a weekend with Jake, Megan, and his ostentatious in-laws at their beach house.

He folded the handkerchief into a perfect rectangle then tucked it back into his suit coat pocket. He retrieved a bottle of *Clos Du Mesnil* off the leather passenger seat then pulled the keys from the ignition.

"Our anniversary?" He smacked the base of the champagne bottle onto his thigh and cursed under his breath. Trust his mother-in-law to remember. "It was great!" He lied with polished fervor, hoping she didn't see through his muse. "Yeah, she'll have to show you what I gave her. You'll love it." He was going to have to go above and beyond his typical generosity to make this look good. "Okay Kat, sounds good. See you Friday night." He gave his car one last look-over then confidently made his way through the parking garage and into the elevator. He was going to need to plan a surprise so grandiose that it'd look like he'd intended to postpone their celebration all along. When he pulled it off, not even Megan would realize that he'd forgotten their anniversary.

He twisted the champagne bottle playfully in his hands and grinned. Based on the incredibly expensive bouquet he'd sent this morning, he anticipated a joyful, apology filled greeting. He pushed the front door open and stepped into the foyer. His cheerful disposition floundered at the unexpected darkness. "Meg?" he called into the silence, setting his keys gently onto the table as his eyes adjusted to the shadows. "Meg? Where are you?"

A glow of light from the master suite pierced through the otherwise dark penthouse, sparking a new excitement within him. He detoured to the bar for some champagne flutes before following the glow into his room. "Hey, baby!" he gloated cockily, pushing the door open. Surprised at the disheveled mess of the bed, his spirits wavered. "Meg?" he called. Setting the bottle and glasses down on the dresser, he stepped further into the room. "Megan?"

Following another glow of light, he stepped into the bathroom. Confused by the lack of tidiness, he walked by the cluttered countertop, knocking a fan of small papers to the ground as he passed by. He disjointedly gathered the stack of postcards into a pile and tapped them on the countertop before mentally connecting their presence in the rest of the clutter.

Adjusting his stare to the empty shelf where his luggage belonged, he threw the cards to the floor then rampaged through the penthouse flipping every light on.

As he moved from empty room after empty room, Matt's fury intensified. Silently he churned punishments through his head as he anticipated his wife's return home. *She's really done it this time*, he snarled as he brisked by the dining room, looking only for signs of life. He paced around the kitchen, not bothering to pick up a wayward shard of glass from the night before as he passed it by. He made mental note of it though, adding it to the ever growing list of things he was going to address when Megan got home.

He poured himself a drink, slamming the bar cabinet closed as he marched towards the living room. He'd wait for her as she'd waited for him, insolent, ungrateful wife that she was. Kicking his way across the floor like a spoiled child, he raised his glass to his lips but stopped short of tossing back the amber liquid.

Adjusting his saunter towards the dining table, Matt was momentarily distracted by the magnificent city skyline that lit up his windows. Wonderful as it was, it wasn't enough to hold his attention. He snapped his gaze back to the room. His vision immediately caught hold of the generous flower arrangement he'd had delivered early that morning. Barely noticing the massive bouquet sticking out of the crystal vase, he set his drink down and, almost hypnotically, picked up Megan's ring. "She wouldn't leave... she wouldn't dare..." he huffed under his breath. Twirling the three-carat diamond solitaire around his pinky finger – a full year's wages for some people, he noted, though it'd been nearly a drop in the bucket for him – his eyes fell to the words on the florist's card. *"I'm sorry. It will never happen again."* The florist's neat penmanship read was followed by two words in Megan's bubbly script: *"You're right!"*

Chapter Four

Ammon Carter let the wind dance across his face as he took in the sweet smell of the moisture-laden landscape. The sun painted stunning hues of gold and red across the mountain crest as it slowly rose to its full spring glory. It'd been a rainy season, more so than a typical Santa Clarita spring, and as Carter watched the sun rise, he was grateful for the previous evening's downpour. The ground was damp and even the smallest of cobwebs stretching from one grass blade to another bore the sparkle of a fresh, clean shower.

Grandma Beth had picked the plots at the Eternal Valley Memorial Park, stating that its name alone was reason enough, but ultimately sold by its accessibility off the Antelope Valley Freeway. Had she known that her final resting spot would be dug at the beginning of one of the wettest winters on record, she may have opted for a plot on a flatter grade. But she'd be pleased now, Carter thought, as he knelt by her headstone and placed a bouquet of fresh cut roses into the attached vase. After six months the sod had almost mended itself seamlessly across the earth.

He wiped the back of his hand across her neatly scrawled name. *Bethany Brown Carter* it read in the same font as the other five headstones lined up in a tight row. Almost ritualistically, he made his way down the line of matching granite markers, gently placing small bouquets at each one. *Ezra, Spencer, Julianne, Joseph,* and *Raychel.*

He took extra pause at Raychel's marker, gracing hers with soft pink carnations as he remembered the beautiful little girl that she'd been. She'd shared his dark, silken hair and golden eyes, though hers enviously bore more of the conversation starting blue flecks than his. She'd been a ball of energy; a constant delight. Hers had been the first arms to greet him each morning and the last to let go and say good bye on that fateful day.

There were times he'd cursed the very God that had taken his family and left him alone in the world, but as the dawn broke, he found himself at peace in the quiet morning. He laced his fingers together and said a silent prayer. Today was a new day, as each one before it had been. He'd keep moving forward... just as he'd always done.

He drove with the window down, letting the cool morning dance across his scratchy, unshaven face and the wind tussle his hair. Bosco filled the passenger seat, his head pressed out the window to drink in the wind as his jowls flapped back like empty parachutes. The dog was more than a pet, he was Carter's friend. And a big one at that. Their weights were nearly equal, although surely the bullmastiff's hundred and seventy five pounds were mostly in his giant head and massive shoulders.

Carter adjusted the radio then glanced at himself in the rearview mirror. Though he'd never been heavy, without Grandma Beth around to keep him fed, he'd lost a bit of weight.

He exited the freeway and turned onto the two lane highway that curved its way towards home. The smell of wet farmland and water-beaded orchards laced the damp air. A sign posting the reduced speed limit was the only indication of Mountainside's border. For about one mile, the highway would become Main Street, then as abruptly as it had started, it would convert back to highway. Anyone not intent on stopping would fly on through without even knowing they'd been there.

Carter pulled his old truck to the side of the road and, leaving the windows down for Bosco, entered the familiar diner. No sooner had his boots touched the establishment's worn tiles then the motherly proprietor's arms embraced him.

"Well looky here what the cat dragged in." She gave him a squeeze and shuffled him to a stool at the bartop.

"Mornin' Ruthy," he smiled at their familiarity. Twice a week he came in for breakfast, a routine he'd kept since high school.

"Thought maybe you weren't goin' to make it by today," she patted his shoulder and scurried happily around the counter.

"Just running a little slow this morning." He hooked his boot heals over the stool's lower bar as he leaned into the counter.

"Now, I don't believe that for a minute." She poured him a tall, thin glass of orange juice. "The regular for you, honey?" she asked.

"Sure, why not," he lifted his glass. "And maybe you should throw an extra slice of bacon on there too."

"Don't have to ask me twice," Ruth smiled. "Your grandma would roll over in her grave if she saw how thin you've gotten. It's a darn right shame, I tell you," she continued without taking a breath. "Boy like you shouldn't be livin' all alone, you know. You need yer self a good lady to take care of you." She scuttled around behind the counter, continuing to chatter as she worked. "My youngest daughter, Julie... you remember Julie, right? Wee bitty thing. Cute too, if I can be so bold as to say so." She smiled at the thought then added, "Heart of gold," for good measure. "If I remember right, she's just about your same age."

"Yes'm, I remember Julie. Red hair, fiery like her mother," he teased.

"That's the one. Well," she talked faster than even her practiced hands could move, "she's 'bout to graduate college in a couple of weeks and you know what that means?"

"She'll have a degree."

"Well, duh," she shook her head. "Such a teaser, aren't you? Just like your grandpa... sure do miss that ol' buck," she diverted for a momentary stroll down memory lane. "He use ta come in here a couple times a week just like you do, wearin' his worn out Stetson and drivin' that same truck." She nodded at the mint green dinosaur just beyond the front windows, then, as quickly as she'd diverted, jumped right back on track. "Julie's graduating," she remembered, "which means she'll be coming home for the summer. Spending some time helping me out around here, in fact. You should come by and get re-acquainted with her. She's really a beauty, you know."

"I'm sure she is." He took another drink of juice, smiling at the stumpy, round woman, suspecting, though he hadn't seen her in years, that Julie's beauty, like her mother's had to come from the inside.

Steam danced off the hotcakes, eggs, and bacon as she slid the plate in front of him. "Can I send a bag of surplus food with you for the Wilsons?" she asked. "Nothin' you'd have to deliver today, or anything, just some time in the next week or so."

"You know I'm always happy to do that for you, Ruth."

"Thanks," she smiled warmly as she leaned her robust body against the counter. "So, you never did tell me why you were late today." Her soft arms nestled comfortably across her equally soft torso.

"Anniversary." Carter tucked his napkin into his collar then dusted his eggs with salt and pepper.

The matron's apple cheeks drew a blank for a moment before they pulled down into a frown. "I'm sorry, Carter. I'd forgotten the date. How dumb am I? I hope you took Beth some nice flowers while you were there. Roses. You know how much she loves those roses."

"You know I did," he answered somberly as he watched the butter melt into a puddle in the center of his hotcake.

"You're a good kid," he heard her say over the thoughts in his head. "I know you haven't exactly always liked it here, but I'm glad you decided to stay."

"Me too," he agreed thoughtfully, remembering his dreams of a life somewhere else. Things hadn't panned out the way he'd once thought they would, but he wasn't the type to complain. He rubbed his fingers across the stubble on his chin, grateful to be in a place where no one judged his tattered boots, unshaved face, or quiet ways.

Chapter Five

The only time Megan had spent at The Peninsula Beverly Hills had been a weekend runaway with Matt - before Jake, before the drinking, before the adultery, before the abuse. The two of them had shopped the stores of Rodeo drive, dined at the Belvedere, and relaxed the weekend away at the spa. That'd been a different time and a seemingly different place. The luxurious hotel, as she quickly learned, was better fit for a romantic getaway than it was for a mother and her small, wiggly son's comfort. Jake needed somewhere to crawl about and make noise. Their first night away from home may have been luxurious - the décor exquisite, the food heavenly - but it wasn't suited for her immediate needs. Sadly, after a less than restful night, she took one last drink of the crystal chandeliers and sophisticated elegance of the suite, then reluctantly checked out.

She paid the hotel clerk with cash, glad for the small stash that she'd put aside. She knew Matt would cut off her money, that was his biggest tether to her, and she expected him to move quickly. No doubt he'd already put a block on her account. Grateful for a full tank of gas, her stash of cash, and shelter from the impending rain, she fired up the engine and headed toward the freeway.

~   ~   ~

"Who does she think I am," Doctor Hamilton grumbled out the side of his mouth as he watched the potential patient walk past the reception desk. "I'm good," he stated matter-of-factly, "but I'm not a freakin' Houdini."

"Doctor!" his stout, no-nonsense nurse smacked him in the arm with the patient file.

"Seriously, Ronda," he continued to grumble. "What am I supposed to do with *that*?" They watched the oversized woman waddle out the office door.

"What's gotten into you?" Ronda glared over her leopard framed glasses. "You could help her and you know it. You didn't need to be mean!"

"I'm not a miracle worker," he squared off with the solid, middle-aged blonde. He may have had a way with most women, but his charm was lost on his assistant. "At least not to *that*!"

Ronda pushed her boss into his office and slammed the door behind her. Her brow creased and her jaw tightened. She threw one hand on her hip and raised the other with an accusing finger. "I don't know what your problem is, *DOCTOR*," she spat the title at him with disgust. "Surely you could've come up with a nicer way to tell that lady you couldn't help her until she lost a few pounds. I'm sure she's fully aware that she could stand to shed some weight."

"My toolbox is full of little razor blades, Ronda, not chainsaws."

"Even so, you could've been nice about it. I don't even care that you just lost what could've been a lucrative client, but you hurt a person. Women are hard enough on themselves, they don't need a doctor to put them down even further. Not acceptable." She tossed the file on his desk. "Not acceptable," she repeated then stomped her way out of the room with a huff.

Matt kicked the door closed before leaning into it. He waited for his nerves to settle, but it was a hopeless fight. He'd brought his personal life to the office and hour after searing hour, he'd finally let it get the best of him. He'd taken his frustration out on a patient and it was all he could do not to take it out on Ronda too. Any other assistant would've found herself with her walking papers for confronting him like she had, but Matt and Ronda both knew how valuable she was to the practice. He was good on his own, but it was her proficiency that made them the best clinic within a hundred miles.

He'd been unprofessional; he knew it and didn't need Ronda to point it out to him. Rage burned in his chest. He needed to get himself under control.

Easier said than done.

"Pull it together," he growled to the walls as he pushed his hands over his eyes then through his hair, but it was a hollow sentiment. He was livid. *Who did Megan think she was?* She had no right to leave him. If anybody was going to leave the marriage, it'd be him. And, in his time frame! She was wrong if she thought he'd just roll over and take a hit from her. He called the shots and when Megan came back – because he was sure she would – he'd make sure she had full understanding that he was in control.

Dropping into his desk chair, he made a mental checklist. *Contain and control*, he thought as he replayed the steps of his day.

Contain. He'd tucked Megan's ridiculous divorce documents, along with her ring and the floral card, securely into his briefcase before leaving the penthouse this morning. Contained. He'd straightened up the disheveled closet and bathroom counter so Alessandra wouldn't become suspicious when she came to take care of her daily routine. Contained. If Alessandra asked, he'd tell her that Megan had taken Jacob to the beach house, but he doubted he'd have to say anything. Alessandra was efficient and quiet and trustworthy. Her devotion could be easily bought. Job security is a powerful thing.

Megan's devotion, on the other hand, needed some work. She couldn't survive without him, of that he was certain. She was a spoiled product of money. Pretty, young, and rich. Never had she wanted for anything, not before they were married and certainly not after. Daddy Warbucks raised a girl who knew nothing of the real world and the thought of her trying to tackle reality on her own was almost enough to make him chuckle despite his fury. He made a mental checkmark next to *Control*. Not only had he blocked her credit cards and bank accounts, he'd used his charm to wrap her mother so tight around his finger Megan didn't have a prayer of getting help from her. Control. Whether she wanted him or not, Megan needed him... almost as much as he needed her.

~   ~   ~

After almost seven hours staring through the rhythmic beat of wind-shield wipers, half a box of graham crackers, and a couple of stops for food and diaper changes, Jacob was done. They'd left Beverly Hills first through Santa Monica then down to Seal Beach before catching the I-5 north again.

Megan had no idea where she was going, but after winding her way through pretty much every leg of the LA county freeway system, she landed on the 405 and navigated her Audi northward.

Gratefully, Jake was a patient baby, but after a dreary, rain-soaked day in the car, his last thirty minutes of whimpering from the back seat had become all Megan could handle.

"Almost there, buddy. Just a couple more minutes," she soothed through tear-glazed eyes. Time meant nothing to a ten month old, but the promise of some hope on the horizon was all she could give him. Really, it was all she could give herself too. The sun – if she'd been able to see it – was still high, but the thick cap of clouds that'd followed their route hung low and heavy.

Unsure of where she was headed, she picked a random exit somewhere near Santa Clarita and headed up a two lane highway into the nearby mountains. Nearly twenty lonely minutes passed on the deserted highway and signs of life were sparse. Doing all she could to sooth her restless child, a sprinkling of lights in the distance caught her attention. She turned off the little highway and apprehensively followed her headlights towards the small hint of civilization. Hoping for food and a dry place to stretch out for the night, she increased the speed of her windshield wipers and crossed her fingers.

She pulled her rain-soaked Audi off the paved road and into a dirt parking lot. Fluorescent lights flickered the word "vacancy" under a relic of a sign that read *Mountainside Motel and Suites*. She sighed, her stomach ready to lurch as she stared at the dilapidated building. Gripping the leather steering wheel intently, she debated turning back towards Santa Clarita. Even the idea of sleeping in the car sounded more inviting than a sleazy, germ infested hotel room. Again, she looked at the flashing vacancy sign then into her rearview mirror. The last thing Jake needed was another minute in the car.

An older lady – just as much a relic as her circa 1952 Motel – offered a toothy smile from behind the front desk. "Can I help you, dear?" Her bouffant hair bounced as she stood slowly and approached the counter.

Adjusting Jacob's weight from one hip to another, Megan dusted the raindrops from his hair. "Can I get a room?" she asked, scoping the time-forgotten office. The linoleum tiles on the floor were pealing up at the corners but, she took small comfort, they sported a new lemon-fresh wax job. Likewise, the countertop sparkled with its 1950's glitter laminate but it, too, was clean.

"Sure, honey." The round lady chomped noisily on a piece of gum while her stumpy hands scribbled something into an old green and white striped ledger. "Will that be one or two beds for ya, sweety?"

"Um," Megan fidgeted with the sock on Jacob's foot. "Do you have some kind of a suite?"

The lady's eyes illuminated under thick caps of mascara and heavy streaks of blue eye shadow. "Sure, for an extra thirty dollars I can hook you up with an extra pillow and all the free shower caps you'd like." Her plump cheeks rounded out as she chuckled. "That's about the best I can do for ya, dear."

"In that case," Megan didn't see the humor, "I guess one bed will be just fine."

"Perfect," the lady smiled warmly. "I just need to swipe your credit card and you're good to go."

"I'll be paying with cash if that's alright." Megan pulled a note out of her purse and unfolded it onto the counter. "Will this be enough?" she asked, running her fingers across Benjamin Franklin's face.

"That'll get you two nights and then some." The lady greedily snatched the bill off the counter and replaced it with a key. "This is one of the best rooms I've got," she winked then reached for Megan's hand and gave it a maternal squeeze. "I don't mean to pry, sweetie, but you're not in trouble with the law or somethin' are you?"

"No," Megan shook her head. "I'm just looking for a change of pace is all."

"Well, in that case, I hope you make yourself right at home here. It may look like there ain't much around this ol' town, but we aren't short on hospitality, that's for sure. By the way," she said, "I'm Marjean... Marjean Richards." She extended her hand across the counter and shook Megan's enthusiastically. "And what can I call you, honey?"

"Megan." She answered quickly while stepping toward the door. Immediately she wanted to kick herself. The first flaw in her plan was not having a definitive place to run to. The second: giving out her real name. She hoped Marjean's crime TV repertoire was big enough to understand the importance of keeping her identity a secret.

"Well then, Megan, if you're hungry, Ruthie's got herself a little diner right next door. Her dinners aren't too bad but I wouldn't miss out on breakfast if I were you. It'll knock them fancy heels right off yer feet."

Megan glanced at her stilettoed toes. "Thanks," she answered, unsure whether the comment was a compliment or a jibe. A tiny bell jingled on the doorknob as she pushed the door open. "We'll be sure to give the food a try."

The lady offered a toothy grin. "I hope you enjoy your stay, hun," she waved.

Megan quickly sized up the room. It was marginally less horrid than she'd expected. In all of its old, distasteful glory, it was surprisingly clean and adequately maintained. The old furnishings were straight out of a John Wayne movie, but the décor looked like maybe they'd attempted an update sometime in the ninety's. A matching pair of wing-backed chairs sat on either side of a small, round table. The upholstery job - dark green with small grizzly bears embroidered into a pattern - coordinated somewhat awkwardly with the deep-red twill curtains and brown striped bedspread. It was a far cry from the five star resorts she was accustomed to, and certainly a step down from the luxury of the night before, but it would have to do. Knowing that Matt would never look for her in a place like this made a night or two almost bearable.

One agonizing trip after another, Megan toted their luggage into the room with Jacob on her hip. How she ended up in a place without a bellhop, she couldn't quite fathom, but after the fourth trip to the car, she knew she'd never take such luxuries for granted again.

Jacob wriggled restlessly in her arms, wanting more than anything to be free after so many hours strapped in his car seat. She pushed the door shut with her foot, secured the locks, then set down the last of their luggage. Improvising with what she could find, Megan pulled the comforter off the bed and spread it over the old carpet. Jacob nearly jumped from her arms and onto the freshly spread quilt, happy to be free of all confines. Reluctant to let her baby crawl around on what was sure to be germ infested filth, she found another blanket on the closet shelf and used it to cover the remaining section of dingy old carpet.

Little Jacob, unaffected by the hideousness of the hotel room, sat on the blankets having the time of his life as he slowly emptied the contents of one of his diaper bags. He clanked together two plastic spoons, giggling at the resulting noise for only a moment before discarding them and reaching into the bag for another treasure. Item by item, he dismantled the bag, leaving a trail of baby food jars, bibs, diapers, and miscellaneous toys strewn behind him.

Megan sat cross legged in the center of the bed watching her son curiously explore the sights and textures of this foreign new world. He ambled about in his tubby little body, opening a drawer here and tossing a ball there.

Reaching into the front pocket of her suitcase, she removed the thicker of the two manila envelopes. Setting it in front of her on the bed, she straightened the metal clasp, turned it upside down then dumped its contents onto the sheets. Tight bundles of green bills bounced lightly off of each other before coming to a rest. She'd been putting away what little bits she could sneak past Matt for several months - cutting back on shopping trips, spa wraps, and facials from the allowance he provided her. Matt was a control freak in every sense of their relationship, from the clothes she wore to the amount of access she had to their finances. He considered everything to be his. His penthouse, his money, his bank accounts. He'd put a cap on her monthly withdrawals, a cap she'd happily maxed out for the last several months. But it wasn't much - enough to keep her floating for a couple of weeks at best. If she wanted freedom, though, it was the only ticket she had.

She took in her surroundings, unsure how it'd all boiled down to this. Matt hadn't always been abusive. In fact, during their courtship and even the first year of their marriage he had been tender and doting. He'd been everything everybody made him out to be: a sweet-talking, suave, and devoted husband. In front of colleagues and patients he was always polite, friendly, and professional. At home, though, something had changed. She couldn't put her finger on the exact moment it started, but over time his disposition had morphed into something different. Something terrifying. His obsessive perfectionism had taken over. Everything had to perfect. Everything: his clothes, his car, his home, his image... and his wife.

His drinking didn't help matters, though she assumed he did it to drown his stress. Maybe the alcohol was the stress. She didn't know. What she did know was that he'd shut her out. Any love he'd once had for her was clearly gone. She couldn't keep buying his lies, couldn't keep caving to his pseudo sympathetic apologies, and most certainly couldn't keep holding out for the hope that he'd magically change back into the carefree, loving man she'd once known.

Despite all the unknowns in her plan, the one thing Megan was sure of was that she was done holding on. Done waiting and hoping for a piece of the man Matt had once been. His obsessions had become unrelenting and his rages brutal. She knew she only had one shot at freedom. She had to disappear – at least until he simmered down enough to agree to the divorce. Like any alpha dog, he needed a little space and time. Time to rage, time to rationalize, and time to lick his wounds in private. He had to decide that the divorce was his idea – that he'd called the shots and made the move – because, more than anything, control was something Matt never gave up and losing was something he simply didn't do.

Chapter Six

Carter hefted the last bulging box into the bed of his truck then dusted his hands before closing the tailgate. Cleaning out Beth's house had been a much bigger task than he'd anticipated. Amazed at how many knickknacks and thing-a-ma-jigs a woman could collect over the course of her years, it'd taken him the better part of six months to separate the sentimental stuff from the junk. The sentimentals were moved to his own home, along with a few select pieces from the kitchen, and Grandpa Ez's rifle collection. Other than a few essential furniture pieces, the rest he'd donated to various charities.

Tossing a ball across the yard, Carter watched his lazy dog stroll after it over the damp lawn. His tail nearly created its own weather pattern, confirming that Bosco's laziness was confined only to his legs. Raising his eyes to the foreboding sky, Carter talked to the canine, "We gotta get this stuff dropped off before the rain swallows up the sunshine again." The dog furrowed his brow as if in confirmation. The ball disappeared momentarily into the folds of his jowls as he met Carter by the back porch. "Gonna lock the place up," he scratched the eager dog's head, "then we'll be on our way."

Stepping through the enclosed porch and into the kitchen, Carter swept his eyes over the empty farmhouse. Even though he'd had months to mourn the loss of his grandma, seeing the home stripped of her stuff made him yearn for just one more witty, quip-filled conversation. For the last nine years she and Grandpa Ez had been his only family. Losing his parents had been tough. Losing Grandpa had been even harder. But nothing compared to losing Grandma. That loss had been almost crippling.

He drew the kitchen blinds, consumed with memories as he stared out the window into the back yard. So much had unfolded out on that lawn; irreplaceable fragments of his life.

He shook off the nostalgia only to be almost taken over by it again as he double checked the lock on the front door. He could count on one hand the number of times he'd actually used the front door to enter or exit the house. Only strangers came up the rose flanked walkway to the front porch and, if they worked themselves into Beth's heart, surely they'd end their visit on the back porch proudly wearing the badge of a friend. Beth was that way; friendly and accepting of everyone. She never turned a needy soul away... except for that one time, he remembered with a grin. Only once had he seen the dark side of his petite little grandma. Even so, the remnant of that little, fire-packed temper was stamped proudly in the form of a frying pan indentation on the back door frame. With a chuckle, he added the repair to his to-do list.

The century old family home definitely had a past, one that was burned deep within his heart, but he wasn't so sure about its future. The floorboards creaked as he moved across them, just one sign of the home's deteriorating state. The windows were drafty, the cupboards needed refinishing, and the bathroom needed a complete makeover.

He ran his fingers one last time over the light switch and locked the door behind him. "Let's go, Boss," he called after his dog. "Time to move on."

~   ~   ~

Matt carefully stacked the patient consult files into a neat pile on the edge of his desk. Gruffly, he logged into his computer and half-heartedly began entering a few final notes for the day. Opening the Hamilton Center of Cosmetic Surgery had proven to be nothing short of genius. Thanks to his skilled hands and attention to detail, business was booming.

He stared at the blinking cursor, unable to shake Megan from his mind. She'd been a child-bride – a twenty-year-old trophy – and a huge asset. At least that's what he thought at the beginning. As it turned out, she'd turned out to be nothing short of a liability.

A liability, in fact, that could potentially cost him more than just a few clients. He hoped she was as miserable as she was making him. Regardless of where she was or what she was doing, he couldn't keep letting the frustration get in the way of his work. It wouldn't be long before she came crawling back; he believed it to his core. But, in the meantime, he needed to do a better job keeping the situation contained. No one needed to know that she was gone.

One by one his assistants left for the day, shutting out most of the lights as they closed up. Still festering about Megan though, he was in no hurry to return to the empty penthouse. Just beyond the glow of his monitor he noticed Ashlee lingering down the hall at the front desk. Her lipstick may have been a shade too bright and her intelligence a shade too dull, but he figured the first person to greet a potential patient should be cute and bubbly. His intelligent staff members were the ones that were hard to keep happy and, while he needed experienced and dependable nurses like Ronda, he always liked to keep a few "Ashlee's" around, if for no other reason than to provide eye candy for both his clientele and himself.

Megan had been one of the first "Ashlee's" he'd hired when he'd opened up his own practice. She was a young, beautiful co-ed with just enough spunk to keep things lively in what could be an otherwise sterile office. Gorgeous as she'd been though, having a rich daddy certainly added to the overall package. But marriage had turned out to be even more monotonous than he'd ever imagined. He made his living surrounded by beautiful women. Megan couldn't possibly understand what his days were like. He capitalized on women's insecurities. A small percentage of his patients were skin grafts and post-trauma reconstructions, but the majority of them were women seeking a more perfect self. And some of them honestly needed the help of a master's hand, but others – a large portion of his clientele, in fact – were pretty, young co-eds seeking the validation of augmentations and enhancements.

He patted himself on the back for maintaining his faithfulness for as long as he had, but honestly he'd never intended to tie himself to a life of fidelity. Some men just aren't cut out for monogamy. He qualified himself as one of them.

He glanced down the hall at Ashlee again, then at the framed family portrait on his desk. Four years ago that was Megan sitting down the hall with her short skirt and flirtatious smile. She wasn't much more than a trophy, void of any real life skills. He chortled at the very thought. She couldn't cook or clean let alone support her or Jacob. She'd never make it. He gave her a week. Two tops.

Smugly, he glared at her photo through the glass, justifying the very thought of infidelity. Megan had nothing to complain about, he concluded. He'd made every effort to provide her with a good life. He'd given her a beautiful home, an incredible car, and designer clothes. He'd taken her around the world to luxury resorts, wined and dined her at the finest restaurants, and made sure she didn't want for anything. Whatever she thought she had a right to complain about was trivial in the big equation. Her devotion, however, was not.

Anger seethed so deeply that he could neither concentrate nor appreciate his day. The very idea that she thought she could just up and leave was infuriating. He slammed the photograph face down and turned back to his computer. Seven new consults with commitments, enough to more than bank roll the new Harley he'd stumbled upon last week, but not enough to make his anger fizzle. All he could see was Megan's face, presumably smug and calm, as she sat with her lawyer. She'd put some obvious thought into this whole thing. What kind of lies had she told him? And what judge on the planet had issued a restraining order anyway? Ridiculous! He hadn't done anything any other husband wouldn't have done. She'd clearly over exaggerated the situation.

Matt shut down his computer and stood from his desk. He needed to clear his mind. Opening his briefcase, he took a swig from his silver flask, then loosened his tie and paraded down the hall.

"How'd your day go, Ashlee?" he peacocked his way to the reception desk.

"Hey Doc," she smiled overtly. "Busy as usual," she snapped a small bubble of gum with her lips as she tossed her hair over her shoulder.

He perched himself tentatively on the edge of her desk and pitched his lure. "Have I ever told you how important you are to our office?" His eyes softened at her blushing cheeks. "You work so hard and do such a good job." He touched the top of her hand gently with his fingertips. "I had a good time the other night and I'd be honored if you'd let me buy you dinner again." He lathered the charm on as thickly as he could. It was time to up the ante on their extracurricular time together.

"What about your wife?" Ashlee's conscience pricked at her.

"She's out of town," he smiled. For once, it wasn't a lie. His eyes bore into hers. His fingers traced softly from her hand, up her arm, and onto her chin. She opened her mouth to speak but he silenced it with his lips. "Let's not over-complicate this," he persuaded. "You're so beautiful," he gently traced his fingers over her cheek. "And smart," he leaned in closer. "And I *want* to be with you." He breathed the words in her ear then brushed her earlobe with his lips. "Isn't that enough?"

His charisma never faltered; not with Ashlee and certainly not with Megan. Whether by her own choice or his persuasion, he knew she'd be back. He'd make sure of it. But in the meantime...

Chapter Seven

By the full light of day the little hiccup of a town would have disappeared unnoticed on the horizon. Without the glittering of its lights in the overcast evening sky, Megan was sure she would have driven right through. It was exactly the type of place that she'd been hoping to stumble upon, but her business-savvy daddy always told her that if something was too good to be true, it probably was. *Maybe I should call Daddy.* The thought left as quickly as it came. He was busy... ever busy. She noted his old counsel then made plans to leave the eight room building and its ten horse town as soon as her second night of lodging expired.

"You must be Megan," she was greeted at the door of the retro fifties diner. "Welcome to town," the stocky, white-haired matron smiled. "Marge told me you'd probably be stoppin' in. I'm Ruth."

Perhaps tomorrow would be too late. It'd taken Marjean, proprietor, manager, and cleaning staff of the Mountainside Motel, all of twelve hours to pass her name on to the neighbor. She wondered how far along the business corridor the gossip had spread. She wondered if there even was a business corridor.

"How about a highchair for that cute little guy?" Ruth offered.

"No, thank you." Megan hesitantly slid onto the red upholstered bench, settling Jacob onto her lap. "He'll just try to stand up in it anyway. I think I'll just hold on to him right here." She kissed his cheek, newly flush with fever.

"How do you take your joe?" Ruth asked, turning a flat-black coffee mug right-side up on the table.

"Actually, can I just get some juice please?" Megan asked, politely placing her hand over the top of the mug.

"Whatever floats your boat," Ruth smiled.

In his obsession with vanity, Matt subscribed to the idea that caffeine accelerated aging. Megan considered taking a cup just to spite him. Unconsciously, she rubbed at one of her bruised arms.

Ruth's breakfast was everything Marjean had made it out to be and, even though she'd gotten accustomed to a diet free of refined carbohydrates and non-organic foods, Megan cleared her plate of two huge hot-cakes, hash browns and scrambled eggs. Jacob picked menacingly at his hot-cake, playfully smashing it into an astonishing mess, and successfully shoveling only a fraction of the resulting chaos into his mouth. His normal insatiable appetite had been replaced with seemingly unquenchable thirst.

"Can we get another refill?" Megan asked, handing Ruth his spill proof sippy-cup.

"Thirsty lad, isn't he?" Ruth asked.

"He's not usually like this." Megan explained. "He's been running a fever since last night."

"Is he teething?"

"I don't know. Maybe." Megan took little comfort in the proposed possibility. He'd never sustained a fever like this when he was cutting teeth. "You don't happen to have a good doctor around here, do you?"

"Just ol' Doc Stone." She grinned, "Actually he ain't all that old – just a snot-nosed kid, really. Same age as my Mitchel." She shoved her hands into the front pocket of her apron. "Anyway," she continued her explanation, "His dad's been the doctor around here since I had my babies - that's been more than a few years, ya know, and I guess he done finally decided to retire." She shrugged her shoulders. "So, he gave the practice to his boy. Bright young man, he is," she nodded, "but still just a kid. Barely thirty and runnin' his own practice."

Megan tried to be polite as she interrupted the chatty restaurateur's babbling, "Is Doctor Stone's office nearby?"

"Sure, honey," Ruth playfully swatted her hand in the air. "About three blocks down Main Street."

"And where's Main Street?" Megan pulled a small bundle of bills out of her purse.

"You're on it!" Ruth's cheeks sparkled when she smiled. "And put your money away. Breakfast is on the house today."

Megan stared incredulously at the proud, small-town proprietor. "Are you sure? I have plenty of money."

"Me too." Ruth smirked, patting Megan's shoulder. "You take care of that baby today and maybe tomorrow I'll let you pay for your meal."

Megan re-adjusted Jacob's weight on her hip as she read the gold italicized lettering on the newel post. After almost a full day of letting Jake crawl around the cool hotel room in nothing but his diaper and a few lukewarm baths, she finally gave up trying to break his fever on her own. He didn't fuss much but Megan's motherly intuition told her that his discomfort was more than a simple teething issue. She counted out what she hoped would be enough money to cover the doctor and tucked it into her purse. She had insurance – wonderful insurance – but Matt might be able to track her if she used it. Cash was best.

"Isaac W. Stone, MD," she read the sign again before climbing the stairs to the old house. A paper sign hung in the screen glass door announcing, "We're Open. Please come in."

She pulled the door open and stepped inside the converted home. Directly in front of the doorway stood a small, unmanned reception desk.

"I'll be with you in just a minute," a squeaky feminine voice sounded from somewhere beyond the reception counter.

"Don't hold your breath." A grey-haired man grumbled from the corner of the waiting room. "See these wrinkles?" He pointed to his aged face, "Didn't have a single one when I came in here."

"Oh, Earl," his elderly wife smacked his knee. "It's not that bad."

"William never made me wait this long," the man grumbled again, unfazed by his wife's chipper spirit.

"I think Isaac's doing a fine job," a young, pregnant mother offered from the corner of the room. "He's normally not this slow." She held a book open for the toddler on her lap while another child, a three or four year old boy, played contently at her feet. "He's just a little under-staffed is all. His receptionist ran off to Vegas with her boyfriend last weekend."

"Would've loved to see ol' Frank's face when he got the happy little bit of news that his daughter ran off," Earl chortled. "Bet he had some un-saintly words to say about that one," his deep, throaty laugh caused him to erupt into a fit of dry coughing.

Jake's hot, round body weighed heavily on her hip as she stood by the reception counter waiting for the high-pitched, faceless voice to come help her. Alert and edgy, she discretely took in her surroundings. Other than the continual ringing of a phone and a collage of framed PHD certificates, there wasn't much to make note of. The waiting area was filled with hideous mauve chairs, a rickety old coffee table, the old couple, and the young mother with her two toddlers. Nothing, she decided, of interest or threat. She let the tension roll off her shoulders.

The phone continued to ring.

A swinging door pushed open, exposing an impishly short, pale skinned nurse. "Mr. Eagan," the newly familiar squeak of her voice called out, "we're ready for you now, if you want to come on back."

"I don't *want* to do anything. I was perfectly happy at home on the couch." He folded his arms like an insolent child.

"Get up off your duff, Earl, and quit being so ornery!" His frail but determined wife smacked his shoulder with her handbag. "Men are such boobs," she said as they wobbled their way past the impish woman and through the open door towards a series of exam rooms.

"Sorry," the young, dark haired woman offered. "Let me get the Eagans situated and then I'll be right back out to help you, okay?"

The swinging door swished closed leaving Jake and Megan alone in the waiting room with the beautiful, smiling young mother, her two small children, and the incessantly ringing phone. She sat down three chairs away from the young family, staging herself where she could comfortably coddle Jacob in her arms. He smiled sleepily, his bright blue eyes glossy from the fever. She traced her finger gently across his brow and watched in awe as he drifted off to sleep.

"How old is he?" the mom asked without diverting her attention from her own young ones. Despite her obvious pregnant belly and the toddler that she bounced on her knee, not a blonde curl was out of place. She was striking and trendy and, unlike Ruth and even Marjean, she didn't fit Megan's stereotype of a small-town girl.

"Almost ten months," Megan answered proudly. "How about yours?"

"Mariah here," she softly patted the peach fuzz on top of the little girls head, "is eighteen months, and Noah," she nodded toward the busy boy on the floor, "just turned three."

Megan did the math in her head, trying to balance her small-town judgments with the pretty lady. *What kind of person had a kid every year and a half or so?* "They're both beautiful," she offered politely. "Especially your daughter. She looks just like you."

"Thanks." The young lady's cheeks flushed with the compliment. "Where'd your son get those fun little curls from?" she asked, obviously eager to divert the attention off of herself.

"From his dad" Megan answered. Other than the commonality of their blonde hair – Jacob's natural, Megan's from a bottle – her son bore no resemblance to her. It was impossible to look at Jake without seeing Matt.

"Well," the lady bubbled, "he's amazingly beautiful... I mean handsome." Her smile filled the room. "My husband always reminds me that boys aren't beautiful, they are handsome."

"I'll have to remember that," Megan smiled, touching Jake's rosy cheeks with the back of her hand. His sleepy body was like jello in her arms... an amazingly limber, soft and pliable, increasingly heavy, ball of jello.

"Are you new in town?" the mother asked. "I don't think I've seen you around before."

"No." Megan was quick to answer. *What was it with these people? Why were they so eager to chit chat with everyone? Couldn't they just enjoy a minute of silence?* "Just passing through," she clarified. This was certainly not the place for her. In her mind, she tallied the reasons she'd be leaving at first light: first, the people were too chatty. She couldn't afford their nosiness. And second, from what she could see, there was no food market, beauty salon, or mall. This hole in the wall was too tiny for even the most desperate of stopping points.

"Oh," the young mother smiled. "Well, I wish you well in your travels then."

Megan accepted the cordiality with a nod as she eyed the magazine collection on the table. Noting that the titles were mostly parenting magazines, she gave up hope that there'd be at least one fashion magazine or tabloid. Yielding to the simplicity of her surroundings, she conceded to boredom and settled deeper into the uncomfortable chair.

They could sure use some decorating help, she judged as her eyes swept the office. The gaudy, over-worn, mauve chairs were just the beginning of their problems. The chair rail needed at minimum a new coat of paint. The wallpaper below it was even worse. Perhaps someone should inform the good doctor that the eighties wanted their fuchsia rose buds back. She sized up the worn linoleum before becoming strangely absorbed by the young mother and her children.

Her heart went out to the lady at first. It had to be hard having so many children at such a young age. Especially as close as they all were. Noah, the well-mannered little boy, kept stacking little wooden blocks into towers then proudly knocking them down. "Look, mama," he'd beam each time the tower would ascend more than five or six blocks high.

"Very nice, buddy," she encouraged, smiling at him as if he'd built the Eiffel Tower.

"Moe," little Mariah gently demanded in her tinkling little fairy voice, leaning ever closer into her mom's protruding stomach with a chunky picture book in hand. "Dog," she annunciated the word, tapping her finger to the page. "CoCo?" her munchkin lips turned up in a grin.

"Yes, Riah," the mom patiently answered. "He looks just like Bosco, doesn't he?"

The phone continued its persistent ringing and the little nurse still hadn't returned. Feeling like an intruder on the young mother's precious moments with her children, Megan resisted the temptation to ignore the incessant ringing for only a minute more before she stood. Snuggling Jake's body as best she could into the crook of one arm, she made her way to the reception desk.

"Doctor Stone's office," she said into the receiver, looking at a stray billing statement to verify that she'd given the correct doctor's name to the caller. "An appointment? Today?" She sifted through some papers on the desk looking for some kind of an appointment book. Unable to find one, she turned to the computer screen. The psychedelic swirls of color that danced their way across the monitor disappeared when she moved the mouse. Relieved, she watched as a time-lined spreadsheet opened up. "It looks like he can get you in at four. Would that work?"

It'd been a few years since she'd fielded calls at Matt's office but Megan fell quickly back into receptionist mode. Her job with Matt had been more than just pure coincidence. Her mother had pulled every string she could to woo successful, prestigious men to her daughter. Intent that Megan's happiness depended on securing a slot in the upper-society that she'd been a part of, Katherine Williams prepared a short list of suitors for her daughter. With Dr. Hamilton's name at the top of that list, Katherine, as any controlling parent would do, pulled every necessary string to get Megan a job in his office. Megan secured not only the job, but ultimately Dr. Hamilton's hand, her place in society, and, most triumphantly, her mother's pride.

Megan set up the appointment for Doctor Stone then worked her way systematically through an onslaught of calls, scheduling appointments over the next several days and jotting down notes about billing inquiries until the phone finally fell silent.

"You're pretty good at that."

Megan had been so busy she hadn't noticed the tall, red-headed man leaning casually in the doorway. "I've had a little bit of practice," she smiled awkwardly.

"Really?" He stood erect. He was a tall, thick man. Not fat, rather thick and muscular. "You wouldn't happen to be lookin' for a job, would you?" he asked before introducing himself as Doctor Stone.

"I'm Megan," she shook his outstretched hand, wondering again if she ought not come up with a fake name. It didn't matter, she quickly concluded. She didn't plan on staying anywhere long enough to leave a trail.

"And who's this little guy?" The doctor gently touched his hand to Jake's forehead.

"Jacob," she swallowed, still in awe at the youth of the man who proclaimed to be a doctor. Ruth had said he was thirty, but in his jeans and white coat he looked closer to twenty. He was nothing like she'd expected. Somehow, in the unconscious webs of her mind, she'd imagined him being more like Matt. But he wasn't anything like Doctor Hamilton. Doctor Stone was so much younger than Matt's thirty-eight years – more like a peer and less like a... well, like a doctor. No wonder Ruth still thought of him as a kid.

"Little Jacob seems to be running a bit of a fever, doesn't he?" Dr. Stone observed.

"It started two days ago but then it went away for a while. I've tried all the tricks to make it break, but it just won't go away."

He listened to Jake's pulse as she talked. "Is he going to be grumpy if I wake him?" he looked at her over his freckled nose.

"Maybe," she said, shifting Jake's weight into her other arm.

"Well, let's give it a try." Doctor Stone lifted Megan's sleeping baby from her arms with a generous smile, relieving her of both his weight and his excessive warmth. Without a second thought, she left the reception desk and followed him and his click-clacketing, flip-flopped feet into an exam room.

"What do you mean, it's all legal?" Matthew stared through his lawyer and out the fifteenth-story window. "She had to have messed up somewhere!" he demanded.

"We've gone through it multiple times, Doctor Hamilton," the well-seasoned attorney explained. "Her lawyer was very thorough. Everything is in order."

"What about the restraining order? What grounds does she have for that?" He was on the edge of his seat now, ready to blow his top.

"I showed you the pictures, Doctor. They're pretty incriminating."

"Yeah, and fake!" Matt stood abruptly, toppling his chair end over end as he pressed his palms to the desk. "I don't know how she managed to doctor those up, but I had nothing to do with any of those bruises or cuts or anything!"

"Our experts think they look pretty real," the lawyer almost cowered behind the words.

"Well," Matt grabbed the folder off the desk, stashing all the loose papers into it, and stormed toward the door. "I don't care what your experts think, I didn't touch the woman! And if you don't believe me, then I'm more than happy to take my business elsewhere." Curse words strung from his mouth as he grabbed for the door knob.

"Please, Matthew, have a seat." The partner dropped his formality as he stood. "How long have we been doing business together?" he asked, trying to smooth out the tension in the room. "It's been well over a decade, hasn't it?"

"And then some," Matt snarled.

"I apologize if I made you feel under attack," he picked up the toppled leather chair and squared it firmly onto its legs. "I didn't say I thought you were guilty," he saved face. "I was merely getting at the fact that she's put together a pretty strong case."

He wasn't about to let Matt walk out the door. Hudson and Hudson was a big firm, with many clients, but one of Doctor Hamilton's position was always good to have in the portfolio. Plastic surgeons with their malpractice tendencies made for great year-end bonuses for all the partners. "Let's look at this again and see what we can figure out," he reached for the folder. Matt pulled it back and tucked it protectively under his arm.

"I'm going to have to sleep on it," he growled, twisting the knob in his ever steady hand. Long sturdy legs carried him confidently through the waiting area and into the hallway where Carl Hudson, senior partner, met him with a confident smile.

"Doctor Hamilton," the stout man took two steps to match every one of Matt's. His junior partner had obviously wasted no time making a call. "Please," he called as the elevator door slid open. "Let me buy you a drink."

"Now we're talking," Matt held the elevator for the stumpy, almost laughingly desperate, old man.

~   ~   ~

"Strep throat?" Megan continued to wonder as she sat cross legged in the center of the hotel bed. She'd picked up a map from the street corner pharmacy when she filled Jake's prescription and begun to plot out possible travel destinations. "Where in the world could you have been exposed to that?" She spoke playfully to her happily playing little boy as the sun outside her hotel window slipped behind the surrounding mountains. "I just don't get it Jake. We haven't been anywhere, except…" She retraced her steps for the last week, "Except the Country Club." She nodded, satisfied to have solved the mystery. He had to have been exposed by some kid while in their childcare center.

Jacob contently used both his hands and feet to smash a disposable plastic cup from the hotel bathroom. Intently studying the crinkled cup, he was fascinated by the popping noise it made with each new movement. He seemed completely unfazed by not only his sore throat but also his new environment. Megan, however, was not coping as well.

Thanks to her father's success and generosity, she'd grown up a child of privilege. The second of her mother's two kids, Megan was raised a virtual only child. Ten years her senior, her brother Sean, was rarely around. For the majority of her childhood, he'd been gone at one pretentious private school or another. Harvard took him even further away and, complete with a Law Degree in hand, he'd settled on the east coast. Katherine loved that her son was smart and successful; however, Megan had never achieved such adoration. Her only claim to her mother's affection came by and through her marriage to Doctor Matthew Hamilton.

Matthew represented everything that Megan's mom ever prayed for in a son-in-law: tall, handsome, well-bred, mature, and significantly well-moneyed. Megan thought that's what she wanted too and, much like every woman that crossed his path, it didn't take long for her to fall head over heels for his steel-blue eyes, golden curls, smooth talk, and romantic gestures. The fact that she was fourteen years his junior meant nothing. Naively, she accepted his advances and absorbed every bit of his doting attention. He'd wined and dined her, gave flamboyant gifts for no reason, and promised her the world. In less than a year, her mom was courting caterers, coordinating with consultants, and planning the wedding event of the decade.

~   ~   ~

"I think we both understand the ramifications if she makes these charges stick." Matt's second round of libations had loosened him up a little. The tension in his chest had been as thick as the smoke in the dark bar room, but nothing a little alcohol hadn't helped loosen up.

"I do. Unfortunately, there's nothing in the law that's going to protect you at this point. Either you get her to come home or..." the senior partner swished the last drop of amber around his glass before throwing it down his throat. His sausage fingers laced around the glass even after it was empty.

"As my lawyer aren't you supposed to tell me that everything's going to be all right?" Matt waived at the bartender to bring another round then crossed his arms hard against his chest.

"As your lawyer I have to tell you to prepare for a battle. We both know how deep her daddy's pockets are."

Matt didn't need the reminder. John William's financial situation was never far from his mind. He could only hope to bring Megan home before John got wind of their fight.

But," he crossed his stubby arms and leaned across the pub table, "as your friend, I'm going to tell you something different." He waited for Matt to lean in so he could lower his voice to a whisper. "These abuse charges are the least of your worries. Let's not forget that you've got bigger things at stake here. You've got to bring Megan home. Swallow your pride. Do some serious groveling if you have to. Just bring her home... and then,

STEPHANIE CONNELLEY WORLTON

don't let her leave again. Do you understand? Whatever it takes, Matt, you have to keep her around. The cost of her leaving is very high."

"Thanks for reminding me of the obvious," Matt straightened in his chair.

"I know a guy," Carl jotted a number onto a napkin. "He's the best around. He can help you find her."

Matt stuffed the napkin into his shirtfront pocket. He watched a group of college co-eds slide into the bar. Unabashedly, he sent a smile and a knowing wink in the direction of a young, boisterous blonde. The flirtatious, playful cherry red of her lipstick was invitation enough.

"Thanks." He diverted his attention from the girl long enough to let Carl know he'd had his fill of talk about the issue.

"And you didn't hear this from me," Carl cleared his throat with a cough, "but if you can't work things out with that wife of yours, I've got another guy," he winked. "I think you know what I mean."

Matt threw a stack of bills on the table. "Hopefully it doesn't come to that," he sighed as he pushed his stool back and stood.

Carl took his new drink from the waitress's tray and stirred it with a greedy grin. "Let me know when she's home."

"Will do," Matt shook the partner's hand then peacocked his way across the dim room.

Chapter Eight

Megan was running. Running so fast the scenery around her was nothing more than a blur. And yet, oddly enough, she could barely feel the pavement beneath her feet. It was almost as if she were floating... floating through the darkness. She was a wreck. Nervously, she scanned through the shadows looking... but, for what? She wasn't sure, but with an intense sense of desperation she continued looking anyway. A single light cut through the darkness. She directed her energy toward it, strangely fascinated by its glow.

Someone, or something, pressed from behind and she jumped, diverting the blow. She jumped so high she could see over the rooftops. The pavement disappeared under her feet as it morphed into a dirt road. Her feet bounced again, this time sending up puffs of dust. Whatever had tried to grab her, disappeared into the blanket of floating sand.

She was on her way, no longer running, but jumping with tremendous strides towards the light. And then, with her target just out of reach, the horizon came to a screeching halt. Everything around her stiffened. Some force held her back. She struggled with all her might, pushing, pulling, kicking her legs, wriggling her arms, but she couldn't break free.

She was sinking. Sinking from one darkness to another. Fear consumed her. Whatever power held her in its grasp was cold, emotionless, and mean. She continued fighting furiously, but still, couldn't break free.

"I knew you'd be back." Matt's voice thundered into the darkness. "You can't make it on your own."

The unseen power that bound her helpless began to take on the shape of his arms. She pried at his newly apparitioned fingers, wrenching them slowly apart. His rumbling laughter echoed as he released his grip. No longer was Megan sinking, she was hurling downward in a full-fledged, uncontrolled freefall. She crashed onto the kitchen floor, its hard slate tiles sending searing pain up her legs.

She tried to stand, but couldn't, her legs were unresponsive. Jacob's soft whimper trickled into the chaos. Matthew was still laughing. She had to move. She *had to get to Jacob. She reached for her legs with a new sense of urgency, but what she found was wrong. Terribly wrong.*

Her legs had ceased to exist.

Megan wrenched over in horror and then, suddenly, she was lying in bed, sweating profusely. It took a minute to get her bearings, but when she did, she let out a sigh of relief. She was back in the hotel room, far, far away from the nightmare that raged through her mind. She reached to her side, feeling for her precious Jacob. He was there, a compact ball of heat, engrossed in peaceful sleep. She rolled out of bed and stumbled through the darkness towards the bathroom.

The fluorescent lighting began to hum as it flickered on. The angry red and purple bruises on her arms had intensified to a deep, blackish purple. They were ugly reminders that she couldn't afford to go crawling back. She couldn't let Matthew tyrant her life. She couldn't let him rule Jacob's either.

Her hands shook as she tried to force a handful of water past her lips. It tasted stale and metallic. She almost gagged but needed the moisture. She'd have done just about anything for a bottle of natural spring water - anything but go back to Matt. She resigned herself to the tap water, knowing it wasn't the only thing she was resigning. Things would never be the same again.

By the time the sun peaked into her hotel room, Megan felt like she'd been hit by a Mac truck. Her head throbbed, her neck ached, her throat was impassible, and her mouth permeated the taste of chrome. After a rough, restless night, all she'd wanted to do was sleep in, but Jacob's little fingers pulling at her nose and lips had been a rude awakening. Attempts to keep him occupied through lazy games of peek-a-boo and tickle-monster only reminded her all the more of how miserable she felt. She tuned the TV to a kids channel hoping by some miracle something in the programming would catch the attention of her restless ten-month old and settle him down enough that she could rest, but it was useless.

By mid-morning, when Jake finally settled into a morning nap, Megan was so full of chills that she could barely relax. What rest she was able to get was unproductive. She felt more and more tired with each passing hour.

Midafternoon found the cleaning staff - aka Marjean - knocking on the door. She followed up shortly with a bowl of steaming hot soup and a plate of pancakes from Ruth. Dr. Stone showed up before the soup had cooled and after confirming her strep test called in his wife to help watch Jake so Megan could rest. Megan was sure she'd somehow landed in one of those old Andy Griffith reruns her dad liked to watch in his den. Only in Mayberry were people this nice. When Ruth's son fumbled in clumsily with a tray for dinner, she couldn't help but inwardly chuckle at his resemblance to Barney Fife.

The whole thing was mind boggling. Her own mother had yet to notice she was gone, let alone ever doted on her when she felt ill, yet complete strangers - people who had no reason to help her other than the kindness in their hearts - had come running to her aid.

Chapter Nine

Twenty-four hours beyond her scheduled departure from no-man's-land, Megan finally felt good enough to reconsider her plans. *These* people wouldn't rat her out, she concluded, though her situation didn't merit her trust towards anyone. If the rest of the town was as compassionate and kind as the handful of residents she'd met, then maybe this really would be a good place to lay low.

Despite her father's voice in her head whispering his doubts, Megan tossed the road map in the trash and, with the help of Marjean, set an appointment to see the only available rental in town. She then retraced her steps down the lazy Main Street to Doctor Stone's office.

The door chimed when she walked in and, amidst the ringing of the phone and the chatter of a handful of patients in the waiting room, a familiar, fairy-like voice echoed from behind the swinging door. "I'll be with you in a minute."

Megan didn't wait for an invitation before sliding into the seat at the reception counter. She settled Jake on her lap and began to field Doctor Stone's phone calls.

"Well, well, what do we have here?" The doctor's voice sounded from the hallway. "Does this mean that you're going to take me up on my offer?" She spun the desk chair around in time to see the glowing smile on his face. Today he'd paired his flip-flops with a pair of khaki shorts and a gaudy hibiscus print Hawaiian shirt.

"Maybe," she grinned at his attire.

"It's Friday," he explained. "I like to keep things casual on Fridays."

"And Mondays, and Tuesdays..." the impish nurse laughed as she passed by him. "Miss Turner?" she pushed the door open and called, "We're ready for you now."

Doctor Stone offered a mischievous smile to his nurse, shook Miss Turner's hand, then turned back to Megan. "Well," his freckled nose crinkled when he smiled, "Is there anything I can do to persuade you?"

"I've been thinking about it and I'd like to take you up on your offer, Doctor Stone, but..."

"Isaac," he interrupted. "Doc Stone was my dad. Please call me Isaac."

"Okay, Isaac," she tried the name on for size. It seemed so informal, but so did everything else in the peanutty little blip of a town. "Like I was saying, I really could use a job, but it seems that I have a bit of a challenge."

"Like?" He raised one eyebrow.

"Like this little guy." She bounced Jacob on her knee. "I can't very well bring him to work with me but I don't know what else to do with him."

"Well that's any easy one." He leaned his lanky frame against the door jamb, "I think we could work out a part time schedule and I happen to know someone who'd just love to watch little Jacob for you."

"Really?" Megan was astounded. It shouldn't be this easy. It couldn't be this easy. "Who?" she wondered.

"My wife," he answered. "All she's talked about for the past two days is how amazingly cute your little Jacob is. I'm sure she'd be thrilled to spend some more time with him."

Megan, although – or perhaps because ‐ she'd been raised by a nanny herself, had sworn off the idea of daycare. She'd wanted to be the kind of mom hers had never been. But her situation had changed. Matt had shut her down financially and she had to supplement her trivial savings with something. If she and Jake were going to survive, she was going to have to make some sacrifices. She supposed as far as care givers were concerned, they didn't come much nicer than Doctor Stone's wife, Emily. Megan had witnessed Emily doting on her own children; she undoubtedly would treat Jake the same way. By noon, it was settled. Megan was set to start on Monday and Emily Stone would watch Jake.

Megan's to-do list was being checked off with almost no effort on her part and, as she drove toward her next destination, she worried that it had all been too easy. She glanced at Jake in the rearview mirror and solidified her resolve. She couldn't keep strapping him in a car and driving every day. It wasn't fair to him. Besides, she reaffirmed her conviction, LA County was a big place. Matt couldn't possibly find her here.

With Marjean's penciled map in hand, Megan navigated to the southernmost end of Main Street, took a right onto a roughly paved road, around a couple of bends, then up a rough graveled canyon road. Out one side of the car acres and acres of farmland and orchards laced the rolling hills, out the other side it was one mountain wall after another.

Just before the odometer turned its second mile from her turn off Main Street, she noticed the rustic wood sign. "High Country" it read, just as Marjean said it would. Megan made a sharp left into what Marge had called a subdivision. Megan wouldn't have been so generous. A narrow dirt road with a handful of homes could hardly be considered a subdivision. The surrounding orchards and farm land did nothing but support her argument.

Though none of the homes looked new or modern, there were definitely some that were older than others. A yellow Victorian two-story caught her eye as she drove by slowly. The home's elegant round turret and wrap-around porch called to her. She could almost imagine herself sipping lemonade on its grand front porch. She read the numbers on the porch post, hoping that by some sweet act of fate they would match with the address Marge had scribbled down. Fortune, although it'd been smiling on her every recent move, had chosen just that moment to retract its bountiful hand. This masterpiece in the middle of nowhere was not fated for her. Its neighbor, however, a tiny white farmhouse with a rickety old porch, a rose filled front yard, and a white picket fence, was.

~   ~   ~

Carter finished supervising the assembly of his troop's fifteen-man tent and was about to set up his own when the text came through. It'd only been a couple of days since he emptied the old farmhouse and somebody was already interested in renting it. He hadn't fixed a single of its flaws or listed it as available, for that matter, but his best friend, Brent, assured him that their elderly neighbor, Sally Rae, had shown it and had a legitimate lease offer. "Whatever," he responded to his long-time friend's text, sure whoever the tenant was wouldn't last long. The old farmhouse needed too much work, but if some recluse wanted to chase away the dust and a field mouse or two, more power to him.

His troop of a dozen twelve-year-olds lost focus of their camp preparations before their gear had even been unloaded from the truck. Like mosquitoes they'd been drawn to the standing water and mud bogs left from the week's rainstorms. Carter supervised from the corner of his eye as he set up his own tent then kicked back in a camping chair beside his assistant scout master and business partner, Roger Whitely.

"They ain't so smart, are they?" Whitely chortled in his rugged slang at the mud soaked boys. His hands were callused from years of working the orchards, first as a hired hand and devoted employee of Carter's grandparents and more recently as a co-owner. His heart was as soft as freshly spun cotton candy.

"Apparently not," Carter chuckled, still wondering about his new tenant as he ran his hand over his dog's back. "Even Bosco here is smart enough to stay out of that mess."

The two men watched as the carefree boys wrestled around in the muck. What started as a light splash with their hands quickly turned into a sloshy mess in their shoes. Complete body submersion followed shortly. Mud wreaked havoc into every inch of their wardrobe as the scouts rambunctiously raced from one end of the sink hole to the next and back again. They splashed and tackled each other, unconcerned by the setting sun or their empty stomachs.

"You don't suppose any of them remembered to pack a spare pair of shoes, do you?" Carter finally asked.

"I reckon not more than two or three of 'em." Whitley took a swig of his soda and propped his cowboy boots up on a nearby rock. "Suppose we ought to get 'em a fire goin' so they can dry them toes off?"

"I think if they want a fire, they should make it themselves."

"So, you just goin' to let them be wet and cold?" the life-long cowboy asked.

"No," Carter relaxed into his chair. "We're supposed to teach them how to survive, not do it for them. When they decide they're cold, they'll figure out a way to get warm."

Whitely nodded. "I sure do like the way you think, Carter. I'm thinkin' good ol' Ez done worn off on you a little bit. Suppose that's why you've been Scoutmaster for so long."

Four years as scoutmaster, Carter thought to himself, and five since Grandpa Ez had been around. He couldn't believe so much time had already past.

Whitley tossed a stick out into the field for Bosco's entertainment, but after only two retrievals, Boss was done. He retired to the far side of

Carter's chair, separating himself adequately away from Whitley's further attention. He plopped his over-sized head onto Carter's knee and lovingly nuzzled into him. He was a lazy, albeit true companion; hungry for a minute or two of attention, but continually content as Carter's shadow.

"You boys hungry yet?" Carter called toward the mud pit as he snuck another tid-bit of beef jerky into his mouth. True to form, a resounding "No" chorused from the scouts as they continued play in the mud. Another text came through. Sally Rae had closed the deal and the new tenant was moving in tonight. He shrugged off his surprise and tucked the phone back into his pocket.

Within minutes, twelve sets of mud bogged shoes stomped their way heavily through the meadow grass. Collectively, they were parched and on what they believed to be the mere brink of teen-aged starvation.

The boys who'd heeded the Boy Scout Motto were prepared with dry clothes and spare shoes, but others had yet to learn the value of preparation, or even the importance of following the recommended packing list. Carter quietly let the young men try to resolve their own predicaments, helping only with the splitting of logs as the older boys taught the younger ones how to build a fire.

The troop gathered around the fire, half of them still soaked and cold to the bone, as they consumed insane quantities of roasted hot dogs and canned chili. Marshmallows and various assortments of candy found their way to the end of roasting sticks. Strange, melted, sugary concoctions emerged, further fueling the energy of the troop.

Two boys perched on the top of stumps playing a tug of war of sorts with a stick. Three other boys set up a makeshift arm wrestling table and were making the rounds to challenge any boy who dared take them on.

Whitley engaged an eager group of stragglers by tossing a handful of sticks and stones randomly into the dirt. "See here, boys," Whitley offered confidently, "the sticks have spoken. A number has been revealed. Who knows what it is?"

Carter chuckled to himself as one gullible boy after another tried to figure out how to decipher Whitley's "secret" pattern. Caleb and Ashton, their two newest scouts, intently watched as the others tried to make order out of chaos.

Carter cherished his role as scout master and hoped he was making a difference for the boys. He took a deep, thoughtful breath as he scanned the circle of faces around him. If nothing else, he could offer some stability and mentorship to some of their difficult young lives.

As the night sky thickened, the stars opened up and the boys began to simmer down. Carter pursed his lips and whistled what the boys knew to be their call to gather. "Find a stump, take a knee, sit on the ground, whatever," Carter instructed as the boys eagerly squished around the warmth of the fire. "Jamison," he nodded toward the oldest boy in the troop, "take charge."

Without batting an eye, Jamison stood to his feet and cupped his hands over his mouth. "Coyote's unite!" he called. In unison, the boys' hands clapped three times as they opened their cantor:

"We are coyotes. Powerful, great coyotes.
We play and discover; there's so much to uncover.
We're proud of our colors, and we respect our mothers. (They always
chuckled at this line.)
We're honest and true in all that we do.
We are coyotes. Powerful, great coyotes!"

A proud howling chorus pierced the night as the boys ended their call then, as quickly as they'd opened up, the troop silenced again.

Carter nodded his approval at the well trained troop. "Very nice," he said. Accepting the influence he could have in these boy's lives, he smiled warmly at them. "Have I ever told you the story of the donkey and the well?"

Heads shook across the fire.

"No," Sam smirked, "but why do all your stories involve donkeys?"

"Yeah," Jeff reciprocated, "why can't they be about dragons?"

"Or dogs?" Jamison teased.

"Or fish?" Sam laughed.

"Because," Carter chuckled, "I like donkeys." He opened his eyes wide, chiseled his face, and broke into his best *Godfather* voice. "You gotta problem with donkeys?"

A few chuckles bounced through the darkness.

"I didn't think so," he winked. "So," he resumed his normal tone.

"Once upon a time?" Sam giggled.

"No," Carter raised his eyebrows, "this ain't no fairytale, boy," he teased. "But if it's a fairytale you're after, maybe Whitley can help you out."

"Don't hold yer breath," Whitely shook his head, "I ain't know any stories 'bout princesses or nothin'."

"I got one," Jeff offered. "Once upon a time there was a beautiful princess named Sam."

Eleven boys laughed; one grimaced. Carter intercepted, "Do you think it would be possible for me to tell my story now, before I grow gray, lose my hair, get old, and die?"

"Alright," the boys conceded, stifling a few chuckles as they did so.

"Okay," Carter looked across the fire, waiting for someone to dare to interrupt him again. "One day a farmer's donkey fell into a well."

"How do you just fall into a well?" Sam started in again.

"I'm 'bout ready to shew you myself," Whitley shuffled his strong, weathered hands. "How's that sound?"

"I'm good, thanks," Sam stilled his sarcastic quips. "Please continue, Carter."

"Thank you, Sam." Carter would've laughed had he not known it would just encourage the other boys. "Okay, let's try this again. One day a farmer's donkey fell into a well...." He waited for an interjection, a quip, or even a giggle, but none came, so he continued. "The farmer looked down the well at the crying animal but didn't know what to do. Finally he decided that the donkey was old and it would be too hard to try to retrieve him. And, since the well had been dry for quite some time, it probably needed to be covered up anyway."

He paused and looked up from the crackling logs. The boy's faces grew somber as they began to piece together the next part of the story.

"So, he buried the donkey alive?" Caleb compassionately asked.

"He did." Carter continued. "He even invited his neighbors to come help him. At first, as the shovel loads of dirt began to dump into the well, the donkey realized what was happening and cried horribly, but after a few minutes he quieted down."

The boy's faces were a mixed bag of shock and sadness at what they presumed was happening. Carter had them right where he wanted them. "The farmer threw a few more shovel loads in then finally looked down into the well. What do you think he saw?"

"A pile of dirt?" came one reply.

"A dead donkey?" came another

"A dog?" Jamison grinned.

"A fish?" Sam played along.

"Close," Carter nodded, ever touched by their wit. "With each load of dirt that hit the donkey's back, he would do something amazing. He would shake it off and step up. As the farmer's neighbors continued to throw dirt on the donkey, he would shake it off and step up."

"So, as the dirt got higher and higher, the donkey got closer and closer to the top?" Ashton asked.

"That's right. Every time something was thrown at him, he shook it off and stepped up." He let the boys stew in silence for a minute before tying up his message. "In your lives do you think you're ever going to have dirt... or trials... thrown at you?"

Twelve bobbing heads replied.

"And what are you going to do when that dirt comes your way? Just like the donkey, you have two choices. You can lie down and let it bury you, or you can shake it off and step up."

The boys processed his message in almost eerie silence. The logs crackled and spewed bursts of flames into the otherwise quiet night. Crimson nuggets of hot ash flashed brilliantly from the fire pit. Warmth from the fire touched Carter's cheeks as a love for each of his boys touched his core.

Despite the heat radiating from what had become an impressive bonfire, a handful of boys continued to shiver. Carter, figuring that he'd maxed out the learning curve of twelve year old boys, reminded them the importance of preparation then pulled a secret stash of blankets from his truck.

The boys took hold of the blankets and dog-piled into their tent seeking to rid themselves of their cold, damp clothes. Carter offered a few extra pairs of wool socks to the boys who'd failed to bring any of their own and even ended up donating his own sleeping bag to the cause. He was sure they'd all sleep well. As for himself, his comfortable bed never sounded so good.

Chapter Ten

Her new home – a very temporary rental, Megan hoped – was by no means a dream abode. In fact, it was a far cry from everything she was accustomed to and, had it not been the only available rental in town, she would have never dropped her standards so low. It didn't take long to understand why it was available and, as she stared at the crumbling plaster walls, she couldn't believe that people really lived in such humble conditions. Who was she kidding? Humble was an understatement; the place was a falling apart, dilapidated excuse of a shack.

With only one bedroom and six-hundred square feet, the cracker box wasn't much bigger than the master closet she'd shared with Matthew. The finish was nearly worn off the creaky wood floor boards, the curtains were musty and old, and the pink sink in the bathroom screamed for a remodel. But, even so, it *was* completely furnished. Tastelessly so, she admitted, but the queen sized bed, orange and brown tweed couch, two mismatched end tables, old wooden coffee table, disheveled looking rocking chair, and a nineteen sixties circa dining table with four matching chairs, each served their purpose.

She wasn't trying to be picky, she rationalized, but as she thought about the posh city penthouse she'd left behind, she couldn't help but grumble about her new quarters. Rolling out of the scratchy old bed sheets and lumpy mattress, she found her resolve faltering and wondered if it'd been enough time for Matt to calm down. She was tempted to return to her comfortable life in the city.

Multiple floorboards creaked in mocking harmony as she stepped into the pepto-puke bathroom. Soon, she thought, could not be soon enough. She analyzed the yellowed linoleum floor for only a moment before deciding to set Jake down on the worn wood floors of the hallway. Pushing a wayward hair off her brow, her fingers skimmed across the still tender wound on her head. She examined it closely in the mirror. The flash of Matt's steel eyes haunted her as she heard his words, "head wounds heal quickly." Luckily, he'd been right about that. The cut was making a quick recovery; the bruises, on the other hand, looked worse with each passing day.

A spider scurried its way across the corner of the mirror and up the wall. Swallowing back the scream that'd nestled itself in her throat, she watched with disgust as it disappeared into the nasty, rusting light fixture. Deal breaker, she thought as she released the breath she'd been holding, but an unsolicited feeling kept her from grabbing Jake, strapping him into his car seat, and heading straight back to the penthouse.

She glanced at the light fixture again, then back at her reflection in the mirror. Sally Rae, the gray haired, weathered faced lady that'd shown her the "house" had grossly underscored its faults. The gravel driveway, dirt roads, outdated furniture, and scratchy sheets were just the tip of the iceberg. Even the word house was a generous term when referring to the worn-down rickety shack.

She added "full of little creepy crawly things" to her ever-growing list of what was better than Matt's wrath, then turned on the water and splashed her face. Even Sally Rae, probably nearing the century mark, had more life and less miles than the pink porcelain sink. Trying to reconcile herself to her new surroundings, she tossed another handful of cool water over her face. She was determined to make the best of a bad situation and, like every other person who'd crossed her path in this little town, the old neighbor lady who'd shown her around was nice and friendly. She could only hope the same about whoever the landlord was.

"Jakey," she scooped him off the floor with a smile. "Would you like to be my date for breakfast?" She welcomed any reason to leave the little shack of a house.

Ruth served up an extra stack of pancakes. "Here ya go, sweetie. Eat up. A girl like you could use a little meat on her bones." She slid the plate in front of Megan and moseyed away before Megan could protest.

Megan looked at the stack of refined carbohydrates hesitantly before surrendering to a few more delightful bites as she jotted down a shopping list on a torn-out page from Ruth's order tablet. Other than toilet tissue in the bathroom, a set of scratchy old sheets on the bed, a few dishes in the kitchen, and the small bag of toiletries she'd brought with her, the house was barren.

She asked Ruth for directions to the nearest retail store and thirty minutes later pulled her car into the parking lot. She sat in the luxury of her car for quite some time, stalled by the idea that stepping inside the retail store would somehow compromise the last thread of her dignity. She'd never set foot in a store that wasn't attached to a mall before, and, other than an occasional stop at the natural foods market, Alessandra did all the household shopping. She wondered if housekeepers could be considered in a custody settlement, then, realizing the absurdity of the idea, shrugged it off.

Following the lead of a pair of giggly, pre-teen girls, she held Jake tight and stepped through the automatic doors. A friendly, old man greeted her from his wheelchair. She tried not to focus on his missing teeth as she forced a smile back at him.

Her standards, however logical they seemed in her mind, were outweighed by the need for a few critical basics – food, bottled water, diapers, and linens. She filled her cart with hair products, soap, and toothpaste, choosing the most expensive brands with the hope that they'd compare closely to the high-end department store products she was accustomed to using. She found towels, cleaning supplies, and a variety of linens, then attempted to stock the remaining space in her cart with groceries.

Inexperience with cooking proved to be her downfall. Beyond fresh produce, she had no idea where to even start. She contemplated the foods she could prepare, realizing how inept in the kitchen she was. She'd mastered the basics: scrambled eggs, boiled water... reservations. If she could afford to eat out she would, but the dwindling stack of bills in her purse and the lack of a response from Matt's attorney, reminded her of the need to be frugal. The deli-prepared meals and the frozen food aisle looked to be her best hope, but the inability to read the ingredients list without tripping over her tongue had her nervous. She picked a few of the least threatening meals then found her way to the book department with the hopes of finding some tutorial on cooking.

Proudly, she pushed the loaded shopping cart across the store, fully aware that her jeans and rhinestone heels probably cost more than the entire contents of her cart. Snugging her Dolce and Gabbana handbag tightly under the cusp of her elbow, she glanced at the ten-dollar fashions, silently committing herself to avoid them at all cost.

After striking out in the cook book arena, Megan picked up every magazine at the check stand that touted healthy family-friendly recipes, hopeful that at least one of them would contain something easy enough for a novice to cook, then headed back to the cracker box home to try her hand at all things domestic.

~   ~   ~

At the first sign of morning, Carter heard the raucous laughter of hungry boys permeating his tent walls. Bosco's tail thumped the ground rhythmically. He patted the dog's head, then crawled off his hammock, threw on a jacket, and met the boys by the fire pit.

Hotcakes were followed by a morning hike, a few wilderness games, then the breaking of camp. By the time his gear and boy laden truck made it back to his home, Carter had completely forgotten about his new tenant. It wasn't until the boys, busily unloading their gear from the bed of his truck, began gawking towards his grandma's house that he remembered the texts from the night before.

"Gotcha some upidy-up rich city boy rentin' Beth's house, huh?" Whitely smirked.

Carter sized up the chrome wheels and tinted windows of the silver Audi parked in the neighboring drive. "Looks that way." He hefted the scouts' tent onto a shelf in his garage.

"Maybe he's a gangster or a mafia boss," Sam imagined. He stepped out of the garage to size up the neighbor's car a second time.

"Or," Whitley laughed as he settled another piece of scout gear onto the shelf, "perhaps something a little less threatening like a movie producer."

What had Sally Rae gotten him into? The only scenario Carter could think of wasn't a good one. "Hope it's not some drug dealer. That's the last thing I need to deal with."

"Whoever it is, he's got himself a lady," Sam quipped.

Whitley stepped out of the garage just in time to see the feminine shadow move away from the window. "And from the looks of things, a mighty fine looking woman at that."

"Great," Carter mumbled sarcastically, pushing off the inevitable meeting until later.

~   ~   ~

After fumbling with the rusty knobs for a good thirty-minutes, Megan finally got the washing machine to fill with water. At the very least, she'd have nice – not great, but at least nicer – sheets to sleep on. The ancient machine roared to life, shaking itself, the back porch, and the kitchen cabinets as it gyrated back and forth. The dryer, too, she soon learned, made a racket of its own, but that was the least of her hurdles. She'd never cleaned before. Not real cleaning anyway. She wished she'd paid more attention to how Alessandra did things. If she'd asked a few "how's" and "why's" when she had the chance maybe she wouldn't have jammed the vacuum, gagged uncontrollably as she cleaned the toilet bowl, or cursed the hard water spots on the kitchen faucet.

Though she should have been proud of her accomplishments, a day full of laundering, cleaning, and organizing only left her with the sour taste of regret in her mouth. *Who could possibly live this way?*

Chapter Eleven

Matt paced restlessly in front of the dining room windows, trying to calculate Megan's plans as he redesigned his own. Twirling the amber liquid over the ice cubes in his glass, he considered the ramifications of her disappearance. Luckily, Megan's father hadn't questioned the validity of his claim that she wasn't feeling well. That lie, at least, had spared him the agony of a weekend with his father-in-law and bought him a little time to put together a plan.

He swallowed back the last drop of his drink and intently set the empty glass on the edge of the dining table with a thud. The spectacular vase of roses he'd so generously sent, sat in full bloom despite Megan's absence. He pulled his phone from his pocket and dialed her number again. A single ring took him to her voicemail.

Cursing aloud, he chucked his phone at the blossoms then ran his hand over the tension in his neck. It'd been nearly a week with no word. Unless someone was helping her, Megan had to be close to her limit. But, who would help her? And, why?

There was only room for one winner in his plan. *She will not screw thing up!* The thought grew as he stared out at the light infused city. Picking up his glass, he sauntered to the bar and topped it off again, then slid into the comfort of his black club chair.

He heard a car door open and close on the street below. A small burst of laughter filtered through the air from a nearby sidewalk. He loved the sounds of the city... busy, industrious, alive. He put his feet up and closed his eyes, allowing the sound of streaming traffic to lull his mind as the alcohol warmed his veins. Clenching her ring in his fist, he surrendered to the night. *I will win this, Megan! I will win!*

~   ~   ~

Other than the whisper of wind through the old wood-framed screens, the only sign of life outside Megan's four walls was the occasional grind of tires as a car or two came and went on the gravel road. Not sure what to do with a Sunday, Megan snuggled with Jake in their fresh, pseudo-luxury sheets and did nothing. If she'd been at home – her old home – she and Matt would be on their way to the country club to meet her parents. The country club crowd wasn't such a great loss – the "regulars" were bitter and haughty anyway – but she longed for the pampering part. The previous day's activities had left her silken soft hands feeling like sandpaper. And, she pouted silently, her forearms ached.

Longing for the comforts she was accustomed to, she found herself thinking that maybe things weren't as bad as they'd seemed with Matt. Maybe things would change if she went back. Maybe she was overreacting. Something inside her gut said she wasn't. That same something whispered that the abuse was only the tip of Matt's iceberg. Maybe he really was ready to change and maybe he wasn't, but every day in this shack was a day too many. What if it took weeks? Months? Years? She didn't have it in her to domesticate the countryside that long.

She imagined the magnificent arrangement of roses that had surely opened up into full blooms on the dining room table. The sun would be slivering across the room by now, painting the giant scarlet blooms in an even more elegant light. Too bad no one was there to appreciate their beauty.

Remembering the finely groomed rose garden of her new home, Megan nestled Jake between two pillows and climbed out of bed. Pulling back the shades, she peered out the picture window. Full splashes of scarlet, violet, salmon, and gold painted the front yard. Someone took a lot of care to make sure they were healthy and pruned. Maybe the landlord, she wondered, though she'd yet to meet the guy. She smiled at the idea of a tough, middle-aged, leather-handed, country man, toting a pair of rose pruners and delicately handling each beautiful little bud.

Allowing the shades to fall back into place, she turned back to her sleeping baby and pressed her lips to his supple cheek. He was her world. She had to protect him at all cost. Even if it meant store-bought dinners, unmanicured nails, and, she sighed, cleaning toilets, she was committed to do whatever it took to keep him safe.

Expecting nothing more from her day except the same solitude and silence as the day before, she filed through her small and simple wardrobe, taking a moment to stroke the scarlet Vera Wang gown longingly before moving on to the more practical dresses in the closet. Figuring the day would be as warm as the one before, she chose a cotton summer dress and pulled it over her head. The ruby hue accentuated her lips and made the blonde of her hair even more vivid. The simple cut of the dress was flattering; it seemed that it was custom made to fit her curves.

She pulled her hair up into a messy bun, grimacing at the exposed yellowing bruises on her arms as she blended makeup over the healing sore on her forehead. She highlighted her eyes, painted her lips, and headed to the kitchen for her first ever attempt at making breakfast.

Toaster waffles and fresh fruit were hardly a meal worth feeling accomplished over, but they were a start. After breakfast, she thumbed through her magazines in search of the easy recipes they advertised on their covers. She wasn't particularly picky, she thought, but as she skimmed over the recipes she was astounded by how fattening they were.

By lunch time she'd dog-eared all of the potential options, intent to find a way to modify them to fit her needs, then pulled a tray of deli-prepared chicken fettuccini-alfredo out of the freezer and carefully followed the instructions for baking.

She set the timer then scooped Jake into her arms and made the rounds opening windows throughout the house. She dug her cell phone out of her purse and powered it on with the intent to contact her lawyer for an update. The device unexpectedly buzzed in her hand. She checked the caller ID, disappointed to see her mother's name on the screen and not her lawyers. She let her mother go straight to voicemail.

Two minutes later, the ringtone sounded again. Avoiding what she knew would be chastisement, for a second time, she let her mother go to voicemail. One or two angry messages from her mother – although cutting and accusatory, she was sure – had to be more pleasant than the dozens of messages building from Matt.

A third call came shortly after she pulled their lunch out of the oven. Again, she happily let it go to voicemail. Before she and Jake had a chance to finish eating though, the phone rang for a fourth time. Apparently Mrs. Katherine Williams wasn't going to give up easily.

Megan pushed aside her lunch, scooted Jake from one knee to the other, and answered the phone. "Hello, Kat," she monotoned. Terms like mom, ma, and mother were strictly forbidden. Katherine said they made her sound old and common.

"Where are you?" Kat demanded in her always proper, debonair manner.

"Yes, *Kat*, I'm fine." The words slid off her tongue sarcastically. "Thanks for asking."

"I'm sure you are, darling. But that wasn't my question. I asked where you are and more importantly why you missed brunch."

"I'm sorry, Kat, I should've called," Megan didn't try to make excuses. Such expenditures would be a mere waste of her breath. Kat simply wouldn't care.

"You know, I didn't raise you to skip out on people. The Williams family doesn't stand people up for anything. We keep our commitments."

"I'm sure nobody even missed me." Megan served a spoon of mashed-up fettuccini noodles into Jake's mouth. "They barely even notice when I'm there anyway."

"There you go, thinking about yourself again," Kat sighed. "Did it ever occur to you how it would make me feel? Did you consider how awkward and embarrassing it would be for me when you didn't show up? What was I supposed to tell the ladies?"

"I said I was sorry." Megan imagined Kat, not a hair out of place under her white visor, nor a spot of dust on her tennis skirt, as she, with one hand on her afternoon tea, shooshed her maid away from the conversation. A bouquet of flowers, fresh cut every Sunday morning, surely adorned the patio table. A glass of rum undoubtedly awaited her father's return from his Sunday morning round of golf.

"Matthew called this morning," Kat sighed, spewing dramatic undertones of *what-are-you-thinking* as she clicked her tongue over her teeth. "I should have known something was up when he canceled your visit to the beach house this weekend."

"We were invited to the beach house?"

Kat ignored Megan's question. "Well it's a good thing you've got such a sweet husband, my dear. He covered and told your dad you were sick and couldn't make it."

"When did lying become a redeemable quality?" Technically she really had been sick, but Matt didn't know that.

"When you started acting like a child, I suppose."

"A child, huh?" Smashing the backside of her fork into Jake's fettuccini, she took out her frustration on the helpless noodles.

"You know, Megan, Matt's such a good man. He stood up for you even when he probably had every reason not to. He didn't want anyone to know what you did."

"And what exactly *did* I do, Kat?" Megan was astounded by Kat's automatic defense of Matt.

"Well, for starters, you decided to go running off on some selfish little adventure. Without your husband, mind you. I don't know where you are or who you're with, but..." she breathed heavily into the receiver. "Tisk, tisk, my dear. Not only was it irresponsible, but that man of yours is a wreck." She sighed again, sparing no expense to lather on the guilt. "He's just sick about this whole thing."

Adventure? Megan recounted the last few days in her mind. Adventure was hardly the word she'd use. "I highly doubt that he's been worried." Megan spooned more food to Jake. "At least not about me," she added.

"Oh, Megan. I don't know who you think you are, but I did not raise you to be such a spoiled brat!" Kat's tone raised only slightly, though her disapproval hung heavy even over the phone. "It's time to quit playing this childish little game and come home to your husband. I mean, really Megan, what would your father think if I told him?"

The muscles in Megan's neck tightened. For as controlling and nosey as her mom was, her father balanced out the other side of the spectrum: chronically uninvolved and aloof. He'd spent the better part of her life chasing money. She doubted that he'd care, or even notice for that matter, that she'd gone anywhere.

"Did Matt tell you why I left?" Megan finally asked, trying to remain calm. Kat was a heartless, controlling, petty excuse of a mother. Clearly, and not surprisingly, she'd already made up her mind to take Matt's side. Megan could only imagine the lies he'd conjured up to defend his role as Kat's beloved, walk-on-water, son-in-law.

"He sure did, Megan, and I understand. People fight. Husbands and wives get into arguments every now and then. But at the end of the day, Matthew's a good man. There was no reason for you to go running off like you did. It doesn't matter what you did, or even who you are with, Matthew loves you and he's willing to forgive you."

Megan's eyes traced over the yellowing bruises exploding against the paleness of her arms. "He loves me and is going to forgive *me*?" she clarified.

"Absolutely, darling," Kat continued confidently, making it more and more clear where her devotions were. Matt knew exactly how to play her. "We both know that you can get a little smart-mouthed at times," she said. "And sometimes you're not quite as mature as you should be, but that's no excuse to go running off. Matt's a good husband. Whatever your issues are, he's willing to work through them."

Did he tell you that he pushed me around? Did he tell you about the bruises on my arms or the cut on my head? There was no sense in wasting her breath to wage a defense. "Matt's been very generous about looking beyond my faults," she bellowed sarcastically. "All of them, that is, except that I'm fat, disrespectful, and possibly even a disgrace to his practice. He was pretty clear about those ones."

"Now that's just plain ridiculous, Megan, darling. Matthew didn't say anything of the sort," she continued to embellish what she considered to be Matt's sainthood.

"Okay."

"Why are you being so snide? We both know that he'd never say anything like that about anybody. He's not that kind of man. You need to drop the theatrics and start acting like an adult. Seriously, Megan, get over yourself. This has gone too far. It's time to come home and work this out like an adult."

"I'm not coming home." Megan dug her bare feet into the wood floor. She didn't know how she was going to make everything work but she was bound and determined to do it.

"Really?"

"Really."

"You are a work of art, young lady. You've got a perfectly loving husband who gives you anything and everything you could ever want and you're too stupid to see it. How long do you think you're going to make it without him? Huh, Megan? Have you thought about that? Where do you think you're going? How are you going to get money?"

"I'll figure it out." Megan spooned the last of the fettuccini into Jake's eagerly awaiting mouth. *Funny how Kat hadn't once mentioned concern for the welfare of her grandson.*

"I hope you don't think that your father and I are going to open up our wallets in support of this silly little game you're playing."

"Believe me, Kat, I don't expect *anything* from you." Standing, she left the dishes on the table and carried Jake to the sink.

"Just come home."

"I can't." Megan wiped the food off Jake's face then set him loose to crawl around the floor. She twisted the wash cloth into a knot, wishing she could confide in someone about Matt's anger and drinking. She longed for a friend. Stories of bruises, broken bones, and masterfully stitched up cuts, would be wasted on Kat.

Still holding the phone to her ear, she retrieved her plate from the table and set it in the sink. Out of the corner of her eye she caught a movement beyond the kitchen window. The sun reflected brightly in her eyes but not enough to prevent her from seeing the silhouette of a man moving across her driveway and over the back lawn. He was tall, not as tall as Matt she measured with quick relief, and definitely more substantial.

The unassuming shadow moved slowly toward her porch as Kat continued. "And what exactly is that supposed to mean, Miss Megan Williams Hamilton?" she yelled so loudly Megan had to pull the phone away from her ear as she watched the silhouetted figure move closer to the back door. Megan noted the use of her full name. Kat was at the end of her patience. "This is absurd. Childish. Preposterous. I'm not going to stand by and let you do this. What on earth will your father say? What will my friends think? Just tell me where you are so I can send someone to get you."

"I can't do that." Megan did a quick inventory to make sure the house looked presentable as the man, presumably the landlord, and his massive dog easily made their way up the back porch steps.

"Don't be ridiculous, Megan," she laughed haughtily. "Of course you can."

The man tapped lightly on the screen. "Listen, Kat," Megan wiped a wayward crumb off the tile counter and into the sink, "I've got to go."

She dropped the phone onto the counter and opened the door.

"Hi," he extended his hand to her with a smile. His arms had to be the size of her thighs and, despite the earliness of the season, were already kissed with sun. "I'm Carter," he introduced himself then clarified, "the landlord. Sorry I didn't make it by earlier. Yesterday ended up being busier than I'd planned."

Megan quickly sized him up as she shook his hand. He was clean-cut and well groomed, in a strange and rugged way. The strength in his handshake surprised her, although based on his bulk it shouldn't have, as did his youth. She'd expected a landlord much older than herself, not someone of about the same age. The top button of his white dress shirt hung open, exposing a white t-shirt underneath. Polished cowboy boots peeked out from under the cuff of his dark, neatly pressed slacks.

"Are you the guy I saw next door yesterday?" she wondered out loud. "The one with all the boys?"

"Ah, my scouts," he smiled at the comment. "Hope they didn't bother you too much." She opened the screen. "They can get a bit loud sometimes, but they really are a good group of boys."

He walked over to the kitchen table and relieved his hand of the small bundle of papers.

His dog, quiet yet formidable, sat in the doorway clearly waiting for an invite of his own. His giant eyes pled for recognition. She let the screen door shut, barricading the beast outside. Even if dogs weren't dirty and unpredictable, this one was wildly intimidating. His head was the size of a watermelon, his feet small continents of their own. His nose was short and his jowls long. He looked mean; meaner than any animal she'd ever seen before. In his black coat he could sneak around in the darkness; with his massive shoulders he could terrorize in the light.

The man sat down at the table. Megan, trying to remember his name, took a passing glance at the beast of a dog, handed a bundle of plastic measuring cups to Jake, and then slid into the remaining chair at the breakfast table.

"So," he opened with a subtle smile. His teeth were bright against his tanned face. "Would you rather I do this with your husband?" He turned to acknowledge Jake crawling about the floor, then glanced at the stack of documents neatly stacked between him and Megan on the table.

"No," Megan picked up the pen. "I think I can handle it."

He thumbed tentatively through the documents, noting the terms of the lease silently to himself. "This was my grandma's house," he explained. "It needs some fixin' up," he clarified as if Megan hadn't already seen the myriad of flaws.

"It will do fine," Megan twisted the pen eagerly in her hand, trying to ignore the brawny forearms staring back at her from across the table.

He glanced at the last sheet of paper in the stack then closed the pile. "I assume Sally Rae told you the terms when she showed you around?" he asked. "The monthly rent and such?"

"Yes," Megan answered, though she wasn't quite sure what the "*and such*" was.

"Good." He picked up the stack of documents, tapped them into a neat stack, then set them aside. "How 'bout we forego all this busy work and just shake on it then?"

Perplexed, she met his extended hand with hers. "I've got your first and last month's rent, if you'd like."

"Sure," he nodded politely.

She left the room long enough to get the allotted deposit from her ever shrinking stash. "Here you go," she offered the small stack of bills to him.

"Thanks," he tucked the cash into his breast pocket without counting it. "No need to worry about Bosco, by the way." He smiled at the door. "He's just a big ol' kitten."

Megan looked over just in time to see the giant tongue swipe over Jacob's face through the screen. "Eww," she rushed to pull Jake away, disgusted by the very idea of dog slobber. "Maybe it'd be best if you just kept the dog away."

"I'm sure that won't be a problem. He's friendly enough, but he's a one owner kind of dog. He doesn't go much of anywhere without me. Do ya, Boss?" He stepped between Megan and the door. "By the way," he nodded towards the cellphone on the counter. "They can track those things, you know." He opened the screen and patted the dogs head "If you need anything," the dog was right on his heals as he stepped off the porch, "you can find me next door."

If he'd worn a hat she was sure he'd have tipped it. None-the-less she watched his head bob in a subtle nod as he walked away. As soon as he'd disappeared into the beautiful yellow Victorian, she removed the battery and sim card from her phone and dropped all three pieces separately into the kitchen drawer.

Chapter Twelve

Fresh cut lumber. Saw dust. Nature's masterpiece molded into form, function, and beauty. This was Carter's passion. Milling, planeing, and mitering creations. He loved the smell of fresh wood; the satisfaction of a job masterfully done. Each project he finished only made him love the work even more – if only he could pay the bills with his handiwork, then life would be perfect. But times were different than when he was a kid. His dad may have been able to make a living with his carpentry skills, but most people didn't appreciate handcrafted workmanship anymore.

The same was true of the produce industry. Though his grandparents had been able to sustain a life with the proceeds of the orchard, the entire farming industry had changed. Competition had grown and international importation had a way of squishing out the little guy. It was a vulnerable market; one that fluctuated with weather, FDA regulations, and politics.

He'd inherited his grandparents apricot orchard and his dad's woodworking tools, but Carter's livelihood was supported mostly on the back of his home-based business of web development and commercial layouts. Not having to report to an office every day allowed him plenty of flexibility to keep his hands dirty helping out on the orchard, but more importantly, it provided him ample time to kick around in the garage with his woodworking tools.

Carter lightly sanded the maple mantelpiece then dusted it off. It was sure to be a conversation piece in the Dean's home and he couldn't wait to stain it and finish the installation so he could move on to one of his personal projects. Tinkering around with the commissioned mantel had sparked an idea for his own home. Over the next few weeks he planned to put the idea into play. The alarm on his watch, however, told him that play time was over for the day. He had an in-office meeting with Zezmer Corp, one of his newest and potentially biggest clients, in an hour. With a forty-five minute commute time, he'd left himself less than fifteen minutes to get cleaned up and out the door.

He made quick work of cleaning up the wood shop. The key to quality work, his dad always said, was an organized shop. "A place for everything and everything in its place." Even the tools he'd added to his father's extensive collection had a home of their own.

"Let's go Boss," he said, sweeping the last of the saw dust into the garden before closing the garage door behind him. The dog didn't budge. "Come on, Boss," he said again, receiving the same disregard as before. Bosco sat alert, eyes and ears pitched across the property line at the giggling toddler next door. "Come on, Boss," he stepped towards the house, "Let's go!" This time it was a command.

Bosco shot a quick look over his shoulder at Carter then sprung forward in a dash towards the excited baby. One hundred and seventy-five pounds of energy bounced away faster than Carter could keep up. "Bossssssssco!" he yelled, hot on the dog's heals.

"I'm sorry," he said, pulling the dog back before his excited tongue could get a second lick across the baby's face.

The color drained from the protective mother's face, making her shocked eyes nearly pop off the top of her cheek bones. She guarded her baby in her arms and scooted toward the back porch with a disgusted sigh. The baby giggled excitedly.

"Megan, right?" he clarified with a nod. She'd been his tenant for less than a week and he was already scaring her off. "I'm really sorry." He was about to explain his bullmastiff's love for kids but the dog beat him to it. Bosco nuzzled his massive head into the baby's side then flopped down on his back and propped his legs straight up in the air anticipating a belly rub.

"Bosco," Carter shook his head, "No! Not now."

"Thought he was obedient?" Megan quipped as she distanced herself and the baby further away from the dog.

"I'm sorry," he said again as he took firm hold of Bosco's collar. "We're going!"

Bosco put his tail between his legs and whimpered away as he obediently followed Carter's lead back to their house. "I don't know what's gotten into you," Carter declared. Bosco slowly shuffled along, sadly looking over his shoulder every couple of steps.

The dog had never disobeyed before and Carter had no idea why he'd chosen now to start, but for some reason he was fixated on the new neighbors. Maybe it was a novelty thing, but Boss had been around babies and kids his whole life. So what was so special about *this* baby? Was it those super round cheeks or that contagious little giggle? Maybe it wasn't the baby he liked. Maybe it was the mother. He didn't know. What he did know, however, was that they – Megan and her baby – didn't belong here. He'd known it the first second he'd laid eyes on her car. He'd known it even more the moment he'd stepped into the kitchen with her. Her hands were soft and manicured; her posture prim and proper. Megan was no country girl. He knew her type; had met one too many of them while finishing his degree in Santa Barbara. Classy. Moneyed. Fast-paced. Eccentric. Egotistical. She wouldn't last long here; people like her never did. There was no elegance or sophistication to be found for miles, just good ol' down-to-earth humanity with a side of old school integrity.

Megan was just passing through, he was sure of it. She was the kind of girl that needed paved roads, sidewalks, groomed yards, meticulous order. Surely she'd move on as soon as those bruises disappeared from her scrawny arms and the cruelty that caused them faded from her memory. He'd sized her up quickly and figured having her sign a lease would've been pointless. When she'd paid the first and last month's rent with cash, he'd known it was the right decision. At least he wouldn't have to worry about bounced checks when she decided to roll her fancy self in her equally fancy car out of town.

He quickly showered and threw on some slacks then, locking the dog in the house, gave his posh new tenant one last apologetic nod as he hopped in his truck and pulled out of the drive.

City parking garages aren't designed for pickup trucks, especially old tanks like Jade, and by the time Carter found a spot on the street, he had to sprint to make his meeting on time. His presentation was a quick sale as he'd come so highly recommended by the owners of Ridgeco Productions. They'd been among his first contracts and were supportive and devoted fans of his work. He made note to send them a thank you gift for their referral and, subsequently, his new contract.

"Thank you," Carter said, taking the hand of George Zezmer into his with a firm shake.

"No, thank you," George countered. "I trust that it's going to be a pleasure doing business with you."

"And you, too." He replied genuinely. "I'll get these proofs back to you by the end of next week and we should be ready to roll the campaign out by month's end."

"Perfect, Carter. That's exactly the kind of thing I like to hear."

Carter swapped pleasantries long enough to be polite then made his way as quickly and as nondescriptly as possible to the elevators. As soon as he made it back to his truck, he shed his suit coat, tossed it gently to the passenger seat, then secured his presentation on the floor of the cab.

Glancing at his wristwatch was only a habit; thanks to all of his years of scouting, he could get a pretty good handle on the time simply by noting the position of the sun in the sky. It was waning more toward the west than he'd hoped, a sign that he'd missed his chance to beat the rest of the commuters out of the city. He was grateful he didn't have to make this drive daily but, even so, found himself disgruntled whenever the occasion arose.

The stop and go travel had his old truck pleading for relief. The transmission groaned each time it had to downshift back into first gear. "Come on Jade," he soothed the vehicle, gently stoking the grip-bare steering wheel. Without an air conditioner, he drank in the exhaust fumes of the other idling vehicles on the interstate. Deciding to give both himself and the old engine a rest, Carter made his way to an exit and pulled off the freeway. Shutting off the engine, he didn't bother to roll up the manual windows before stepping into a familiar ma-and-pa Mexican restaurant just outside of Santa Clarita.

After dining alone, he hopped back in the cab, grateful for the fresh air and the settling temperature of the day. Not convinced that the traffic had dissipated, however, he began to guide his relic of a truck through the less congested back streets. Every now and then, often without conscious thought, he was drawn back to the streets of the quiet Santa Clarita suburbs. Eventually he'd end up slowly cruising through the most familiar of them. The trees were bigger than their concrete images in his memory and some of the storefronts had changed too, but for the most part, things remained static. Even the taste of spring in the air was the same.

He took the long way around the neighborhood, avoiding the intersection on Singing Hills Drive, as he turned up the hill and into his childhood neighborhood. It always surprised him how small the elementary school was – the image in his mind had it so much bigger. Even more surprising though, was how short the distance between it and the humble house on Poppy Way was. So many days had been spent walking that stretch of asphalt. So many memories tied up in the walls of that simple stucco home.

An unfamiliar car took up the drive and an equally unfamiliar shadow moved across the window. He didn't know who lived there now, but in his mind he could still walk every square foot of the house. The front window belonged to his childhood bedroom; he liked to think it was the best room in the house. If it wasn't, at least he could honestly claim that it had the best view of the distant city lights.

He shrugged off the memory, replacing it with another and then again another. He'd expected that over time some of the memories would have faded, but with each passing year, they seemed only to intensify.

Chapter Thirteen

It'd been a long week full of tasks she'd never imagined herself conquering, but conquer Megan did and she felt a new sense of pride with each little victory. Her first measure had been to start working out a routine. She'd resigned herself to the fact that even with that awful ring around the drain, the bath tub was indeed clean. The toilet made a funny noise until the tank was full, the television had only two stations, and it took about five minutes for the hot water to reach the shower in the morning. The gas stove worked perfectly though, even though cooking meals for one and a half people was a chore of its own. Day by day she made new amends. With no dishwasher, she washed all the dishes by hand. With no salons nearby she groomed her own fingernails. With a dirt driveway, she learned how to walk more carefully in her heals and resorted to cleaning the dust off them daily.

And, more than ever, Megan cherished the moments of Jake's precious life. She hadn't thought she was ready to be a mom nor was she sure it was what she'd wanted for her life plan, but as fate would have it, Jake had turned out to be the best decision she'd ever made. Though unplanned, she'd seen her pregnancy as an opportunity to bandaid her broken marriage. Unfortunately, Matt hadn't seen things the same way. Starting a family wasn't in his carefully charted plans. As early as med school he'd begun mapping out his life. Internship, partnership, and ultimately his own practice - those were in the plans, but a baby was not. Frankly, Megan often wondered if marriage had ever been on his list.

Gravel crunched under her tires as she thanked fate for the amazing gift of motherhood. She slid the transmission into park and pulled the keys from the ignition.

"Well, hello there," a feminine voice called from the driveway, stopping Megan as she stepped from her car. "Remember me?" the lady asked, helping her two toddlers out of the tandem stroller. "I never got the chance to introduce myself last week at the doctor's office."

The front gate creaked open smoothly as the young pregnant mother ushered her kids past her enlarged belly and into the confines of Megan's rose encircled front yard. As soon as she released it, the gate sprung closed with a loud snap. Megan flinched at the sudden sound.

"I'm Brianna," the familiar lady said, unfazed by the quick recoil of the gate.

"I'm Megan." She lifted Jacob from his seat then settled his limp body into one arm so she could shake the hand of the lady she'd informally met her first day in town.

"I thought you were just passing through," Brianna said, retrieving a plate of cookies from the bottom of her stroller.

"I thought I was." Megan smiled in anticipation of the homemade treats. It'd been a long week of food experimentation and she was looking forward to something undoubtedly edible.

"Well, I'm glad you decided to give us a chance." Brianna hitched her cookie-free hand on her hip, accentuating the roundness of her belly.

With Jacob asleep in her arms, Megan pushed her car door shut with her hip. He flinched at the noise, crinkling his brow and puckering his lips at the sound, but didn't wake. "Do you want to sit down?" Megan invited her new friend to the rickety old front porch swing.

The second step squeaked under her foot and the wooden porch was in need of some minor repair, but the beautifully groomed yard of perennials and roses in early bloom was inarguably the best feature of her new little house.

Under the shade of the covered porch, Megan snuggled Jake into her as she watched Brianna's toddlers run around the yard. Jake, still trying to adjust to his new early morning schedule and six busy hours of day care, was worn out. Their new schedule was taking an unplanned toll on Megan too. She sunk deep into the wooden seat, losing her last breath of energy to the swing.

"He's so precious," Brianna smiled at Jake's peaceful, round face.

"Precious but heavy." She answered with a smile then, mindful not to share too much personal information, diverted the conversation away from her and Jacob. "You've got to be exhausted." She eyed the two rambunctious toddlers running, bouncing, spinning, and giggling across the front lawn.

"I have my moments," Brianna traced the curve of Jacob's face with her pinky finger. "His curls are absolutely amazing." She smiled at Jacob then patted the top of her own belly, "I sure hope this little guy gets some just like that."

Megan nodded at the comment. Neither Noah nor Mariah had inherited their mother's blonde hair, let alone her curls. She looked like a pregnant, curly-headed Barbie doll. Minus, of course, the stilettos, the penthouse, and the plastic smile. "When are you due?"

"Fifteen more weeks," she sighed. "At least I only have to go through half of the summer with this melon," she smiled.

Jacob slowly stirred to life and perked his ears at the sound of Brianna's children in the yard. His cuddle was short lived as he became excited by the energy of other children and wanted to get down and play. Hesitating for a curious moment when his hands touched the grass, he looked at Megan questioningly then charged forward on his knees.

"This is all so new to him," Megan explained before realizing that the novelty of grass surely had to sound stupid.

"Kids are pretty resilient," Brianna smiled genuinely. "He seems to be adjusting just fine."

"I hope so," Megan assumed she was referring to their change of address. Bri knew nothing of their current situation. Jake did seem to be handling all the change much better than she was.

"The real question," Brianna turned to Megan with a smile, "is how are you adjusting?"

Megan wondered only briefly as to why Brianna would think she had some adjusting to do then, noting the contrast of her stilettoed feet on the weathered porch, she realized how obviously out of place she must look. "Well, this certainly isn't Rodeo Drive," she quipped through a twisted grin.

"No," Brianna laughed, "it's better."

The swing gently rocked beneath the two new friends as the sun began to fall over the horizon. Their friendship felt so natural and comfortable that when Brianna opened up about her life, Megan was tempted to do the same. Maybe Brianna would be the confidant she craved... but, she sighed, it'd be short lived. Ten days had to have been ample time for Matt to stew. She called her lawyer every day from the doctor's office and anticipated positive news soon.

"I spent most of my childhood at our beach house," Megan finally offered when Brianna told her she'd grown up on a ranch just outside of Chula Vista. It was harmless information, she concluded.

"That must've been heavenly," Brianna basked in the idea. "While I was kickin' around in boots, you were lavishing the sand between your toes."

Sand between your toes isn't all that dreamy when the only person you have to share it with is a nanny, but Megan let her new friend hold on to her fairytale image anyway.

"What do people around here do for fun?" she asked at the first sign of a lull in Brianna's stories of ranching, motherhood, and the simple nature of her life.

"I don't know," Brianna scrunched her face in thought. "I read a lot of books, I keep a mothering blog, and I just started learning how to sew, but mostly," she absorbed every detail of her kids in the yard. "I just like to hang out with my family." She resituated herself on the hard wood of the swing. "Wow," she chuckled, "that sounds pretty lame, doesn't it?"

"It actually doesn't sound all that bad," Megan answered. "If you have someone to share it with, that is."

Growing up, Megan rarely saw either of her parents. When her dad wasn't busy pulling late hours at the office, he was either tucked away in his private den or out on the golf course. Her mother, too, though not employed, pawned Megan's care onto one nanny after another while she floundered her time away at tennis lessons and country club lunches. Motherhood had been a burden to Kat. Like Brianna, Megan found it to be a delight.

Brianna gently patted her new friend's knee. "I know it's probably hard to see from your perspective, but this really isn't a bad life."

The soft fiddle of crickets played from the shadows of the porch as the breeze picked up the tender taste of early rose buds and delivered it to Megan's nose. She had a momentary itch for the smell of the surf and the tranquility of waves breaking on the beach before realizing that her current surroundings were equally beautiful in their own right. Reds and oranges spilled their way over the mountain crest as silence painted the air. Sunsets were a thing of clichés and poetry, Megan had always thought, but as the day slipped over the mountain, she drank it in.

"What do *you* do for fun?" Bri turned the question back on her.

"Fun?" Megan churned the word over in her mind. She'd grown up thinking the whole country club scene must be fun, but as an adult found it less than exciting. And, unless facials and mani-pedis were considered hobbies, she didn't really have any of those either. "I danced in college," she finally answered.

"Dancing? Really?" Brianna hitched herself up straighter in the swing. "Well, then, you might just be in luck."

"How so?" Megan anticipated.

Brianna smiled. "Our annual Strawberry Carnival is just around the corner."

"Okay?" Megan had no idea what that even meant. Pensively she pursued, "And there's dancing?"

"Yep. A real live hoe-down."

"You can't be serious. People still do that?"

"Uh, huh. Cowboy hats, denim skirts, plaid shirts, belt buckles, and the whole works." Brianna shifted her feet under the swing. "There are even carnival games and rides, cotton candy, and the annual Strawberry Gala."

"Do I want to know what that is?"

"It's a bake-off. Pies, cakes, casseroles – if you can imagine it, it'll be there. The only rule is that it has to have strawberries in it."

"Sounds like all that's missing is a demolition derby."

"Nah. Every red-neck in town's got you covered with that one. But you're going to have to wait to the first part of July for it. The Strawberry Gala is in May but Apricot Days don't start until the first of July. It's a whole week of eatin' and celebratin'. Starts with the Apricot Parade and ends with our Independence Festival for the Fourth of July."

"So let me get this straight. First you celebrate strawberries? Then you celebrate apricots? For four days? How is that even possible?"

"When that's the means by which your city was founded, you find a way. Pretty much everyone around here is connected to the strawberry fields or the apricot orchards in one way or another. My husband, Brent, is a fifth generation strawberry grower, although, the only fruit he ever touches are the bushels he brings home for our family. His dad and brother run the operation and many of the locals help out in one way or another."

"I see," Megan glanced over the neighboring homes toward the orchard, knowing that on the far side of it strawberry plants were bursting with red splashes of fruit.

"So if Brent's family owns the strawberry field, why doesn't he work there?"

"I guess because farming's just not for everybody. He grew up with his hands in the dirt and at some point realized that it wasn't the life for him."

"So, if he's not a strawberry farmer, what does he do that keeps your family around here?"

"I think his career decided on him," she grinned. "Perhaps you've seen the SUV down the street with the Sheriff logo on it?"

Megan shook her head. She didn't recall seeing it, but she hadn't looked either. Rural, dirt streets were much longer and sparse than the city streets she was accustomed to. Just down the street, she'd learned, could mean a couple of football fields or even a couple of miles. Carter was her closest neighbor, Sally Rae's house was hidden away somewhere at the end of a long drive across the street. She didn't realize there was anyone else close enough to be called a neighbor.

"Well," Brianna continued, "that's my Brent... or Deputy Tall, if you want to get technical."

The conversation lulled for a moment, giving the pair of mothers a chance to bask in their children's joy. There was nothing that Noah touched, be it a toy truck, a rock, or even a fleck of dirt, that didn't fascinate Jake. Mariah, though not much bigger than Jake, took on a natural motherly affection toward him. He soaked it up and was only slightly hesitant when she continually tried to carry him.

"What are you doing Sunday evening?" Brianna stood and stretched her back.

"I'll have to check my schedule," Megan teased, wishing for an ounce of the natural beauty her new friend possessed. "Oh, wait," she smiled, "I don't have one."

"Perfect," Brianna pushed her belly out and rubbed her hips. "Then why don't you and Jacob come over for dinner? Brent's been dying to meet this girl they call *Hollywood*."

"Hollywood? What? Who are *they*? And why do they call me *Hollywood*?" Megan stepped from the porch swing to do some leg stretching of her own.

"Umm, don't know if you've noticed, but people don't exactly drive fancy cars around here," she chuckled. "When one shows up everyone seems to notice."

"I guess that could be a problem," Megan thought out loud.

"I wouldn't worry about it much," Bri seemed to notice the concern on Megan's face. "Soon as someone does something stupid - which believe me, happens all the time - you and your car will be old news."

Megan played the nickname over and over in her mind the next few days. Maybe the car was too conspicuous. Maybe she needed to get rid of it. Maybe it was too "Hollywood" for Mountainside. And, maybe that meant she was, too. As she pushed Jake's stroller down the dirt road towards Brianna's house, she considered the possible ramifications and, subsequently, her options.

"It's so good to finally meet you," the dark green door rushed open before Megan had a chance to knock. "I'm Brent." Even without the biceps bulging from his shirt, the massive man was opposing. The gun on his hip did nothing to ease her trepidation. "Brianna's been talking about you non-stop all weekend," he reached for her hand and took it warmly - gently - into his.

"Don't believe him. He's exaggerating," Brianna interjected her tiny frame around her substantial husband and welcomed Megan and Jake into their modest farm house.

"I'm not," he chuckled. "You'd think she'd found her long lost sister or something," Brent wrapped his arms around his wife tenderly. He was equally as handsome as his wife was beautiful, but Megan could see immediately that their love was far deeper than anything physical. His eyes pierced Brianna's longingly; unspoken words moved through the air. "Nothing matters more to me than her happiness, you know." He looked first at his wife then at Megan. "And, if you make her happy, then consider yourself welcome here anytime."

"He's not lying," a familiar voice echoed from the porch.

"I never do, brother."

Megan turned in time to see Brent grasp Carter's hand then pull him into a hug. She didn't realize he'd been invited to dinner too. "Are they really brothers?" she whispered to Brianna. The two grown men bore absolutely no resemblance to each other. They were equally tall but Carter had dark, warm features and ample amounts of lustrous coffee colored hair.

Brent's cool-eyed, fair-skinned head had a luster of its own – one caused by the light reflecting off of its perfectly shined smoothness.

"Not by blood, but in every other way," Bri answered. "You know," she offered with a smile, "they didn't even like each other the first time they met. May or may not have ended in a little brawl between the two of them. Isn't that right, boys?"

Brent slugged Carter's shoulder. "Something like that." They both laughed like adolescent boys.

"Unca Amma," Mariah burst through the room and jumped into his arms. Her big round eyes glistened as she wrapped her tiny arms around his neck.

"Princess Mariah, I think you get more and more beautiful every time I see you." Carter kissed the toddler's blushing round cheek as she giggled. He tickled her bare toes and she giggled even louder.

"Where Co?" she wriggled around in his arms trying to sneak a peek out the open door.

"Boss?" he shook his head. "Is that all you care about? Huh, little monster? What about me?" he nuzzled into her neck and made a growling sound.

"Co," she repeated, "Co!" The word giggled off her tongue.

"No way, missy," Carter teased, "there's no way that dog is gettin' a kiss before I do."

Mariah's eyes lit up and her cheeks rose into little pink balls as she sighed. "Daddy says I no kiss boys," she frowned at him.

"Not even Uncle Ammon?" he frowned back.

Ammon? Megan wondered. She thought his name was Carter.

Mariah sighed and tilted her head towards her dad. "Eben Unca Amma, daddy?" she questioned with broken hearted eyes.

Brianna stroked Brent's arm then answered for him, "Only Uncle Ammon," she said.

"But no one else," Brent nodded with a grin. "Besides, if you don't humor him, who will?"

"What's that supposed to mean?" Carter asked as Mariah pressed her lips to his cheek.

"It means, you aint kissin' any ladies and we all know it," Brent's face lit up with laughter.

"And," Carter defended as he slid Mariah out of his arms, "what makes you the expert on my love life?"

"Love life is a pretty generous term to be flingin' around, bro. Betcha can't tell me the last time you had dinner with a lady."

"Betcha I can." Carter mused.

"For the record, Grandma Beth doesn't count." Brent challenged. "And neither do your meals at Ruth's Diner."

"Also for the record, its none of your business," Carter played.

"Okay, boys," Brianna interrupted. "I don't see any reason why you can't continue this while you're setting the table."

"Because," Brent started.

"That would fall under the heading of multi-tasking," Carter finished.

"And you know, baby, that we don't do that very well," Brent pulled Brianna into him and kissed her forehead.

"Well," she watched Mariah run out the front door to meet the ginormous dog, "I suppose now would be a good time to start practicing, don't ya think?" She pushed the boys toward the kitchen then followed Mariah onto the front porch.

Megan watched the grown men grunt and tease each other out of the corner of one eye while she kept tabs on the beastly dog out of the other. *Was this whole dinner thing some weird attempt at a set up? Or,* she wondered, *we're Brent and Bri just being neighborly?*

"Guess I should've told you that Ammon would be here," Bri seemed to read her thoughts. "We feed him almost every Sunday."

"It's fine," Megan answered with a relieved shrug as she turned her attention back to the big dog. "Yuck," she flinched as Bosco's giant, slobber tongue consumed Mariah's little face. "Doesn't that bother you?" Jake giggled in her arms and reached for the dog.

"Boss?" Brianna asked. "He wouldn't hurt a fly."

"That's what Carter said," Megan tightened her hold on Jake as he tried to maneuver out of her arms. "But I don't believe it. A dog that size could do some serious damage," she shook her head. "He's got to weigh at least a hundred pounds."

"One-seventy-five," Carter's voice sounded from the kitchen.

Megan and Brianna looked at each other and giggled. "Seriously," Brianna hollered back, "what do a pair of ladies have to do to have a private conversation around here?"

"There's no such thing as privacy in a small town, baby," Brent called back with a snicker. "You should know that by now."

Megan had never been to a dinner party before that didn't consist of fine china, polished silver, alcohol consumption, or a surplus of posturing. She'd never started a meal with a prayer or sat around a dining table full of adults as well as kids. She'd never seen milk served so freely or water served from the tap. She'd never eaten fruit salad made with lemon pudding and marshmallows, barbequed corn on the cob, or chicken breasts slathered with barbeque sauce. She'd also never laughed as hard, ate so abundantly, or felt so welcome.

"Brianna," she asked, handing over a stack of half-empty plastic kids' plates, "I know this must sound crazy," she felt like an idiot for asking, "but why does your family keep calling Carter Ammon?" She'd waited all night for Brent and Carter to be out of earshot so she could ask the question. They'd taken the kids to the back yard to play.

"It's really not a big deal," Bri explained, rinsing the dishes and placing them in the dishwasher. "His family calls him by his first name, which is Ammon, but everyone else calls him by his last name, Carter."

"Oh," Megan pondered the information for a minute. "Why?" she continued clearing the table, uncertain why she even cared.

"I think it started when he first came to live with his grandparents, though I didn't live here then. Brent said that he was a pretty quiet kid and nobody really knew his name, but everybody knew his grandpa Ez." She rinsed the dishes as she explained. "So they started calling him the Carter kid, and I guess it just stuck."

Megan left the rest of her questions unasked as she glanced out the window at their subject matter. Carter was sprawled on the grass, buried with children. They giggled in unison as one by one Carter lifted them into the air on the soles of his feet. They stretched their arms forward like Super Man, maintaining balance for as long as they could while hysterically laughing. Not one of the three children in the yard was immune to him. He was a kid magnet. Even Jacob, who was a mama's boy and had never taken to any man, was hypnotized by Carter's apparent charms.

Or, was it the dog? That stupid dog. Always at Carter's side.

Noah's bare feet successfully touched down on the sod as he landed his Super Man flight. The setting sun prismed off his spiked hair as he pulled his t-shirt back over his belly-button, giggled, applauded himself, and made a bee-line to the dog.

Jacob, more and more comfortable with his bare knees on the lawn, followed Noah as quickly as his crawl would take him. Megan flinched toward the door but Brianna's hand took hold of her sleeve and pulled her back. "Just watch."

"But...."

"It'll be okay." She swung her arm over Megan's shoulder and held vigil in front of the window.

Jacob stopped short of the dog, planting his bottom with a thud on the lawn. Bosco's tail thumped the ground excitedly. Noah's arms wrapped around the gigantic furry neck and the dog responded by swiping his enormous tongue over the small boy. Noah giggled and nuzzled in closer. Jake giggled and lunged forward. Megan held her breath.

Noah bounced up to his feet and took off with all the energy of a three year old, leaving Jake alone with the mammoth beast. Megan's heart raced. Jake reached his pudgy hand towards the dog's mouth.

Then, in a movement that made Megan's heart stand still, the dog rose to his feet and stepped towards her little Jacob. The beast leaned over her baby, swamping him under his shadow. He nudged him first with a gentle tap of his nose, then again with a whop that knocked Jake backward. The towering dog drug his tongue over Jake's face then smashed his jowls into his chest. The dog's head was as big as her baby's entire body; his muscular shoulders broader than her own. He could easily snarf Jake down in a single bite. Maternal instinct had Megan wanting to bolt out the door to his rescue; Brianna's hold had her pinned to the window, motionless.

The dog's tail thumped wildly as he continued to press into Jake's chest. Without an ounce of grace, the colossal animal dropped to the ground and planted his head gently into Jake's lap. Jake giggled then roughly patted the dog's forehead. The beast didn't flinch at what had to be an unpleasant wallop. Instead, he closed his eyes and, if it was possible for a dog to smile, Megan was sure his jowls were doing such.

Carter reached over and helped roll Jake back to a sitting position. The dog – his head still on Jake's lap - rolled to his back and flung his legs toward the sky. Jake smacked the dog again, this time right between the eyes. The beast looked up and kissed Jake's entire face with his tongue.

Carter knelt down and patted his dog's belly, then tenderly took Jake's assaulting hand in his. He whispered something in the baby's ear, touched Jake's fingers softly with his, then gently guided his tiny hand over the dog's ears. Jake's face lit up like the morning sun as the dog kissed him again.

"Wait up a sec and Ammon will walk with you." Bri followed Megan onto the front porch after a long evening of games, dessert, and conversation.

"He doesn't have to do that." Megan fastened the stroller belt around Jake's exhausted body. "Believe me, downtown L.A. has scarier streets than this. I'm sure I'll be just fine."

"And I'm sure the coyotes would agree." Brent hung his arm around Brianna. Brianna jabbed his ribs with her elbow.

"For some reason I don't feel inclined to believe you." Megan shook her head. The subsequent hours of joking and quick quips had her questioning the validity of anything either Carter or Brent said.

"I wouldn't worry so much about the coyotes as I would the snipes." Carter's eyes gleamed under the porch light as he joined them.

"What's a snipe?" Megan asked as Carter descended the porch steps.

"An elusive little creature," Carter answered smugly.

"Tricky little buggers," Brent added. "Fast too. If you ever see one, you'll know it."

"Hmm?" she pondered the suggestion, wondering how dangerous an animal she'd never heard of could really be. She thanked Brent and Bri yet again for the evening, then put Jake's stroller into motion down the dark, dirt road.

Carter fell quietly into step beside her, seemingly intent to keep an honest distance from her side. Bosco rushed to the head, confidently leading the pack.

"What about the coyotes?" She took it upon herself to break the awkward silence. "Why aren't *you* afraid of the coyotes?" she asked, sure the threat more of their good natured teasing, but not ready to drop the possibility that they were being serious.

"We've got a mutual understanding," he shrugged. "They leave me alone and I'll leave them alone."

"Funny," she smirked feeling privy to his game. "There aren't really coyotes around here, are there?"

"Sure there are, but you don't stand a chance of outrunning them in those shoes."

Megan tipped her head towards her leather Gucci pumps. "You'd be surprised what I can do in heels," she defended. Of course a man like Carter wouldn't appreciate such feats of style.

"If you say so," Carter shrugged before tipping his ear toward the mountain cliff. "Every now and then you'll hear them howling – the coyotes, not the small starving village you could've fed for the cost of those shoes." She flinched at the accusation, but he didn't give her time to refute. "You probably don't really need to worry about 'em, though. They kinda keep to themselves.... Well," he chuckled under his breath, "unless you're a bunny or a chicken that is."

Megan was too engrossed in the enormity of the star-freckled sky to notice his smile. Though trying to dismiss the idea of carnivorous animals in the vicinity, she was suddenly grateful to be accompanied by Carter and his big, intimidating dog. Even if the tales of coyotes proved to be false, the darkness of the night was heavy and quiet... too quiet. The only light came from the dim glow of distant porch lights and the blush of the moon. The smell of newly blossoming lavender and jasmine from nearby gardens interlaced the air, tickling her nose. The melodic chirp of crickets touched her ears.

"You sure seem to have a way with kids." The quiet made her uncomfortable.

"Nah," he shrugged. "I think they have a way with me."

Megan didn't ask the next question that popped into her mind. Carter's relationship status and subsequent paternal status was none of her business. She couldn't help but wonder, though, about the drive that had him rolling on the grass in laughter with the kids. It struck her as odd: a seemingly tough, single man so engaged with children. And, for that matter, equally odd was the swarm of twelve-year-old boys that frequented his company. *Don't judge*, the warning formed itself in her mind at the same time that she caught herself staring at the shadow on his ruggedly handsome jaw line.

"Thanks for walking me home," she pushed the stroller up the drive. Gravel grated at the tires, making them difficult to turn. The smell of roses replaced that of lavender. She shook off the sudden memory of Matt and his overrated, ridiculous bouquets.

"No problem," Carter nodded. He folded his arms across his chest and waited in the drive as his dog walked Megan and Jake to the door.

Chapter Fourteen

Carter had spent nearly every ounce of his free time for the last three years trying to finish up the details of his house. When Grandpa Ez passed away, the last thing Grandma Beth wanted was for him to move in and take care of her. She was as independent and sharp as they came and she wasn't about to let anyone become her babysitter. Similarly, and although he'd spent his adolescence there, Carter wasn't exactly aching to move back onto his grandma's enclosed back porch. When she granted him a portion of her land, he immediately began construction of his own house.

A hundred percent product of his own hands, the exterior shell had gone up in no time. Within six-months, the basic structure of his home was ready for occupancy. He moved in at almost the same time that Grandma Beth got sick. Her cancer came on quickly and with a vengeance, leaving Carter's project to stew while he took care of her. After a two year fight, she succumbed, leaving everything she had to the care of her burned-out, broken-hearted, and completely alone grandson.

Regrouping had been a slow process. Beth was the last piece of family Carter had left, so he did what he did best – escaped into the world of sawdust and creativity. The results were impeccable, even by his own high standards. Every intricate detail of every room told a story of labor and love. One by one he'd adorned the rooms with custom moldings and hand-scraped wood floors. All that was left were the final details of his master suite.

He unloaded the raw mahogany from the bed of his old truck, stacking it carefully in the front of his garage. Oak and pine were easy to come by, but for mahogany of such great quality he'd spent the better part of his day driving to the mill and back. Such sacrifices wouldn't have been worth it if he'd only hoped to replicate the mantel he'd built for the Deans. Theirs had turned out beautiful, but his would be a masterpiece.

"Hey guys," he called as he slammed the tailgate shut. Sam had been coming around an awful lot lately. Things must've been getting rough again at home.

"Hey Carter," the pair of boys rode their bikes up his drive.

"Whatcha' building?" Jamison asked, repositioning the glasses on his nose as he skidded to a stop.

"I'll bet it's a boat," Sam quipped. His stocky build seemed out of proportion to his old BMX bike.

"A boat? What in the world would I do with a boat?" With the pre-teen boys in tow, Carter stepped into his open garage wood shop and organized the newly acquired wood next to his work bench.

"Well, the way I see it," Sam hopped off his bike, letting it drop roughly to the ground as he continued, "a boat is good for one of two things." He raised two thick fingers definitively for Jamison and Carter to see. "One," he announced, waving his hand as he folded a finger down, "would be to float it."

"You don't say?" Carter wheeled his table saw out of it storage cubby.

"As a matter of fact," Sam laughed at himself, "I do." He resituated the tattered ball cap over his dark, buzz cut hair.

"And," Carter blew at the sawdust on the saw, sending it rippling up into a cloud. "Do I dare ask what the second option is?" He looked up at the boys and caught a glimpse of his grandma's kitchen window behind them. He thought he saw Megan watching, but immediately shrugged off the idea.

"Now, stay with me here," Sam said. "I was thinking we could put wheels on it."

"And tow it behind your four-wheeler," Jamison kicked the toe of his sneaker at the sawdust on the garage floor.

"To the top of that mountain," Sam pointed past the back border of Carter's property.

Carter followed their glances to the top of the mountain, surmising its slope and altitude. He'd ridden his ATV to the top several times but doubted a boat ride down would be a realistic venture, wheels or not. He smiled at the boys then, still listening to their excited banter, went back to work.

"Then," Jamison's lanky frame bounced with excitement as he caught the vision, "we could ride it all the way down."

Sam nodded his approval. "Yeah, kinda like a sled but with wheels."

"Haha, that'd be awesome."

"I'll bet we could make it go really fast."

"So fast we'll have to pick bugs out of our teeth!"

"And, how do you plan to steer it?" Carter asked, gently throwing wisdom into the boys' slapdash plan. "There are a lot of rocks and trees on that mountain." For a second time, in passing glance, he thought he saw Megan at the window. Even though she was admittedly beautiful, he still didn't know what to make of her.

"With a steering wheel, of course," Sam answered with the cockiness of a twelve-year-old know-it-all.

"Of course," Carter smirked. He shook the thought of Megan from his head. The last person she'd ever be interested in was a guy like him. The feeling was mutual.

"We'd only need to avoid the trees, the rocks we could jump," Sam would never be accused of being boring. Carter grinned at his animation.

"Yeah, with like super shocks or something," Jamison contributed.

"Oh, and we could install a rocket booster too."

"Or a jet pack!"

"And light the fuse like a firecracker," Sam made a swooshing sound as his hands mimicked the striking of a match.

"Fire!" Their eyes sparkled in unison.

"We could blow it up!" Sam exclaimed.

"And how are you going to do that if you're in it?" Carter offered with a chuckle.

The boys snapped their heads towards each other, piecing together another facet to their plan. "With a remote control," they quickly agreed.

Carter listened silently as the boys' plan continued to evolve from boats, to fires, and then on to blowing things up. It hadn't seemed like all that long ago that he was trying to score some ether from Grandpa Ez in his own young fascination with fire. Next thing he knew they'd be asking him about rifles, then machine guns, then bazookas.

"Where do you think we can get a cannon?" Sam asked too sullenly for Carter to believe that he was kidding.

Cannons. Carter chastised himself for not thinking big enough. Of course, he thought, what twelve-year-old's project doesn't need a cannon?

"What for?" He shrugged off the outlandish request and went back to measuring out where he needed to make a cut to the wood.

"Well," Sam swaggered confidently, "if we're going to blow up a boat, maybe we should do it pirate-style."

"Pirate-style?" Carter smiled at the term, knowing full well where this idea was heading.

"Yeah, like with a cannon," Jamison clarified.

"So, let me clarify," Carter stopped his work and eyed the boys. "You want me to build you a boat then help you blow it up?"

"Uh, huh," Sam pulled the stool out from under the workbench and immediately began spinning around on it.

"And explain to me why exactly I would want to do that?"

"Cause it'd be cool," Sam stopped spinning long enough to nod.

"Starting forest fires is cool?" Carter solicited.

"We're not going to start a forest fire," Sam defended. "We just want to shoot a cannon at a boat."

"And blow it up!" Jamison added.

"And," Carter chuckled despite himself, "what happens when you miss?"

"We won't," Sam answered cockily. "We could get some heat-seeker radar stuff like those Apache helicopters have."

"Sounds logical enough," Carter played along. "But exactly what heat would it be seeking?" he asked.

"The fire that we light in the back of the boat," Sam shook his head as if it were the obvious answer.

Carter wiped the last of the saw dust off the table then set his rag down. "How 'bout this," he led the boys out the open garage door. "I've got this pile of scrap wood over here. Why don't you two build your own boat? Research it, design it, and build it. Then, after we float it, we'll see how you feel about blowing it up."

"Sweet!" Sam kicked at the pile of wood. "You mean we can use all this?"

"Nothin' but scrap to me," Carter shrugged. "Have at it!"

The boys smiled in elation. "Thanks," they echoed in unison then, with wide eyes, turned to each other and began plotting a plan.

"Hey, boys," Carter called across his yard. It was hard not to laugh at the half-brained concoction taking form just beyond the groomed part of his yard. "It's time to clean up for the day." He was afraid to even ask what their thought process was, because, he figured, it was unlikely that there had been any. "Why don't you start hauling all your tools back so I can lock up the shed," he called again, wiping at the furniture stain on his hands.

"Just a little longer?" Sam pled.

"Can't do it," Carter hollered back. "We've got scouts tonight, remember?"

"Uh," Sam argued, "do we have to go?"

"To scouts?" Carter asked making his way towards the lean-to whatchamadinger they'd built. "I thought you liked scouts."

"Yeah, usually I do." Sam tapped at an invisible nail with his hammer. "But, why do we have to go to the old-people place? I don't like it there. That's not fun."

"I like it there," Jamison contributed. His arms were full of wayward tools. "The people are really nice."

"I agree, Jamison. They are nice." Carter slipped the hammer out of Sam's hand, slung his arm over the boy's shoulder, and guided him toward the garage. They put all the tools away, closed up shop, and loaded the boys' bikes into the back of Carter's truck.

"I'll be back to pick you up in about an hour," he instructed as he pulled up to Jamison's house. He gave the same instruction at Sam's house with the addition of, "and don't forget your scout shirt."

"Why didn't you tell Jamison that, too?" Sam smirked.

"Because," Carter lightly slugged his arm, "Jamison isn't the one who forgets it all the time."

Chuckling, Sam jumped out of the open door. "By the way," he leaned back into the cab, "my mom said to tell you thanks for the box of food last week."

"No prob," Carter answered.

"And she said to let you know that..." With one hand on his hip and the other twisting a pretend strand of hair, he struck an awkward pose and pitched his voice falsetto, "... if there's ever *anything* she can do for you," he guffawed an exaggerated wink, "the door is always open."

Carter rolled his eyes. *How do you respond to that? Especially to a kid?* Luckily, Sam didn't wait for a response before he slammed the truck door and ran across the patch of weeds that at one point had been a lawn.

~   ~   ~

Megan wondered about the man beyond her window. Why those boys flocked to his house, she could only speculate. It didn't make sense that a semi-decent looking, muscle brandishing man like Carter was single. He wasn't exactly her type, just a bit too rough around the edges for her liking, but she imagined in a small town he could probably have his pick of ladies. So, *why hadn't he?* Other than his scouts, he was a classic recluse – not that she was stalking him or anything, she defended to herself. But why didn't she ever see women visit? Why didn't she ever see him dress up and go out? And, maybe more of a bother, why was he so indifferent to her?

It's not like she wanted him to want her, or anything of the sort. The very idea was ridiculous, she thought, as she noticed how flattering his scout shirt looked over his well-defined arms. The short, khakis sleeves almost cut into his tan biceps; she noticed purely under the context that the color of his uniform accentuated his tan, not because she was checking him out, she rationalized yet again.

The wind tousled the carefree locks of his hair as he stepped off his porch and strode to his truck. The truck rumbled to life and he turned toward her with a sheepish smile. She tripped over the rug as she quickly stepped into the shadow of her kitchen. She hoped he didn't think she was watching him, because she wasn't. He was so far from her type the very idea was humiliating.

She picked her empty glass up from the counter and turned on the kitchen tap. Directing her attention to washing her glass, she pretended not to notice the commotion the scouts made just beyond her window. Drying the freshly cleaned cup, she positioned it tidily in the cupboard, then skirted to the table with her notepad. Carter's old green truck thundered out of the drive and down the dirt lane.

Chapter Fifteen

Matt listened to the voicemail for a second time, smiling at Kat's adoration and hoping his decision to entrust her with Megan's little make-believe tryst wouldn't come back to bite him. What his mother-in-law didn't know certainly couldn't hurt her. In fact, what he'd led her to believe could actually play out to help him in the end. He was sure Megan wasn't having an affair, but what other excuse could he come up with to make Kat think he was the victim? What other way to anchor her devotions to him even deeper than they already were?

He slipped his loafers off and meticulously arranged them with the rest of his designer shoe collection in his closet. He shrugged out of his tie and repeated the meticulous act of putting it where it belonged. He had to admit that not having Megan around did have its pleasantries. His hand floated across the top of his clothes hangers. Each designer shirt hung on a cedar hanger and was arranged by style, cut, and color. Each hanger faced the same direction, equally spaced, and in perfect order. Megan's side of the closet, in her absence, maintained the same level of perfection. There were no randomly scattered socks to deal with, no dresses hanging in the wrong color order, no backwards hangers disrupting the model, and, maybe best of all, no baby paraphernalia disrupting his peace and tidiness.

He loosened his top buttons and touched the digital key pad to turn his shower to an optimal 108 degrees Fahrenheit. Steam began to fill the room, but it wasn't enough to loosen the knots in his neck. Matt's house may have been in perfect order but without Megan, his life was in shambles.

He had to find her... and quick. Even a loveless marriage, sour and cold as it was, was better than the hell that awaited him without her.

~   ~   ~

Megan logged out of her email and stared blankly at her reflection in the computer monitor. What was Matt's problem? Why wouldn't he respond to her attorney's requests? It'd been just over three weeks and still no response. Knowing just how petty the *amazing* Doctor Hamilton was, she was impressed that he hadn't figured out how to flip the situation on its head and take control. *Or,* she ran a nervous hand through her overgrown bangs, *maybe he had.*

"Megan," Brianna smiled over the receptionist counter, pulling her from her stupor. "You look like you need a break."

"You're probably right," Megan smiled at her new, and honestly, probably only real friend in the world. The girls in her private school, tennis club, and even dance team had always been friendly, but she figured the draw was simply the appeal of the Williams family financial and social status. Like her mother, image and money meant everything to most of the girls who'd claimed her friendship over the years, but where were they now?

"How'd your check up go?" Megan brushed aside her personal worries and smiled over the reception desk at her friend.

"Still got twelve weeks left," Bri grimaced a crooked smile at her belly. "This little guy's gonna come out walking if he keeps growing the way he is. Either that, or they're gonna have to roll me into the delivery room with a fork-lift," she laughed.

"Well, I think you look beautiful!" Megan offered genuinely, wishing someone had provided her the same compliment when she'd felt like a pregnant barge.

"Thanks," she beamed. "It's probably my new haircut. I changed it up a bit. Do you like it?" she flipped her head from side to side, showing off the flirtatious layers she'd had cut in.

"It looks great, Bri. Fun and light and..." she looked for the right word before settling on, "summery."

"It's amazing how a little trim and color can make you feel so fabulous." She flipped her hair again. "You know what you need?" she leaned on to the counter. "You need a little pampering party."

Megan's reflection screamed back at her from the computer monitor. Bri was more right than she could possibly know. She was so many weeks over-due for a root-touchup that she'd quit keeping track. "You're probably right," she swiped her hand through her overgrown bangs. "But what's a girl gonna do? Between work and Jake I just don't have two seconds to myself." Not to mention the tightness of her budget, but she didn't mention that part. She assumed her money concerns would seem petty to most of her new neighbors.

Bri fished through her purse and pulled out her cell phone. "I need another doctor's appointment in four weeks," she stated to Megan as her fingers began typing into her phone. She became engrossed in whatever she was doing on the screen for a few minutes then added, "You better call Emily and let her know I'm picking up Jake today."

"What?" Megan's fingers froze on the keyboard. "Why would you..."

"You have a hair appointment," she pulled one of Doc Stone's cards from the stack and, after briefly referencing her phone, jotted down an address on the back of it. "Five-fifteen. Her name's Annita." She slapped the card down in front of Megan. "And she's fabulous."

After almost two hours in Annita's chair, Megan agreed. She was fabulous. And, as she stroked her hair in the rear view mirror she wondered why she'd ever let Kat convince her that she looked better as a blonde. How had she ever believed that her amber eyes were suited for bleached-out hair?

It was the same catalyst, she realized, that had defined most of her adult life. She'd never done anything but follow Kat's every call. She was done being a blonde. Done hanging out with pretentious snobs. Done following Kat's lead. If only she could be done with Matt too, she'd have cause to celebrate. He, however, still had more control over her than she could handle. If only he'd sign those divorce papers, then she could check him off her "done" list as well.

Clouds hung low over the mountains, smothering the evening sun with their weight, but even the dismal sky couldn't dampen her mood. Bri had been right. A little bit of pampering was exactly what she needed. She stole another peek at herself in the rearview mirror, touching the silken, russet colored strands that touched her neck, then took the turn-off out of town and headed up the mountain road.

The closer she got to home, the heavier the clouds hung. If she didn't hurry she'd be making a mad, rain-pelleted, dash across Brianna's yard to pick up Jake and then again to get into her own house. Surely such a dash would ruin her freshly styled hair then neither she nor Bri would fully get to appreciate the beautiful miracle Annita had performed. And, as if her hair wasn't reason enough to out-run the rain, the fact that even a little bit of mud would ruin her shoes was enough to make her toe press down harder on the accelerator.

A single, brilliant rush of lightning lit up the horizon as she approached the first of the strawberry fields. The surge reflected off the strawberry leaves like little disco balls. She quickened her pace, accelerating faster than usual around each newly familiar bend. She could make it, she was sure, if she just moved a little faster. In the distance ahead, the clouds had begun to form grey streaks toward the ground. *Almost there*, she thought, passing the field's entrance. A few more twists in the road and she'd be past the fields all together. A few more after that and the orchards would be behind her as well. Just a few more...

The Audi jolted slightly, tugging at the wheel in her hands. Something was wrong. Despite her strong hold on the wheel, the car pulled ferociously towards the side of the road. She let up on the gas and, cursing at whatever the problem was, lightly engaged her brakes. A subtle alarm sounded, drawing her attention to the control panel. The low-tire-pressure indicator lit up her dash.

She settled the car as far off the road as she could with its minimal shoulder, stopping the passenger side just inches away from the mountain wall. Her good mood officially blown, she stomped out of the car to assess the situation. Sure enough, just as the car's intelligence system had suggested, she'd blown a tire.

"Stupid car!" she snarled, kicking the flat with the toe of her Italian leather pump. Grumbling under her breath, she analyzed her options as she looked up at the threatening sky.

A quick survey confirmed that her options weren't just limited, they were nearly nonexistent. If the rain held off long enough she could make it to the small office at the gate of the strawberry fields. She could see it just behind her, maybe a half a mile down the road. If she could make it, they'd surely have a phone, that is, if anyone were even there. She glanced up the mountain road, then down it again. Other than the rolling cloak of grey sky, there was no sign of life as far as she could see. She tucked her handbag under her arm and, kicking the tire one more time, started down the road toward the small office.

Another flash of lightning lit up the sky. Whether it was really bigger than the first Megan didn't know, but her complete vulnerability made it seem so. The thunder on its tail didn't help matters either. With the sound still ricocheting off the canyon walls, the sky opened up. The office that just moments before had seemed to be her answer became, in another flash of the sky, an impossibility. As fast as she could move her stilettos across the newly forming mud, she reversed her course back up the mountain road.

Back in the shelter of her car, the rain pummeled down around her. She grumbled out loud, cursing the rain, the muddy road, the stupid foreign car with stupid wimpy tires, her stupid husband and his stupid temper for making her leave her home, and her stupid mother for making her marry Matt in the first place. If only she had a stupid phone, or at least a stupid umbrella, she might have a stitch of hope, but as the rain rhythmically pelleted her car, she knew she was stuck. She cursed the sky then buried her head into her steering wheel and opened up a down-pour of her own.

Chapter Sixteen

Wishing he'd paid more attention to the forecast, Carter kicked himself for not driving his truck down to the orchard. Most days he preferred to ride his Polaris 700 from his house and through the orchard to check on things, but with a storm on the horizon he always opted to take ol' Jade. Today he'd made a bad judgment call, leaving the pickup parked at home in the driveway, but as the sky continued to darken, he was at least grateful for the raingear he kept packed in the four-wheeler's cargo box.

Securing his cowboy hat over his head, he grabbed a ragged old jacket off the back of Whitley's chair and bolted out of the office into the rain. Water puddled on the brim of his hat before diverting down his back as he hitched open the cargo box and quickly retrieved the rain suit. The office door swung closed behind him as he ran back inside and shed the now soaked cowboy hat and jacket. He hung them to dry then, like a suit of armor, he pulled the heavy plastic pants over his jeans and slid the matching shell over his shoulders.

Snugging a ball cap over his head, he pulled the plastic poncho over his ears then, appropriately geared for the downpour, Carter locked up the office and pulled his ATV to the main gate of the orchard. He started to take a left onto the main road when a strange feeling prodded him to go toward the strawberry fields. He hesitated for a moment, questioning the illogical feeling. His intuition didn't often lead him astray, so he decided to follow it. He pulled the handlebars to the right, flipped a u-turn across the muddy road, and headed the opposite direction of his house.

Within minutes, the brim of his ball cap was soaked clean through. Cold droplets of rain pelted his face then dripped down to the handlebars.

He thumbed the throttle and steered the machine with ease down the puddled mountain road. Just beyond the third bend, a pair of headlights blurrily cut through the downpour.

His mud tires slid to a graceful stop in front of the crippled Audi. Just inches from the mountain wall, her tire lay completely flat. Cutting his way through the dark sky, he approached the silhouette in the driver's seat.

"You have a flat," he offered as Megan cracked her window down just a hair.

She wiped the tears from her eyes, "I know. Can you fix it?"

"Now?" He raised a leery brow. "I don't ..." he shook his head without finishing the rebuke. Did she really expect him to fix it now? A pair of somber, amber eyes told him the answer.

"I'm afraid it's too wet and," he glanced at the sheer mountain wall, "you're parked too close to the mountain. We're going to have to move the car before I can fix it."

"Okay," she reached for the ignition key.

"No," he shook his head. "Not now. Even if you moved it, the road is like a river. We're going to have to wait til the storm stops."

"I can't do that," her lip quivered. "I have to get home to Jacob."

Rain ran off Carter's gear and down to the puddle laden ground as Megan's eyes welled up with moisture. "Jacob's not with you?" He peered through the rain drenched window at the empty back seat.

"No, he's with Bri," she didn't break contact with the sheet of water running down her windshield.

"Well, then," he smiled. "This just got a whole lot easier." His heal sunk in the mud as he turned and headed back to his four-wheeler.

~   ~   ~

Megan watched in horror as her sole rescuer walked away. The rain poured so hard that everything beyond the glass of her windshield looked like a melted chalk drawing. Maybe it wasn't all rain, she conceded, wiping the fog of tears from her eyes. "Jerk!" she grumbled through shaking lips. She turned the radio up and pushed her aching head back into the leather head rest.

She closed her eyes just long enough to be startled by the sudden rapping on her window. "Had a change of heart, huh?" she growled as she slowly descended her window again.

"What?" He tugged at the brim of his hat, pulling it tighter across his forehead to deflect the water from his face. "Here," he slid an olive colored packet through the window slot.

"What am I supposed to do with that?" she flinched at the horrendous color.

"It's a poncho." He shook his head. "Put it on."

"Why?"

"Just a hunch," he smiled, "but I thought you might like to get out of here and get back to your baby."

"On that?" she nodded towards his hillbilly machine.

"That's all I got."

"I'll get soaked out there," she mumbled.

"Look, Megan, you've got two choices: You can either ride back with me or sit here til the storm stops. What's it gonna be?"

Her jaw tightened and little drops of tears began to form in her eyes. She looked at the machine, looked at the rain, then slowly turned her head and stubbornly locked his eyes with hers.

"Well, what's it gonna be?" He knocked the rain from his shoulders.

She stared off through the windshield.

"I know it doesn't have a designer label," he finally offered with a frustrated sigh, "but this will do a pretty good job keeping you dry." He offered the poncho through the window again. "You can put that on and join me for a little ride back to Bri's house or you can sit here all night. Your choice." He tossed the poncho through her window and splashed his way back to the four-wheeler.

Megan didn't think it could storm any harder than it already had been, but not thirty seconds after sliding into the ugly, military stock parka, throwing her shoes into her handbag, and exiting the dryness of the car with bare feet, the heavens opened up with a vengeance.

"You sure you don't want to put your shoes back on?" Carter asked as she awkwardly climbed to the back of his ATV.

"I'm fine," she snarled, pretending the metal footgaurds didn't bother the soles of her feet. "Just get me to my baby," she mumbled irritably as she situated herself on the wire rack at the back of the machine. "Please," she added for good measure, although she didn't really feel like being gracious.

"You might be a little more comfortable up here," he straddled the seat then patted the sliver of padding left behind him.

She scooted further back on the metal rack and laced her fingers of one hand around the cold steel bars while grasping her shoe-filled handbag with the other. "I'm fine," she reassured herself as much as him.

"Okay," Carter shrugged as the engine rumbled to life.

The machine sprung forward, knocking Megan off balance. She white-knuckle gripped the metal rack, holding her breath in anticipation of every turn and growl of the throttle. Rain pelted her forehead abusively before running down her face and ultimately dripping onto her lap. Her bare feet were painfully cold. Blinking the water out of her eyes, she couldn't see a thing, let alone their progress. Every rock and bump in the road bore its witness on her boney buttocks as she bounced on the cold, unforgiving metal.

"Can you slow down?" she yelled into the wind.

No response.

"Can you slow down?" she yelled again, this time with a hint of irritation.

Carter turned his head toward her. "Did you say something?" he bellowed. "I can't hear up here."

"Yeah," she yelled again, "Can you please slow this thing down?"

Carter retracted his thumb from the throttle to honor her request. The engine quieted minutely as the speedometer dipped to a slower speed.

Megan watched as he wiped the back of his wet jacket sleeve over his goggles; the intensity of the rain against her face made her doubt whether his effort had really made much of a difference.

"Thanks," she yelled to the back of his head. When he didn't respond, she yelled louder, "Thank you!"

"No prob," he cocked his head to the side as he talked. "Is this a better speed for you?"

She considered her answer before responding. Even at a slower pace, she found the ride terrifying and uncomfortable. "Yes," she replied through labored nerves, "this is much better."

"Do you mind if we take a short cut?" he hollered over his shoulder.

"Sounds great," Megan agreed easily. Anything to get off the stupid bike sooner.

Carter turned a hard left, veering the machine onto a narrow path through the apricot orchard. "Hold on!"

He yelled the words too late to spare Megan her horror as the bike bounced down into a gulch, through a massive puddle, and caught what she believed to be several feet of air on the other side. She almost lost hold of her purse as she grabbed hold of Carter for security.

"Sorry," he laughed as her body smashed into his back.

"Somehow I don't think you are." Repositioning her purse on her lap, she sandwiched it in the gap between their parka-smocked bodies then wrapped her free arm around him. "I think you enjoyed it."

"Maybe just a little." She was sure he smiled at the remark.

She grumbled at the sight of another puddle ahead and tightened her grip. Her shoes poked through her handbag and into his back. She assumed it had to be uncomfortable, but he didn't complain. Instead, he smashed her arms into his side with his elbows to anchor her.

"Hold on again!" he hollered.

Mud splashed over their heads, covering every inch of her parka before dripping onto her bare feet. They bounced through a third puddle then a fourth, each time Carter assuring that her arms were securely anchored around him. He was much more substantial than she'd suspected, not that she'd really suspected anything.

By the fifth jump Megan quit offering her muffled pleas for him to divert around the puddles. Had her face not been buried between his shoulder blades, he'd probably have interpreted the silence as a sign that she was enjoying their little ride.

"Are you sure this was a shortcut?" she lifted her head just long enough to throw the words over his shoulder. By the rumble of laughter in his chest she assumed that he'd heard her.

He anchored her arms with his elbows again, a sign that they were about to hit another rough spot, then answered, "Yep. We're just about there."

A few more bumps and jostles later, the machine throttled to a stop. She didn't dare open her eyes. "Are we there?" she whispered into his shoulder. "Or are we dead?"

"Well, I'm feeling pretty alive," he laughed, "and judging by the monster grip you have on my chest, I'm guessing you're still alive too."

"Sorry," embarrassed, she retracted her arms.

"It's okay," he dismounted the machine. "Bri would probably appreciate it if you shed the muddy parka on the porch." He offered her a hand off the bike. "Not sure what she's gonna want to do about those muddy feet though."

Chapter Seventeen

Carter turned down Bri's dinner offer but left the less-than-happy Megan in her care. Supposing he'd given the spoiled princess a hard enough time for one day, he was more than happy to leave her behind while he did a little playing in the rain. About an hour after he'd parked his four-wheeler in the garage, he heard the crunching of Bri's van in Megan's driveway. The prima-donna made it home, safe and dry.

The rain didn't stop until well after midnight.

Despite the fact that Megan probably wouldn't appreciate his efforts, Carter couldn't stand the idea of leaving a mother and her child stranded without transportation. As with any other Saturday, he was up before dawn, but instead of heading to his wood shed, Carter hitched a ride with Whitley to retrieve and repair Megan's stranded Audi.

Before first light he rolled Megan's car into the driveway, new tire and all. Then, feeling energized by the freshly christened spring morning air, he decided to take care of a few needed repairs on his grandma's house. Realizing Megan and the baby were probably still asleep, he determined not to wake her majesty and contained his repair list to the outdoor projects.

Tool belt loaded up and ball cap on, he made quick work of adjusting the overactive gate hinges then moved on to the squeaky porch steps. He fixed the stairs then walked the entire surface of the porch, tightening all the loose boards as he went. By nine he'd already slathered on a coat of primer and was starting in on his first coat of paint.

"Morning," Megan grumbled from behind the screen door. Anchored to the floor with bare feet – notably more delicate than he'd remembered them being when they were slathered with mud - her slight legs poked out from the ivory hem of her satin bathrobe. Jake sat on her hip, still in his pajamas, twisting his fingers through her tussled hair. Even without makeup, the newly introduced reddish browns in her hair made her delicate lips, rich, luminous eyes, and petite features hard to ignore.

"Morning," he smiled at her long enough to be polite, but not long enough to be awkward, then looked back at his work. "I fixed your car," he nodded towards the mud covered auto in the driveway. "The keys are on the dash."

"You sure don't waste any time getting around to stuff, do you?" she muttered.

"Why do tomorrow what you can do today?" He smiled at the line. It was a favorite of his grandpa's. He dipped his brush into the paint can then wiped the excess off the bristles before spreading it over the railing.

"Thanks," she finally offered, clearly still upset about their muddy little ride. "I was about to make some breakfast. Would you like some?"

"No thank you, ma'am, I already ate."

"Are you sure?" she asked. "I've got to cook something for myself and Jake anyway."

"Really, I'm okay." He deliberately kept his focus on the porch. "I had a bowl of cereal earlier this morning."

She pitched her hip. "Please let me prepare something for you. It's the least I can do." She nodded toward the fresh tire on her Audi.

Carter turned long enough to see a faint smile brush across her face. She untangled Jake's hands from her hair then shook the knot out. Sun-touched locks feathered her face as she kissed her baby's sausage fingers. "Since you put it that way," he nodded, recognizing her attempt at a peace offering, "how can I say no?"

She almost smiled. "Give me about thirty minutes." She started to turn then added, "I can't promise anything fantastic, but it'll be edible.... Or, at least I hope so."

Megan didn't linger long enough for him to counter. "I hope so too," he mumbled into the wind. "And," he smirked at her still simmering attitude, "I hope you're not trying to poison me, lady."

When he seated himself at the old farm table, he was stifled by the culinary presentation she delivered. He indulged every bite of the omelet. Bacon, spinach, and avocado meshed together in a symphony of delicious harmony. It was like nothing he'd ever eaten before. And, when he thought it couldn't get any better, he tasted his first bite of heaven. The strawberry cream cheese blintz danced across his tongue, entertaining his taste buds as if he'd never eaten a strawberry before. "I think I've died and gone to heaven," he managed the compliment between eager bites. "Where in the world did you learn to cook like this?"

"Mostly the internet," she thwarted the compliment.

"The internet?" he looked up quizzically. Jake sat on her lap, eagerly awaiting his next bite. This girl might have more layers than he'd given her credit for.

"And a few magazines," she shrugged. "And a whole lot of trial and error."

"You got these recipes off the internet?" he asked again, perplexed by the idea that such masterpieces were just floating out in cyberspace for any taker.

"Not exactly," she gave Jake another bite. "I spend my lunch break browsing the internet, then I modge-podge recipes together and Jake and I experiment with them until they become our own. I like to try to keep things organic and sugar free."

"This is sugar free?" he asked, pointing to the strawberry concoction.

"Yes," she shrugged nonchalantly.

He took another anxious bite of the omelet, savoring its flavors as they melted on his palette. "Is everything you make this incredible?"

"Umm..." she chuckled at the compliment. "I'd have to say, no. Unfortunately my learning curve often leaves me with a full trash can. Believe it or not, just a few weeks ago I barely knew how to boil water."

"I don't believe that for a second. This is amazing. Really? How long have you been cooking?"

"Honestly?" she blushed. "About three and a half weeks."

"Well," he wasn't sure if she was kidding or not. "Either you're a real quick study or an out-right liar." He savored his last bite of blintz. "You should enter this in the Gala."

"Funny," she smirked. "The Gala is next week isn't it? Other than Jake, you're the first person who's ever tried my cooking. What if I kill someone? Seriously," she chuckled, "I'm still learning the basics."

"Well," he returned her smile, "you've got a few days to fine tune your skills. Besides, nobody's ever created something like this before. Whether you're a master chef or not, if you make this exact recipe, that trophy is yours."

Carter tried to read her reaction to his compliment. She didn't seem to know how to take it. Maybe she wasn't as pretentious as he'd made her out to be.

"It was really good," he offered the compliment one more time as he excused himself back to the work waiting on the porch. "Thank you."

The paint grated over the aged boards like butter on whole grain bread. The timbers were spotted with the cancerous signs of weather and age but not so much that they were candidates for replacement. A fresh coat of paint could do wonders to smooth the wrinkled surface.

"Can I help?" Megan appeared again behind the rickety screen door. She'd pulled her hair back into a pony tail and slid into a figure fitting, Bruins t-shirt.

Carter chuckled under his breath, or at least he thought he did until he saw the look on her face. The furrow in her brow suggested that he must have vocalized the snicker. "Sorry," he felt like a jerk. "I didn't mean..."

"Is there something wrong with the way I'm dressed?" she analyzed her outfit.

"Sorry," he apologized again. "You look fine. It's just..." He shook the grin off his face. "You just don't strike me as the painting type. I apologize. I should have never assumed."

"It's okay," she shrugged her thin shoulders. "You were probably right to assume. Honestly, I've never touched a paint brush before," she sheepishly grinned.

The dark screen did nothing to hide her perfectly aligned teeth. Carter smiled back. "But," he continued to make amends, "that doesn't mean you couldn't do it, if..." he dropped his paintbrush into the almost empty can. "If it wasn't done already."

"Bummer," she smirked, though her feigned disappointment was obvious, "I was looking forward to getting my hands dirty."

"If you have your heart set," he teased, "I'm sure I can still make that happen." He stood up and dusted off his jeans then gathered his tools. "Meet me out back," he instructed.

Half way around the house, as he kicked his way over the gravel drive, it occurred to Carter that perhaps the request had come out more like a command than an invitation. He'd become accustomed to and even comfortable with a life of solidarity. He had Bosco, his scouts, Whitely, and the Tall family. His life was pretty full and a fleeting friendship with a down-and-out, trying-to-make-the- most-of-county-life, square peg in a round hole, rich girl wasn't exactly on the top of his to-do list. Even if she was beautiful.

"You don't need to help me if you don't want to," he clarified when he reached the back yard.

Megan tied tidy little bows in the top of her crisp, clean athletic shoes. Carter figured she didn't make a habit of wearing much other than fancy high heels, hence the sparkly newness of the runners. "I don't have anything else to do," she smiled, finishing up the last knot. "It's morning nap time. Jake will be down for at least the next hour."

He accepted her bid as merely a way to occupy her time and was happy to oblige the offer. He led her to the back of the driveway and unlocked the padlocked garage door. The rollers were stiff and even a little rusty as he pushed the door up. Unlike his adjacent garage, which he frequented as often as possible, this one hadn't seen the light of day in years.

"What is all this stuff?" Megan hung back on the driveway, taking in the dusty, cob-webbed contents.

"Mostly junk." He stepped inside and plugged in a utility light, illuminating the tall stacks of furniture and cardboard boxes. Scanning the mountains of dusty memories, he identified what he'd come for and plotted a route through the strategically stacked assortment of household items.

"Can I get you to hold this for me?" He waved the light at Megan, trying to swamp the tide of emotions rising in his chest before they swamped him. "Please?" he smiled.

She took hold of the lamp and aimed it towards the back corner of the garage. "If it's junk," she asked matter-of-factly as he crawled his way gingerly across the carefully stacked piles, "then why don't you just get rid of it?"

"It's sentimental," he finally answered, hoping the spoiled princess didn't feel the need to pry any further. He stretched across the width of a coffee table and nudged at the finely spindled piece of wood until it wedged loose.

"Are you sure?" Megan admired the handcrafted high chair first in the driveway then again in her kitchen.

"Someone ought to use it," Carter shrugged, wiping the last of the dust off its tray. It'd been tucked so deep in the shed it hadn't seen the light of day for more years than Carter cared to do the math for. "Doesn't do anyone any good sitting in the back of that dusty garage."

"But it's so beautiful," she traced her hand over it as if it would crumble at her touch.

"It survived three children," Carter rinsed the dusty rag out in the sink. "I don't think there's anything Jake can do to it that hasn't already been done."

"Your grandparent's had three children?" Megan asked, still admiring the handiwork.

"No," he leaned against the counter. "They tried to give my dad a sibling, but they never could. He was an only child." He hoped to leave his explanation at that then realized he needed to provide a touch more clarification. "My dad made the highchair," he sighed. "For his kids."

"Oh," she said, seemingly content with the answer. He was happy not to expand.

"So," Carter smiled at her t-shirt. "UCLA, huh?"

"Good guess," she nodded, pulling a container of disinfecting wipes out of the cupboard.

"I know, I'm a regular Sherlock Holmes, aren't I?"

"It must be a gift." Although Carter had successfully removed any visible signs of dust, Megan gave the high chair a thorough wipe with the antibacterial soaked, disposable cloth.

"Yes, ma'am," he grinned, still trying to figure this girl out. "What did you major in?"

"Business management."

"Really?" he wondered out loud. "I would have put my money on cheerleading."

"Well, Sherlock," she cocked her jaw, "you would have lost your shirt and the whole farm too."

"Funny," he shrugged, discreetly noting her physique. Though lacking the height to be a fashion model, her arms and legs were long and slim. Her torso tapered with the curves of someone with a practiced fitness routine, though not one of a die-hard athlete. She was neither overly toned nor scrawny, but healthy and lean. "I had you pegged for a dancer."

"Dancer, yes. Cheerleader, no." She pulled a second wipe from the canister and gave the high chair tray one last swipe.

"Is there a difference?" he chided playfully.

"That's like confusing a football player with a golfer."Her eyes lit up and a hint of reserved laughter trilled past her lips.

"You know," he chuckled back, "such things can co-exist."

"Maybe at one of your back woods country boy schools."

"Yes," he nodded, "because it doesn't get much more back woods than the U.C. Santa Barbara."

She closed the disinfectant canister and placed it back in the cupboard. "I didn't know they had a handy-man degree there."

"Indeed, they do." He tried not to take offense to her chiding, after all, he'd heard both sides of the coin; lived both sides of the spectrum. City boy in the country; country boy in the city. "But that was just my minor," he teased. "Somehow I managed to walk away with a BS in Graphic Design."

"The BS part I believe, but the Graphic Design part might be pushing it." She crossed her arms.

"Really? And what's so hard to believe about it?" He noted her eyes as they trailed from his boots to his baseball hat.

"Honestly?" she snapped her eyes up to his. "That's just a lot for one person to have on his plate." "You're an athlete, a handy-man, and an artsy-fartsy, too?"

"Yes, ma'am," he nodded. Pretending not to notice the golden spheres staring back at him, he leaned casually against the counter.

"Alright, Carter," she skirted across the floor and opened the fridge. "If you call me ma'am one more time I'm going to un-invite you to my kitchen."

He smiled at her, strangely drawn in by her aggrandized sense of self. He found humor in her all too serious take on reality. Equally so, he was curious about her fairy-tale existence. Not to mention her beauty. Even if she hadn't been perfectly framed in designer jeans and a Hollywood hairstyle, she would've easily drawn attention.

"What am I suppose to call you then?" he asked, turning his glance away from her and out the window. The tulips, no longer perky flame-shaped accents around the willow tree, were starting to peel open into two dimensional shadows of their early season magnificence. Poppies and lilies had begun to fill the space.

"I don't know," she shrugged. "For some reason I've always been drawn to Megan." She pulled a cutting board out of the cabinet and set two chicken breasts on it. "Either that, or Bob."

"Well, Bob," he smirked at her attempt at humor, then nodding toward the yard added, "It would appear that we have ourselves a little visitor."

"What?"

"Shhhh. You're going to startle him." Carter drew his finger to his lips and looked back over his shoulder at her. He wondered for a moment at her sudden tenseness. The color had washed from her face and her feet seemed to have anchored themselves to the floor. Gently, he put his hand on her shoulder and nudged her closer to the window. Her shoulders were tense and he thought he noticed her breath still. He directed her attention to the corner of the porch.

"Is that a...?"

"Squirrel." He finished quietly, still questioning her sudden change in demeanor. She was scared, he resolved, remembering the bruises at their first meeting. Scared. But of what? Or, better yet, who?

The fluffy tailed visitor climbed up the wooden porch post and perched on top of the railing. His head bobbed subtly as he sniffed around at the air. He pawed at some fleck of dust then rocked back on his hind end and smoothly elevated into a sitting stance. His nose wiggled slightly; his tail rolled up the curve of his back and stood at full, fluffy attention.

"It's so cute," she whispered. He heard the deep breath release from her. "You know," she spoke softly to Carter's shoulder, though her attention never seemed to divert from the scene outside the window. "I've never seen a squirrel in real life before. I can't believe how cute he is."

"We've got a few that live around here." Carter whispered, not nearly as affected by the frequent visitor as his city-girl renter was. "Boss thinks they're the greatest toy on the planet."

"I hope he doesn't hurt them."

Realizing his inadvertent encroachment on her personal space, Carter took a step back. "Nah. It's just a game of chase. Sometimes I think they come around just to drive him nuts. They sit up there on the porch railing, or back there on one of those big rocks, and stare at the house like they're entire goal in life is to torment him."

"They're that smart huh?"

"Well, I don't know how much smarts it takes to tease a dog," he tucked his hands into his jean pockets. "I'll tell you what I do know, though. If you ever want to find out just what annoying little pests those squirrels can be, go ahead and leave the screen open one evening and..."

111

"Where *is* your dog?" Megan turned abruptly.

"I don't know," Carter shrugged. "Probably asleep under a tree somewhere." He stepped closer to the window so he could get a better look around the perimeter of the yard. "I haven't seen him since we went into the garage."

"Me either," Megan's brow furrowed. She glanced at her watch. "It's been well over an hour since I put Jake down. He should be up by now, but..." She backed away from the window and quickly moved toward the bedroom.

Megan's voice squealed in an octave Carter had only heard once on a PBS opera segment. Suddenly the pieces started adding up. Rich girl showing up in her fancy car. Bruises on her arms. A cash only rental deal. Jumpy. Paranoid. Insecure... New hair color. She wasn't just running away. She was hiding.

In a quick five paces he crossed the entirety of the small home before his cowboy boots slid to a stop on the wood floor in the hallway. Megan – in what appeared to be the full stages of shock – stood fixed in the doorway. He was sure she was breathing but her body showed no signs of life. Her face, drained to a milky void of color, cocked towards him accusingly, then just as quickly turned back to the room. If the very room had disappeared into a black hole, she couldn't have looked more horrified. Prepared for the worst, Carter scooted behind Megan and peeked over her shoulder.

"Well, I'll be," he rested his hands on her rigid shoulders.

"How'd he get in here?" she whimpered, clearly horrified.

"I don't know," Carter shook his head, trying simultaneously to neither laugh out loud nor wake up the baby. "Did you leave the back door open?"

"No, I don't think so. I'm pretty sure I heard it snap behind me when I went out."

"Hmm," he, despite Megan's apparent horror, couldn't help but smile at the scene.

"And," she added, "I know I closed the bedroom door."

"You gotta admit, that's pretty cute." Carter nodded toward the lump of blankets, pillows, and snuggly bodies on the bed.

"Absolutely precious," she grumbled sarcastically. "Are you going to just stand there or are you going to help me save my baby." Her attempt to lunge forward was thwarted by Carter's gently grasp on her shoulders.

"Does he really look like he's in any danger?" Carter whispered softly into her ear. Bosco's eyes were drawn tight and his jowls jiggled loosely as the rhythmic growl of his snore slipped into the silence. His massive, hairy body curled into a crescent moon, one paw tucked loosely under his head and the other resting lightly across Jake.

"That dog could swallow him in one bite."

"If that was his plan don't you think he would've done it already?" He tugged lightly at her shoulders, pulling her out of the room. "I'm pretty sure their arrangement was mutual. Come on," he nudged, "let the boys rest."

Chapter Eighteen

Megan spent the next several nights wondering how the stupid dog kept getting into her house. Having the dog in her house was one thing and having it protectively shadow her child was another, but having it shed and drool and make a mess of her bed was completely out of the question. Fortunately for Megan's sanity - and Bosco's life - Carter had come up with a solution. Somewhere in that garage of treasures he rescued yet another piece of his childhood from a life of dust bunnies and dry rot. Like the highchair, it was exquisitely crafted of the most beautiful cherry wood Megan had ever laid her eyes on. Nothing she'd ever seen in a department store or even a special order catalogue could hold a candle to the beauty and love Carter's dad had molded into a crib. And it was solid. So solid, in fact, that had Bosco decided to join Jake inside its barred walls, it would've easily held him.

After several weeks of restlessly sleeping with her baby in the crook of her arm, Megan was finally getting at least a few hours of quality sleep each night. Bosco's invasions and Jake's body heat were only part of the problem, though. The lingering trouble existed in the fear of Matt and the persistence of her nightmares. It was the same dream over and over, but on some level it molded and changed – even if only in minuscule increments – each night. She was running and jumping higher with each replay. She was making it further and further down the road; covering more and more terrain. The horizon called to her and safety seemed just one big bound away. But she never could reach it. Just when she'd get her hopes up, Matt's burley, mean hands would snag her. Before she knew it she'd be on her knees. Sometimes she'd try to reason with him, others she'd fight back, yet more often than not she'd cower.

"*What do you mean you don't want to be a doctor?*" The story line shifted again. "*Hamliton's are doctors, Jacob. That's what we are. That's what you are. Quit being a baby about it. Grow up and be a man!*"

"*But, he's only five!*" Megan yelled, desperately trying to climb out of the piles of sugar on the floor.

"*And your point is what?*" Matthew pushed her face into the sugar, suffocating her in its stench. She grasped for strength and when she finally found it, the sugar ran through her fingers and came out as sand.

"*It's time to cut the apron strings, Megan. You're holding him back. It's time to let him go.*" His callous voice echoed over the vast desert; his aura hung in the air like a mirage. She tried to stand and, as seemed to be a theme, found that she had no legs. The strength in her arms wasn't enough to sustain her, though, and after a few fruitless movements her face smacked back into the mountain of sand. But it wasn't sand after all. Slowly, helplessly, her body floated down as a tsunami of water engulfed her.

"*You're such a loser,*" Matthew's voice chortled through the water. "*And if there's one thing Hamilton's are not, Megan, it is losers!*"

Darkness. Silence. Nothingness.

Megan's eyes sprung open. Her heart raced. Just enough light from the early summer moon sifted through the window coverings for her to get her bearings. She took a couple of deep breaths and pushed back the covers. She gathered her wits enough to settle her trembling hands then moved quietly across the small room to Jake's crib. The rise and fall of his chest told her that everything was okay. Her baby was safe.

Careful not to disturb his sleep, she tiptoed out of her room and did a quick inventory of the house. All the doors were locked, the windows were closed, and everything was in order. She padded into the kitchen, satisfied that her nightmares were unfounded, and pulled a bottle of water from the fridge. As she opened the cupboard for a glass, she realized that she'd inadvertently organized the dishes exactly as Matt would have expected them. Small glasses to the right, large ones to the left. Each subsequent cupboard that she opened told the same story. Jake's plastic cups were in a different cupboard than the glass ones. His plastic plates in a different one than the stoneware.

Matthew was still in control.

She emptied the entire contents of the kitchen cupboards, rearranging them more logically. There was no reason Jake's plastic plates couldn't coexist with hers. No logic to having his sippy cups in a different location than the other glasses. It was quick work and as soon as she finished in the kitchen she moved on to the bathroom. She pulled her toothbrush out of the drawer and set it on the counter. She took every towel out of the linen closet and refolded them in halves rather than thirds, then moved them down a shelf and randomized their organization. She'd do the same with her clothes – mixing up their color-coded order – as soon as Jake was up in the morning.

She wandered back to the kitchen, her mind too restless to sleep, and began seeking ingredients in the fridge. Fresh strawberries from the Tall's fields and a couple of early season apricots from Carter's orchard sat front and center. She pulled them both out and set them on the counter. Wishing she had a computer, or even access to a cooking show on her antenna-only TV, she was left to her own devices to pull together a recipe.

Time passed almost effortlessly when Megan baked. It lifted her spirits and soothed her worried mind. Forgetting the horror she was running from and relishing in some sort of normalcy were the immediate byproducts of her work. Tasting the fruits of her labors – and hopefully enjoying them – was also a plus. She wondered if other people used cooking as an escape and, as the sun began to form over the mountains, an idea began to form in her head.

She pulled the experimental pastry from the oven – a strawberry apricot breakfast cake of sorts – and placed it on the stovetop to cool down. The smell wafting from it was amazing, but the true test would come only when she took a bite. She was unsure how the flavors would meld together – whether harmony would strike or a flavor riot would breakout – but that was half the fun of experimenting in the kitchen. She was proof enough that anybody could make a cake from a tried and true recipe. The true trick was to take raw ingredients and create something new. Something unexpected. Something divine.

Megan cracked the kitchen window open, the stagnancy of the old home quickly filled with fresh morning air, carrying the smell of her cake on its soft currant. Dew softly sat in tiny little droplets on the tips of the lawn and the daylilies were starting to crown. Summer was clearly stepping in the door and she was excited for its entrance. She drank the air, cool and clean in her chest, then took her notebook out of her handbag and flipped to the first blank page. Taking a seat at the table, she jotted down the latest recipe before she forgot it, making notes to remind herself of each particular step. Sure to leave room for future notes and adjustments as needed, she left the recipe untitled and opened up another blank page.

"Do other people use cooking as an escape?" she underlined the question then, staring out the window, watched the sun rise one incremental step at a time until it's light spilled into the kitchen and it's warmth touched her cheeks.

~   ~   ~

Sam and Jamison were at the door minutes after the sun was up, their faces beaming with more excitement than Carter imagined possible. "We've got it!" Sam burst as soon as the door swung open, waving a tattered piece of paper through the screen. "We figured it out!"

"Well then," Carter swung the screen door open, stepping onto the porch with the boys. "Let's see what you've got."

"I Googled it last night," Jamison made sure to take the credit before Sam could claim it, although Carter would have assumed as much. Sam's family didn't have a home phone, let alone a computer or internet access; the printed document couldn't have been his doing.

"What do ya think?" Sam asked as Carter sat down on the top step.

"Well," he studied the drawing. "It's a nice plan and all, and I definitely think we can pull it off..." he traced his finger over the step-by-step instructions, "but it's going to take a lot of time." He peered up at both boys, still overflowing with excitement. "And a lot of patience. A drift-boat like this is a big project. Do you have it in you?"

"We've got the whole summer, duh!" Sam jumped off the porch, over the hedges, and stuck a perfect landing on the front lawn.

"And," Carter looked from one boy to the other, knowing he'd have to make this point clear at least a dozen more times before summer's end, "you understand that I'll only be able to help you with it when I don't have other work to do, right?"

"Sure," Jamison nodded.

"Obviously," Sam added. Then bouncing toward the driveway smirked, "Let's get started. I'm not getting any younger, you know!"

~   ~   ~

Megan heard the boys before she saw them. One of them was so boisterous and sarcastic she couldn't help but smile. "It's true," she heard him defend. "Every word of it."

"Whatever, Sam," she recognized Carter's tenor. "Think about it for a minute. Do you really think an outhouse would blow up like that?"

"But I was there," the boy defended, "and when the kid threw the match in the hole it was like boom, bang, rumble!"

"And you saw it?" Carter asked. "You saw the explosion?"

"Well..." the kid hesitated for only a moment. "No, I didn't see it, but I heard it. It was the loudest thing I've ever heard! Kaboom!" He animated the explosion with his arms. "Nearly blew my eardrums out. And then everyone was like 'whoa'," another full animation, "and 'wow' and they were running and screaming and trying to get out of the way of the flying...."

"Okay," Carter interrupted. "Let me get this straight. A kid threw a match in the outhouse and it just blew up?"

"Exactly!" The boy bolstered. "And then..."

"Hold on," Carter interrupted again, a smile smeared across his face. "So you expect me to believe that a single match blew an outhouse to smithereens?"

"Um, yeah," the boy shrugged cockily, "cause that's what happened."

"Okay," Carter played along, "and you didn't see it, but you heard it?"

"Yep! Made my eardrums burst right open!" he expanded his story. "Couldn't hear a thing for days!"

"But you heard all the *whoas* and *wows*?" Carter laughed.

The boy's expression, void of emotion, froze as he locked his eyes on Carter. For a moment they stood quietly staring at each other, then almost on cue, laughter ripped from both of them. The other boy hesitated briefly then, unable to control himself any longer, added his snort to the hysterics.

Megan found herself chuckling too as she washed up the last of her baking and breakfast dishes. Jacob, busily emptying the kitchen drawers, froze and studied his mother. Hands still wet, she swooped him into her arms and kissed the baby soft curls on his head.

Unaffected by her kisses, he reached longingly for the sudsy dish water. She snuggled his soft cheek against hers then set him on the counter and watched tentatively as, one toe at a time, he dipped his feet into the bubbles. His innocent laughter brought tears to her eyes. He was such a joyful kid; full of life and curiosity. She imagined his life back in the penthouse. Matt didn't allow him to touch or explore anything. Could he have ever been this happy there?

Jake caught sight of Bosco through the window and giggled out a series of unidentifiable words. The dog must've seen him too because he sprang to life and, barking excitedly, ran towards the back door.

"Boss!" she heard Carter call then, looking up, caught hold of his smile.

She couldn't figure out why she'd become drawn to this rugged landlord of hers. There was something about him that was different than any other guy she'd ever known. "How bout we pull ourselves together and go for a little walk?" she whispered to Jake, returning Carter's wave as she pulled the drain on the kitchen sink.

~   ~   ~

"Wow, I see why they call her Hollywood." Sam overtly stared across the yard.

Carter's hand stopped moving, catching the planer on a small knot in the wood grain. He looked first at Sam then followed his glance toward the driveway. "Her name is Megan," Carter stated, as he raised his free hand in greeting. "Either that or Bob," he smirked at the boys confused faces.

"Morning," Megan called, clearly trying to ignore Bosco's eager shadow at her side. Jake sat on her hip, struggling to get down. She balanced a cake pan in her free hand.

At Carter's command, Bosco obediently sat but didn't take his eyes off the baby. The baby, in return, didn't take his eyes off Boss. "That's a nice dog you've got there lady," Carter teased.

"Thanks," she smiled. "I'll sell him to you," she teased back. "Dirt cheap."

Carter set his tool down and stepped out of the garage. "Traitor," he furrowed his brow at his dog then asked Megan, "Where are you off to this morning?"

She glanced at her dust speckled Audi. "Thinking about finding a car wash today," she answered. "Then Bri is going to take me to check out this infamous Strawberry Gala of yours."

"Not a bad idea," Carter nodded, not mentioning the obvious fact that her Audi, even dirty, was a bit too shiny to ever fit in around here. "Did you decide to enter your blintz then?" He nodded toward the pan.

"Not this year," she smiled sheepishly.

"Well, that's too bad," he shrugged, and then, remembering the boys in the garage, likely still gawking at the pretty lady, made introductions.

"Nice to meet you," Megan nodded, her hands too full to shake theirs. "Do you boys like cake?" she asked.

Jamison nodded bashfully, politely. Sam quipped out loudly, "Do whales breathe air?"

Megan turned to Carter. "I guess that means yes?"

"I think so," Carter laughed, taking the pan as Megan offered it.

"Give it a try and let me know what you think," her eyes twinkled with pride as she smiled. "It's a new recipe," she explained. "I made it up this morning."

"Must be terrible if you already ate half of it," Carter joked as he peaked under the foil.

"It was my breakfast," she shyly looked to the ground. "But not all of it," she quickly recovered. "I'm taking some over to Brianna." She pointed to a foil covered plate glistening from the stroller by her back porch.

They made small talk for only a minute, though Carter sensed she'd have stayed longer if the invitation had been offered.

"Vavavoom," Sam grinned when Megan was out of sight. "I think I've got a genuine shot with a babe like that," he stated matter-of-factly. "I should ask her out."

"Let me know how that goes," Carter tapped the boy's shoulder then, picking up his planer went back to work.

Hours passed easily but with disappointingly little progress for the boys. They'd picked an easy enough boat plan but the time and effort involved was more than they'd anticipated. Each step took a grueling amount of patience and Carter could only laugh as their boredom began to set in.

"It's probably time to call it a day," Carter announced as his belly rumbled. They'd worked through lunch, picking at Megan's amazing cake as they labored. The boys hadn't said as much, but their snarfing was indication enough that they liked it too. He'd be sure to let her know their approval.

"Will you drive us to the Gala?" Sam asked.

"What makes you think I'm headed that way?" Carter teased.

"Snakes don't live in ant holes," Sam swaggered.

Carter and Jamison exchanged confused glances. "I don't even know what that means, Sam."

Chapter Nineteen

"You don't have to buy my dinner," Megan reached her hand into her handbag in search of her wallet. One themed booth after another, they'd spent the day meeting nearly every vender west of the Rockies. The children, of course, preferred the blow up slides and small carnival rides, but Megan had a special fondness for the free mani-pedi booth and the discount jewelry peddlers. If only a Gucci vender had shown up, she'd have been in near heaven.

"I told you," Bri defended, "this is my mad money. I can spend it however I want," she swatted her friend's shoulder. "And I want to buy you and Jake some dinner."

"But," Megan deflected, "you don't have to..."

"Stop it already," Bri refused the offered cash. "Now, you have to try the strawberry bisque and the strawberry chicken wrap. Is there anything else you want? Maybe some strawberry popcorn, strawberry funnel-cake, or deep-fried strawberries?"

"I think I'll stick with the wrap," Megan gawked at the carnival stand menu. *Strawberry Nachos? Strawberry Ricotta Empanadas? Strawberry tarts, cookies, and popsicles?* Apparently, just like the parade floats this morning, there wasn't anything they couldn't strawberry.

Bri ordered two large strawberry lemonades, two wraps, two bisques, and a couple of cookies before turning back to her friend. "It's not like this money comes out of my family budget or anything," she explained. "It's completely side stuff. Don't worry about it."

"Side stuff?" Megan asked.

"Yeah. Advertising endorsements," Bri shrugged. "No big deal."

Megan helped rustle the kids to a table and unfastened the buckle of Jake's stroller before asking, "Bri, where in the world are you getting advertising endorsements?"

"Oh," she chuckled, "just my good looks." She sashayed awkwardly in her rubber flip-flops and maternity capris. Accentuating her round belly, she added, "I *am* a top fashion model, you know."

"Clearly," Megan smiled at her lively friend.

"If only," she chuckled as she gracelessly slid into the picnic table bench. "Remember that little blogging hobby I told you about?"

"Sure." Megan dipped an apprehensive spoon into her strawberry bisque.

"Well, it seems there are other moms out there who like to hear what I say... Uh, err, write. They frequent my site and share my posts with other moms. I don't see a ton of traffic, but it's enough to interest advertisers. Like I said, it's not much, but every time someone clicks on the advertising link, I get a paycheck."

"Good for you," Megan nodded with a grin as she spooned the strawberry bisque into her mouth. It was smooth and cool on her tongue. Jake yammered for another bite and she graciously obliged. "This is sooooo good," Megan smiled at her friend. "Thank you."

"No," Bri smiled, "thank you. The Gala is a lot more fun when you have a friend to share it with and, frankly, Brent would've been a bear in all those booths."

"You mean he's not into all that glitzy stuff?" Megan teased. "I think a little bling might just be what his uniform is missing."

"Maybe I should bedazzle his holster. I think he'd really appreciate the effort."

"Not to mention all those bad guys he's gotta take down. Surely they'd take him a whole lot more seriously if his gun had a little sparkle to it, right?"

Absorbed in the ease of their friendship, the two ladies burst into laughter.

~   ~   ~

"I kissed a girl and I liked it," Sam and Jamison bellowed in offbeat, unharmonious unison. "The taste of her cherry chapstick." Sam bobbed his head with animated swagger and licked his lips. "I kissed a girl just to try it..." He blew an energetic kiss out the window and toward an unsuspecting group of teenage girls. Six sets of unimpressed eyes rolled back at him.

Carter, trying to stifle his laughter, pulled the truck into a field that was roped off to serve as a makeshift carnival parking lot. It never got old, watching pre-pubescent boys get all excited at the lyrics of Katy Perry's "I Kissed a Girl." Even when competing with the crackling of the truck's old speakers, the boys' boisterous singing was disastrous at best. Disastrously funny.

"It felt so wrong. It felt so right." Sam pounded an open palm across his chest. "Don't mean I'm in love tonight!" His lips pursed; his shoulders swaggered.

Carter hitched the transmission into park and killed the engine. Despite the loss of the radio's lead, the boys finished out their unharmonious accolade.

"I kissed a girl and I liked it...." With big round eyes, Sam stared boldly at Carter as he, with unwavered confidence, belted out the last refrain, "I LIKED IT!"

"The question is," Carter slid out of the cab, "did she?"

"Of course she did," Sam's sneakers hit the dry dirt with a thud. "What lady on the planet wouldn't want a piece of this action?" He puffed his husky chest out with pride. "I's hot stuff, Carter!" he proclaimed.

"If you say so," their fearless leader conceded as he tucked his truck keys in his pocket. "I'm leaving here at nine-o-clock sharp," he reminded. "If you don't want to take the heel-toe express home, I suggest you be back here by then."

"Yes, sir," Jamison nodded with his typical reserve.

"Aye, aye, captain," Sam saluted.

~   ~   ~

"I bring you to a hoe-down and all you do is sit on the sidelines and watch?" Bri taunted.

"I use to think I could dance, but now I'm not so sure." Megan watched the cowboy hats bob across the makeshift stage. Girls in cutoff jean-shorts flung from one partner to another in choreographed perfection. "It looks so confusing. I'm pretty sure I'll end up on my face."

"Now that'd be a shame." The sudden touch of a man's hand on her shoulder caused her to spill her strawberry lemonade. His long willowy shadow blanketed the ground in front of her. Her breath hitched. Her heart pounded brutally in her chest. She turned her head slowly, pensively towards the large, agile fingers.

"Sorry," the man's face softly plead as Megan's heart resumed its normal beat. "Didn't mean to startle you." He smiled warmly. "Can I buy you a new drink?"

"No," Megan brushed at the sticky liquid on her designer jeans. "It's okay." Coaxing herself to relax, she returned his smile.

"In that case," the stringy man curtseyed, "can I interest you in a dance?"

"Yes," Bri enthusiastically answered for her. "She'd love to dance!"

"But, I..."

"Go," Bri pushed her to her feet. "I've got the kid situation under control." She glanced at the sleeping toddlers in their strollers. "Go dance!"

Megan's trepidation fizzled as soon as her heels hit the floor. Square-dancing, she quickly learned, was all about patterns. The tall stranger who led her to the floor only remained her partner for a matter of seconds before she was swooped away into the lead of an older gentleman. He graced her with a hearty grin, then following the caller's instructions, lead her first in a do-si-do then across the stage in a lively promenade.

She caught on quickly, eagerly watching the other dancers for guidance. "Circle right, circle left, chasse'," the caller instructed. She followed vigilantly, pleased with each new call she mastered.

"I had no idea city girls could dance like that." Her fourth partner hooked her from behind.

The familiar vibrato of Carter's voice soothed her.

"This might surprise you," she mused defense at her newest partner, who, at the direction of the caller, spun her around. "But," she continued, "there are a lot of things city girls can do." She raised a brow as an invitation for him to refute, but he didn't. Instead, he offered a crooked smile.

What was it about him that pulled her in? And why didn't he seem to reciprocate the interest? Was he only being nice because that's who he was? Mr. Nice-guy? She didn't know, but as she followed his lead through the dance moves, she felt her guard go down. He pulled her in to him, close enough to smell his aftershave. She didn't realize normal men even wore aftershave anymore. *Maybe its deodorant,* she thought. Then, *maybe he's not normal.*

Chapter Twenty

Matt lifted his head from the fold of his arm, leaving behind a small puddle of drool. Maybe if he could shake the nausea the room would stop spinning. Squinting through blood shot eyes, he cursed the computer's light. He'd reached a new low, he realized, lifting his aching head only enough to reach for the amber bottle. Drinking alone was something he rarely did. Passing out in his office was a disgraceful first.

Pressing the empty bottle to his lips, he willed it to yield even just a drop of its nectar. Its inability to deliver found it flying across the room. His mouth was like cotton; his entire body ached. Even the glow of his desktop's screensaver seemed to mock him. "Shut up," he cursed, swiping a limp arm into the keyboard and sending it the same direction as the discarded bottle. The screensaver disappeared, revealing the infuriating remnants of his drunken idiocy. *Fifty grand?* His stomach knotted at the thought.

He stood up quickly only to buckle back into his desk chair. The keyboard was out of his reach, he concluded angrily as his heavy head plopped back down on the desk. His back and neck were like rusty machine parts, non-conducive to moving.

Crawling his way gingerly across the floor, he finally slithered himself onto the leather sofa. He was thirsty; dry to the bone. But, he concluded, the water cooler was too far away. He'd just sleep it off – if he could. His heart raced. Its incessant pounding reverberated in his ears. He draped his arm over his head hoping to mute the sound, but it only caused it to echo out louder.

"Shut up," he yelled out again, swatting at the silence in the room. "Look what you've done to me!" He scowled at Megan's photo, wishing it'd been close enough to throw. He cursed her name out loud. "This is all your fault!" He grumbled a string of profanities. "I *will* find you," he promised the smiling beauty in the frame. "And when I do...." He drifted to unconsciousness before finishing the threat.

~   ~   ~

Carter dropped the boys at their homes then hunkered down in front of his computer to get some much needed work done. With a deadline pressing he shouldn't have spent the better part of his day helping the boys and, even more-so, he should've skipped out on the evening festivities at the Gala.

The cuckoo clock chimed once, then again, and a third time until it played out twelve rings. Its jingly song echoed from the living room, the only witness he had to the deepening night. His belly rumbled again, sending him to the kitchen for a snack. A pb and j sandwich in hand, he moved Megan's empty cake pan into the sink and wondered what kind of delicacy she'd be preparing for breakfast. Certainly something better than the bowl of cold cereal that awaited him.

He took a second sandwich back to his office, determined to keep focused on the project until it was complete. The cuckoo clock sang and danced a few more times then, as his eyes began to tire, he at long last deemed the project done. He logged off the computer, picked up his dirty dishes, and closed the office door behind him.

Rinsing his crumb speckled plate in the sink, Carter noticed light radiating softly from Megan's kitchen window. Her silhouette anchored the kitchen table. He glanced at the late hour, placed his plate in his dishwasher, washed her empty cake pan, and stepped out into the darkness.

~   ~   ~

Everything Megan had left behind embittered her as she sat in the confines of her cracker-box excuse of a kitchen. Her parking garage, her cell phone, her spa days. Even her new cooking fetish – which less than an hour before had seemed so exciting – had become the object of her scrutiny. Questions came quickly – the same ones that had surfaced over the past few weeks any time things got a little tough. *Why had she left? Was this – any of this – really worth it? How long could she keep up this charade?* Sooner or later she was going to break. She was most definitely not a country girl. Maybe it was time to crawl back to Matt... or even worse, to her mother.

A soft tap on the screen door startled her from her thoughts. Her breath hitched as she looked up from the kitchen table.

"Hey," Carter offered her a pleasant smile. He raised the empty cake pan to the screen. "It was great," he waived the pan in the air then let himself in.

"Thanks," she forced a grin. Her hair was tussled and her makeup smudged softly under her eyes. "I'm not sure what to call it," she shrugged, gathering the mess of papers strewn before her.

"Well," he set the pan on the counter then slid into a chair across the table from her. "How 'bout Apricot Berry Delight?"

"Maybe," she grinned again, this time less forcibly.

"Or Apri-berry Goodness," he smiled, "or perhaps Berry-cot Temptation," he teased. "It's two a.m.," he looked at the clock. "What are you still doing up?"

She gathered the papers in front of her. "I could ask the same of you," she answered.

"If you're still bitter about me stepping on your toe tonight, I really am sorry," he smiled at the remark. "Here," he offered her his stocking foot, "stomp on mine as hard as you want."

"Carter," she shook her head, wiping at her eyes.

"No, really, do it!" he played. "Put on your most pointy, life-threatening shoes and pounce away."

She stared, steel-faced into his mocking eyes. "Is that supposed to be funny?"

"Um," he hedged back in his chair. "I guess not."

A tear escaped her eye, despite her desire to keep it contained.

"Sorry, Megan, I shouldn't have laughed. Are you okay?" he prodded.

"Everything's fine," she lied, crossing her arms on the table to disguise the writing on the papers. "Just having one of those days," she finally released.

"I think your Audi will forgive you for not making it to the car wash," he grinned again.

His attempt to lighten the mood didn't work. A stone-cold look was all the response she could muster.

"Oh, one of *those* kind of days." He settled deeper into the chair. "Is there anything I can do to help?"

"Not unless you've got a couple grand lying around," she offered flippantly, as if it was a joke.

"I know this is none of my business," he hesitated, "but if you need money, why don't you ask your ex-husband, or Jake's dad, or whoever's responsible for that fancy car of yours. Surely you've got someone who can help?"

"You're right," she sniffled, "it's none of your business. Besides," she continued much to her own surprise, "he wouldn't give it to me anyway. *He*," the word jumped off her tongue with exaggerated vibrato, "won't give me a divorce let alone child support or alimony. And," she chuckled with frustration, "I don't want his stinking money anyway!"

With that, she pushed her chair back and rose, trying to anchor her declaration of independence, but the quiver in her lip exposed her. "Do you want a drink?" she forced a smile, hoping her obstinacy would be enough to change the subject.

"Sure." He rocked his chair back on its two back legs. "I'll take a tall glass of water."

"That's good," she guffawed at his cool, carefree, almost cocky attitude, "because that's about all I've got." She pulled two glasses from the newly re-arranged cupboard. "Bottled or tap?" she asked.

"Tap is good enough for me," he continued to smile. "You're still married?"

She handed him his glass. "One extra tall glass of fresh tap water for the cowboy," she smiled, a newly formed tear hanging on the rim of her lower lid. "Can I get you anything else?"

"No ma'am," he drawled the words sarcastically. She swatted his shoulder. "Sorry," he laughed. "I meant, Bob."

"To answer your question," she didn't so much as crack a grin, "as of yesterday, yes." She glided back into her chair, focusing on the label of her water bottle as she whimpered the sobering fact. "According to the law, I'm still married." The situation with Matt wasn't worthy of being termed a legal battle, it was simply a one-sided standoff. She called her lawyer weekly from Doctor Stone's office, hoping each time for good news – that Matt had signed the papers - but instead, learned time and time again that he was still stalling. "I just don't get it," she sipped at her water, "I'm not asking for anything but a clean break. Why won't he sign those papers?"

"Maybe he's realized what he stands to lose and he doesn't want to let go without a fight,"

"Oh, he's had his fight," Megan pushed the hair off her forehead and pointed out the faded remnants of not one, but three wounds. "And how about this one?" she flipped her wrist to show another scar. "Pins," she clarified. "And that doesn't include all the stuff that's healed without scars. The black eyes and bruises. The fat lips and... and the mean words." She wiped at the tears again, still trying to be tough.

"What about Jake?" he asked hesitantly. "Did he ever hurt Jake?"

"No," she wiped her nose with a napkin. "That's why I left. For Jake. I don't ever want him to touch Jake."

"I'm sorry, Megan," he touched her hand tenderly. "What can I do to help you?"

His honey-colored eyes looked at her. She yearned for safety and, if she was willing to be honest with herself, the security of companionship. She needed someone to hold her and tell her that everything would be alright. She curled her lower lip into her teeth, gnawing at it as she processed her thoughts. "Nothing, Carter," she broke contact with his eyes. "There's really nothing you can do."

He kept his hand on hers. "These aren't legal documents," he finally broke the silence. "Not divorce documents, anyway," he pointed to the torn out notebook pages. "What are they?"

"I was just brainstorming a little," she grinned sheepishly, shrugging off the idea. "But it's stupid really. Just a crazy idea. Nothing that'd work anyway." She pulled her arms off the papers, exposing an explosion of bubbled ideas and a series of scratched out mathematical equations.

"What kind of idea?" he leaned across the table.

"A website," she shrugged. "To share my cooking ideas... and, er... foibles. You know, something that would show other moms out there that feeding your family doesn't have to be as difficult and, well, perfect as the magazines and other websites make it out to be."

"Hmmm," Carter followed the brainstorm bubbles with his eyes.

"Honestly, what it's really about... what sparked the idea," she paused long enough to stall the hitch in her voice, "... well, I just don't like leaving Jake all day. And the pay pretty much sucks anyway, so I thought maybe I could get this web thing going and then," she released hope of her dream in a single sigh, realizing the full gravity of its ridiculousness as it hit the air. "Maybe I could get a bunch of advertising sponsors and then I could quit the doctor's office and just work at home. Stupid, right? I know. It'd never work."

"I don't know," Carter pulled the scribble filled paper. "This looks interesting. I think you've got a pretty good idea going on here. It might actually work."

"Might," Megan scoffed, "if I had two cents to get it off the ground."

"Ah ha. The couple grand comment makes a whole lot more sense now. And here I thought you were just being facetious."

"I'm flattered," she simpered, "but really, I'm not that clever." Her mood lifted as she watched the corners of his mouth turn up into a grin. Her heart rushed at the appearance of his smile.

"That's too bad," Carter winked at her. "Clever girls are hard to come by, and if I'm going to build this website for you, you're going to have to bring your brain to the table too. I don't know a thing about how to make cooking appealing."

"You're going to build me a website, huh?" she raised a suspicious brow as he nodded the affirmative. "Do I want to know how much that's going to cost me?" she asked. She glared at the numbers screaming from her page.

"Well, how much did you figure you were going to need for the other stuff?" he leaned his elbow onto the table.

"I'm not sure. First off, I'd need to get a computer and maybe some internet service." She scooted back into her seat opening the conversation again.

"You can always piggyback my wifi, but the computer would probably be important." His lips curled up into a grin as he started to throw out ideas. "Ok, so why don't you ask your parents?"

She met him with a vacant stare.

"Could you sell something?"

She glanced around the room. "Like what?" she shrugged. Her lack of abundance should've been obvious.

"Point taken," he nodded. "Maybe you could hit your savings or take out a loan?"

"If I go to a bank," she somberly reminded, "*he* might find me."

"Good call." He scrunched his brow for a moment. "I guess you could always try my tried and true method."

"Which is?" she waited eagerly.

"When all else fails, I like to pray."

"Pray? That's your answer? Pray." The very idea seemed ridiculous. He fell a notch off the pedestal she'd slowly constructed for him.

"Sure, why not?" he shrugged.

"Why?" Megan was adamant. "If there is a God... and that's a big IF... Why would he care about me? I'm just a nobody. Surely He's got bigger stuff to take care of then little old me."

"I don't know about that. He never seems to let me down," Carter crossed his arms. "And I'm about as big of a nobody as it gets."

All of his confidence only brought Megan back to square one. Moist eyes, trembling lip. She was looking for a concrete, tangible solution, not one based in the clouds.

"How 'bout this," he set her schematic back on the table and engaged his eyes with hers. "You figure out how to pay for the computer and I'll donate the website, pro bono."

She took in his grin, unsure whether he was to be taken serious or if he was just playing with her. "People don't do stuff just to be nice," Megan started. "Business doesn't work that way."

He leaned across the table. "Maybe business relationships don't work that way, but friendships do."

She stopped herself from jumping across the table and throwing her arms around him, even though the invitation was clearly in his eyes. Or at least she thought it was. She was probably wrong. His eyes were just enticing by nature. Their perceived invitation was just that, perceived.. Besides, finding the money – even if it was only a couple thousand dollars – was impossible.

Carter's phone vibrated loudly in his pocket. "Excuse me," he nodded, completely oblivious to the moment she thought they were having. "I've got to take this."

"Hey," he smiled at Megan as he talked into the device. Whoever was on the other end had a lot to say and Carter, ever smiling, listened intently. "Okay. Make yourself comfortable," he finally responded. "I'll be home in a few minutes."

He ended the call and dropped the phone back into his pocket. "Sorry," he said to Megan. He took his glass of water as he stood from the table. "I've got to go," he nodded towards the door. "But we're not done with this conversation," he said, dumping his water down the sink. "Let's talk about it again tomorrow." The porch door bounced twice behind him before finally clicking shut.

"I guess daddy was right after all," Megan whispered. Her growing feelings for Carter, she was now sure, were one sided. "When things seem too good to be true, they probably are."

Stacking the papers, she moved them to the kitchen counter and watched Carter's silhouette move across her yard. For a moment she'd been honored by his presence, lifted by his friendship. She'd even let herself believe that she'd seen something new in his eyes; something special. But – just like Matt – as soon as something better presented itself, he was gone.

She buried her head in her hands, wondering again if Matt might be her best solution. Between her almost non-existent money stash, her bare-minimum income, and her current rate of spending, there was no way to make her crazy new reality work.

Wishing she had something stronger than water to wash down her frustration, Megan sunk down on the kitchen floor and embraced her knees as her eyes opened their faucets.

The distant cry of a coyote joined her reverie. "Coyotes..." she whimpered through even heavier tears. "Well, isn't that great."

She bowed her head and whispered God's name for the first time in her life. After all, she sighed, what did she have to lose?

Chapter Twenty-One

"I've got it." Megan burst through Carter's back door and into his kitchen. Realizing it'd been a bit forward to just rush in, she stepped back on the porch and knocked on the door.

"Got what?" Carter's voice sounded from another room. She took it as an invitation to let herself in.

A bit unexpected for a bachelor pad, every inch of the Victorian-style abode was immaculate. The paint was fresh and inviting; the molding intricate and exact. The craftsmanship seemed to speak of years gone by, yet everything was surprisingly new. The kitchen was more gourmet than her penthouse's. It was clearly designed to feed masses.

"A solution," she said, making her way through the kitchen and down the hall toward his voice.

She passed a console in the hall and didn't even bother to wonder its origin. She'd seen enough of Carter's work in his garage to know that it either came from himself or from that shed of his dad's. "Where are you?" she called out, again surprised by the size of the house. Its street presence was humble enough; she'd never imagined its square footage to be quite so substantial.

"In here," he called again.

Jake must've sensed Bosco's presence. "Dow," he slurred, wiggling his body around in her arms. "Dow," he repeated the request again, insistent on growing up by the minute. He'd turn one in a couple weeks; she stalled at the thought. How had time stolen her baby so quickly? In just the last few days he'd added a few choppy words to his vocabulary, all of which made her smile with pride, but none of which resembled "ma" or "mama" or even "mom." She slid him off her hip, took his hands in hers, and securing him as he wobbled down the hall on his unsteady feet, led him towards the sound of Carter's voice.

Bosco greeted them in the doorway of the living room with an exuberantly thumping tail and a deep, baritone yawn. His giant tongue kissed Jake's face. Megan flinched with disgust but did nothing to stop the exchange. Blankets were strewn about the floor, the virtual reminders of a sleepover party. Megan looked for evidence of a beautiful, tussled woman, but instead found two disheveled kids.

"Hey," Carter greeted from behind her. She turned quick enough to see him emerging from what appeared to be his home office. "Why don't you let Jake go hang out with the kids," he motioned to the blanketed room. "I've got something to show you."

"Okay," she hesitated, not sure if she should ask the question in her mind or let it go. The young girl, noticing Jake, bounced from her sleeping bag. "I'll watch him," she flashed a toothless smile.

"Thanks, Sarah," Carter smiled then motioned Megan into his office as if suddenly having two kids in his home was no big deal. "What do you think?" he asked, pointing to his computer screen. "I don't know what you want to name it," his cheeks warmed at her smile, "but it could be ready to roll out by next week if you're ready."

"Next week?" she beamed, still wondering about the kids in the front room. Carter spent a lot of time with his scouts, this she knew, but kids too? Whose were they? "Carter, I don't know what to say." She smiled at the web page glowing back from the screen. It was a rough layout, but he'd captured her vision more clearly than she could've ever drawn it out for him.

"Thanks would be good," he teased, settling her into his chair to get a closer look. She followed his prods, clicking buttons and scrolling through the pages.

"I love it," she said. "But I don't think I'll be ready to go in a week," she sighed.

"Well that's not a very positive attitude, is it?" He leaned over and clicked another link. It directed them to an online computer store. "I think this one would be good for what you want to do," he pointed to a laptop near the bottom of the screen. "What do you think?"

His smile was so eager she didn't feel right breaking his spirit. "It's nice," she grinned. "But I still don't have any money."

"What if I lend you a little," he offered. "Just until you get up and going."

"No," she answered quickly. She noted the simplicity of his clothes, his office, and even the rusty old truck in the driveway. The offer was quite generous, but she couldn't take it. "I don't want your charity," she finally answered though the softness in his eyes made it hard for her to stay strong. "But, I've got an idea."

"Yeah," he said, settling onto the edge of his desk. "I'm all ears."

Opening the clasp on her handbag, Megan pulled out a wisp of red fabric, revealing a gorgeous evening gown. "It's a Vera Wang," she explained, though she assumed the term had no meaning to Carter. "I think I can sell it for a couple thousand."

"Two grand!" He gasped. "Who on earth would pay two grand for a dress?"

"It's worth more than that," she defended. "It's never even been worn."

"But seriously, two grand?" he asked again several times as he helped create a sales listing for it. Within ten minutes and despite his reluctance at the price, the cherished Vera Wang was posted online, a reserve set, and a "buy it now" price of two-thousand dollars anchored.

"We're hungry," the little girl smiled from the doorway. Megan quickly sized her up, deciding that she must be about six or seven. She balanced against the doorframe with Jake on her hip. His chunky baby body was almost as heavy as her petite one.

"I can make some breakfast," Megan offered, reaching to relieve the small girl from the weight of her baby. Jake acknowledged her but didn't reach back. He was engrossed in the young girl's attention.

"Nah," Carter rested his hand on her shoulder. "You're a guest in my house this morning. Let me feed you."

Following him to the kitchen, she protested.

"You don't think I can cook, do you?" he finally questioned.

"It's not that..." she started. With a sigh, she backed off. "I'm happy to help," she smiled graciously.

"Not today," he pulled a barstool out and motioned for her to sit in it. "I've totally got this under control but, if it will make you feel better, I suppose you can watch."

Hesitantly, she situated herself on the stool and scooted it closer to the breakfast-island. Giggles echoed from the front room where the kids continued to build forts with their blankets. Again, she swallowed her questions about them. "I'm expecting a good show," she teased instead.

One of Carter's eyebrows peaked. "You can't afford the price of admission," he teased back as his stocking feet glided gracefully across the wood floor. "What?" He turned in time to catch her laughing to herself.

"Nothing," she silenced her chuckle but left the smile on her lips.

"I think she's laughing at your dance moves," the boy sniggered his way into the room.

"These moves?" Carter puckered his face as he playfully shimmied his hips. His stocking feet slid from one end of the kitchen to the other causing Megan to laugh again. "Why you laugh at me?" he tossed grammar out the door and lowered his voice a mischievous octave as he shimmied towards her.

"Cause you're doing it all wrong," the strangely familiar boy answered for her. He stepped into line with Carter and proceeded to shake his hips mockingly. "You look like a broken robot," he criticized his mentor with a smile. "You gotta move 'em like this." Exaggeratingly, the boy's hips swayed effortlessly from one side to the other. "Graceful. Smooth," he laughed.

"Like this?" Carter lunged his hip into the boy, knocking him off balance with a laugh. Their banter erupted into a playful wrestling match, both boys – adult and youth – laughing until tears ran down their cheeks. Megan watched, momentarily feeling like an intruder. Carter, she concluded, was some kind of paternal figure to this kid. Engrossed in their antics, sudden recognition of the boy hit. He was one of the scouts she'd met the day before. *Sam*, she nodded the confirmation to herself silently.

Carter served up a breakfast of pancakes and bacon, all the while exchanging hilarious conversation with Sam. Megan could barely get a word in edgewise, not that she wanted to, she was completely entertained with Sam's ability to tell a story. She was riveted by his detail and exuberance; whole heartedly entertained by his mannerisms and sound effects.

"That sure is the nicest car I've ever seen." Sam gawked out the kitchen window towards Megan's Audi. "I'll bet it goes really fast," he added before jumping into another one of his stories. "When I was a kid my grandpa taught me how to drive his truck."

"Wow," Carter teased. "Way back in the day when you were a kid, huh?"

Sam ignored the jibe. "It had a big engine and even bigger tires," he leveled his hand out at his waist. "Like clear up to here. When I'd go to church with him, he'd let me drive home. And," he used his entire body to narrate, "there was this big bump and we'd hit it and it'd be like 'whoa'. Then Grandpa would say 'way to go, Sam. You're the bestest driver ever.'"

"The bestest?" Carter grinned.

"The very bestest," Sam grinned back. "I'm almost thirteen now, you know." He was batting his eyes at Megan. "I'd be real gentle," the balls of his cheeks rounded out as his face lit up.

"I think he's trying to ask if he can drive your car," Carter nodded towards Megan as he stood to clear the table.

Megan looked first at the eager boy then out the window at her car. She didn't value it as much as Matt did – in fact, to her it was merely transportation, but it was all she had. "When you're *almost* twenty we'll talk." She wiped Jake's sticky hands clean of syrup then released him off her lap to follow the giddy calls of cute little Sarah.

"Ah," Sam kicked at the floor. "Can I at least ride in it?" He batted his eyes again.

"Does that eye-stuff work on your mother?" Megan laughed at his theatrics. "Cause it's pretty persuasive."

"Don't cave too easily," Carter warned. "First it's a car ride, then the next thing you know he's showing up on your doorstep at two a.m."

"And eating all your candy," Sam chuckled, pulling a handful of empty candy wrappers out of his pocket.

"Was that before or after you emptied out my pantry?" Carter messed up the boy's hair.

"It's more like a simultaneous act." Sam nestled under Carter's arm. "I'm not just a great driver," he grinned, "I'm world-renowned for my multi-tasking abilities."

"Is that a fact?" Megan asked.

Carter handed him a dish cloth. "Then why are we letting those skills go to waste?"

Megan sat at the table as the boys cleaned up after breakfast. She'd offered her help but was immediately turned away on the premise that she was still a guest. Watching them, however, made for good entertainment. Not a moment of silence passed. Sam simply couldn't breathe without talking, and Carter happily fueled his stories. Their talk floated from one subject to the next disjointedly. Somehow what started as a car discussion morphed into something about jackrabbits, then squirrels, then shotguns and boats. Before she knew it, they were back to cars.

"I'd be glad to help you take the kids home," Megan found herself offering, still curious about the situation but too reserved to ask. "You know," she clarified, "so Sam can have a chance to ride in my car."

"You really don't have to," Carter put the last of the dishes away. "I've got some other errands to run while I'm out anyway."

"I can take you," Megan surprised herself with the bold offer. "I don't have anything going on today," she explained. "And I could really use a day away from the cracker box," she grinned out the window towards the farmhouse. "No offense or anything."

"None taken." Carter folded the damp towel over the oven door handle. "If you're really up to it," he unwittingly slid his feet across the kitchen floor again, "I'd love the company."

Megan pulled her Audi hesitantly into the dirt driveway. For all the flaws she saw in her little farmhouse, Sam and Sarah's was much worse off. Nothing was living in the yard except a rogue elm tree. What use to be a carport was nothing more than a sagging section of fallen roofing. The screen door hung limply from its frame and the front walk was pocked with holes.

"Sam and Sarah," Carter opened the car door, "why don't you two stay with Jake for a second while I take Megan in to meet your mother?"

Simultaneously, the children nodded in unspoken understanding. Hesitantly, she followed him out of the car. A rusty mailbox hung half-hinged beside the front door. Haphazardly, tattered sticker squares formed a crooked line, spelling out the name Wilson.

Carter turned the rickety front knob and directed her into the house. Flinching first at the stench of alcohol and stagnant smoke, then again at the random bodies strewn about the furniture and on the floor, she stalled just inside the threshold. Carter gently moved around her concrete feet and made his move into the room. He pulled the shades open, blinding the hung-over partiers with the late morning light.

"Time to get out," he pulled one man then another off the sofa. "Party's over," he helped a passed-out lady off the floor. "Keep moving," he ushered them out the door as he worked his way through the house opening up blinds and windows and picking up empty bottles and burnt out cigarette stubs.

"Megan?" He called from the top of the stairs. "Can I get your help up here please?" Her feet had anchored themselves in the front room, stunned at the scene in front of her, heartbroken for Sarah and Sam.

"Sure," she followed the sound of his voice, absorbing all the pitiful details of the sad little house. Stepping over a stain in the carpet, she resisted the urge to touch the rickety handrail as she ascended the stairs.

The lady was thin - probably too much so - and gaunt. Carter had her propped up against the wall, but the crusted chunks in her hair suggested that he'd found her passed out in a puddle of her own vomit. "You can't keep doing this," he squatted down in front of her.

Apparently still working the alcohol out of her system, she reached her feeble hand up to his cheek and stroked it gently. "You," she stuttered. "You are always... You are so good to me."

"Nadine," Carter ignored the lady's adulation and pointed over his shoulder at Megan, "this is my friend Megan. She's going to help you to the shower, okay?"

Voided eyes sized Megan up before turning their attention back to Carter. "I. Want. You. To." She loosely grinned, giving him the same trusting regard that her children did.

He pulled her to her feet and reached for Megan. "Megan's going to help you today."

Any compassion Megan should've had was embittered by the memory of Matt's binges. The thought of Sarah and Sam was all that pushed her forward. She swung the lady's skeleton arm over her neck and hooked her own around her emaciated waist.

"You're Carter's friend, huh?" Nadine's cold body melted into her.

"Sure," Megan glanced into each of the open doorways on their way to the bathroom at the end of the hall. Both the kids' rooms were clean and appeared to be untouched by whatever party had unfolded the night before. They were the only two rooms in the house that didn't make Megan shudder. Whatever faults this mother had, clearly she - or someone - had been trying to take care of the kids.

"I thought so." The uncontrolled weight of her head bobbed. "Saw you dancin' at the Gal... Gal... Gala," she scowled her lips and swallowed back her previous night's entertainment as it tried to resurface. Megan turned her head away from the stench.

"Well," Nadine cackled, regaining a small semblance of composure, "don't get yur heart set on being an'thin more than that with him," she cackled again. "Carter don't go hookin' up with da ladies, you know. Believe me, I've tried. So just don't go waistin' yur time tryin' to git with him, ya hear." Blood shot eyes stared into Megan's. She cackled again, then vomited, this time at least it hit the bathroom tile.

Chapter Twenty-Two

"Are they going to be okay?" Megan watched the porch door close behind Sam and Sarah. She clenched her car keys in her hand, still shaken from the scene inside the house.

"They'll be fine," Carter cocked his head and presented a forced half-grin, as if he didn't quite believe the words himself.

"Here," she said, offering him the keys to her car. "I don't feel much like driving."

Carter raised his brow. "That car is worth more than the contents of my home. Are you sure you want me to drive it?"

"It's just a car," she shrugged.

"But," he started.

She tossed him the keys. "You know your way around here better than me anyway. This is just easier."

She opened the passenger door and slid inside.

"If you insist," he said as the car purred to life.

"What kind of mother gets smashed like that?" Megan hurled the words as soon as they were at the end of Nadine's street. "Shouldn't we call Child Services or something?"

"I know it's hard to believe," Carter navigated his words as carefully as he did the road, "but Nadine really is trying to be a good mother." When Megan didn't respond, he elaborated. "She never drinks in front of them," he explained. "That's why they were at my house last night. She doesn't want them to see her like that anymore than you or I do."

"Then why doesn't she quit?" Megan spat the words, though she knew addiction was a hard master to leave behind.

"Basic human weakness," he answered without condemnation.

"Who are you?" she glared at him in wonder. "Saint Carter?"

"No. I'm pretty sure that was my grandma," he said matter-of-factly. He stared out the glass, easily navigating the rural roads.

She watched him out of the corner of her eye, waiting through an uncomfortable stretch of silence for him to expand before realizing he wasn't going to offer information without her asking for it.

"So," she gently slipped her query into the silence. "What's the story? How did you meet Nadine? And more importantly, how did you become the keeper of her children?" She asked about Sam and Sarah, but what she really sought was a better understanding of the mysterious manifestation of humanity that sat beside her.

He raised a menacing eyebrow at her. "The keeper of her children? That sounds a bit cryptic, don't you think?"

"Not to burst your bubble here, Carter, but this situation – whatever it is - isn't exactly normal."

"Point taken, I guess." He shrugged his shoulders and seemed to disappear into his thoughts.

Megan waited – almost impatiently – for him to finally answer her question. "I was fifteen when I moved in with my grandparents," he started. She resisted the urge to ask why, but tucked the question into her memory for another time. "Nadine was a few years older than me – I think she was about eighteen or so. And Sam... Well, he was a toddler. Two and a half, three maybe."

"She had a three year old when she was eighteen?" Megan choked over the words.

"Don't judge what you don't know, Megan." Carter sighed. "That's exactly what everyone else in town did. They judged her... and ultimately condemned her. Can't say I don't blame them or even that I didn't throw my own stones. Honestly, I didn't like her much. I never quite understood why my grandma felt like she had to take in every lost soul around here. I'm almost ashamed to admit it, but back then it was almost like punishment for me. You have no idea how much I hated having to come home from school to help take care of her little boy."

"Then why did you?"

"Didn't really have a choice. My grandparents made me." He turned the car off the dirt road and headed south on Main Street.

"Oh," she wondered if that was it. The end of the story.

Carter surprised her when he continued. "Every day I took care of that little boy and eventually he rubbed off on me. His mother, on the other hand, took a little longer." He shook his head. "I was just about to graduate when I found out her secret. She'd never told anyone who Sam's father was. She kept it festering inside her for all those years. Then one day I overheard her talking to my grandma. They were both crying but the name I heard her whisper was as clear as day and, honestly, it shocked me." His chest rose as he let the words work their way out. "Sam's dad wasn't another kid – or even a random one-night stand as all the naysayers had supposed." He shook his head and swallowed the lump in his throat. "Nadine was taken advantage of by a well-respected adult member of our community. To this day she carries his secret."

Megan let the words sink into the silence that followed, feeling sudden compassion for the young girl who'd had her virtue stolen and her innocence and reputation destroyed. She blinked the moisture out of her eyes at the realization that the gangly mess of a woman that she'd pretty much thrown into the shower was in fact a tender, broken, human being.

"By the time Sam started school he'd learned to cope by using wit and sarcasm." Megan nodded. This explained the quirky kid she'd briefly gotten to know. "And by the time I left for college, he'd earned a piece of real-estate in this rock-hard heart of mine."

"Yeah," the corners of her mouth turned up at the memory of him dancing with both Sam and Sarah, "You're just one big ol' ornery grizzly bear, aren't you?"

"You know it," his smile illuminated the interior of the car. "And don't you go starting any rumors otherwise."

Megan wondered where Sarah fit into the story but didn't find it necessary to ask. Carter had given her far more information than she needed to put things into perspective. "I can't imagine having to deal with so much," she offered almost as an apology for her misguided judgments. "Those kids sure are lucky to have you."

Humbly shrugging off the compliment, he pulled the Audi up to a road-side flower market. "Everybody deserves to have someone who cares." He turned off the engine and pushed the hair off his brow thoughtfully. "She'll pull herself back together, I'm sure of it."

"And in the meantime you'll take care of her kids?"

"They shouldn't have to suffer because of her problems." He opened the car door and slid his feet out to the pavement then walked around to the passenger side. "I usually like to cut flowers from Grandma's garden," he left the subject of Nadine behind them as he pulled Megan's door open. "But we've had such a busy morning, I forgot."

"Flowers for what?" Megan wondered out loud as she opened the door to retrieve Jake from the back seat.

"For a friend." Matt simply answered. "It's her birthday."

Chapter Twenty-Three

You can learn a lot about a person in the course of a day. For instance, Carter learned that Megan liked her bacon extra crunchy, her orange juice ice cold, and barely any butter on her pancakes. He also learned that she preferred pretty much any flower to roses.

"What's wrong with roses?" he'd dared to ask as they walked through the rows of fresh cut flowers. He'd always liked roses - thought that's what all girls liked - but now found himself questioning his resolve.

"They're too pretentious," she sniffed a bouquet of carnations. Then, moving Jake to her opposite hip, picked up a bouquet of daisies.

"Pretentious?" he wondered, taking in her designer shoes and coordinating handbag. "You're right. I just can't imagine you being interested in anything that would indicate the slightest bit of propriety."

"You're funny," she almost laughed at his jibe. "But roses - I don't know - A single rose is okay I suppose. Alone it says *"I love you."* Simple, plain, beautiful. But a whole bouquet is too much. Too loud. Too cocky. You know, like, *"Hey, here I am! Look at me! I've got something to prove!""*

"That's what they say, huh?" He set the bouquet down and moved towards the daisies. "And what about daisies? What do they say?"

Megan thought about it for a minute then answered, "They say, *"Hi, I'm cute and friendly and fun. I'm not trying to be proper or impress you with my magnificence. I like you just the way you are. And I want you to like me for who I am.""*

"Wow," he picked up a bundle and turned to pay the vendor. "I guess I'll be getting some daisies," he said with a sideways smirk.

"Looks like you just got schooled, young man." The proprietor accepted Carter's cash.

"I know." Carter laughed. "Flowerfoliadialect 1010. Who knew?"

"Flowerfolia-whojadahwhatsa?" Megan questioned as soon as they were back in the car. "Remind me where you went to school again so I don't send my children there," she laughed.

"We've already been down that road," he laughed at himself. "No need to go back there again."

"Then, where exactly *are* we going?" she asked, taking in the unfamiliar buildings and landscaping as they passed by the passenger side window.

"Here." He pulled her car onto a residential road then rolled to a stop in front of a little red brick home. "This is the place," he grinned, taking the bouquet into his hands.

"Is this where you keep all your lady friends hidden?" Megan teased.

"Just one of them," he teased back. "Her name's Roxie and she's a spry little lady. I think you'll really like her."

He rang the bell and, with a rock in his step, waited for it to open.

"Well, hello there," the gray haired lady smiled through the crack as she unlatched a series of chains. "I was just in the kitchen baking up some rolls for dinner." She released the last chain and pulled the door open with an excited gesture. "My family is coming over for dinner in a bit," she clarified. "The kids always come for my birthday."

"That's great, Roxie." He stepped towards the spunky older lady and placed a kiss on her cheek as she stretched her arms eagerly around him.

"Megan," he finally said as they stepped into the brightly decorated room, "this is my friend Roxie." He pulled Megan further into the room and made proper introductions before handing over the bouquet of daisies. "These are for you," he smiled.

"They're beautiful," her voice was animated as she spoke.

"They're for your birthday. Megan picked them out for you. She said they are fun and friendly, just like you."

"You're such a good boy," Roxie smiled.

~   ~   ~

"Who is she?" Megan finally dared ask as she buckled Jake into his car seat. Even after spending an hour around Roxie's table catching up on all her latest gossip, Megan still couldn't piece together the spry lady's connection to Carter. She'd looked for evidence of a familial connection - pictures, mannerisms, mention of a common aunt or cousin or anyone - but hadn't gleaned anything.

"Just a friend," he answered, then asked, "Are you sure you still want me to drive? I'm really okay being a passenger."

"I'm a good passenger too, she answered."

"But it's your car."

"I know. And I get to drive it all the time. Maybe you should stop complaining and be happy about my generosity," she teased.

"Wow," he shrugged. "Not going to say another word." He turned the key in the ignition.

"So," she brought the conversation back to Roxy, "you said she's a friend. What kind of friend?" She slid into the passenger seat.

"I don't know. A friend kind of friend."

"Ok, I see how this is going. Apparently I need to be more specific in my questioning, for instance, how did you meet? Unless you've aged masterfully, it's not like you went to school together."

"Well, if you must know," he winked at himself in the rearview mirror, "there's nothing a good plastic surgeon can't fix."

Her stomach lurched. She knew the comment was meant to be a joke but it brought unsolicited - and unwanted - thoughts of Matt. She knotted her hands into fists and, with a deep breath, released them.

"Come on," he slipped the transmission into drive, apparently unaware of her sudden discomfort. "Does it really matter?"

"No, but..." she snapped her seatbelt into place, realizing his innocence in the remark. She'd have never dared push Matt on any issue, even one as trivial as this, but Carter was the most laid back person she'd ever met. She decided to playfully pursue an answer, if for no other reason than to tease him with her adamancy. "Maybe it does matter," she spewed playfully. "Maybe someday somewhere someone will need to know. Maybe it will be the final link to keep civilization alive. Maybe it'll be the million dollar question."

"And maybe you'll be the next President."

"Maybe," she smiled. "In which case, I'd probably need to know everything about everyone. Like why you're friends with a lady three times your age. And why you hang out so much with twelve year olds. And why you live out in po-dunk-ville all alone in a big yellow house."

"Oh, well that's an easy one." He weaved the car through the winding neighborhood streets. "I live in po-dunk-ville because that's where the mother ship dumped me. The yellow house is just a disguise for my rocket, and nobody lives with me because I morph into a droid as soon as the sun goes down."

Seriously? Was he twelve? She shook her head and went along with it. "See, now we're getting somewhere. And what about the twelve year old boys? How do they fit into the story?"

"Well, they're really the key to my return to my planet. I'm on a mission to steal their energy and their advanced knowledge to harness the moon, which in turn will fulfill my mission and I'll be exalted back to the planet GRRR where I will be pronounced king."

"And you do that with the *advanced* knowledge of twelve year olds?"

"Not just any twelve year olds," he laughed. "Scouts. They have to be scouts. Honest. True. Brave."

"To the planet GRRR. I've got it. This all makes so much sense now. All the missing pieces to the Carter story are starting to come together." She shook her head again. *Why was he being so vague?*

"The only piece that's missing is that one." He pointed to a roadside car lot.

"The red one?" Megan played along looking at the lot full of SUVs.

"No, I like the yellow one," Carter pulled into the lot. "The red one would be a good fit for you though," he grinned.

"What's wrong with the car I have?" she asked.

He raised a playful brow, "Nothing really. It drives like a dream. Just one little problem."

"What's that," she wondered. She was pretty sure it was flawless.

"It's not really designed for all the dirt and gravel roads you've been driving on. Not to mention the fact that it's a little fancy for the likes of a small town. But whatever."

"Hmm," she grumbled, not ready to admit that he'd made a good point.

"What do you think?" he asked as he pulled the Audi alongside the Jeep.

"Well, I don't know." She pretended to size up the SUV. "Maybe we should get out and see."

Carter made quite the show about pointing out every feature he deemed essential on the Jeep: durability, off-road capabilities, traction control, anti-lock brakes, and of course the highly coveted convertible top. Megan checked out the price tag. A quick guess at the numbers had her figuring she could probably trade in her Audi and leave with any two vehicles she wanted. The salesman's drool confirmed her suspicions.

"Lookin' to make a trade?" He asked, salivating over his beady little bottle cap glasses at the mere prospect.

"Probably not today," Carter answered, still looking at the equipment list on the Jeep window.

"Can I at least pull some numbers for you? You know, give you a ball park figure so you know what you've got to work with?"

"Sure," Megan answered before Carter could. "That'd be great."

"What are you doing?" Carter asked as soon as the hungry salesman wobbled into his office with the car's VIN number.

"I'm just curious." Megan defended. "Maybe this is my plan B. You know, the answer to my prayers."

"You prayed, huh?"

"Why is that so hard for you to believe?"

"I guess it's not," he kicked the tires of the Jeep. "Should we take this baby for a ride?"

"Maybe one of us ought to just take it home," she laughed, pulling the door open. She handed Jake to Carter then climbed up the round chrome step to the driver's seat.

"I don't know about you, but I'm not ready yet." He held the wiggly baby with ease as he leaned into the open doorframe, making the jacked up height seem like nothing.

"Ah, another piece to the puzzle: commitment issues," Megan assessed.

"Seriously? Commitment issues?" He shook his head. "In case you haven't noticed, that beauty of a truck I drive is more than forty years old. If that's not commitment, I don't know what is."

"No offense, but don't you think it's time to let it die? Maybe Billy Bob Smoozer over there would take it as a trade in," she nodded toward the salesman's office. "You know, '*work up some figures for you*,'" she mocked the man's scratchy voice.

"I'm afraid Jade will be a part of me forever."

"Jade? You named your truck Jade?" She fidgeted with the rearview mirror.

"Jade is more than an old, rusted piece of metal. She's a living breathing piece of history. The Carter family legacy," he defended. "Grandpa ordered her straight from the factory in 1972."

"Custom, huh?" she flipped the Jeep's visor down and opened the vanity mirror.

"One of the finest of its day," he answered. "It's the last of Chevy's glamour series pickups, you know."

"Well, I certainly do now," she gave her eyes a quick glance then pushed the visor back into place. "But, if it's such a relic," the sentimental sparkle in his eye told her she was treading on tender territory, "wouldn't it make more sense to drive something else so you can keep it preserved?"

"Perhaps," he chuckled. "I've got myself some other priorities right now, but one day..." he touched the leather steering wheel. "One day this baby will be mine."

"Great news," the lerpy little salesman returned with a grin. He handed the number sheet to Megan. "Looks like this puppy's paid for. Which means, working a deal just got a whole lot easier." He gave a wink that sent spiders up Megan's back then started throwing around numbers like they were parade candy.

She was grateful for Carter's company, because without it she was just desperate enough that she may have walked away with two cars that she didn't need. If Nadine's habit was drinking, Megan's was spending... and it'd been a long, hard, dry withdrawal.

"Let's think it over, sweetheart," Carter, pretending to be her significant other, nearly dragged Megan out of the dealer's office. "We're going to have to discuss this over lunch," he offered to the eager commission-hungry sales manager. He welcomed Jake into the crook of one arm then, wrapping his other arm around Megan, nudged her toward her car.

"Thanks." She snapped out of her near spending coma as she slid into the passenger seat. The rush of making such a big transaction would've surely been short lived when the reality of the less than favorable deal had time to settle. Either she needed an influx of money or she had a lot to learn about budgeting. She preferred the first but Matt's stubbornness could mean that she just might have a long haul of settling for the second.

~   ~   ~

"What's next?" Carter asked over their fast food lunch.

"I don't know," Megan handed Jake another French fry. "Something that doesn't cost any money."

He looked at her quizzically.

"Look," she defended, "a girl can't spend her life buying anything she wants and then, in the blink of an eye, be expected to live on a tight," she chuckled, "no, an almost nonexistent budget and be okay."

"Then I suppose it's a good thing that I'm broke too." He finished the last of his burger and patiently sat back while Megan slowly did the same.

"Can I take you somewhere?" he finally asked. "Somewhere kind of special to me?"

"Sure," Megan sipped at her water. "I'm game for whatever."

"I just don't want this to become 'Carter' day," he sighed. "I feel like everything today has been about me."

"I'll make you a deal," Megan stirred the ketchup puddle intently with her fry, "you can take me to this 'somewhere' if you promise to tell me why it's special. None of this she's 'a friend kind of friend' baloney."

Chapter Twenty-Four

"Somebody had to take over the family property and orchard when my grandparents died." Carter knelt beside the granite memorials. "By default, that somebody was me."

Megan wiped the tears from her eyes as she watched Carter glaze over the row of grave markers. She'd had him all wrong, this quiet, confident, almost cocky loner. It'd been easy for him to have compassion for Nadine because, to some extent, his life had been even harder than hers.

"I was fourteen," he took a deep breath as if pulling the story from deep within his chest. "Almost fifteen," he clarified. "And, I'm not going to lie, I was a jerk. I thought I was so much better than my family. Smarter than my dad. Too cool to hang out with my mom. And I let them know it."

Megan, intent to hear him out, didn't throw in her doubts, but it was hard to believe the charitable man standing before her was anything close to a malicious juvenile. "When they left that night I was extra mouthy," he continued. "I didn't want to be with them but I didn't like the alternative either. Dad grounded me to my room, like that ever stopped a kid. As soon as my family pulled out of the driveway, I walked out the front door and disappeared with my friends."

His hands were trembling as he picked a blade of grass and held it tightly in his hand.

"For years I told myself that I should've been with them. I didn't deserve to be here. I should've been in the car that night."

Megan reached for his hand. "I'm so sorry," she said, feeling completely helpless at his pain.

"The worst part was that I'd yelled at them. All of them. I told Joe that I hated him. That he was the worst little brother in the world."

Megan read the inscription on his headstone. *Joseph Alan Carter*, followed by the dates of his short life. She choked as she did the math. He'd only been ten.

"I told my dad that I never wanted to be like him. That he was the worst dad and scout master ever." He lifted his head and slowly followed Jacob's brisk crawl toward the reflection pond with his eyes.

Megan glanced at the markers again, making quick note of their names and ages before following the slowly migrating boys. Spencer – 42. Julianne – 38. Joseph – 10. Raychel – 7. Plus Beth and Ezra. A whole family memorialized across the cusp of the hill. Carter's family.

She fell smoothly into step beside Carter, just a pace behind the speedily crawling Jacob. "My whole life changed that night and I spent a lot of time blaming other people. I didn't want to leave my home and friends in Santa Clarita. And the last thing I wanted was to go live with my grandparents in – what did you call it? Po-dunk-ville?" He turned to her with a grave smile as he shoved his hands in his pockets.

"Somebody else's mistake turned my life upside down. Somebody else's stupidity took away the people I needed most. The man," he paused for a moment, "Roxie's husband." He paused again, giving Megan time to absorb the detail about the woman they'd visited earlier. "He'd lost his job that day and decided to console himself at the bar. He took that intersection full speed. He was so drunk he didn't even try to stop. Dad and Raychel died on impact, but mom... Mom and Joe fought it out for a few days. Grandma told me if we prayed, God would make it all right. I believed her and for a time I thought they were going to make it."

Jake had made it to the pond and pulled himself up to stand at its stone edge. Megan and Carter watched as he playfully splashed his hand into the clear water, oblivious to anything else around him.

"When they didn't pull through I got really bitter. I was mad at the world. Mad at God. And I took it out on everybody... especially myself."

"So what changed?" Megan hesitated to break his story.

"What do you mean?" He pulled his hands out of his pockets and crossed them over his chest.

"Well, how'd you get from that rebellious, heartbroken kid to the caring, kind, uber-responsible adult you are now?"

"Uber-responsible?" He laughed at the term. "Now, that's funny." He nudged her playfully with his shoulder. "I guess you can credit Beth and Ez... or blame them as may be the better case. They loved me even when I didn't deserve it."

"This sounds a little familiar," Megan nudged him back. "I recall someone telling me early today that everyone deserves to have someone who cares."

"Redundant, huh?" he grinned.

"Refreshingly so," she returned his smile.

"For the record," he added. "Grandma was right about a lot of things. She was right about God. Even though it took me a lot of years to realize it, He did hear our prayers. He didn't answer them the way I thought He should, but in His own way. Because of His love, things have turned out pretty alright." He stepped over to Jacob's side then sat down on the edge of the rock wall.

Megan stayed back, happy to be an observer as she processed everything Carter had unfolded to her. Jake's butterball cheeks radiated as he splashed in the fountain. His curls reflected the sun angelically and his giggle danced through the air. Carter lifted Jake to his lap and removed his sandals before settling him down where his feet could reach the sparkling water. The air lightened and the sun seemed to shine brighter as both boys graced the air with their giggles. Playfully, they splashed in unison, committing Megan's heart a little deeper to each of them.

"Did I answer all of your questions, Madame President Bob?" Carter asked as he pulled the Audi back into Megan's dirt drive.

"For the most part," she unbuckled Jacob from the back seat. "You did leave a few danglers however."

"My boot size is eleven." He grinned, handing her the keys. "And yes, this is my natural hair color," he added with a wink.

"And what about Roxie? You told me who she was, but how did you go about becoming her friend? Seems to me like that's a relationship that would've been okay not happening."

"Gotta thank Ez for that one," he shrugged. "The way he put it was that she lost someone that night too. He said that her someone might have been to blame but that didn't mean she was. He dragged me to her house for years – sometimes kicking and screaming – to help with odd projects. Funny thing is, when you serve someone, you learn to love them."

Megan's chin had to have been scraping the ground as Carter kept pulling things out of his seemingly bottomless Mary Poppin's bag of surprises. He was a saint and she wasn't sure how that factored in to the feelings she was developing for him.

"And," he called over his shoulder with a chuckle as he greeted Bosco at his own back door, "The house is yellow cause I like it like that. And I live alone cause I'm an onery ol' bear that talks to his dog."

Chapter Twenty-Five

Matt glanced at the name on the top of the patient file then, without reading its contents, smiled at Ronda. "I think I can handle this one on my own," he said. "Why don't you go ahead and take a long lunch today."

"Are you sure?" she asked.

"Absolutely," his blue eyes twinkled their approval as he left her in the hall and stepped alone into the small procedure room.

"Have you heard anything?" Kat asked eagerly from the patient chair. She had her hair pulled back and her face scrubbed clean.

"Nothing." He grimaced as he pulled the Botox supplies from a locked cabinet and began preparing them. "Her lawyers know where she is, I'm sure of it," he cussed. "But they won't tell me a blasted thing."

"It's been two months," she sighed, as if he didn't know. "And it's Jake's birthday. Did you tell her attorney that?" She relaxed into the chair as Matt covered her forehead with the cool, smooth anesthetic cream.

"I did," he swabbed the corners of her eyes with the topical. "They're not being very accommodating," he lied, not disclosing the offer they'd made to deliver a gift to his son. That was information she didn't need to know; information that might lead to the divulgence of Megan's ridiculous restraining order. He didn't wish to defend nor explain anything to Kat that might sway her devotion.

He swabbed the corners of her eyes then the laugh lines around her mouth. "I looked into her phone records," he admitted. "Apparently she's turned the thing off." Again, he didn't tell his mother-in-law that the last ping on her GPS was in the Santa Clarita area or that he'd hired someone to dig into it.

He left the topical to settle as he reconstituted a small bottle of wrinkle filling solution.

"I'm sorry, Matt," Kat sighed. "She's just like her father. Once she set's her mind to something, she just can't let go. I'm sure she'll be back soon, it's just..." She trailed off at the thought then presented it. "I'm not sure how much longer I can keep all this from John," she finally said.

Matt cursed under his breath. *John could not know!* "I appreciate your keeping it a secret from him. I know he's not always been my biggest fan." That was a gross understatement and they both knew it. Nobody, however, knew the depth of their mutual disdain. Family peace required civility and loyalty – even if it was all for show.

His back to Kat, Matt masked his irritation and filled his syringe with the miracle filler.

"He's just jealous, is all," Kat defended the man who funded her gregarious lifestyle. "You stole his little girl from him, you know."

Matt tried to take the comment at face value, but knew that there was so much more to John's disregard than the cliché and over-simplified stealing-of-his-princess argument. Kat wasn't the only one keeping secrets in the Williams' marriage.

"Megan will be home soon." He turned with a smile. "I miss her so much," he straddled his stool and winked at Kat. "And Jake. I can't imagine how much he's grown." That, too, was a lie. He hadn't lost a single minute of sleep worried about the child that bore his name.

"I know," she smiled through numb lips and cheeks. "John was asking about him the other day," her frustration was as evident as his own.

"And what did you tell him?" Matt rolled his chair up to her side.

"I didn't." She flinched at the first light push of the tiny needle into her forehead. "I changed the subject just like I always do. Lucky for me he's always wanting to talk about money. Whenever he brings up Megan, I simply change the conversation to the Dow."

"Thanks," Matt meticulously made small injections into her facial muscles as he envisioned his money-driven father-in-law. "You know, Kat," he jumped to change the subject, worried that his fury at Megan might make itself known if he wasn't careful. "I don't know why you insist on coming in here," he charmed her with his smooth accolades. "A woman as beautiful and timeless as you really doesn't need to have any of this done." His steel eyes continued to flatter as he added, "If you weren't my mother-in-law, I just might have to take you out for a drink."

By the time she left his office, Kat's face was as spry as her adulation for her son-in-law. Even if it was fake, Matt certainly wasn't shy about laying his praise on thick. He watched her enter the elevator and waited for the doors to close before kicking his way down the hall and into his private office. Picking up Megan's photo from the corner of his desk he cursed her name along with a string of obscenities. His steady hands shook as he smashed the frame over the edge of his desk. Shards of glass and broken wood split like the sound waves they created. The very thought of her made him want to hit the wall, which he did, after kicking it first.

"Doctor Hamilton?" He heard the query through his closed door. "Is everything okay in there?" Ashlee's voice penetrated the solid wood.

"Um," he quickly picked his way across the carpet gathering what he could of the broken photo. "Yes, Ashlee, I'm okay," he glazed his voice as he called back. Embarrassed that she'd heard his tantrum, he tossed the broken pieces into the trash, smoothed his dress shirt, and opened the door with an overt smile. "We had lunch plans," he smoothly covered, "didn't we?"

"We did," she leaned to the side, trying to peak around him and into the room. "But I can take a rain check if I need to."

"Now don't be ridiculous," he played coy as he reached behind him and flipped the light switch off. "Are you ready?" he flirted, touching her shoulder softly with his palm.

"Uh, huh," she nodded, still trying to work her eyes around him to catch a glimpse into the now dark office.

He slid his hand to the backside of the door knob and turned the lock quietly before draping his arm over Ashlee and leading her down the hall.

~   ~   ~

Megan clocked out, picked Jake up from Emily's, and headed home with a smile on her face and a determination to make today extra special for her little guy. She was in a completely different place - in a very literal and figurative sense – than she'd been at the beginning of Jake's sweet little life just a year ago... Already a year!

She couldn't believe how fast the time had gone. Especially the last two months of it. The very essence of her one room farm house was screaming proof of the vulnerability of all that she'd once taken for granted. The very smile on Jake's face, testimony that she'd made the right decision to take him away from the dangers of that life.

"It's not much," Megan consoled herself as she greeted Bri on the back porch. She'd filled the yard with colorful streamers, balloons, and a handful of rambunctious kids.

"It's great, Megan. You've done a really nice job." Bri waddled down the stairs to the lawn where the children were already at play.

Megan's own birthday parties had been nothing short of carnivals, designed as much for the adults as they were for the children. She reassured herself that Jake's second birthday would be better. A year was a long time. Surely within that time Matt would come around. She'd be safely back in LA well before the year expired, easily living off her savings fund and child support, and amply spoiling her son with all the things he deserved.

Carter pulled a folding banquet table out of his shed of treasures. Upon it, makeshift decorations and colorfully wrapped gifts adorned the paw-printed table cloth she'd scored at the discount store. At the center was Jake's cake - a puppy-shaped concoction, decorated by Megan with extensive help from Bri.

"Thanks for helping me with the frosting," Megan situated a stack of dog-themed paper plates and napkins beside their masterpiece.

"You'd never guess it was your first time," Bri slid into a folding chair and cupped her hands over her belly. Every day she seemed to grow exponentially.

"Are you sure you didn't miscalculate your due date?" Megan asked, handing her friend a glass of lemonade.

Bri kicked her shoes off and rolled her toes through the grass. "This is just normal for me," she shrugged. "Only a few more weeks, though," she smiled.

"You're a trooper, Bri." Megan admired her friend. One baby had been a lot for her to handle, she couldn't even begin to comprehend what it must be like to be expecting her third. But that was the key. She couldn't comprehend because her life had been so much different than Brianna's. In so many ways Bri's had been harder - she and Brent didn't have a lot of money, they had to budget and sacrifice and sometimes just do without. They didn't go on fancy vacations or drive expensive cars. They didn't even own a flat-screen TV. - But in other ways, ways Megan was just beginning to understand, Bri's life had been easier. She had a loving, caring, compassionate husband. He worked hard, pulling late nights and double shifts and overtime, but at the end of the day, his family always came first. Bri had a family that supported her. And most of all, she had faith. Faith that things would always work out.

"You've done a beautiful job," Emily Stone set her children free to run with the others and threw her arm over Megan's shoulder. "So much fun!" she smiled as she turned to admire the large dog-shaped birthday cake and its tiny companion. "They look too good to eat," she grinned.

"Believe me," Carter interjected, his arms full of folding chairs, "you are most definitely going to want to eat it. And lots of it too." He opened a pair of chairs and offered them to the ladies. "If there's one thing this woman can do," he smiled at their hostess, "its cook."

"You don't say," Emily watched her children out of the corner of her eye as she took a seat beside Bri.

Megan dusted her chair off with a napkin before sitting in it. She smoothed her hands down the front of her jeans, weighing the details she should be attending to rather than chatting with her friends.

"Did you know she's about to launch a website?" Carter offered. "A cooking one. This week."

"This week?" Megan blushed at the unexpected announcement. She smiled at her friends and, standing quickly, grabbed Carter by the arm. She pulled him away from the group with a silent grunt. "We can't do it this week," she lowered her voice so everyone didn't hear their conversation.

"Why not?" Carter beamed, his enthusiastic smile fodder for drawing more attention from the party-goers.

"Moolah," Megan rubbed her fingers together. "We don't have any moolah." She hitched her hands on her hips and assumed the "mom" stance.

"Sure you do," Carter looked over her shoulder to evaluate the condition of Emily and Bri's attention. They pretended to be watching their children but their cocked heads told him that their ears were fully devoted to him and Megan. "I forgot to tell you," he stepped in close enough that his breath warmed her neck. "Your dress sold."

"What?" She took a clumsy step backward, twisting her ankle in the grass and almost tripping. She steadied her hand on the table, pretending to straighten the tablecloth. "Already?" she gasped, embarrassed that Carter had such an effect on her. His words, that is. His words had a heart-racing, mind-boggling effect on her. *Not him. Not his breath on her cheek. Not his deep, tender voice. Not his sturdy hand on her shoulder.*

As soon as Carter was done explaining that the money for the dress would hit his account by week's end, he caved to Mariah's pleas for attention and scampered off into the bundle of kids. As if he were some kind of superstar, kids stopped what they were doing to pile on him. They squealed and laughed and teased him for attention – and he obliged.

Bosco quickly joined his master. Between the two of them Megan didn't need to provide any entertainment. Together they captured the attention of every kid in the yard. Though strangely baffled by it, she was grateful because her entertainment budget rounded out at a whopping null.

"Who invited the clown?" Brent appeared from seemingly nowhere, still outfitted in his sheriff's uniform, as he strolled into the yard.

"I think he just comes with the territory," Bri smiled. Brent leaned in with a kiss.

"I heard that!" Carter hollered from his position on the grass. The banter died there though, as he was swarmed by an onslaught of happy kids.

Megan tried to be sociable but felt her attention pulled by the action of wresting and racing and tickling at center stage in her back yard. Before she knew it, Carter was pulling a wagon out of his shed. When she thought the kids couldn't possibly have more fun, Carter and Doc Stone were lashing a tire over the branch of the giant sycamore and had kids screaming for joy as they swung over everyone's heads.

"He's pretty amazing with those kids," Doctor Stone offered as he finally pulled away from the action and took a seat next to his wife.

"Quite a catch, that one is," Emily offered. "Gonna make someone a fine husband one day."

Megan brushed away the idea. "I think it's time for cake," she said before the conversation could continue any further.

"Do you have a camera?" Bri reminded as Megan slid a bib over Jake's shirt and set him into his highchair. "Do you want Brent to run home and get ours?" she offered.

Megan tussled Jake's curls while she thought about it. "No," she finally answered. "I've got one. Hold on just a sec."

She ran into the house and pulled open the kitchen drawer. She grabbed the cell phone and its battery, hoping after several weeks of being separate it would have enough charge. Sliding the battery into place, she opened the back door with her foot, and skipped down the patio steps.

"Let me get the two of you together," Bri offered as Megan lit a candle in the individual sized cake.

"Okay," She handed the phone to Bri, placed the candled cake on Jake's highchair tray, and balanced the neatly decorated dog-shaped cake on her palm. She flipped her hair off her shoulder then shared her most poised smile with the camera.

"One more," Bri called after they sung the birthday song and laughed as Jake tried to blow out the candle. The shutter clicked just as a begging Bosco plopped his head on the edge of Jake's tray. Megan thought for sure Jake's little cake was a goner. She quickly lunged towards it, grabbing the edge of the plate. In almost the same movement that she saved the tiny cake, she felt the weight of the larger one shift in her other hand. The dog-shaped cake was slowly on the move. In a split moment decision, she released her hold on the little cake, hoping the hungry dog would leave it alone, and dove to save the one shimmying out of her grasp.

It happened so fast, she couldn't have drawn a replay if she'd tried. One knee hit the grass, then the other. The momentum sent her body lunging forward and for a fearful, uncontrollable moment, she thought she was going to face plant into the cake. But something held her back. Something stabilized her. Which in turn stabilized the cake. Crisis averted. She didn't need to look to see who her rescuer had been. There was no doubt who the strong hands belonged to. The only doubt she had was her ability to stifle the growing desire to feel their warmth again.

Chapter Twenty-Six

"It really is amazing," he heard her say across the table, though he'd lost as much interest in the conversation as he had with Ashlee in general. Not only was Matt's mind preoccupied with the Megan situation, his arrangement with Ashlee had reached a point where she clearly considered it a relationship, which meant, for Matthew it had run its course.

"Ash," he took her hands in his, interrupting whatever rambling, one-sided conversation she'd been having. "I've got some bad news," he wooed her with his sincerity. "I know I told you that my wife and I like to keep an open marriage, and that was true," he buttered her up for the lie of all lies, "but it's just not working for me."

"What are you saying?" Ashlee's lips had already begun to shake. Moisture instantly coated her eyes.

"Don't get me wrong," he laced every word with slick persuasion, "you're a beautiful girl and I've had an amazing time with you..."

"But you love your wife," she finished for him.

Matt could see what was sure to be the ugliest of all ugly cries form on her face. "I do." He lied, hoping to get over with the theatrics as quickly as possible. This was exactly why he didn't like relationships. Women were too emotional. Eventually they all started to believe that they were that someone special. Everything was about love and commitment - and he didn't want any part of any of it.

"Why don't you take the rest of the day off," he warmed her with his touch as soon as her fanatic crying settled to a whimper. "Or, better yet," he sucked her in with his smile, "just take the rest of the week off. Paid of course."

165

"But who will answer the phones?" her voice quivered.

"We'll find someone," he answered. "Here," he handed her a fold of money, "Go buy yourself something nice." After years of practice he had this routine down to a science. "I'll call you a taxi."

As he escorted Ashlee out of the restaurant, he discretely tucked the waitress's number into his breast pocket, hoping he'd get things wrapped up in time to call her tonight. If not, then maybe by week's end. He made a few calls and by the time he got back to the office, the temp company had a receptionist sitting in Ashlee's chair.

"Not again," Ronda huffed at the arrival of the new temp.

He cockily disregarded his nurse's disapproval and introduced himself to the pretty, young coed. He took note of her empty ring finger as he shook her hand, thrilled at the possibility of making her his newest pet.

"You have a message," the new temp smiled through perfectly painted lips. "He said it's important." She handed him the note then shyly looked away, breaking the hypnotic power of his stare.

"Thanks." He was admittedly too distracted by her innocence to make anything of her note the first time he read it. He liked a good challenge and she looked to be one. He imagined the coming weeks of playful banter as he stepped slowly down the hall, working the scribed annotation through his mind for a second time.

He unlocked his office door and, making sure nobody was watching, stepped inside. There was still a dent in the drywall that was in need of repair before anybody would be welcome in here again. He checked his watch before deciding he had time to return the call before his next appointment.

The door securely locked behind him, he made his way to the far side of the room and dialed the number. "This is Matthew Hamilton," he whispered into the quiet line when the ringing stopped. "You have a message about my wife?"

~   ~   ~

"Okay, are we ready to do this?" Carter greeted Megan the second she pulled into the drive after work. She'd spent the day shaking off the embarrassment of the near cake-fiasco and the night trying to work through her feelings for this man who so freely gave of his friendship.

"Do what?" She swung her legs out of the car and gently settled her four-inch heals into the dirt. After an all-too-familiar restless night and an eight hour shift the only thing she wanted to do was cook, eat, and snuggle on the porch swing with Jake.

"Make your first video," he smiled as he reached through the rear door to unbuckle Jake from his carseat.

"Naturally," she smirked at his tenacity. He seemed more excited about her idea than she did. "I haven't even thought about it. I don't even know what to make."

"Why not just stick to whatever you were going to make for dinner?" he suggested, handing a wiggly Jake into her arms. "I mean, you've gotta cook anyway. Why not just film that?"

"Okay," she agreed easily as she kissed Jake's cheek. "And you're going to film it, right? Then edit it?"

"Absolutely," he smiled. Without hesitation, he added, "But I think we should do it in my kitchen."

"Why?" Megan was already half way up her own back steps.

"Because I've got that big breakfast island." He'd clearly spent some time thinking about the logistics. "It'd just make it a lot easier to show all the steps. You know, like on those cooking shows."

Megan digested his information then decided he was probably right. "Okay," she smiled easily. She was bubbling with a new eagerness to share his company. "Can I freshen up first?"

"Sure," he said, taking Jake from her arms. "Jake and I will meet you in my kitchen when you're ready."

Megan checked the girl in the mirror before deciding to reapply a fresh coat of makeup and spruce up her hair. Her clothes, too, needed some spicing up and before she knew it she was twisting and turning in front of the mirror in an entirely new outfit. She wanted to look good for the camera from all angles, she rationalized, as she checked out the backside of her jeans.

She gathered her cooking supplies and piled them into a laundry basket for the short walk to Carter's. Her kitchen would've been a lot easier, but he was right, his was a lot better suited for filming.

"What are we making?" he asked with exuberance as she entered with her basket of food. He already had the camera situated on its tripod and Jake entertained on the floor with a ball and Bosco.

"Balsamic chicken and pears," she answered, sliding her shoes off by the door and pushing them neatly next to Carter's with her toes.

"Darn," he smiled as she padded her way across the kitchen and set the basket down on the bar. "I was hoping for chili cheese dogs."

Megan rolled her eyes but didn't grace him with a response. She unloaded the couscous, fresh organic Bosch pears, olive oil, and chicken breasts onto his counter.

"Let's try to get this in one take." Carter hopped behind the camera.

Megan was inexplicably nervous though. For a kid that'd done her fair share of photo shoots, she expected more from herself. But live action was different than smiling... not to mention the talking.

"Just relax," Carter coached as she sliced a pear with her shaky hands.

"Maybe we should prep everything first," she said. "That way I don't cut my fingers off on film."

"Whatever you want," he turned the camera off. "This is your show."

Okay, I want you. The thought came in to her mind quite uninvited. They were words she knew her egotistical husband would've thrown out without so much as a blush, but she wasn't like that. She believed in fidelity. And, had she not been convinced that her marriage was over, she'd have pushed them quickly aside. But she didn't. She let them reside. Maybe it was time to stop fighting her growing feelings.

"Will you help me?" she asked. He was already sliding up next to her.

"Put me to work."

He smiled innocently enough but she still had to take a deep breath to settle herself. Why all of a sudden was she so twitter-pated by him? He was so far from her type it was ridiculous. She was pretty sure she wasn't his type either.

"Here," she said, sliding the cutting board in front of him. She set the knife on the surface then plopped the bowl of pears down. "Can you cut these?"

"Like how?" he asked.

"Like with the knife," she pointed at its red handle.

"Genius!" he smirked, nudging her softly with his elbow. "I meant, what shape would you like me to cut them into?"

She brushed her hand across his purposefully as she retrieved the knife and a pear. "Like this," she instructed, slicing a long, thin spear. Her hands were still shaky.

"The camera is off, you know," he smiled and took the knife from her unstable hand. "You can relax now." He gently slid the pear out of her hand and copied her technique, minus the trembling nerves. "Am I doing it right?" he asked.

"Perfect," she answered. *Too perfect,* she sighed.

It didn't take long to prep all the ingredients and display them in the pretty little bowls Carter pulled from his china hutch. "They were my grandma's," he was quick to explain when Megan raised her brow. She hadn't even wondered though. If there was one thing she'd figured out about Carter, he was sentimental.

He slid around the bar and behind the camera again, raising his eyes to pose the question of whether or not she was ready. Her nerves had finally started to settle. She took an exaggeratedly deep breath, closed her eyes for a moment and then let the air flow out her lips.

With calculated ease, he stepped from behind the camera and beckoned her with his finger. "What?" she wondered as she stepped towards him. "Do I have something on my face?" she swiped her cheek with the back of her hand.

"Just come here," he teased with more power than he knew he had over her. She followed his call. Hopeful, ever hopeful.

She stopped a step in front of him and braced herself for what she hoped was coming. He rested his hands onto her shoulders and stepped into her personal space. "You can do this," he said, looking into her eyes. "I believe in you." He leaned in and softly grazed the top of her head with his lips.

You've got to be kidding me, she thought as he resumed his position behind the camera. *A forehead kiss? Ugh!* She screamed inside her head, intent not to let him see her frazzled. "Let's do this," she said, resituating herself behind the bar.

From behind the camera Carter continued to frazzle her with his smile. She did everything in her power to ignore him. She had no more business with him than he had with a girl like her. But... But he was so nice and cute and genuine and...

~   ~   ~

Carter tried to coax Megan to relax. She was a shaky ball of nerves. *Must be the camera,* he thought as he smiled gently across the room at her.

She lifted the prepared casserole dish off the counter. "Now that we've got everything assembled," she smiled at the camera, "we are going to bake it for forty-five minutes in a three-hundred- and fifty..." She didn't finish getting the sentence out before the dish slid from her hands, split into three pieces as it hit the edge of the counter, then fell to the floor. Chicken and pears and glass were everywhere.

Megan let out an exasperated scream and fell to her knees beside the mess. "I'm sorry," she wept as she began to gather the shattered glass from the floor. "I'm so sorry."

Carter glanced quickly in the direction of Jake and Bosco before racing around the bar. With the baby thoroughly occupied by the dog, he grabbed the trash bin and set it near the biggest portion of the mess before coming to a stop beside Megan.

Frantically, she tried to scoop the chicken up into a large shard of glass, apologizing constantly as she did so. "I'm sorry. I'm so, so, so sorry."

He reached his hand toward her and, as she flinched away, he saw fear behind the tears in her eyes. "It's okay," he sidled down beside her, taking the debris from her hands and tossing it into the trash can. *That husband of hers was a real piece of work.* He couldn't even begin to imagine the kind of monster that would hurt a girl like Megan. Or any girl for that matter.

She turned away from him and defensively raised her arms over her face. "I'm sorry," she shuttered between sobs. "I'll make it right," she cried. "I'll fix it."

"Megan," he reached for her again. She'd rolled her body into a ball, clearly preparing for a blow. "Megan," he repeated her name gently as he reached around her defenses. "It's okay." He leaned against the cabinet beside her and softly pulled her balled up frame into him.

"I'll clean it up," she cried. "And..." she forced each syllable out between whimpers, "and... and I know that was probably your grandma's casserole dish, which means it's not replaceable, but... but, I'll buy you a new one anyway. And..."

"And," he interrupted, "it's just stuff. It doesn't matter." He pulled her sobbing body in closer. "It doesn't matter," he reiterated.

"But," she started again.

"Listen to me," he cupped her face in his hands, "it doesn't matter."

She stared up at him through tear streaked eyes. "How can you say that?" she trembled. "Look at this mess."

Balsamic vinegar dripped off the edge of the counter, down the cabinet face, and finally to the floor. Chicken breasts lay in soggy heaps peppered with shards of glass. Pear slivers clung to the front of the fridge and onto nearly every surface to be seen. "Yep," he grinned, "looks like a mess alright." He wiped a tear from her cheek. "Good thing messes clean up, huh?"

She melted into him with another sob. "I'll clean it up spotless," she sniffled into his chest. "I promise."

"How 'bout we do it together," he said as he worked his way to his feet.

"No," she argued as he began tossing what he could into the trash can. She pulled herself slowly to her feet. "I can do it," she sighed.

"I know you can," he smiled. "And, believe it or not, so can I."

Megan moistened a dish cloth with hot water. "I'm sorry for ruining your dinner," she gained composure as she began wiping the cabinet face.

"It's probably a good thing this ended the way it did," Carter smirked. "I mean, seriously, I'm not sure how I feel about eating a chicken that apparently doesn't know how to fly." He picked up the last floppy breast from the floor and tossed it with a thud into the trash.

"Looks like it flew okay to me," she followed his playful cues with a tinge of hesitancy.

"Nah," he shrugged. "That wasn't flying. This is flying." He picked up a pear spear and masterfully sent it flying like a paper airplane. "Looks like we're going to need a plan B for dinner," he turned the oven off.

"I'll take you out," Megan offered. "How does *Ruth's* sound? My treat."

"I've got a better idea," he nodded.

Chapter Twenty-Seven

Before Megan could sufficiently object, Carter had her and Jake in the cab of his truck. "Where are we going?" she asked as she eyed the brown paper bag near her feat. She was confused by his understanding and generosity. Nobody was this nice, she thought, feeling herself fall deeper for him by the second. Nobody was this perfect, she considered. He had to have a flaw. Some big secret. Some hidden weakness.

She ran her fingers across the metal dashboard plaque. *Custom build for Ezra Carter.*

Nervously, she shifted her attention out the windshield at the dirt road. Rocks framed the path on one side, there was a steep and steady drop off the other. "I've never," she sighed, looking for the right words as she braced herself for the onslaught of bumps and jostles. "I've never done anything like this before." Her white knuckle grip on the armrest did nothing to calm her nerves.

"Like what?" he seemed completely relaxed as he navigated the truck over the mountain road.

"Like drive into a shady dark canyon on a barely existent dirt road with a guy I barely know."

"Ah," Carter teased. "So, you've only done it with guys you know well?"

She gawked at him from the passenger seat, wondering if he realized what his comment had implied.

"I meant," he quickly clarified, "that you've gone four-wheeling up a canyon with guys you know."

"No," she grinned. "That is, to the second question." She didn't try to hide the blush on her cheeks as she thought about the first. Somehow not one of the guys she'd ever dated seemed as important as the one navigating his truck, and subsequently her and her baby's lives, up the questionably curvy canyon trail.

"Well, if it makes you feel any better," he glanced at her nervously twitching fingers on the arm rest. "We're just about there."

"That's good," she touched Jake's toes, "because I'm kind of freaking out over here."

"Yeah," he laughed, "I've kind of noticed."

She held her breath around a few last perilous curves before Carter pulled the truck onto a grassy turnout. "We're here," he turned to her with a smile as he tugged at the door handle.

"And where exactly is *here?*" she asked.

"I like to think of it as my own little piece of heaven," he gloated as he hopped out of the cab. He stopped at the bed of the truck to drop the tailgate for Bosco then continued around and opened Megan's door.

"Guess I should've listened when you told me to change my shoes," she said, taking his hand as she jumped out of the cab. The long wild grasses tickled her ankles as her four-inch heels touched down on the soft earth.

"I know. I surprise myself with my genius sometimes." He dropped her hand and retrieved the brown paper sack off the floor of the cab.

Megan took a deep breath of the summer air, surprised at the noticeable chill it held at their increased altitude. She savored another breath then unbuckled Jake and pulled him from his seat. "Are you hungry?" she asked him as she squeezed his warm body into hers.

"Coco," he answered, ever intrigued by the dog. She snuggled him for a long minute, taking in his sweet baby smell and his addicting softness before sliding his arms into a jacket and setting him down to love Bosco.

"Well," she answered herself, "I'm starving." She pushed the truck door closed and, keeping an eye on Jake, tiptoed her way through the grass towards Carter. "Can I help?" she asked as she approached him from behind.

"Nope." He stood and dusted off his knees, exposing the small beginnings of a fire in a rock encircled pit. "Dinner will be ready in about fifteen minutes." He reached into the back of his truck and pulled out a blanket. "Why don't you take a seat and enjoy the scenery," he said, pointing to a large rock.

"Wow," Megan couldn't help but laugh, "you are quite the entertainer, aren't you?" she teased. She dusted the rock off with her hand then hesitantly sat down.

"I do my best." With a rapid shake the blanket unfolded in his hands and billowed into the air. Easing it slowly to the ground, it spread open across the grass.

"Impressive," Megan teased from her post on the rock. "You're pretty good at that."

"Years of practice," he guffawed with pretend conceit.

"I guess that means I'm not the first girl you've drug up here to your *little piece of heaven*?" she baited. "And here I was starting to think I was someone special," she teased.

"Oh, you're special, Megan," he teased back. "And by special, I mean that you're the only person who's ever been up here in high heels."

"But they're cute," she defended, dusting off the toe.

"Yes, we clarified that in the driveway," he smiled, "when I suggested you opt for something a little more durable."

"These are durable," she played. "I could run a marathon in them for sure."

"I'll bet." He picked up Jake and set him on the blanket then handed him a cracker from the paper sack. Bosco begged for a cracker, swallowed it without chewing, then with a giant thud made himself comfortable beside Jake.

"How's that fire looking?" Carter asked as he spread the remaining contents of the bag onto his tailgate.

"Like a fire," Megan shrugged, more impressed with the view beyond the fire than the glowing flame itself. She tried to be discrete as she watched Carter, even though part of her hoped he'd catch her staring. *This is ridiculous*, she told herself, shaking off the juvenile gape. "Is that your orchard?" she asked, diverting her gaze into the valley below.

"Yup," he stabbed a hotdog onto the end of a metal stick. "Pretty nice view up here, isn't it?"

"Yeah it is." Her words were laced with more insinuation than she'd intended. *Calm down*, she chided herself.

Carter seemed to miss the innuendo. "Here." He handed her the hotdog flanked stick.

"What am I supposed to do with this?"

"Roast it," he answered, squatting down beside the fire with a roasting stick in each of his hands.

Megan didn't know if she should be insulted or embarrassed. "People really do this?" she asked as she watched him slowly turn his hotdogs over the fire.

"Yup," he answered.

"Okay," she hesitated. "Not that you don't already think I'm *special* or anything, but," she blushed, "I have no idea what I'm doing."

"Why am I not surprised," he smiled. He slowly stood from the fire and rested his sticks against the truck's tailgate. Bosco drooled at the partially roasted hotdogs saluting him in the air. A quick look told the obedient dog to leave them alone.

Carter pulled a second blanket from the back of the truck and partially unfolded it near the fire pit. "Come here," he patted the newly blanketed ground as he smiled at Megan. "It's my turn to dazzle you with my cooking abilities."

"Dazzle away," she chuckled as she settled onto the blanket. He took her hand and patiently instructed her on proper roasting techniques. Though she doubted that she'd like the hotdog, she enjoyed the lesson. Or maybe it was the teacher.

Jake ambled over and took position on her lap, enthralled by both the fire and the crackers that Carter kept slipping him.

"Now go build a bun," he instructed when she'd achieved roasting perfection. He lifted Jake off her lap and into his own.

"Build a bun?" she grinned as she stretched up from the blanket.

"You know," he smiled, "get it ready for your dog?"

"I figured," she bumped playfully into him as she passed. "I'd just never heard it referred to as *building* before."

"Well then, madam, it would appear that I've got a lot to teach you."

And so he did. He introduced Jake and Megan to their first roasted hotdogs. He taught Megan how to make a s'more and, though it made himself a sticky mess, fed one to Jake bite by patient bite. He nestled Jake on his lap, holding him a safe distance from the fire as he explained that it was "hot" and not to touch because it would give him an "owey." He told stories of Indian lore and other outdoor tales he'd surely shared with his scouts.

Jake drifted to sleep in her arms. She enveloped him in one of Carter's blankets then lay him beside her. Relieved of his weight, she wrapped her shoulders in the other blanket with a heavy sigh. "What am I doing here?" she exhaled as the night unfolded around her.

"As I recall," Carter poked a stick at the dancing flame, "some crazy, out-doorsy kind of guy dragged you up here."

"Indeed," she said, nodding at him as she grinned. "Good thing he decided against dumping my body in the wilderness," she teased, trusting him more fully than she probably should have.

"The night is young yet." The fire played shadows across his rugged face, softening his eyes and his smile to the point of near irresistibility.

Look up at me, she willed, hoping to distract him away from the fire long enough to validate her rush of feelings.

"You really like it out here, don't you?" she finally asked. She was becoming more and more enamored by the minute.

"I do," he radiated.

She wondered what it was about this isolation and quiet that he liked, but didn't ask. "I kind of miss home." She shifted her weight on the blanket and stared out across the light speckled valley.

Carter turned to her in earnest. "What's it like, you know, where you're from?"

The valley lights began to blur under the threat of tears as she conjured up the memories. "I have a penthouse," she grinned, bursting with pride at the very thought of it. "Everything's new and clean and trendy. And my bed," she sighed, "my bed is soft and comfortable, with sheets as smooth as butter. I could spend a whole day there and not feel a bit sorry about it." She walked through the penthouse in her mind, one room at a time. "We've got this super shaggy rug that tickles your toes, and the biggest flat screen TV you've ever seen." A thought of the haughty glass dining table adorned with exuberant bouquets came to mind. She pushed it aside to make room for the pleasant thoughts. "I have..." she swallowed back the emotion. "I mean, I had a housekeeper," she mumbled with the realization of how ridiculous that must sound to a do-it-yourselfer like Carter. She drew her knees into her chest. "And I don't have to worry about mice or squirrels," she forced a smile Carter's direction, "or snipes."

"It sounds nice," he returned her smile.

"It's beautiful." She restrained herself from letting the emotion quiver out, but as it settled in her gut she wondered out loud, "Maybe it's time to go home."

"Can I ask you something?" He didn't turn from the fire as he spoke.

"Sure."

"What's the cost of that lifestyle?"

The unexpected question caught her off guard. "I don't know. Matt handled all the finances."

Carter shifted his stare from the fire to the valley. "That's not what I meant." He continued slowly, thoughtfully, "What's the cost to *you*?" He tossed a small rock over the fire and into the grass.

"I don't know what you mean," she answered without thinking. "I just told you that Matt took care of everything."

"Megan," he finally turned to look at her. "I know this may be none of my business, but I saw the way you reacted earlier. You were scared. You thought I was going to hit you."

Her lip started to tremble. The emotion she'd pitted began to scramble to the surface.

"Is that lifestyle – all of those fancy *things* - worth the price *you* pay to have them? Don't you think you deserve something better?"

"Better than a penthouse?" her voice quivered.

"Better than fear?"

The silence was almost suffocating. Neither party did so much as take a deep breath. Megan broke free of Carter's gaze and shifted her eyes to the dirt. "I'm just not very good at this country-type life," she finally said. "I mean, look at me." She kicked her foot towards the light of the fire. "What kind of country girl wears shoes like this? And in the mountains, no less?"

"Just because you're in the country, as you call it, doesn't mean you can't have style. And I can't fault you for your fashion sense. In fact, it's kind of refreshing."

"You don't need to humor me," she mumbled.

"I'm not," he scooted next to her. "But I think you should know that you're doing okay. You've made some big changes and you're handling it like a champ."

"Yeah," she chortled, "I'm a regular Rocky Balboa."

He threw his arm across her shoulders and laughed. "Now I wouldn't go that far, ma'am. Not yet anyway. But," he squeezed her gently, "if you keep working at it, it'll come. Don't give up quite yet. Besides," he said, pulling her to her feet, "I don't think I've properly taught you how to relax yet."

He unraveled the blanket from her shoulders then shook it to the ground in perfect form. She stood, shocked at his boldness as he settled himself onto the blanket. "Are you coming?" he asked, patting the space beside him.

Her eyes gawked in wonder.

"I promise I'm not going to touch you," he patted the blanket again. "I just want to show you something."

Butterflies overtook the sadness in her gut as she slowly settled in beside him. Hoping that perhaps he'd been lying when he promised not to touch her, at his insistence, she melted back flat on the ground and stared upwards.

"Have you ever seen our galaxy before?" he whispered as if it were some amazing secret. He raised his hand to the sky and pointed at the mass of freckled lights in the heavens. "I'll bet you never saw anything as wonderful as that from your buttery soft penthouse bed."

Megan stared up with wonder at the thousands... no, millions of sparkling lights in the sky. "Which one is planet GRRR?" she asked with a grin. "You know, in case I ever want to visit you there."

Chapter Twenty-Eight

Megan watched intently from behind her reception desk, slightly annoyed to have her thoughts pulled away from the pleasantries of her newfound desires. She'd never considered hot dogs to be a romantic gesture, but for the last few days she hadn't been able to shake thoughts about Carter and the star-filled heavens from her mind.

"Doc," she finally called over her shoulder, surrendering her romantic dreams to the unshakeable uneasiness in her gut. Even on a busy day, the car that'd been parked across the street for the last thirty minutes was anything but normal. Behind its tinted windows she could see a shadow. A man, she concluded. Definitely a man.

"Hmm?" he peered around the corner.

"What do you make of this?" she nodded out the front windows toward the street. "He's been sitting there since I got back from lunch."

"Interesting. Maybe he's lost," Doctor Stone shrugged.

"I don't know," Megan said.

"Just keep your eye on him," Doc patted her shoulder. "If he moves, let me know."

As soon as he stepped away, the car door swung open and a big, burly man thumped his foot onto the pavement. "He's moving," Megan called out nervously. There was nothing normal about his movement across the street. Boxy. Methodic.

Doc planted himself behind Megan. "How 'bout you step into the hall," he offered. "Let me handle this."

"Not going to argue with that," she scuttled just far enough around the corner to stay in earshot.

"Excuse me," the man waited for the door chime to silence before he spoke. "I'm looking for the owner of that Audi around back." His lips curled up in a forcibly innocent smile, revealing a gold set of lower teeth.

"May I ask why?" Doc asked casually.

"I just came from a car dealership down the road a bit and he said he knew of someone 'round about these parts looking to sell their Audi." He leaned casually against the counter. "I'm a wholesaler," he explained as he tossed a business card onto the counter. "I was hoping she – or he – would be willing to talk numbers with me."

"You know," Doc inspected the card, "I don't really think the car is for sale."

"Is it yours?" The boxy man asked.

"Sorry," Doc shrugged. "It's not. Belongs to one of my employees, though. She's unavailable right now, but I will happily pass your card on to her."

"That'd be great." His eyes made one more sweep of the office. "Make sure she knows I'm quite good at what I do," his palm smacked the counter. "My clients have deep pockets," he added as he slowly exited the front door.

"Is he gone?" Megan didn't dare poke her head out quite yet.

"Almost," Doc watched the man closely. "He's almost to the other side of the street," he narrated each movement. "Opened his car door... Looking back over his shoulder... Getting in the car... Pulling out... And, he's gone."

Megan's feet were planted in the hall; her back glued to the wall.

"What do you reckin' that was all about?" Doc stole the words from her mouth as he stepped into the hall.

"I don't know." She calculated the man. Something didn't feel right. She reconstructed her visit to the car dealership several weeks prior. She knew she hadn't given out her new address or anything, for that matter, about her whereabouts. *Why would he send someone looking for her?*

~   ~   ~

"I think you're making too much out of it," Bri comforted. "Maybe he was legit. It is a nice car, you know."

"But it didn't feel right," Megan sighed. "It was so... random."

"Why would he give you a card if he wasn't for real?" Bri sipped her lemonade.

"I don't know." Megan turned the card through her fingers. "People do weird things." She reconstructed the afternoon yet again. "He really was a creeper."

"Here," Bri snagged the card. The edges were worn soft from Megan's nervous handling. "How bout I pass this on to Brent?"

Megan let out an exasperated sigh. "Maybe I'm just paranoid," she shrugged. "It's probably nothing, you're right, but thanks for having Brent check it out anyway."

"Well, maybe it'll free up some time for you to do a little checking out of your own."

"What are you talking about?" Megan pretended to be focused on the happily playing children in her yard.

"Give me a break! If you keep staring at *him* like that he's going to think you're a creeper."

"I'm not staring," Megan defended. She took another thirsty peek at Carter then returned her glance to the kids. Jake was doing everything he could to keep up with Noah. Mariah was content to hug and kiss him anytime his unstable legs sent him falling to the ground.

Sitting uncomfortably on the top stair of the porch, Bri took another swallow of her lemonade. "Then what *are* you doing?" she asked.

Megan leaned back into the wooden stairs. "Observing," she smiled, unabashedly shrugging off her infatuation.

"Okay," Bri nudged her with a grin. "Quit *observing* so intently or you're going to freak him out."

"I doubt it," Megan remembered the softness of his innocent touch. "Carter's not easily stirred. Besides, I'm not sure he wasn't trying to kill me with that truck ride the other night. A girl can't ever be too careful, you know," she smirked.

"If you keep *watching him* like that," Bri nodded towards the sound of Carter's sawing in the garage, "he's going to wish he'd left you on that mountain."

Noah hoisted Jake into the little red wagon then waited patiently for Mariah to follow.

"There's got to be something wrong with him," Megan twisted her lips in thought.

"What do you mean?" Bri asked.

Megan perched on the edge of the step, waiting for Noah to tip the wagon over. "It's not like I need his approval or anything," she said. Taking in an exaggerated breath, she added, "But, seriously, there's gotta be something wrong with him."

"Still not following you," Bri rolled her naked toes around in the air. "I feel like I'm going to pop," she mumbled.

"Not to be insensitive," Megan jostled her friend with her shoulder, "but quit trying to change the subject here." She paused long enough to exchange smirks then continued. "He's too nice. Too perfect. There's got to be a flaw. Some kind of weakness. I'm curious to know what makes his knees buckle, Bri, because it certainly isn't me."

"Why are you so quick to assume that?" She continued to roll her swollen toes and adjust her colossally pregnant body awkwardly on the step.

"It's pretty obvious." Megan kept focus on the conversation while she watched the wagon slowly drag across the lawn. "Not to sound conceited or anything, but I've never had a guy turn me down before." She hesitated at Bri's muffled smirk. "I'm being serious here, Bri. I don't get it. I've done everything but strip down and dance on the kitchen table and he hasn't so much as tried to kiss me. It just doesn't make any sense."

"Maybe you should try that."

"Really?"

"No." Bri put her hand on Megan's knee. "Please don't."

Megan considered pushing the idea because if Bri thought it would work she just might do it. Instead, she decided to take a different route. "I can only think of one reason he won't acknowledge me," she started. "He must be gay."

Chapter Twenty-Nine

"She thinks you're gay," Brent laughed as the two men hefted the heavy mantel up Carter's stairs.

"She does not." Carter defended, heaving the solid mass of wood from one rise to the next.

"She does," Brent laughed again. "Either that or there's something wrong with you, if you know what I mean." His deep-throated chortle echoed up the stairway.

"Whatever." Carter shook off the ruse. Since he'd taken Megan to roast hot dogs up the canyon, her overt flirtation had become obvious. So had, he assumed, his blatant evasion of it. "What does it matter anyway? Whether I want her or not, I can't have her."

They reached the top of the stairs and used the landing to readjust their hold before making the turn towards the master doorway. "Can't, huh? Are you sure *won't* isn't a better word? As far as she's concerned you *can* have her, but you don't seem to want to. She's all but thrown herself in your lap and all you do is ignore her."

They secured their hold on the awkward slab of wood and started moving again. "Men don't generally turn women down... especially smokin' hot ones. No wonder she thinks there's something wrong with you."

"I have no interest in a married woman and somehow that means there's something wrong with me?" Carter guided the mahogany mantle through his bedroom door.

"You have no interest in a very beautiful woman. That definitely qualifies under the *something is wrong with you* category. Either that, or you're gay."

"That's ridiculous," Carter defended again as they slid the mantel into place over the fireplace.

"No, you're ridiculous." Brent brushed his hands together with satisfaction then pointed to the ornate piece of work. "And that's ridiculous too."

"And what's so ridiculous about it?" Carter eyed his masterpiece. Hours of hard work and excruciating precision had been poured into every hand carved detail. It was a work even his father's critical eye would've appreciated. He engaged his drill to attach it to the wall.

"You're telling me you don't see the irony here?" Brent didn't wait for an answer. "You've got an outrageous master suite, with an amazing fireplace, and coffered, hand-molded ceilings, but nobody ever sees them but you." He sat on the bottom edge of his friend's bed then with almost forced animation threw himself backwards onto it. "Oh, Ammon," he squealed in a squeaky falsetto, "I can't believe you finally brought me to your room." He sunk himself into the mattress, twisting his imaginary hair around his finger. "You are so hot," he lisped as delicately as he could while stifling his laughter, "Oh my, look at that fireplace. Is it hand carved? And that molding - its every detail is so delicate. I'll bet you're good with your hands, Ammon."

Carter watched his friend with bated disgust. "Get off my bed, you moron." He placed a level across the top of the mantel to insure it's exactness before attaching the final screws.

"You know she wants you," Brent continued as he sat up from the bed. "And, whether you're going to admit it or not, you know you want her too."

Carter turned away and looked out the window. Megan's car was missing from the drive but he knew it'd be back soon. Admittedly, he'd come to anticipate her return from work each day. And, though he wasn't about to break down and kiss her, there were times he wished he could. There were some things he just couldn't do.

"You've got a three bedroom house, immaculate and well-built, but you live alone." Brent couldn't leave well enough alone. He stood and walked across the room then, leaning on the door frame to the master bathroom, flipped the light on. "Look at this. You've got a freakin' bathroom for a princess. Jetted tub, double sinks - it looks like some fancy spa in here. And for who?" he asked. "I'd be willing to bet *you* don't light candles and soak in bubbles up to your chin." He hit the light switch again and stepped towards Carter. "Or... maybe you do. Heck, who am I to judge?" He smacked his friend's shoulder.

"You're about to catch a flying lesson," Carter jostled. He stepped back to admire his handiwork, the sting of his loneliness ever present.

"It's just a little weird, you know. You've got a home for a family, bro, but no family."

"And you think that's by choice?"

"No, but she does."

"I'm over this conversation," Carter shifted his eyes discretely back out the window, reminded full well who the proffered *she* he was referring to was.

"That's fine with me," Brent lamented. "I don't want to talk 'bout any of this touchy-feely stuff with you anyway, but," he stomped out the door and onto the landing, "you probably should talk to *her* about it."

"Whatever," Carter lamented. "It's really a non-issue," he said, though recent encounters with Megan told him otherwise. As if the way she laughed and teased and smiled wasn't enough, her comfortable nudges and subtle touches where almost unbearable. He didn't know how much more he could take. "Wanna help me pull my camping gear out of the garage before you leave?" he asked, needing a change of subject.

"Don't really wanna," Brent took the stairs two at a time, "but if we're quick I will anyway. Gotta get home to my pretty lil' lady," he smirked. "Maybe someday you'll know what that's like."

Chapter Thirty

Megan's car rolled up just as the last of the scouts arrived with their gear. Carter offered her a smile and a quick wave – just enough to be friendly, he reminded himself. *Can't give her anything more. Just friends.*

Bosco, however, saw things differently. Before the car even came to a stop he'd planted himself on the back lawn, tail wagging with ferocious excitement as he waited to greet Jake. It was no use calling him back and Carter knew it. The dog wouldn't be appeased until he'd sufficiently been loved by Jake's pudgy little hands.

"Hey Carter," Sam called as he threw his backpack into the truck bed. "Can we take the boat out soon?"

"Is it ready?" Carter turned from Megan and focused on his boys. He knew the answer to the question without having to ask. The boys had barely spent any time on the project.

"Not yet," Sam skirted up beside him with a swooshing sound, "but soon, right?"

"Right," he nodded at the ambitious kid. "If you want to finish it by summer's end, you're going to have to work on it more often, you know."

"I know," he bounced from one foot anxiously to the other. "Can I go work on it now?" he moved towards the garage.

Carter grabbed the collar of his shirt and stopped him from dashing off in a dusty storm. "Um, no!" he laughed. "We're about to leave on a campout, remember?" He bobbed his head towards the loaded truck and the troop of boys gathered on the front lawn.

"I know," he bounced excitedly, "but can't I work on it for just a minute?"

"Sam," Carter took him under his arm and directed him toward the other boys. "You can work on it later. Right now it's time to hit the road."

He made one last glance towards Megan's house as the excited boys dispersed into his truck and Whitley's van. "Boss," he called across the yard before settling into the driver's seat. "Let's go!"

~ ~ ~

Megan jotted down the last of her recipe notes as she watched out the window. The porch light was the sole beacon of life from Carter's empty house and in its stillness she felt a cloak of isolation settle over her. Jake was settled in bed but she had no desire to retire just yet. She was still unsure what to do with the apricot sauce she had simmering on the stove. With a kick of Worcestershire sauce, it would be amazing as a meat or poultry sauce. With a pinch of cinnamon and sugar, however, it would make a delightful drizzle for a cake. She wished Carter hadn't rolled out of town with his scouts because, if nothing more, he'd proven to be a sound bearer of advice for her culinary endeavors. If she couldn't figure out what to do with the sauce, his taste buds surely would.

She glanced out the window one last time then turned the stove off. Hopeful that a good night's sleep would help her make a decision about it, she moved the unfinished sauce to the fridge. Grabbing a fresh apricot from the basket Whitley delivered before he and Carter left with the scouts, she stepped onto the porch and took in the immensity of the star speckled sky. Until Carter pointed them out, she had never noticed what she'd been missing beyond the glare of the city lights, but for the past two weeks, she'd found herself in awe at their magnitude.

Finishing her apricot, she stepped back in the house and locked the door behind her before shimming across the quiet little house to her bed. Carter may have made fun of her buttery soft sheets, but as she slid into bed, she missed them with a new intensity. Maybe if she could save enough money she could get a new set. Or, better yet, maybe Matt would cave soon and not only would she have money available, she could get a real home. She liked that idea better.

She lay in bed for a minute, staring at the diffused glow of the moon on her ceiling, then had an uneasy feeling that she'd forgotten to lock up. Padding her way out of the bedroom, she checked the front and back doors then returned to bed. Even then it was hard to turn her mind off. The ongoing nightmares frequented her and she rarely got a restful night sleep. She rolled to her side and snuggled her blanket up to her chin. Maybe if she clouded her mind with pleasant thoughts she'd be able to avert the nightmares. Maybe if she thought about shopping, or getting a massage, or relaxing on the beach, or bubble baths... or Carter. Maybe if she thought enough about Carter.

It was only a dream she knew, because despite her newfound infatuation with him, he was clearly not interested in her. But, for the sake of pleasant thoughts, she took the time to dwell. Since their hotdog roasting rendezvous, they'd successfully made four cooking videos for her website and tomorrow would be their fifth. And, after several almost desperate attempts throwing herself at him, he'd successfully communicated with unwearied resistance that he was not interested. He was always patient and kind, but blatantly not interested all the same. Perhaps it was that loneliness that made her think of Matt. Perhaps it was that desperation to feel wanted that made the nightmares so real...

Her eyes shot open and she sat straight up in bed like a spring had pushed her there. Just as she'd succumbed to sleep something had awakened her. A sound, she thought. A bump.

She steadied her breathing and perked her ears toward the darkness. The gentle rise and fall of Jake's breath lightly touched the air. She turned her head to the window as if to catch glimpse of something through its draperies, but was greeted by nothing more than the same shadow of the moon that'd helped soothe her to sleep.

She froze for a moment, hoping the effort would more highly tune her senses and help put her racing heart at ease. As soon as she did so, however, she heard the bump again... towards the back of the house. It was louder now, more persistent. Thump, bump, scratch. Thump, bump, scratch, bump. Squeak, clank, slam... silence. Her heart stopped.

Poised on her bed with nothing more than a blanket for protection, she looked around, horrified by her isolation. She could scream, but with Bosco and Carter gone, no one would hear her. She could dial 911 but by time she put her phone together and powered it on, she'd likely be laying in a pool of blood. Her imagination went crazy with thoughts of knives, guns, and kidnappings. The boxy man who'd inquired about her car flashed through her mind.

The silence was broken again, this time by a soft clicking sound. Slowly the sound ticked towards her closed bedroom door. Her heart jumped into her throat. Her jaw tightened. Her mind raced. *What do I do?*

She remained frozen on her bed.

The clicking stopped just outside her door. She looked around for something she could use to defend herself then silently slipped off the bed. In the darkness, the shoe found her almost before she found it. She picked it up and poised herself, five-inch stiletto in hand, against the wall. On bated breath, she waited for the intruder to push the door open, poised to take him out with the sharp heal of her favorite shoe. With enough blows she was sure she could cause enough damage to at least afford her the time to grab her baby and make a run for Bri's house.

A moment of excruciating silence erupted with a hollow, floor shaking thud. She flinched at the sound, rethinking her shoe defense against whatever giant mass stood outside her door.

Across the room, she heard Jake flinch inside his crib. She snapped her eyes toward him, praying that he'd stay asleep. A new terror enveloped her. *What if Matt had sent someone to take Jake?*

Her lip, raw from biting it, began to taste like metal. She wanted to wipe it to see if it were actually bleeding, but didn't dare move. She had to be ready to defend herself – and Jacob. Especially Jacob.

Each quiet moment found her shaking with more fear. If the intruder's idea had been to debilitate her through psychological warfare, he'd certainly been successful. Every muscle in her body was on lock down. Even her lungs were hesitant to work. With each detained breath, she felt herself lose strength. With each racing thought, she felt herself lose hope.

She was no stranger to violence, but she'd never hit back. *Could she now? Could she deliver a blow?* She doubted her strength but not her determination. She had to protect Jake.

Morning found Megan pretzeled against the wall. Her legs were stiffly squished into her torso, her bare feet cold against the wood floor. She rolled her head from one side then the other, certain she was only dreaming.

She closed her eyes again, hoping to wake up comfortably in her bed, but as her lids unfolded, the terror returned.

She snapped her eyes open. The curtains were still drawn, but the morning pushed its way through them anyway. She rolled her head again, this time cracking it from one side to the other. Pulling her hands into her chin for a yawn, she realized the intensity of her grip on her shoe. Slowly she released it to the ground and flexed the kinks out of her hand. She had a solid imprint of its toe embedded in her palm.

She pulled herself up off the floor, taking in her surroundings with grateful familiarity. Jake's little round body mounded in his crib. Mellow snores lightly sounded from his throat. Whatever had come in the night had apparently left without either of them. She sighed a breath of relief and turned to the door. "Gotta use the ladies room," she mumbled to herself, "then I'm going back to bed until noon."

Running one hand through her hair, she turned the knob with the other and stepped into the hall.

"Ahhh!" she screamed as she tripped her way to the floor. Her palms caught the brunt of the fall, but not before her knee smacked into the door frame. "Ugh," she cursed, pulling her knee into her as she rolled over. "You've got to be kidding me!"

A pair of big round eyes looked at her from the base of the door. Sad eyes. Repentant eyes. "Bosco," she growled through clenched teeth. "I should have known."

Chapter Thirty-One

"Where's your dog?" Whitley asked as the scout troop broke camp.

"Darn dog's got himself a new master, I guess," Carter laughed. "I invited him to get in the truck and instead he planted himself on Megan's porch." Carter shook his head as he pulled a tent stake out of the ground.

"If you ask me, I think that dog's got things figured out, replacing you for a woman and all." Whitley laughed a full-belly laugh.

"Not for a woman," Carter moved around his tent, pulling at each stake effortlessly with the hammer. "He's got a thing for that baby of hers. I've never seen anything quite like it. First place he goes every morning is to their back porch. When they're not there he stalks the place all day, then he hears her car from a mile away and meets them in the driveway with his tail going a million miles an hour."

"Dog just might be smarter than his owner," Whitley mumbled. "Maybe it's time you found yourself a new best friend," Whitley laughed again, pulling out a stake of his own.

Carter yanked at the last stake. "You're not kidding. I'm not sure if I should laugh at his new found devotion or be hurt by it? Stupid animal falls asleep each night with his head on the window sill."

"Maybe he's just reminding you that someone other than him should be keeping you warm at night." Whitley folded the tent into thirds.

"Sounds like you've been talking to Brent." Carter folded his own tent and started rolling it up.

"Nope, but maybe I should."

"Or maybe you should do something important like supervise those boys in packing up their stuff." Carter squished his tent back into its bag.

"Ah, listen to you gettin' all authoritative and all. Was beginin' to wonder if you had it in ya," Whitley teased.

"I haven't hit a man since I was seventeen, Whitley, but if you're sportin' to break that streak, I just might be happy to oblige," Carter joked back.

"Sweet!" his elder companion laughed. "I ain't had a good brawl for years either. Let's do it!"

Rough as he was, Carter doubted Whitley had ever raised a fist to anyone, though Grandpa Ez had spun some wild tales about the young, destitute farm hand who'd stumbled onto the orchard years before Carter existed. "Don't tempt me," he teased, squaring his fists in front of him. The man in Grandpa's tales surely wasn't the gentle, gray haired giant who stood before him now.

"Oh, I'm goin' to tempt you. And then I'm goin' to kick yer white hide."

"You and what army?" Carter teased.

Whitley looked over his shoulder at the rambunctious boys. "How 'bout that one," he smiled.

"What makes you so sure they'd take your side?"

"Food," he answered smugly. "Boys think with their bellies," he laughed. "And I've got all the food packed in my van."

"You've got me there, friend," he lightly punched his long-time ally's shoulder. After their morning hike, the scouts were surely hungry, especially since they'd been told they had to break camp before they could eat lunch. "Tell me about your younger years," he prodded, suddenly curious about the stories of his youth.

"If you think I'm going to spill some outlaw secrets, you're wrong." The creases around his eyes feathered deeply when he chuckled, revealing years of hard work and harsh weather. "But, I'd be willing to do a little barterin' if you like."

The scouts had yet to finish taking down their tent, despite the number of hands available to help. "Come on, guys!" Carter beckoned to the boys cavorting around in the field. "Get over here and help get this tent down before we starve to death!" He waved his hands at the half pitched mass of canvas. "Bartering?" he picked up his conversation with Whitley. "Are you serious? I already gave you half my orchard, old man, what else could you possibly want from me?" he cajoled.

"The dish on that hottie you've got shackin' up in Beth and Ez's house."

"The dish? Hottie?" He kept his voice low and stifled his amusement. "Don't you think you're a bit old for her?"

"Age is relative, young man. If you ain't got no business with her," he lowered his voice so the boys wouldn't hear his crude remark, "then somebody oughta." He winked. "And far as I figure, there ain't no reason why that somebody ought not be me."

"Far as I figure," Carter copied his friend's country slang, "she's goin' to leave this town first chance she gets."

"Yessir," Whitley made a clicking sound with his upturned cheek, "and it's goin' to be with the likes of me."

"Well," Carter considered the idea. "I suppose if we have a good enough season you could sell your portion of the orchard and buy her a little house somewhere near the city. Not a big one, mind you, at least not like the penthouse she's been missing so desperately," he swatted Whitley's back. "But with your rugged good looks and all, as long as you hooked her up with some buttery soft sheets, I'm sure she'd be happy with a two-bedroom bungalow with shag carpets and a detached carport."

"Don't know a woman who wouldn't," Whitley smirked.

"Carter," Jamison hobbled away from the tent distressed. "Nobody's helping and I'm getting hungry."

"I think I found my first recruit," Whitley chortled with a crooked grin. "My army's officially bigger than yours now."

"So what does that make us?" Carter played along. "Team Whitley two, team Carter one?"

"If you count that pretty lady," Whitley handed a stick of beef jerky to Jamison, "I'd figure we're something like Whitley *three*, Carter zilch."

"If you ever need woman advice," Carter addressed the skittish twelve-year-old, "please don't go to Whitley. Apparently, he's a sucker for a pretty face."

~ ~ ~

Megan watched Bosco raise his huge paws to the knob then, after swiping multiple times, achieve just the right angle to knock the door open. His canine persistence had turned the knob, but what she still couldn't figure out was how he managed to do it when it was locked.

"Either your dog's Houdini or there's a problem with the lock." Megan rubbed at her sore knee. "That stupid mutt about gave me a heart attack. You're lucky I didn't just keel over right there."

"How many times do I need to apologize?" Carter examined the dented door frame.

"At least twenty more," she smiled. Even with its skewed jam, the lock seemed perfectly stable.

"I don't know what happened," he shrugged. "I guess I'm going to have to go with the Houdini theory."

"Really?" she grinned. "Then why don't you just throw some voodoo dust at it or something?"

"I suppose I could, if you think it will help," he sashayed his hips from side to side and tossed a handful of pretend sparkle at the door.

"This is serious!" Megan put her foot down. "What if someone other than your beast had gotten in? What if..." she let the thought trail off.

"I'll take care of it," he promised with a smile. "As soon as I finish the entertainment center for the Jensens, I will tear this whole frame out and build a new one, okay?"

She did her best to milk his sympathy. "And just how long is it going to take to do that?" She batted her eyes flirtatiously.

He grinned at her persistence. "If you quit distracting me, I think I can have it done by the end of the day."

"And exactly how am I distracting you?" she played along.

"By pouting your lips and batting your eyes, that's how."

"Like this?" She sulked her lips into a frown and fluttered her long eyelashes against her cheeks.

"Exactly. *Very* distracting."

"That's where we'll have to disagree." She angled into him and softly brushed her hand over his shoulder. "If only I could persuade you to deeper distraction," she teased his eyes with hers, "then I might cut you some slack on the door repair."

Carter quickly pulled away. Megan lit up a grin.

"Look, Megan," he shifted uneasily.

"I know, I know," she interjected with a smile. "And just because you don't want your friends to know, doesn't mean it's not okay."

"What?"

"For you to be gay," she grinned. "It's okay."

"I *am not* gay!" He turned away from her and swiped his hands though his hair. "For heaven's sake, Megan, I am not gay."

"Do I dare ask why you don't want anything to do with me, then?" She didn't want to sound cocky, but his continued indifference was unsettling... unnatural even. "Do you not find me attractive?" Her lower lip quivered.

"Listen Megan," he tucked his hands in his pockets.

"It's okay," she turned away. "You don't have to explain."

"You're married."

"Yeah, yeah, yeah..." she trailed towards the living room. "Saint Carter. Got it."

"Megan," he placed his hand on her shoulder. "Can I explain?"

"No need," she froze. "A scout is honest, trustworthy, yada, yada, yada. I got it."

"No, I don't think you do." He gave her shoulder a soft squeeze.

"Well then, please enlighten me," she pushed his hand off her shoulder and crossed her arms adamantly. Fire sparked in her eyes. "There's nothing I'd love more than another pathetic piece to the Carter puzzle."

"You think I'm pathetic?" He mumbled.

"I *think* it's time for me to go home," she quivered.

"I was hoping this was your home."

"Why do you care? It's not like *this*," she waived her hand flippantly between the two of them, "is ever going to go anywhere."

"Megan, we're from two different worlds."

"I know, remember? Planet GRRR just might want its stupid cowboy back one day."

"There are things you don't know about me."

"Also understood." She paced the worn floor, purposefully rocking on each squeaky spot.

"I was engaged once."

"Well, looky here. Now we're getting somewhere." She stopped pacing and leaned against the doorframe. "Let me guess, she was a beast of a woman. Horrible. Wretched. Mean."

"No." His typical confidence waned. "She was beautiful. Smart." He sighed. "Funny." He pulled a chair out from under the kitchen table then, like a rag doll, folded into it. "When I came home to take care of Grandma Beth, I thought Kristina would come with me, but she didn't. She said she wasn't ready for marriage. There were still things she wanted to see... wanted to do."

"Great," Megan growled, "she broke your heart. Happens to the best of us, Carter. Move on."

"But that's just it, Megan," he traced his finger across the grain of the table. "This wasn't the life for her. She had her goals set on all the finer things: fancy cars, designer clothes, penthouse in the city." He raised his brow. "I could buy her all the silky sheets she wanted, but I could never leave the orchard."

"And you think I'm just like her?" Megan postured.

"Look, Megan. I'm not saying that you're not beautiful or that I'm not attracted to you. The complete opposite is true. You have no idea how bad I wish this would work, but you're completely crazy if you think it would. Your car is worth more than this house is, your jeans could feed a family for a week, and your shoes... I don't even know what to say about your shoes," he sighed.

"There's nothing wrong with my shoes," she defended.

"We're from two completely different worlds."

"We don't have to be."

"You'd never be happy here."

"How do you know that?"

He didn't need to answer.

"So, tell me more about this ex-fiance?" she dug, still not ready to let it drop.

"Why does it matter?" he ran his hand over his forehead and through his hair.

"I don't know," she sulked. "Maybe so I can know who to thank for ruining you."

"So I'm ruined now?"

"Apparently so," she scoffed.

He stared at her for several long, quiet moments. She watched his chest rise and fall; his jaw tightened.

"There's not much to tell," he finally offered. "Except..." his chest rose as he filled it with air, held it for a long moment, then released it.

"Except that when I went back to get my mother's ring from her, she'd pawned it." He pounded the table half-heartedly with his fist.

"She pawned your mother's ring?" Megan asked in shock. She could almost feel his pain. *How had this girl not known how sentimental he was?*

"Yes," he grimaced, "to buy herself some *improvements*... Body work," he continued as he signaled to his chest. "Of all the selfish...."

Is that what he thought of her? That she was selfish? "Matt's a plastic surgeon," Megan mumbled. *Maybe he already knew that. Maybe that was the problem.*

"What?" Carter's forehead crowned.

"He's a plastic surgeon," she sighed. "You know, my husband. He does lots of those 'improvements'." She stood erect and threw her hands to her hips. "Is that why you don't like me? Is that why you think I'm so much like that *other girl*? You think I'm shallow? Or a fake?"

Carter rocked backwards, about falling off of his chair. "That wasn't what I was getting at. I don't think you're fake at all. But I do think you're naïve if you think you'd be happy here."

"Well, you're wrong," Megan was still stuck on the "fake" comment. She raised her voice, "For your information, there isn't a single thing about me that's fake!" She signaled to her chest.

"Wow," Carter stammered. "I, uh..." He searched her eyes, perhaps looking for a touch of sarcasm or humor. There was none. She was unashamedly serious. He took a long, formulated breath. "Umm. Thanks for sharing." He blushed.

Silence hung in the air for several awkward minutes before he finally slid out of the chair and tucked it back under the table. "I don't know how they do things in the big city, but I'm not one to play games." He flashed his arms open in front of him, "This is all I've got, Megan. What you see is what you get. And, frankly, I don't think you're willing to trade in your life of luxury for poor, pathetic, broken me."

His eyes pierced hers. She swallowed the lump in her throat, unable to come up with a response.

"Tell me I'm wrong." He whispered.

She broke his gaze and, rubbing her fingers across her forehead, looked at the floor.

"I'll get that door fixed by week's end," he promised. He offered a nod then let himself out.

Chapter Thirty-Two

"Why do you keep looking at her like that?" Ruth topped off Carter's water for what had to have been the tenth time.

"I don't know what you're talking about," Carter sawed intently at the grilled pork chop. Even after several hours of stewing on it, he was still unsure how Megan's plea to have the door fixed had ended up so far off track.

"Like a puppy that done dug a big ol' hole in his mistress's garden." She crossed her portly arms and leaned into the bar top. "Sure is a pretty lil' thing. Not as pretty as my Julie, but pretty nonetheless."

"How is Julie?" Carter tried to divert Ruth's attention from the nearby booth that sat Megan and Jacob. Perhaps he and Megan should've communicated their dinner plans so as not to converge at Ruth's. Although, short of a bowl of cereal, the diner had been his only real option.

"Smart as a goosenecked donkey," Ruth quipped. "And pretty as a pumpkin pie."

Nodding as if he understood both references, he slid his fork into the butter pit of his mashed potatoes.

"Remind me," Ruth leaned in closer, "What's her name?"

Carter glanced over his shoulder at the back of Megan's head. She, too, played sloppily with her mashed potatoes. "Megan," he answered sullenly.

"Didn't expect her to stick around this long," Ruth mused. "Girls like her typically run after the first coyote call."

"Maybe she's tougher than we give her credit for." He took another methodic bite of his potatoes. "Or maybe what awaits her at home is worse than threat of some far-off coyote."

Ruth piqued her penciled brows. "You know what I think?" she offered with a mysterious grin. "I think she's gone got herself a hankerin' for the likes of one of our young cowboys."

"Yeah," he couldn't resist the quip, "seems old Whitley's got himself a hankerin' for her too."

Ruth smacked his arm playfully. "Always a comedian. Just like yer Pa," she laughed. "Maybe if you'd quit makin' her so comfortable, she'd have half a mind to hitch up that fancy car of hers and drive off into the sunset with Whitley," she teased.

"She has taken quite a liking to Beth's house," he replied sarcastically as he took a sip of water.

"It is a mighty nice house." Ruth topped off his glass again then peered back at Megan. "But seriously, what'd you do to tick her off so bad?"

"I don't know what you're talking about." Carter shrugged.

Ruth's thick fingers touched his chin and pushed his head toward Megan. "You see that," she pointed with her other hand. "That girl is simmerin' about somethin'. Somebody done gone fluffed her panties." The matronly lady glared accusingly into his eyes.

"Why do you automatically think I'm the one who did something?" Carter defended.

"Cause, sweetie," she tapped his hand, "you're a man."

"Order's up!" a voice crackled from the kitchen. The call sent Ruth spinning her heals to retrieve a platter of fries and a perfectly golden grilled cheese sandwich. Carter sawed another bite of pork chop. He missed Megan's cooking. Maybe that alone constituted an apology.

"Will you be seeing the Wilsons this week?" Ruth asked, sliding a box of food onto the bar top.

"I'm sure I will," Carter answered. "At least Sam," he smiled at her generosity. "You don't have to do this," he said, tapping on the box.

"It's the least I can do," Ruth patted her heart. "Kinda got me a soft spot right here for that Sam kid. The older he gets, the more I see his father."

Carter acknowledged the gesture. "You're a good woman, Ruth."

"You know, nothin' I do will ever make things right for them," she drifted into her thoughts for a moment. "Never did understand what made that man do what he did," she mumbled. "But I loved him anyway."

Carter settled the tab then tucked the box under his arm and scooted out the door.

"You didn't have to pay for my dinner," Megan followed quickly behind him.

"I know," he nodded. "And you didn't need to tell me about your boobs," he grinned.

"About that," she leaned on the hood of his truck, letting Jake fiddle with the side mirror.

"Wait," he placed a cautionary hand on her forearm. "I'm okay if we never want to bring any of that up again."

"You don't like booby talk?" she teased.

There was no safe way to answer. "How 'bout we just call a truce," he offered.

"Just like that?" Her brow furrowed. "You don't need to be right, or defend your cause, or anything macho like that?"

"Megan," he shook his head. "I'm not really even sure what happened. Can we just erase it and..."

"And at least give this a try?" Her eyes plead as much as her words.

Her hair danced on the breeze as he considered the idea. "One thing at a time, okay?"

"You know I'm not going to quit trying," her eyes drilled into him.

No matter how optimistic she was, he knew she'd never be happy with his lifestyle. Not wanting to hurt her twice in one day, he swallowed his refute. "Truce?" he offered.

"Truce," she smiled back.

Chapter Thirty-Three

"Has Megan mentioned anything to you about the car salesman guy?" Brent kicked the truck's tire.

Carter rolled his car dolly out from under the carriage. "You mean the piranha in San Clemente? I took her there to look at a Jeep." He wiped his greasy hands on his coveralls then hoisted himself up off the ground.

"No, not that guy. The one that dropped by Isaac Stone's office a few weeks back looking to buy her car." He peered into the open hood. "Said he was some wholesale dealer or some other blabber."

"No," Carter set his wrench into his tool box, "she hasn't said anything. What's this all about?"

"I don't know. Still trying to get to the bottom of it. The number on his card was bogus, and his name and dealer number don't check out either. He said he'd gotten her info from the lot in San Clemente, but no one on the lot knew anything about it," he shook his head and glanced back under the hood. "Transmission again?"

"Yeah, I think it may be time to just park her in the pasture."

"I can help you look at it next weekend if you'd like," Brent offered.

"Thanks. If I can just keep her holding transmission fluid, I'm sure I can squeeze a few more miles out of her." He leaned against the fender. "I want to know more about this car guy."

"You and me both," Brent said. He adjusted his ball cap then asked, "How much do you know about Megan's past?"

"I don't know," Carter shrugged. "I know that when she showed up in my grandma's kitchen she had an ugly set of bruises on her arms and a series of scars on her head. She said her husband gave them to her. That's why she's here. Trying to keep Jake safe."

"Is there any reason to believe that she's not who she says she is?"

"Are you kidding?" he asked. "She can't even keep a straight face long enough to make a ten minute cooking segment. There's no way she could put on a summer-long con. No way," he shook his head again. "Not even possible."

"What do you know about her ex?"

"He's a plastic surgeon," he offered the newly acquired information first. "He's controlling and abusive," he used a clean corner of his rag to wipe the sweat off his neck. "And, he's not her ex."

~   ~   ~

"This is the one," Carter smiled behind his camera. "I just know it."

"I hope so," Megan pureed the last of the apricots in the blender then added them to the stock pot on the stove.

"How are you going to choose which ones to enter?" He directed the camera across the table full of apricot themed foods.

"I like the desserts best," she wiped her nectared hands across her apron. "But Bri said there are usually a lot of entries in the dessert category."

"The crockpot chicken one wasn't bad," he offered. "And the apricot encrusted tilapia was pretty surprising, too."

"Surprising? That's hopeful." She pulled a package of fresh cut pork chops from the fridge. "*And the award for most surprising dish goes to the lady in the red Gucci heals.*"

"They're all good, Megan. And I'm not just saying that because my tummy's rumbling," he smiled. "Right, Jake?" He picked the busy toddler up off the floor. "Tell your mama that it's all good."

"Co." He clapped his hands excitedly. The dog perked his ears at the sound of his name.

"One track mind," Carter grinned.

"Good thing Bri and Brent are coming over to help with all the taste testing." She rinsed the pork chops under the tap, then gently lay them on a broiling pan. "You two are hopeless."

"Um," Carter tapped his finger gently on the top of the camera. "Just a reminder: you're on camera, Megs. You know, maybe you want to stay in character."

"Ugh," she sighed. "I've been in character all week. Can't we just turn it off and have a conversation that doesn't involve me monotoning something about 'buying only the finest cut of meat' or 'using fresh, locally grown fruit'?"

"It's your show. You can do whatever you want."

"Well, I want to be done for the day. Is that okay?" She tossed a touch of cinnamon and another touch of garlic to the apricot mixture on the stove.

"Yup," he stalled the record button.

"I thought all this Apricot Festival stuff was supposed to be fun," she sprinkled sea salt on the pork.

"You're just stressed." Carter scooted up next to her. "You took on a lot of different recipes. It's been a busy week. If you take it too seriously, it's not going to be any fun."

"And if I don't, it's going to be yucky!"

"Like that braised potato concoction," he twisted his mouth in disgust.

"It wasn't *that* bad," she defended, sliding the roasting tray into the oven.

"Yeah, it was." He dodged the hot pad as it flew at his head.

"Well," she cocked her hip, "we'll just have to let Brent and Bri decide, won't we?"

"You didn't?" He swung his head toward the collection of covered dishes on the table. "It's not in there," panic struck his playful eyes. "Is it?" He searched her eyes, looked at the table, then turned back to her. "No, Megan. You can't." He shook his head. "You can't do that to our friends."

Simultaneously, they sprung from their positions and toward the kitchen table. Carter reached for a piece of foil and tore it off the first dish. Apricot-blueberry cobbler. Delish. He tossed the foil to the side and grabbed another one. Pasta shells with apricot sauce. Not his favorite, but edible. He tossed the foil to the side. He reached for a third dish, but got distracted by Megan quietly trying to sleuth a dish away from the table.

"Oh, no you don't," he swept down on her like a hawk.

She quickly slid around the breakfast island, snuggling the dish to her hip as she dodged his advance.

"Give it to me," he demanded with a laugh.

"Not on your life," she cut to the right.

Reaching across the bar, he mirrored her movement. She darted left. Back and forth they bobbed, stretching bug eyes and making faces at each other. "You can't have it," Megan balked.

"Wanna bet?" he countered. Calculating her next movement, he dashed in front of her and cut her off. Gripping the dish tightly, she ducked to her knees and tried to slide between his legs. He caught hold of her bare foot and pulled her back in front of him. Laughter infused tears leaked from his eyes.

Wriggling to get away, she backed herself into the cabinet doors. Still laughing, he reached for the dish. She tucked it behind her back and presented her tongue in a childish raspberry.

"Really?" He leaned over her and raspberried back.

"Not giving it to you," the words trilled out with amusement.

"That's what you said." He pinned her to the floor. "Engaging Tickle-Monster," he announced.

"Stop," she screamed through her giggles as his fingers poked into her sides. "I'm not letting you have it," she squealed.

"Are we interrupting something?" Brent paused in the doorway, holding the door for his wife.

"Nope." Carter scooped the dish from behind Megan's back and stood. "Situation under control."

"Are you sure?" Bri observed the scene. "We can come back later if we need to," she winked at Megan.

Carter popped the trash can open and dumped the potato-apricot-mush mess into it. "You're welcome," he nodded to Brent as he set the empty dish in the sink then offered a hand to Megan. "The rest is good," he postured toward the buffet spread. "That," he gazed at the trash can, "was not."

Chapter Thirty-Four

"I think you made some good choices," Bri helped Megan tote four dishes to the judging station. "The apricot pork chops are a sure winner."

"I hope I added enough Worcestershire to them," Megan began to doubt herself.

"Any more," Bri confessed, "and the mere smell of them would give the judges heartburn."

"Point taken." Megan set the foil covered concoctions on their assigned tables. Two on the dessert table, and the other two on the one for main courses. "I didn't think anything could conjure up more celebration than strawberries," she assessed the booth packed park, "but it looks like apricots might actually have them beat."

"It's the derby," she pointed to the makeshift stadium then at a tattered piece of plywood advertising the 47th Annual Apricot Festival Demolition Derby. "People come from all over to watch the derby."

"You're kidding, right?" A flatbed truck was unloading what she assumed was one of the derby cars. It had no windows or, from what she could see, a dashboard. The hood and body were adorned with spray paint skulls and the words "The Executioner." The number seven monopolized the rusty roof.

"Trust me," Bri leaned against the table and rubbed her belly. "It's a lot more entertaining than you might imagine."

"I think I'm going to have to take your word for it."

"No, you're not. You get to experience it all for yourself," she fluttered her eyebrows in unison across her tired face. "Carter hooked us all up with tickets."

"And how'd he do that?" Megan turned to see her friend wipe the moisture off her forehead. "Are you okay?" she asked, noting the enormity of Bri's swollen feet.

"I'll be fine," she reached to the bottom of her tandem stroller and pulled out a large bottle of water. "Just hot," she swigged at the refreshment. "And tired," she added.

"Do you want to find somewhere to sit?" Megan offered.

"Already got a place." She pulled a stack of tickets from her pocket. "Show doesn't start for an hour, but it's general admission, so if we want a good seat, we ought to go in soon."

"Okay," Megan agreed easily, though she wasn't overly excited about watching cars purposefully crash into each other. "Seems barbaric," she observed after she and Bri had the three little ones secured on a wooden bench.

"Just good ol' crazy fun," a fully uniformed Brent slid on the bench. "You look beat." He planted a kiss on his wife's cheek. "Do you want some nachos or something?"

"Nope," she pulled a nutrition bar out of her diaper bag. "This is probably better for all of us involved."

"Heartburn again?" he guessed. She nodded the affirmative. "I'm sorry, baby," he snuggled up beside her.

"Before your snuggle fest gets too intense, will someone explain to me why that guy out there looks an awful lot like Carter?" Megan pointed to the sidelines at a man in red overalls. She leaned forward and squinted her eyes at the image. Same rugged build. Same tussled hair. Same cocky swagger.

"Oh," Bri propped her swollen ankles on the bench in front of her. "I forgot to tell you, Carter's a driver."

Megan absorbed Carter with unexplained fascination as he methodically walked around the old rust bucket excuse of a car. He was decidedly the most red-neck person she'd ever laid eyes on, yet for whatever reasons she couldn't wrap her refined, educated mind around, he continued to intrigue her. Attempting to ward off the growing heat – a combination of the early evening sun and the unrequited anticipation of Carter's attention - she accepted Brent's offer to get her a diet Coke then pulled the hair up off her neck and continued to silently observe this man she'd so quickly fallen for.

~ ~ ~

Matt slid his Jaguar into the roadside parking stall, taking care to double check his hair in the rearview mirror before killing the engine. Checking the private eye's hen scratched note against the roadside diner's sign, he folded it into perfect thirds then tossed it to the empty passenger seat. A quick assessment of the little nowhere town convinced him it was safe to leave the convertible top down. He wiped the fingerprints off his steering wheel, tucked his phone in his pocket, and swung the door open.

His boat shoes crunched on the gravely road base as he stepped out of the car. Despite his hesitations about the food, he pushed his keys in his pocket and stepped through the door.

"Well, hello there," a homely young redhead greeted him before the door swung to a close. "Just you today?" she asked, smoothing down the front of her apron.

"Yes," he nodded. He examined the retro décor, wondering if it was intentional or if the owners had just never dared to venture out of 1954.

The young hostess smacked her gum. "Would you like to sit at the bar or..."

"No," he answered abruptly, offended by the mere suggestion of sitting at a breakfast bar. "I'll take a booth." Then, remembering his purpose for dropping in to this hole in the wall, he added a forced and overtly polite, "Please."

"Absolutely," she popped a crackly series of little gum bubbles in her mouth. "How's this one look?" she asked, slapping a menu down on one of the many empty tables.

"It'll be perfect," he piled on the charm as he slid into the red upholstered bench, wondering why a place that was supposed to have the best food around only hosted a handful of people. It was a nationally observed holiday, after all. People should be off of work and out playing.

Ignoring the tear in the seat's fabric and the dingy overall feeling of the joint, he painted on his most enticing smile. "Thank you."

"No prob," she pulled a napkin enclosed set of utensils from her apron and set them on the table. "Ruth will be right with you to take your order," she smacked her gum again and headed off toward the kitchen.

From his position inside the diner, Matt studied the little town. The diner sat on what he considered the lamest excuse for a Main Street he'd ever seen. There were maybe a dozen businesses and about that many homes. People didn't really live here, he thought. They couldn't.

"What's going on down there?" he pointed out the window when his waitress appeared. About a half-mile down the road he could see a field full of cars.

She set a glass of ice water in front of him. Tap, he assumed. He pushed it aside.

"Apricot Festival," she leaned in with a smile. She was an older lady, gray haired and round. A perfect fit for the diner. "And Independence Day," she shrugged. He looked down the street again. "Kinda a two-fer."

"Apricot Festival, huh?" He sized up his waitress, hoping to gain her favor before his meal was through. Her eyes boasted crow's-feet like he'd never before seen. Her skin was weathered and her hips more than supple. Categorically, he assessed her from head to toe, calculating the plethora of work he would recommend for her, though he knew he'd never see her in his office. Despite her simple dress and lack of makeup, she seemed nice enough. Enough, at least, to make his task doable.

"Happens every year," she boasted. "S'pose that's what you get when you live in the middle of all them apricot orchards."

"I suppose so," he pretended to like her, even though the mole on her cheek was already driving him crazy.

"What's it goin' to be today, son?" Her teeth were surprisingly straight, though her smile was not.

"I don't know," he left the unopened menu on the table. "What do you recommend?"

"Well, shoot," she grinned, sliding her hands into her apron pocket. "It's all good."

"Okay," he relaxed back and smiled up at her, "what's your favorite?"

"Darn," she puckered her lips in thought, "that's a toughy. Up until this mornin' I didn't think it got any better than the double bacon bleu cheese crumble burger, but after judgin' some of those entries at the festival, I may be havin' to shake up my menu with an apricot pork chop or two."

"The burger sounds great, Ruth." He familiarized himself with her nametag, realizing the diner must be her namesake.

"Perfect," she bobbled on stubby little feet. "I'll get that goin' for ya." He watched her walk away wishing she'd smooth the wrinkles out of her apron instead of chatting up every occupied table that she passed by. She turned back with a smile and, as she slipped into the kitchen, he nodded with satisfaction. Ruth was going to be easy game. He pulled his ring out of his pocket and, keeping it hidden beneath the table, slid it onto his finger.

"Oh, my," he flattered as Ruth returned with his order. "That's got to be the biggest burger I've ever seen." He stared down at the overflowing bun. Thick cut bacon dripped over the edges of the giant patty. Bleu cheese crumbles oozed from the sides. His stomach almost lurched at the sight. It was a far cry from anything he generally considered edible.

"I guarantee it'll be the best burger you've ever sunk your teeth into," she set the burger filled plate and a basket of fries in front of him. "If you don't like it," she smiled, "it's on me," she winked.

"Thank you," he unraveled his knife from the napkin and rubbed the water spots off of it before proportioning the burger in perfect halves. Then, settling the paper napkin on his lap, he leaned towards the burger and willed himself to take one bite then, apprehensively, another.

"This Apricot Festival looks like a pretty big deal," Matt opened up as the last of Ruth's patrons waved good bye and slipped out the door. "How come you're not down there?"

"Been down there all day," she smiled. "But I ain't much for the demo derby or the dancin'. Besides, somebody's got to work the dinner shift."

He looked around the diner. Other than himself and Ruth, the place had completely emptied out. Even the gum-crackling, oafish, young redhead was nowhere to be seen. "Well," he folded his paper napkin in half and set it on top of his half eaten meal, "I'm glad that someone is you."

"Thanks," she smiled proudly, eyeing his untouched water. "Did everything taste all right?" She looked at his half eaten meal. "Can I get you anything else?"

"Oh," he glanced down at the plate. "Everything was great, I just don't seem to have much of an appetite today," he shrugged.

"Well," she reached for his discarded plate, "that's too bad. Would you like me to box it up for you to eat later?"

He intercepted her hand before she could pull the plate away. "Actually," he baited for her pity, "What I really need is someone to talk to." He let out a despondent sigh and gently encircled her hand in his.

"Not like I got anythin' else to do," she looked around the empty dining room.

Keep her nibbling, he thought as she slid into the booth in front of him.

"What seems to be on your mind?" she asked. "And, mind you, this better be good," she laughed and pointed to his burger, "cause nobody turns away from my cooking."

"Do you mind if I ask you a question?" he asked with artificial interest.

"Well, shoot, I don't see why not,"

"What's a pretty lady like yourself doing in a little town like this?"

"Lived here most my life," she rocked back and crossed her arms over her ample middle.

"Is that so?" He leaned into the shiny red upholstery and draped his arm casually over the edge of the booth. "I'd have never guessed," he lied with ease. "And here I had you pegged as an actress just taking a quiet little sabbatical."

"Well aren't you the charmer?" she flushed with the compliment.

"Pretty young thing like you has got to be married, right?" he asked nonchalantly.

Her face painted scarlet as her cheeks balled up with a grin. "Now, son," she swatted at his flattering, "don't you think I'm a bit old for you?"

"I don't see how that could be possible." He had her right where he wanted her. Soft. Gullible. Charmed. "Fortunately for you, Ruth, I'm already taken," he presented his ring finger.

She snickered, "I don't know many ladies who'd consider your unavailability to be their fortune."

"Well," he grinned, "who's the charmer now?"

"I'm not trying to charm you, mister," she chuckled. "But any girl who didn't try to land a ride in that fancy car of yours would be a fool."

Matt looked out the window, noticing how out of place his Jaguar looked amongst the weather worn buildings and simple cars. "Sticks out a bit, doesn't it?" he shrugged, hoping to stun her with his humility.

"Nah," she beamed, "we see all kinds of fancy cars round here. In fact," she brushed away his pretend chagrin, "got ourselves some sweet little city girl driving around a fancy new German car. Beemer or something."

Or *Audi.* The thought excited him. "Those Germans sure make pretty cars, don't they?"

"I s'pose they do," she nodded.

He let the silence speak for a moment, chewing thoughtfully on his lip. He hoped to bate her into trusting him with more information. "Do you think..." He purposefully stumbled over his words though he knew exactly what it was he wanted to say. "If you..." he calculated another moment of silence. "If your husband made a stupid mistake, would you forgive him?"

"Not to be rude," she chuckled, "but when referring to men and stupidity, the proper term is *when* not *if*."

He pouted his lip with such precision she didn't stand a chance. "But you'd forgive him, right?"

"Absolutely," she melted into his performance. "Any good woman would."

He leaned forward, resting his elbows on the table, and sighed, "Mine won't." He paused long enough to penetrate Ruth's eyes with his. Satisfied that he had her undivided devotion, he started again. "I screwed up and she left." He folded his shoulders down.

"Well, dear," Ruth patted his hand. "Give 'er time to cool off and she'll be back."

"I don't know," he shrugged. Rehearsed tears clouded his eyes. "It's been a couple of months and she still won't talk to me." He hoped the quiver in his lip didn't look overdone. Regardless, Ruth seemed to buy it.

"Now, there, there, sweetie," she patted his hand. "You poor thing," she continued to pat. "Sometimes women are kinda fickle, I guess. Maybe I can help you," she offered. "Why don't you tell me what you did and I'll see if I can figure out a way to help you fix it."

"Are you sure?" Hook, line, and sinker.

"Well, come on now," she prodded.

"Okay," he started with a sigh. "This is really embarrassing," he stalled again, further wrangling her in with his charm. "And stupid. There's just no good explanation."

"Are you going to tell me already, or what?" she seemed excited at the prospect of fresh gossip.

Matt stifled his pleasure. Ruth was going to give him everything he needed. He was sure of it. "I... I forgot our anniversary," he laid the confession on her with enough fake remorse to convince any juror of his sorrow.

"And?" Ruth pried.

"That's it," he pouted. "I got all wrapped up in work and forgot our anniversary."

"So she left?" Ruth scrunched her penciled brows to such a hideous point on her forehead Matt had to turn away.

He swallowed hard and nodded. "Her and the baby. They," he forced the quiver in his lip again. "They both left. And," he laid it on as heavy as he could. "I'm completely lost without them. I don't know what to do. I can't eat," he pointed to the half consumed burger. "I can't sleep. I'm a complete mess."

Ruth reached for both of his hands, and holding them in hers, fell into his plea. "You poor thing," she shook her head. "Every woman should have such a loving man at home. You need to go to her. You need to show her how much you love her."

"I know," he whimpered. "But I don't know where she is." He sucked Ruth into his arctic eyes. "Maybe you can help me," he submitted to her eagerly awaiting eyes. "She's got friends around these parts. Maybe," he pulled a snapshot out of his wallet with a shrug. "Maybe you've seen her?"

~   ~   ~

"Thanks for dancing with me," Julie's freckled face beamed with joy. She crackled her gum in a series of annoying bubbles.

"My pleasure," Carter tipped his cowboy hat with feigned delight as he scanned the dance floor for refuge. Though she'd shed her uniform in favor of a pair of shorts and a tailored t-shirt, she still smelled of the diner. "Excuse me," he nodded. Politely declining a chance for a second dance, he stepped away from her reach. "I promised a dance to a friend of mine," he explained as he watched Megan break away from her current dance partner. She was a fireball of energy. He'd observed her bouncing from one eager dance partner to another since the band started playing and, though she clearly didn't need his charity, he needed hers.

"May I have this dance?" he interjected before a beady eyed ranch hand had the chance to beat him to it.

"Absolutely," Megan inserted her hand in Carter's as the dejected, still hopeful man stepped aside. "Thanks," she whispered, warily eyeing the haphazardly groomed rancher out of the corner of her eye.

"My pleasure," Carter offered the same sentiment he had to Julie, but this time he meant it. There was no doubt why she'd had men lining up to dance with her all night. Megan looked amazing in her tailored gingham top and riveted capris. Her normally perfectly styled hair, tussled about her face invitingly. And, for the first time since he'd met her, the sassy little high-heeled numbers strapped to her feet seemed almost appropriate.

The band opened up a high spirited rendition of *The Devil Went Down to Georgia*. Megan fell in line beside Carter as the lead singer called out instructions for the line dance. She caught on quickly, adding a new grace to the traditional country song. Within moments, her high heeled shoes blended seamlessly into the crowd of beat stomping cowboy boots. Carter was sure she'd run out of energy before the song was over. To his surprise, however, she wasn't half as winded as he was. A quick moving country two-step and two fast paced country swings later, he wasn't sure if he could keep up with her much longer.

He rested his hands on his hips long enough to notice the sun's position on the horizon. "Probably got time for one more," he assessed through exaggerated breath, "before they start handing out the cooking awards... or I pass out. Whichever comes first," he forced a deep, exhausted lungful of air past his smiling lips.

"Well, you just might be in luck," Megan bobbed her head as she recognized the first few notes of the next song. "Looks like the band is in the mood for a slow one." With a shrug, she turned away and stepped off the makeshift dance floor.

"Where are you going?" Carter snagged her hand as she retreated. Since the door repair-Houdini-booby awkwardness, her overt flirtations had ended almost as abruptly as they'd started. "I promised you one last dance," he plead with his eyes.

She hesitated only briefly before following his lead back to the floor. He enveloped one of her hands in his then slid his other one to her hip. Against his better judgment, he pulled her into him.

"Where exactly does a country boy learn to dance like that?"

"I suppose you can thank my grandma," he tried to stay focused on his footwork. "Either that, or MTV," he smirked.

"MTV taught you the box step?" she asked with doubt as he led her gracefully to the right.

"No, that one was definitely my grandma," he counted the steps in his mind. *Forward. Side. Together.* "But I wouldn't get too excited just yet. Slow dancin' takes a bit more refinement than hip shakin'. I'll only consider this a success when we've made it through the dance without me leavin' a boot print on one of your pretty little shoes."

"I see," she teasingly resisted his lead. "Am I throwing you off?" she tried to make him misstep.

He shuffled his boots "Gonna take more than that," he conceded.

She grinned, "I think I'll let you off easy this time."

"Good plan."

She fell back into his lead and, as she nestled into his chest, he found himself welcoming her touch. The song ended too soon and Carter hoped for another but he followed Megan off the floor without asking.

His boots hit the grass and he immediately diverted his thoughts about the beautiful girl he'd committed to friendship. "What'd you think of the demolition derby?" he asked as he scanned the crowded lawn for Brent and Bri.

"Still trying to figure out how you walked away from it without so much as a scratch."

"Piece of cake," he grinned.

"And," she expanded, "why you want to do submit yourself to that in the first place."

"Tradition," he answered with a shrug. "The orchard's always sponsored a car. Somebody's got to drive it, right?" Across the sea of blankets, Carter spotted Brent's bald head and pointed to it. "Looks like they've saved us a spot right there."

Sliding her shoes off her feet, Megan clenched them in her hand. "Where?" she asked, looking into the sea of people.

"See that," he pointed towards the stage platform. "Just below the stage. Right there," he pointed again. "Brent's head has a special kind of shine to it." He took her hand in his and pulled her through the thick crowd.

Megan was almost yelling even though she was only inches away from his ear, "I'm still not sure about the whole smashed-up car driving thing. It has to be the epitome of this whole redneck lifestyle." They were directly below the live band's sound system. Music loudly ricocheted through at least a dozen speakers. "I've got to admit, it shocked me to see you out there. Makes me wonder what other surprises you have hiding in your closet."

"Knitting," he hollered back. "Grandma made me learn how to knit." He stepped over the edge of an abandoned blanket and around a little girl with cotton candy hands.

"No, really," Megan grinned, almost tripping over the small girl.

"Really," he looked over his shoulder in time to catch her suspicious smirk then smacked a salutary hand to Brent's as he and Megan approached the blanket.

"Was she trying to keep you single? I mean, knitting doesn't exactly give you points towards your man-card." Megan knelt onto Brianna's neatly spread blanket and welcomed a hyper Jake into her arms.

"Man-card?" Brent chuckled. "You realize who you're talking to, right?"

"What's that supposed to mean?" Carter glared at his friend, his eyes warning him not to contribute to Megan's banter. Brent chose to ignore the cautionary suggestion.

"For starters, you've got a princess bathroom and..."

"And someday he'd like to have a princess to go with it." Bri elbowed her husband in the ribs.

"Well that shouldn't be a problem," Megan said as she wrestled her excited toddler to his back and began to blow raspberries onto is belly. "Every single lady in this town's got her eyes on you."

"You don't know what you're talking about." He'd no more settled onto an open spot on the blanket before Mariah accosted him with giggles and hugs.

"Really?" Bri jumped in.

Carter rolled his eyes.

"Like who?" Brent asked as he creased the festival program lengthwise then with another fold, created a point.

"Yeah, like who?" Carter followed. Watching the paper airplane take shape in Brent's hands, he hugged Mariah's little form, lifted her bare feet in the air, and kissed her cheek. She giggled away then took his face in her miniature hands and squeezed until his lips puckered. "Name one," the words lisped through his gathered lips.

"I can do better than one," Megan piped in. "For starters you've got Nadine. And then there's Julie. You know Ruth gets all googley eyed about the possibility of the two of you. And, let's see. How about all those ladies who were watching us dance?"

"Nobody was watching us dance," he interrupted. "You're just making stuff up now."

"No way. They were there. Lots of them. And they couldn't keep their eyes off you. Especially Nadine. She's got a *bad* sort of something for you!"

"Okay, for clarification, Nadine is just *lonely*. I think sometimes our friendship clouds her judgment," Carter defended.

"More than her judgment is clouded, but that's beside the point," Brent smirked. "Megan's right. She wants you. Plain and simple,"

Snuggling Jake into her, Megan turned to face Carter. "I know I've only met Nadine once, but it's pretty obvious how she regards you."

"Hmmm?" Carter pseudo listened to her persuasion.

"She thinks you walk on water." Megan offered.

"Yeah, she does," Brent agreed with pleasure. "And Megan's right about Julie too. She harasses every officer in the department for info about you."

"Whatever," Carter shrugged off their teasing. "Not exactly the pick of the crop, now are they?"

"Beggars can't be choosers," Brent laughed.

"Now let's be fair," Megan stretched her legs out in front of her and offered a taunting defense of her friend. "I mean, Carter's not exactly a beggar, you know. Give him some credit. He is a hardworking, friendly, and marginally good-looking guy, afterall."

"*Marginally* good looking?" Carter snorted. "I like to consider myself somewhat more than marginal."

"The cocky train has officially arrived!" Bri tossed a cookie at Carter. It bounced off his shoulder and onto the blanket where Mariah was more than happy to rescue it for him.

"Come on, hun." Brent playfully defended his friend. "I think he's at least *reasonably* good looking, right?"

"Getting closer." Carter smiled, taking a bite of the snickerdoodle.

"Insanely?" Brent threw out for approval.

"Now you're on to something." Carter bumped knuckles with his friend.

"Okay, Mr. Insanely Attractive," Megan smirked. "So, how come your calendar isn't bursting with dates?"

"Cause he's all doe-eyed about someone he can't have," Brent offered.

Carter tightened his jaw at the remark. *Not cool*, he thought, *not cool.*

"I mean," Brent tried to dig his way out, "he could have her if he really wanted her, but..."

Daggers shot from Carter's eyes as he glared first at Brent, then directed his attention toward to the stage. "Look," he welcomed the respite from conversation pertaining to his dating life, "they're getting ready to announce the winners of the cook-off."

The mayor tapped the microphone into his hand until it buzzed through the loudspeaker and, with a squelch, came to life. As if a giant mute button was pushed, the entire crowd silenced and the cook-off judges were introduced. Bri settled Noah and Mariah with a cookie then reclined back to listen. Megan arranged Jake on her lap as she awaited the results. Carter and Brent continued to have a quiet conversation with their eyes – one that in their younger years would have undoubtedly been taking place with their fists.

A surprise only to Megan, she won two of the five categories. "Best Main Course" for her spicy apricot pork chops and the coveted "Best Dessert" for her apricot-ricotta tarts.

"I told you they were good," Carter nudged her when she returned to the blanket with her first-place ribbons and prize package.

"You tell me that about everything I make," she shrugged off the compliment. "I'm beginning to wonder what you ate before I showed up."

"I can cook" he defended with a smile.

"Don't let him fool you," Bri rubbed at her bulging baby belly. "He use to do most of his eating at our house or Ruth's Diner." She reached over and patted her husband's hand. "Honey," she enticed him with a smile, "I'm parched. Do we have anything left in the cooler?"

"Sorry, dear," he was on his feet already. "I'll go get you something."

Carter was on his feet too. "Do you want anything?" he asked Megan.

Megan thought for a moment, then asked, "Can you get me some cotton candy?" She pulled a small bundle of cash out of her pocket and tried to hand it off to Carter. He raised his hand, "It's on me today."

~   ~   ~

The minivan had just enough seats to accommodate all seven of them and with the surprising turn out at the festival Megan was grateful she hadn't had to drive herself.

"Thanks for the ride." She shimmied out the sliding door then reached through Bri's open window and hugged her. "And for the drinks and the cotton candy..."

"And the heartburn," Bri smiled. "I'm glad you came with us. It was a fun night."

Megan retrieved her purse and all of her cook-off prizes from the back seat. "This has been the best Fourth of July I've ever had." She wasn't just slathering on the compliments for the sake of being nice. In all its simplicity, the home-grown celebration was better than a lifetime of beachside barbeques and wine-buzzed firework displays.

"It's cause I was there," Brent winked from the driver's seat before his wife's elbow caught him in the ribs. "What?" he played innocently, watching through his rearview mirror as Carter unbuckled Jake from his car seat.

Megan took her sleeping babe from Carter's outreached hands and snuggled him into her. She kissed the top of his head. He was warm and soft and perfect. She couldn't imagine a more perfect day with more perfect company.

"Go ahead and take him in," Carter offered. "I'll grab his seat and bring it up." With three car seats smashed across the back bench it was a tight fit and Megan imagined her slender hands would probably have had an easier time at it then Carter's, but watching him struggle with it was touching and albeit humorous. She kept her adoration to herself, however. She'd been trying to be content with a friendship, but found herself continually falling. At least now his disinterest made sense thanks to Brent's little reveal. If Carter had just told her there was someone else in the first place, she'd have saved herself a lot of wasted, pining hours fueling her infatuation.

"Need some help there?" Brent teased, obviously finding his own enjoyment from the spectacle.

"Nope," Carter emerged from the sliding door. "It's a bit of a tight squeeze, but I got it." He held the seat victoriously in one hand and pulled the van door closed with his other.

"You know," Brent caressed Bri's belly. "When this little guy shows up you guys are on your own for transportation. Maybe you ought to look into getting your own minivan, Ammon, cause that ol' truck's not going to do the job." He chuckled that deep, inviting belly laugh that Megan had grown to adore and, with a wave, pulled off toward his own home.

"He's getting pretty big." Carter ignored Brent's parting jibe and, with the empty car seat in one hand and a half eaten cotton candy in the other, pushed the swinging gate open with his hip.

"You're telling me." She shifted Jake's sleeping head further up onto her shoulder and stepped through the gate. Adjusting Jake again, she dug her hand into her purse in search of her keys as she ascended the porch stairs.

"Can I help you?" Carter set the car seat on the porch and lay the cotton candy bag in it. "Here," he leaned across her body and gently reached for Jake.

"Thanks," she froze at the warmth of his breath on her cheek. He tenderly peeled Jake out of her arms relieving her of his weight.

"Anytime." His hazel eyes, only inches away from hers, pierced through the darkness, sending a rush of heat into the already smoldering night. She'd never noticed the yellow and blue flecks in his eyes before. Breathtaking.

Reaching into her purse again, she fumbled for her keys with an inexplicable lack of urgency. Something in his hazel eyes had sent her heart racing. A chill ran from her toes up to her neck causing her hands to tremble. She lost hold of her purse and watched it fall to the ground.

Snapping out of her trance, she knelt down to get it but, even with her sleeping babe in his arms, Carter beat her to it.

"Megan," his cheeks turned up in a grin as they locked eyes again.

"Hmm?" she swallowed the twitter-pated lump in her throat.

She felt the rumble of his deep voice in the silence almost as much as she heard it. "You dropped your purse," he sighed, slipping the open parcel back into her trembling hands. His breath tickled her nose as he spoke. It was sweet. Simple. Inviting.

"Thanks," she answered hypnotically, still intent on the magical depth of his eyes. She remembered the feel of his hands on her hips when they were dancing. She let go of her caution and fully engaged her anticipation as he reached his hand towards her ear.

His fingers lightly breezed by her cheek. He touched her hair softly. She clenched her fists willing them to stop shaking.

"I think Jake got you with his cotton candy slobber," he said as he pulled his hand away.

She broke her eye-piercing stare and reached for the clump of hair in question. Sure enough, it was a sticky, sugary mess. "Thanks," she smiled, reaching into her purse with renewed interest. She slid the key into the lock and pushed the door open before turning to Carter one last hopeful time.

"Do you want me to carry him in to bed?" he offered. If it'd ever really existed, the power she thought she'd felt from him was gone.

"No," she reached for her baby. "I think I can handle it from here." She swiped Jake out of Carter's arms, offered him one last thank you and a goodnight, shut the door, and quietly cursed the embarrassment she felt for herself.

Chewing herself out for so desperately wanting him, she gingerly tucked Jake into bed and, quietly pulling the bedroom door closed behind her, stepped into the bathroom. With her darker hair color, the cotton candy wasn't as noticeable as it would've been in her bleached state, but its pink chunks were in obvious need of a shampooing.

She started the shower then stepped softly back into her and Jake's shared room to grab her essentials. Over the rush of water she thought she heard the screen door jiggle. A moment later it made the unmistakable sound of slamming shut.

"Bosco!" she huffed out of her room. "I am *so* not in the mood!"

"Well hello, baby." His smug grin froze her in her tracks. His gait – clearly intoxicated - swaggered stoically into the living room. "I was beginning to think that hick friend of yours was never going to leave."

"What are you doing here?"

"Ah, baby," he took another unstable step towards her. "I thought you'd be so happy to see me. Why aren't you happy to see me?"

"How did you find me?" She stumbled back, crashing into the door jam.

"I'm a smart man," he tapped at his temple as the words slurred out. "Ed-u-ca-ted," he pronounced every syllable. He chuckled for his own benefit, "I've got connections."

"You need to leave." She gained composure and stepped towards the front door.

"But I just got here, baby." His breath wreaked unfamiliar alcohols. "Are you expecting someone?" He looked out the front window. "Is it that smooth dancin' hick boyfriend of yours?"

She glared at him through pursed lips.

"That's it, isn't it?" He stepped in closer. "You're hoping that he's coming back, aren't you?"

"He's not my boyfriend." Megan announced with bitterness. "And he's not coming back, but you're leaving!" She reached for the knob.

"No," Matthew grabbed her hand ferociously. "I'm not leaving, baby." He pulled her into him, squeezing her wrists with an intensity she'd somehow managed to forget. "Not without you anyway."

"No, Matt," she tried to pull her hands away. His grip burned her flesh. "This is my home now. I'm not going anywhere."

He twisted her arms and hurled her into the couch. The back of her knees buckled as she crashed into the worn cushion and fell onto the seat. "I don't know what kind of game you're trying to play with your hillbilly boyfriend and your salvaged, junk-yard furniture, but it's over now. This is *not* your home, Megan. You don't belong here. I'm taking you home."

She knotted her hands into his chest as he perched over her. "Get away from me!" she screamed.

"Oh, baby, I've missed you." He locked her wrists in his hands again but she didn't give in.

She twisted and pivoted with every muscle she could engage. "Get away from me!" she screamed again, praying as she looked through Matt that her cry didn't wake up Jake.

"Shh." Matt's breath burned her face as if he'd read her thoughts. "Wouldn't wanna wake up the baby, now would we?"

"Get out!" She pushed with a ferocity that had him rolling off of her and onto the floor. She leapt from the sofa, jumping over his drunken body and ran towards the kitchen.

"What do you think you're doing?" He stumbled into the kitchen as Megan shakily tried to manipulate the child lock she'd placed on the knife drawer. In two paces he had her pinned against the counter. He swung at her jaw. Her head flailed to the side as the focus shattered from her eyes and the stability drained from her legs. "Seems like you've already forgotten who's in charge, Megan dear!" He grabbed the back of her neck and pushed her to the ground.

"Leave!" She recomposed her vision and kicked at his legs.

He grabbed one of the dinette chairs and pinned its legs over her body. "You don't seem to get it," he straddled the chair and leaned into the back of it as he spoke. "You are my wife and that makes me the head of our household. This," he swiped a shaky hand across the room, "is not my house. Therefore, my darling Megan, this is not your house either." His chest heaved heavily with each alcohol hindered breath. "You can come peacefully or you can come kicking and screaming, but one way or another, you *are* coming!"

She scanned the room for a weapon, catching sight of the broom tucked beside the fridge. Calculating her reach, she grabbed for it and in the same movement wacked him across the face.

He cupped his hands over his nose, mumbling profanities as the blood started to flow. She took advantage of his diversion and snaked her way out from under the chair.

"It really is unfortunate that you're such a slow learner." His powerful fist grabbed her collar as soon as she hit her feet. She pulled away, hoping the fabric would tear before it choked her, but instead, it cut into her neck, burning the flesh. She relinquished her pull and, crashing back into him, put all of her force into sending a backwards elbow into his ribs.

He barely flinched. "Megan, baby," he shook his condescending head. "I find this new feistiness fascinating. I never knew you had it in you. And honestly," he spun her around and cupped her face in his hands, "it's kind of hot." Eyes of cold, brazen metal penetrated hers. "Maybe we should continue this conversation in the bedroom," he said, ignoring the blood dripping from his nose and over his lips. "Come morning I think you'll find yourself feeling much more reasonable." He pressed his mouth over hers, digging his fingers into the back of her neck to hold her in place.

Her arms never ceased hitting and pushing him away as she gagged on his tongue. He pressed in harder, anger and passion fueling his fire. His tongue pressed past her teeth a second time, but this time she was ready. She bit down - hard.

Matt screamed obscenities, blood oozing from both his nose and his tongue. Megan wiped his blood and slobber from her face as she turned to run. She gained about three steps before something hard hit her in the back of the head. Her knees smacked the floor. Warmth filled her hair. She tried to stand, but even with the help of the sofa, she couldn't gain her balance. The room spun in kaleidoscoping rays around her. She pressed her eyelids tightly closed and took a deep breath.

"Are we on the same page yet?" Matt huffed.

"No," Megan spat the words out. "Because you're still here."

She'd hoped to turn around and face her tormenter head on, but didn't get the chance. His shoe caught her solidly in the back. She buckled over, burying her head in the aged plaid of the sofa. Slowly, painfully, she twisted around and slid into a slump on the floor.

"Now that's better," he smiled at her broken body. "Now, what do ya say? Let's go home," he offered his hand.

"No." The word strained past her lips.

He dropped to his knee by her side. "Excuse me?" He leaned into her.

"I said no." It was barely a whisper. Her focus fought to find something to steady on. The back of her head throbbed.

He replied with a hook to the side of her face. Blood splattered from around her eye as her head jerked sideways and took another blow on the corner of the coffee table. She gave up any immediate hope of fighting back and slumped limply to the floor.

"Get up!" He stood up and accentuated his demand by kicking her in the ribs. His voice echoed in her aching head. She didn't respond.

"Get up!" He yelled louder as he threw his foot into her ribs again and again.

"Stop," she gurgled the word softly. "Please..."

He straddled her limp body. "What was that?" he demanded. "I didn't hear you."

"Pl... plea... please." It took her three tries to get the word out.

The ringing in her ears was deafening; the pain in her side suffocating. She wrapped her arms around her torso, curling over in agony as she coughed. The metallic taste of blood lined her mouth. She closed her eyes, caving to the crushing pain ravaging through her. She could feel Matt's weight pressing on her, but she'd lost her strength. There was no fight left in her – only the torturous burn of anguish curling its way from her gut to her head.

She thought she heard the shower running but wasn't sure over the humming in her ears. *Turn it off,* she thought as darkness swirled around her. Unable to take a second more of the torture, she closed her eyes to the pain and allowed herself to succumb to the shadows. In a last touch of consciousness, she prayed for Jake.

Chapter Thirty-Five

Carter left his boots by the door. The prospect of kicking himself was far less intimidating without their sharp leather toes. Leaning into the kitchen sink, he splashed his face with cool water. Honor, integrity, respect – these were the things he taught his scouts. They were the same virtues his grandfather had spent so much time drilling into his head. Sometimes – like when Megan absorbed him into her sweet honey eyes – he wished they hadn't anchored so deep.

"Hey buddy," Carter welcomed Bosco's nudge with a few strokes behind his ears. The dog pressed his muzzle into Carter's thigh, pleading for more attention. "What have you been up to all day?" he questioned the canine, glad for the distraction. "Where's your toy?" he asked, locking his arms around Bosco's shoulders as the dog pressed for more love. "Go get your toy," he pushed Bosco's hesitant body away. "Go get it, buddy, and we'll play."

The dog didn't budge, instead he pressed his muzzle harder into Carter's thigh, then let out a single bark. "What?" Carter conceded to the dog's plea for attention. "Do you want some water?" he asked.

The hair on Bosco's neck rose to attention as his ears peaked. He barked again then, snarling like Carter had never heard him do before, ran to the back door. Impatiently, he swiped his paw at the knob a couple of times then ran through the house to the front door.

"My word, Boss, what's gotten into you?"

Unsuccessful in his attempt at the front door, Bosco bolted back into the kitchen. Knocking over a barstool and about taking out Carter, he slid into the back door.

"Okay, okay." Carter reached across the dog to unlock the deadbolt. "Settle down," he'd barely turned the knob before Bosco was muscling his way out and barreling across the yard to Megan's house.

"Boss..." he called after his intent dog, ready to command him to freeze. His throat, however, froze first.

Even under the shadow of the waxing summer moon, the car was an unmistakable misfit in Megan's dirt drive. Carter didn't take time to identify the brand, suspecting by its pomposity that it could only have one owner. He bolted behind his dog, ignoring the beating his bare feet were taking as he ran across the yard. Boss burst through Megan's back door as Carter jumped the railing and landed hard on the wood decking. He didn't pause to pull the sliver from his sock as he rushed into the kitchen.

Nearly tripping over a sideways chair in the middle of the kitchen floor, he pushed it aside and rushed toward the deep snarl of Bosco's growl. The headstrong dog had already used his bulk to pin the intruder to the ground.

The man, cowering to the dog's seething teeth, called out angrily, "Get this beast off me!"

"Good boy!" Carter acknowledged his dog with a nod as he rushed toward Megan's limp body. Ignoring the man's pleas, he knelt into the puddle of blood and unfolded Megan's buckled frame onto his lap. Her eyes opened for a moment, blankly voiding out before they closed again. He caught her bobbing head in the cusp of his arm and, pushing the warm, wet hair off her face, began looking for the source of all the blood. Her breath was labored, even crackling, but at least it was present. A small victory, he realized as he sponged the blood off her face with his shirt.

"Megan?" he softly appealed. Her skin was graying by the second, her breath becoming more and more faint. The man continued to throw profanities, but they might as well have been intended for the furniture, because neither Carter nor Bosco reciprocated.

"Megan," he pressed the palm of his hand to a crack in the back of her head and, shrugging out of his shirt, used it on the giant gash under her eye. They weren't the only wounds, he was afraid, but they seemed to be the source of most of the spilling.

"Hang on, Megan." She needed help immediately. He scooped her limp body into his arms before thinking of Jake. "Help's on its way," he said to her nearly unconscious body as he set her back on the floor. He pulled his phone from his pocket and speed dialed Brent. "Megan's house. Now!" he hollered at his friend, hoping he hadn't already left for his shift.

The moments seemed like an eternity before Brent's cruiser lights flashed through the front window. Gun drawn, he burst through the front door.

"She can't wait for an ambulance," Carter scooped Megan into his arms again. "She needs help now!" The flow of blood had slowed but the color had continued to drain from her flesh. He glowered at the perpetrator as Brent rushed to cuff him. His lip twitched with fury. Words formed but decidedly he didn't give the satisfaction to Megan's monster.

"Jake's in the bedroom," he directed with a nod. "I've got to get her to the hospital." He stepped past Brent. "She can't breathe!"

"Put her in my cruiser," Brent pressed his Glock into the perp's back. "Backup's about thirty-seconds away." He turned to the intruder as Carter rushed out the door. "You oughta be more careful when you go waiving pictures around," he accused. "Not sure if you've heard, but word spreads quickly through a small town."

The street filled with sirens as Carter settled Megan onto his lap in the back of Brent's cruiser. Uniforms ran by, glancing his way as they followed Brent's commands to hurry inside the house. Brent passed the perp on to another officer and dashed for his car.

The hard plastic seat in the back of the cruiser wasn't exactly comfortable, but it was far easier than trying to hold Megan, monitor her breathing, control her blood flow, and drive himself. Brent's sirens and lead foot were much more efficient than his old rickety truck, too. With each turn of the car, though, Megan's face grimaced with some unvoiced pain. She was in and out of consciousness, opening her eyes long enough to make her eyelashes flutter but not long enough to shower Carter with hope.

Brent was on the radio frantically ordering the officers to carefully remove Jake from the scene. He suggested they drop him off to Brianna, called his wife to prepare her, then radioed the county ER. "How's the bleeding?" Brent called over his shoulder, trying to relay information to the ER staff.

"Going to need some serious stitches." Carter's shirt was long past its absorption capacity. "In her head," he clarified.

Brent relayed the information. "Is she still breathing?"

Carter watched her chest labor. "Barely." He caught the quiver in his own voice as he stared at the helpless frame in his lap. Every delicate feature bore testimony of trauma. Dried blood flecked from her head to her toes. Streaks from his sopped t-shirt smeared along her cheek. Her entire eye socket was already taking on the angry hues of abuse. Her skin continued transforming through varying shades of gray.

He traced his shaky hand across the soft skin of her jaw as he fought the emotional cocktail of anger and tears simmering ever closer to the surface. All the survival training in the world couldn't have prepared him to watch her life – another in his long list of "losts" – fade out.

Chapter Thirty-Six

Dr. Matthew Hamilton had thought he'd met his match in the gargantuan beast of a dog when it ripped the lower half of his pant-leg off and left teeth marks in his calf, but that had only been the beginning of his woes. The dog-inflicted injury was so superficial he'd only been granted the opportunity to have some sorry excuse of a small-town doctor look at it. The whole time he'd plead for a real doctor, neither the sheriff nor the doctor broke their conversation.

"How are Emily and the twins?" the country officer asked.

"They're doin' good," the doctor – dressed in shorts and a Hawaiian shirt answered. "How 'bout that family of yours, Ben? I sure enjoyed Celia's Sunday-school lesson last week."

Matt didn't want to hear about the small-town adventures of two stupid strangers any more than he wanted to hear about their families or their church services. Unfortunately, as they booked him into the rinky-dink jail, they didn't seem to care what he wanted.

He paced the concrete floors of the five-by-eight cage, wishing for a bottle of cognac or even a shot of some cheap whiskey. He wasn't as inebriated as the sheriff or the breathalyzer had made him out to be – not enough to touch any of the disgusting features of his closet-sized cell or to numb out the reality of its mildew stench, anyway. By morning he was sure his lawyer would set things straight and both he and Megan would be headed back to the comfort of his penthouse. That was the only option. They had to reconcile. And if they didn't?

The consequences would be costly.

~　　　~　　　~

Megan willed her eyes open at the sound of her name on a stranger's voice then quickly closed them against the brightness.

"Megan," the soft voice queried again, "can you hear me?"

"Mmmhuh," she whispered.

"Megan," the lady posed in front of her. "Can you see me?"

She strained against the light to open her eyes again. "Kind of," she answered, realizing her left eye didn't open all the way. She raised her hand to her cheek, feeling the heat and swelling. "It hurts," she said.

"Your eye?" a familiar, unsympathetic voice asked. She turned her head to the side hoping to dispel the sudden frustration in her gut. "Everything," she clarified before closing her eyes again. "What are *you* doing here?"

"Were you expecting someone else?" Megan sensed her beside the bed, though her head hurt too much to open her eyes and confirm. "I *am* your mother," she said, as if that'd ever meant anything.

"Jake?" she whispered. "Where's Jake?"

"Your friend has him." Kat answered. "Brenda, or something like that," she shrugged.

"Bri?" Megan mumbled, wishing Kat had paid better attention to the details pertaining to her grandson. "What about Carter?" she whispered softly. The back of her head pounded but it was her torso that hurt the most.

"Your father?" Kat misunderstood. "He's in the hall,' she straightened the sheets into a taught crease across Megan's chest. "Would you like the nurse to go get him?"

"Whatever," Megan sighed. The strange lady, whom she assumed must be a nurse, lifted her wrist, held it for a few moments, and then set it down gently on the bed.

"Everything is stable," the nurse said to Kat. "I'll go get your husband. I'm sure the officers are going to want to talk to her now that she's awake, too."

"Why do I hurt so bad?" Megan tried to ignore her mother's fidgeting as three men walked into the room.

"You've been through a lot," Brent's voice soothed her. She strained her eyes to see him better. Fully uniformed, he stepped up to the side of her bed and squeezed her hand tenderly. "Carter and Bri will be happy to hear that you're finally awake." He hooked a nearby stool with his foot and dragged it within his reach. Situating himself on it, he leaned in with a smile. "Sergeant Springer and I need you to tell us what you remember. Do you think you can do that, Megan?"

She looked around the room, sore from one end of her body to the other, and took in her audience. Her dad, dressed in a full suit and tie, perched stiffly beside Kat on the far side of the cold room. Brent's partner held vigil near the door. A clipboard waited in his hands eager, she assumed, to record her statement.

Turning to Brent, she took a painful breath. "What's wrong with me?" she motioned towards the pain in her torso.

"I'm afraid I'd botch up all the medical lingo," he smiled. "So how 'bout you tell me what happened and then we'll let the doctor explain everything else?"

She nodded in agreement then replayed the horrific details of Matt's visit. Purposefully, she skipped over the bit on the porch with Carter, but not before remembering how much she'd hoped he'd have kissed her. "Where's Carter?" she whispered when she'd finished recounting her tale.

"He didn't leave your side," Brent assured her with a smile, "until your parents arrived and the doctors kicked him out. Said he couldn't stay unless he was family." He glanced accusingly at the rigid couple across the room then shrugged apologetically at Megan. "I told 'em he might as well be, but your mother wouldn't hear anything of it."

She let herself relax back into the pillow, emotionally drained, but grateful to be alive.

"I'll go look for the doctor, okay." He squeezed her hand, "I'll find Carter, too."

Most of what the doctor said failed to register with Megan. Based on the pain that radiated through her body, she latched onto the words: broken, concussion, and lucky, though she was unsure what was so lucky about her situation.

"Three broken ribs?" Kat questioned the doctor for a third time. "I don't know Doctor. What did you say your credentials are? She looks just fine to me."

"And that's why you're not a doctor," the doctor ignored Kat's insolence and turned the remainder of his comments to John. "We'll keep her here for another day or two, just to make sure we didn't miss anything, but after that, she's still going to be down for a while. Could be six weeks or more, every body heals a little differently."

"I understand." John, all business, noted every detail the doctor gave him.

"Now, Megan," the doctor turned to her, "I know you're in a lot of pain so I'm going to give you some more pain meds." He pulled a syringe from his breast pocket and injected into the IV line. Megan felt the instant warming.

"Thank you," she mumbled.

"You're welcome," the doctor smiled. "The meds are going to make you want to sleep and that's exactly what we want you to do, okay? Just relax and let your body mend."

"Okay," Megan easily agreed.

Kat shook her head as the doctor left the room. "The way everyone's babying you, you'd think you'd lost a lung or something." With a huff, she crossed her arms deliberately across her chest.

"Did you hear what he said, Kat?" John confronted his wife. "Luckily her lungs weren't punctured but that doesn't mean they were spared from some pretty severe bruising! This is serious stuff, my dear, and she needs to be taken care of."

"I just don't get it," she spewed as if Megan couldn't hear. "Her story doesn't add up. Why would *he* hit her? And how could he hit her *that* hard?" She paced the floor, still holding on to the hope of Matt's innocence. Both Megan and John stared past her and out the window.

"By the way," Kat raised her chin toward Megan, "while you were out, your father and I went over and saw that dump you've been living in." She looked at her husband hoping for back up. Busily, he typed into his phone, only vaguely aware that she was talking. "We probably need to get Jacob into a doctor," she eyed her daughter with disgust. "I'm sure that furniture is full of all kinds of germs and diseases. And... oh my word, what is this?" She pulled Megan's gingham top out of her bag of personal items and dangled it from the tips of her fingers with disgust. The shirt had been Brianna's idea and, though Megan had hesitated at first, she had to admit it looked surprisingly cute... *and country.*

Country. Megan played with the word as Kat continued to grumble at the blood stained shirt. She couldn't wait for the meds to kick in and put her out of this misery. Or, better yet, maybe they had a little special something that could put Kat out of *her* misery.

"John, I'm going to need you to get your daughter a change of clothes," she commanded. "She certainly can't wear these." She tossed the blood stained clothes in the trash can.

"I've got a business matter to attend to," John nodded. "I'm going to go for a little walk." His face was buried in his phone before he was out of the room.

Megan gingerly resituated herself in the bed as her mother went about her ranting. The words flowing past her collagen-filled lips struck a familiar cord. Cheep sheets. Lumpy mattress. Ugly curtains. "I'll have your father send someone over to get you packed up and out of that shanty." She didn't stop moving. "I'll bet you can't wait to sleep in a real bed and eat in a real dining room again."

Megan took a deep breath, mindful of her injuries. "Sure," she shrugged, watching the pattern of shadowed feet through the sliver in her door. She missed her baby.

"They can just pack up your clothes and leave the rest behind." Kat was busy opening and closing every cupboard in the tiny hospital room. "None of it looked like it's worth the hassle anyway."

Megan was only half listening to her mother when she heard the familiar stride in the hall. Well before she saw the shadow of his boots, she anticipated his distraction. His deep voice laughed just outside her door. Jake followed with a giggle. Megan's heart did a somersault.

"Hey," Carter smiled as he swung the door open, "I've got a special delivery for one Megan Hamilton." Jake wiggled in his arms. "I think someone really misses you," he grinned.

For what seemed like the best minutes of her life, Jake wrapped his arms around her neck and held on tight. He didn't seem fazed by the sterile surroundings. He didn't even seem to notice the cut below her eye or the fact that it was raging purple and black. All he cared about was holding her. And despite the pain that encompassed her, all she cared about was holding him too.

"How's my little man?" Megan kissed the top of his head over and over again.

"He's been really good." Carter leaned against the edge of the bed. "Not that that should be a surprise or anything. He's always good."

Megan watched Carter's eyes move up and down her haggard face. "I'm sorry," she said, stroking her uncombed hair.

"No," he pushed a wayward lock off her brow and more deeply examined her sore eye. "I'm the one who's sorry."

Megan felt a rush of warm through her body. *Was it the meds or Carter?*

She kissed Jake's head one last time then set him free to wiggle around on her bed. Carter quickly filled the void with the warmth of his embrace. "I'm not even going to ask how you're feeling, cause if you feel as crappy as you look I already know the answer!"

"Mr. Clementine," Kat interrupted. "That is no way to talk to my daughter."

"Carter," Carter gently reminded.

Megan didn't wait for her mother to offer Carter an apology. "That bad, huh?" She touched the bruise under her eye. It was swollen and hot. "It feels like it's going to explode." She tried to laugh but found herself bracing her ribs at the attempt. Her head swirled.

"Brent filled me in," Carter frowned. "Guess this means you'll be takin' it easy with Bri for the next little bit."

"Megan will be taking it easy at home." Kat balked as she lifted the energy packed toddler from the bed and tried to smother him in her arms. "No reason to hang around that old dump when she can lounge around the pool and be properly taken care of at my place." She didn't try to mask the insult.

"She can receive proper care here, too." He didn't dignify Kat with as much as a glance. "You don't have to leave," he offered softly. "We can take care of you. Between me and Bri I'm pretty sure we can keep you alive," his lip turned up in a half grin. "And Jake too," he added. "For at least a couple of weeks anyway."

"Thanks for all your kindness, Mr. Cardwell," Kat positioned herself and Jake in front of Carter. "But my daughter doesn't need your charity. Megan will be coming home where her father and I can see to it that she receives the kind of care that she and Jacob deserve."

Megan looked through her mother at Carter's dispirited face. "What if I don't want to?"

"Don't be ridiculous. Say your goodbyes and as soon as they release you, we'll take you home."

"I can do it," Carter reaffirmed. His eyes softly locked hers. "All you have to do is say the word."

Megan could feel her limbs getting heavier. The medication was slowly kicking in. "Come here," she signaled Carter with a heavy finger. He edged his way up to the side of the bed. Kat scoffed.

"Closer," Megan's finger beckoned.

He raised an eyebrow and moved in tighter. "Close enough?" he smirked, touching his cheek to hers. Though unshaven, his face was soft.

"Almost," she teased as she absorbed the vibration of his voice in her ear. "I'll make you a deal," she offered hopefully.

"And, what's that?"

"There are three little words that will make me stay." His whiskers tickled her cheek.

"Ten-thousand-count Egyptian cotton?" he teased.

"Nice, but not quite."

"Megan, honey," her dad burst back into the room. "I hate to interrupt, but there's a matter of business I need to discuss with you."

"Can I have a minute, daddy?" Megan gripped Carter's shirt to hold him in place.

"I'm sorry, baby," he sauntered up to the edge of the bed, "but I'm afraid I don't have a minute. This needs to happen now."

Carter stood up straight and shrugged.

"In private," John added as he looked at the disheveled cowboy.

"No problem," Carter nodded politely. "I suppose Jake and I can go get an ice cream cone while we wait," he smiled and offered to relieve Kat of her apparently stressful grandma duties.

Jake reached for Carter's outstretched arms only to be denied by Kat's sudden possessiveness. "Mr. Cleatus," the slaughter was intentional this time, "I think I am capable of handling my own grandson."

"Kat, let him take the child. This is no place for children anyway." Ignoring her impertinence as she handed the baby over, John looked sternly at his wife. "Now, dear, I'd like to speak to our daughter for a moment." He added "please" as a formality, gingerly smiling across the stale room at her. "In private."

"Whatever you've got to say, you can say in front of me." She hastily rearranged the display of flowers in the window, moving aside the two smaller arrangements in order to put her own contributed vase of pink and white roses central.

"Kat!" The deep cut of John's voice was enough to turn her on her heel. The two met eyes, exchanging a silent dialogue. Kat picked up the blanket at Megan's feet, creased it into thirds then tossed it back onto the foot of the bed. Poutingly, she shuffled her stiletto heels across the hospital floor and followed Carter out of the room.

The look of defeat on Kat's face would've been enough to make Megan laugh had her ribs not hurt so bad. Though the pain meds had started to take the edge off, every breath still felt like a blunt dagger pressing in and out of her sternum. Laughing was definitely out of the question. So, apparently, was smiling. She quickly wiped the smirk off her face as her dad's steely-eyed seriousness enveloped the room.

"Seems like a nice enough guy," he watched Carter's shadow disappear down the hall, then pushed the door closed and waited for the sound of the latch before speaking. "I wish you would've come to me about this," he stared at the crisp creases in his slacks.

"Why? It's not like you could've done anything about it. You can't just throw money at everything and hope to fix it." Megan took the biggest breath she could muster and let it roll noisily past her vocal chords. Her heavy eyelids bobbed. Her body sunk deeper into the mattress.

"I know." He loosened the knot in his tie. "I'm sorry. I'm sorry that I haven't exactly been the best dad. I know I wasn't around a lot when you were little, and it may have seemed like I didn't care about you, but Megan, I did." He pushed open his suit coat and slid his hands into the pockets of his slacks. "I do," he looked at the floor.

The only thing more uncomfortable than the stiff hospital bed was the pacification of her otherwise confident father. When he finally looked at her, Megan thought she saw tears in his eyes. Impossible. John Williams didn't cry. John Williams didn't have feelings.

"I should've protected you better. All I've ever wanted is for you to have a good life. I wanted you to be safe. And happy too." He managed to crack the corner of his mouth into what may have been easily mistaken for a grin. "Megan," he straightened his posture, cleared the unsolicited moment of emotion, and got back to business. "There's something I need to tell you. Something I should've told you a couple of years ago." Calm, cool, and professional, he pulled his hands from his pockets and clasped them intently behind his back.

At first she was unsure whether she was lucid or not. *What were those meds they'd given her and why had they chosen now to kick in?* She listened as intently as she could as the weight of sleep threatened to consume her. The details were sketchy... *Money? Secrets? Debts?... Blackmail?*

"I was trying to protect you, Megan." She thought his eyes softened. Maybe he did have a heart. Maybe it was just the drugs. "I thought that's what I was doing. Protecting you." He stuffed his hands into his trousers and connected his eyes pleadingly with hers. "If I'd had any idea he was hurting you," he choked as he looked at his broken daughter – swollen eye, bruised face, wires, tubes, and monitors. "If I'd known he was capable of this level of brutality, I'd have pulled the plug on him years ago."

"We can't rewind time." She reached a heavy hand towards his and, for the first time in her memory, he wrapped his fingers around hers.

"So..." He puffed his chest and erected his posture again. "What are we going to do about this whole Matt situation?"

~ ~ ~

Carter polished vanilla ice cream off Jake's face as the door opened and a confident John exited. No words were exchanged, but the nod of a head let Carter know he was free to go in.

"Hey," Carter strolled into the cold, dark room. "I think we have a conversation to fini..." he trailed off. Megan's eyes were closed and her chest moved rhythmically with the monitor beside the bed.

Stepping up to her side, he nestled Jake into him. "Looks like mommy needed a nap," he whispered.

"The doctor said to let her sleep," Kat haughtily cut the silence.

Securing Jake to his side, he used his free hand to tenderly push the hair off Megan's forehead. Paying no heed to Kat's arrogant glare, he leaned down and gently kissed Megan's crown. "I think the words you were looking for," he whispered into her incoherent ear, "are 'I love you.'"

236

Chapter Thirty-Seven

"Tough couple of nights, huh?"

Nauseous and haggard, Matt shielded his eyes from the morning sun as it slivered through the tiny window and into his cell. He cursed under his breath. "What are you doing here?"

"She lost a lot of blood." John glared through the bars. "So much trauma, in fact, she slept all day yesterday. Don't worry though, she finally woke up this morning. Looks like she went through the garbage disposal." He locked his jaw and squared his shoulders. "They're keeping her fairly sedated so she can heal, thanks for asking."

The men locked eyes. Not even the dust mites dared move.

"I suppose it's time we had a little talk."

"About what?"

"About my daughter. About our deal. About fair play... and betrayal."

Matt turned his back to his visitor and growled a string of profanities to the damp cinderblock wall.

"You know, Matthew, I think I underestimated you." An unresponsive back side was all the acknowledgment his comment construed. "And not in a good way. You really are an invalid."

"I don't know what you're talking about."

John chortled. "You know exactly what I'm talking about. Since the day we met I had my reservations about you... but my daughter saw something," he shrugged. "Don't know what, exactly, but I prayed that it wouldn't last."

"Thanks for the vote of confidence," Matt guffawed. He hated his father-in-law with every fiber of his being.

"I knew from the get-go that you were a perpetual womanizer. It killed me to see my daughter fall for such a baboon. But then," his chest lifted as he sucked in a giant breath. He shook his head, "I now know that the only reason you married her was to get at my money."

"Well, John, you're clearly delusional."

"Come on Matt. Have you no regard for my intellect? You think I'm oblivious to your game?" He raised his brows.

"Just business, right John? All business." Matt shrugged.

"No. This is personal. You messed with my family, Matt." His leather loafers drifted across the concrete floor, stopping just short of the cell bars. "You're a greedy, self-absorbed, sorry excuse of a man. I should've put a stop to things the first time you came to me for money." He pulled an envelope out from his breast pocket and flashed it through the bars. "Megan seemed so happy, though, and I didn't want to break her heart. I should've never given you the benefit of the doubt."

John snugged the envelope under his arm and shrugged his hands into the front pockets of his slacks. "I'm intrigued, young man, to know how you thought you were smart enough to cheat me."

"Cheat you?" Matt growled through clenched teeth. "I didn't cheat you out of anything. Every penny I ever got from you was in good faith. A loan."

"If it was just the loans, Matt, this would be a different conversation."

Matt flinched. His neck stiffened. John didn't know the half of it... at least Matt hoped not.

"Did you really think I was stupid enough to blindly follow your diagnosis? Smart as you think you are, *Doctor*, you should have known I'd seek a second opinion."

"Okay," Matt spat the word through clenched teeth. He'd knowingly misdiagnosed and treated John's cancer as something lesser than what it was, but he wasn't about to admit it. "I told you that you had cancer. Was I wrong?"

"No. You didn't lie about that part. It's cancer alright. Funny thing is, its melanoma not basal cell. Not sure if you know this, but it turns out there's quite a difference between the two and, well, that little slice and dice you did to me wasn't nearly enough to take care of things. I mean, really Matthew, a doctor of your caliber should know the difference."

Matt opened his mouth to respond but John overpowered him with his accusation.

"Don't even!" John raised his voice. "I can't believe you'd think I'd blindly trust you with anything... especially my life. You know what I think? I think you purposely misdiagnosed me. You didn't want me to know how bad it was. You didn't want me to get chemo. You were hoping it'd get out of control and spread to my other organs before we caught it. You were hoping I'd hurry and die."

"And why would I do that?" Matt scowled.

"Simple. You're a greedy man, Matthew. You saw dollar signs and couldn't control yourself. In fact, it seems self-control is something you really struggle with."

"Hmmph!" Matt's heart raced.

"I've got to hand it to you, Matt, it was quite the clever plan. Kill me off, absolve your debt to me, make Megan's inheritance yours... except," his eyes pierced through the cell bars. "Except it was too hard," he scoffed. "You couldn't control Megan. She messed up your perfect little existence and you couldn't take it. You got impatient. And then you broke. You screwed it all up."

"You don't know what you're talking about," Matt accused. He knotted his sweaty hands together.

"You know, at first I thought you'd missed an important step in your plan," John waved his finger towards Matt. "Not a dime of Megan's inheritance would be yours. Unless," his brows furrowed into a tight pitch. "Unless Megan... and little Jacob, were gone too."

He kicked his loafer into the cell bar and glared at Matt. "I didn't think you had it in you, Matt." He shook his head. "Obviously I was wrong."

"You can't prove anything." Matt ran his fingers through his hair noticing for the first time that his hands were shaking.

John leaned casually against the bars. "Well, I accept the challenge," he grinned for the second time in twenty-four hours. "And, in the meantime, I think your recent actions with my daughter are due cause to void our agreement."

"I don't have what you want." Matt hung his head low. John unquestionably had the upper hand. Without John's mercy, Matt was bound to lose his practice to his gambling debts. John had bailed him out a few times; he knew the debt was great. Megan, unfortunately, had been his security to the deed.

"What you did to my daughter is unforgivable." John leaned in closer and dropped his voice low enough that the guard couldn't hear him. "I'm done playing your little games, Matt. Now is not the best time to test my generosity." He waved the envelope in front of Matt's face then dropped it through the bars. Watching it spin its way to the floor he said, "I took the liberty of having my lawyer draft new divorce papers for you. I want you out of my daughter's life."

Matt watched the packet come to a stop on the filthy concrete then tightened his jaw and shuffled into whispering range. "And if I don't?" He kicked the unopened envelope back through the bars. He wasn't going to cower that easy. Megan's inheritance was too much to walk away from without a fight.

John lifted the envelope and fanned it in front of Matt's face. "Then I call my loan due," he exacted with careful ease. "Effective immediately."

"And if I do? If I sign the divorce and walk away?" Matt reeled at the idea.

John shrugged. "I'm a business man, Matt. Deals are what I do. So, here's what I've got for you: sign the divorce papers, walk out of her life, and I'll give you ninety days to make good on your debt."

"Ninety days isn't enough," Matt's neck turned red and his fists balled. "I don't exactly have a million in cash laying around."

"Well, I think it's a pretty generous offer. And," he drew his mouth into a tight line, "it's certainly better than the alternative."

"Which is?"

John smacked the envelope repeatedly into his palm. "If you choose not to sign these papers, I will send someone to collect my money on Friday." John tossed the envelope back into the cell.

"Collect from where, John? I can't give you something I don't have."

"You've got at least twice that much tied up in your penthouse. If I were you, I'd get it on the market ASAP!" John turned to walk away. "Oh," he spun back to look at his writhing target. "And just so we're clear, our financial matter is between you and me, but if you think you can beat up my daughter and get away with it, you are wrong. Expect to hear from the DA about it... And, you might want to scramble together a PR team. The media generally has a hay-day with this kind of stuff."

John crossed his arms affirmatively across his chest and turned his back, leaving Matt to stew over the predicament in silence. He'd let too much ride on Megan. How had he let his impatience blow a hole in the rest of his brilliant plan? A call to repay his gambling deed meant the death of his finances. A press release of any merit would mean the overnight death of his practice. He'd grossly underestimated John.

Chapter Thirty-Eight

Carter encouraged the old truck along. It'd been a decent season on the orchard so far– enough to cover his and Whitley's needs plus the payroll, and a little left to spare ‑ but the idea of parking his grandfather's legacy tugged at him. The sputtering engine and accompanying squeal told him his hopes were far from realistic though.

"I think it's the timing belt," he told his passengers. As always, Jake cared more about the wind-flapped dog in the passenger seat than he did Carter's babble. "Either that or something with the fuel line," he continued. He watched the dash dials bounce around like the back and forth of a tennis match, noting the newly acquired rust ring around the speedometer. "Probably both," he conceded as he continued to coax the truck down the road.

"I guess it's time to admit defeat," he turned to his toddler companion and gently patted his little knee. Jake giggled at the attention. Bosco's tail did a single thump as his eyes and ears poised out the window. Carter didn't stand a chance at being his dog's best friend as long as Jake was around. Somehow the pint-sized little Jacob had managed to steal all of Boss's love.

Truth be told, as long as it meant Megan was around, Carter was happy to share the dog's attention. The jury was still out on that though. With her in the hospital and her obsessive mother in charge, he could only guess where she might end up going. Hoping she'd choose a farm house over a penthouse may have been too much to ask for. He held out for the impossible.

The old farm house had taken on a vacancy that it had never known before. Even after Grandma Beth passed on, the home still had a presence, but for the last few days... well, it'd been dead.

Watching the police move in and out had been hard but cleaning up the aftermath of the horror had been worse. He threw away the old couch, committing it to the grave it should've met years earlier and, after trying to scrub the bloodstains out, ended up refinishing the floor. He fixed the porch door, though it was admittedly too late to do any good. If nothing else, between the cleanup work and taking care of Jake, his mind had stayed occupied. It was the quiet moments he dreaded. The ones where his mind let his heart believe that she might not come back.

The truck sputtered past the last of the summer orchards. Bosco's ears peeked and he jumped his paws to the dash with a throaty cry. His tail whipped ferociously from one side to the other, pelting the seat with its energy. His paws bounced from the dash to the armrest and back again. "Sit down Bosco!" Carter commanded, still trying to diagnose the truck's problem.

For a half a second the dog's tail stilled and his back side hit the bench seat, then like a cannon, he was up again. "Boss!" Carter asserted, "Sit down!"

The stubborn canine didn't even bother to look at his master, instead he turned to Jake and smothered him with a big, slobbery kiss. Jake squeezed the dog's head. "CoCo," he giggled, enjoying every pass of the dog's tongue.

"What in the world has gotten into you?" Carter started as he turned the truck onto his street. The dog's tail flogged back and forth across the cab and he let out another high pitched yelp.

For the second time in less than a week, a police cruiser was stationed in front of Carter's house. Pulling his crippled truck into the drive, he wondered what the officers could possibly want.

As soon as the truck slowed to a stop, the cruiser's doors opened. Two uniformed officers crossed the lawn. Sam and Sarah followed.

"Evening Carter," the first officer called as he approached the old truck. Though not good friends, the two men were familiar. Jim McDermet had been on the force since Carter was a kid.

"Evening Jim," Carter shook his hand before turning to Sam. "What's going on?" he asked the boy.

"Nadine's been in a drunken stupor since Monday," Jim shrugged.

"DCFS has been called," the other officer, a clear rooky, offered. "They'll be lookin' to put the kids in foster care, I'm sure, but for tonight they need somewhere to crash."

"I'll take them." Carter didn't hesitate. "For however long they need me."

"They took my mom," Sarah tried to hold back her tears.

"It'll be okay," Carter took her in his arms. He brushed the hair off her cheek. "Your mom loves you very much. I promise she's not leaving you."

"They'll probably be lookin' to place them with family," the unfamiliar officer said.

"He is my family," Sam said. He stepped along Carter's side and slid his hand around Carter's. "This is where we want to stay."

Jim crouched down to Sam's eye level. "Unfortunately, Sam, it'll be up to the judge. But I'll put in a good word for you. Carter's got a good place here. I'll do my best to make sure the judge knows that."

"Thank you." Carter extended his hand. Jim took it into his grasp and shook it boldly.

"Sorry to just unload them on you like this," Jim said. "But I knew you'd be good for it." He smiled at each of the kids then nodded at Carter. "We'll be in touch," he said, then set his hand atop his holster and sauntered back to the cruiser. The rooky quickly followed.

"Do you want to unbuckle Jake and help get him out of the truck?" Carter asked Sarah as they watched the officers walk away.

She wiped the tears from her eyes and nodded, then climbed into the cab. "Hi, Jake," she smiled at him as her hands worked their way over his car seat buckles.

Carter did the math. There was no way his old truck, functioning properly or not, was going to do the job now.

Chapter Thirty-Nine

Megan adjusted her legs again, trying to find a comfortable position in the hospital bed. Five days of this agony was more than enough. Admittedly she'd loved the attention at first, needing the time to rest and heal, but with each passing day she itched to do something different. Something more. She couldn't wait for a change of scenery and a real meal.

She picked the TV remote up off the bed. The glow from the screen illuminated the small, dark room. One-hundred-thirty-two channels of absolutely nothing. She scrolled through every one of them then turned the TV back off and relaxed her head into the pillow.

The smell of sterile metal and the subtle sound of nurses' feet in the hall did little to excite her senses. She closed her eyes, not really tired, but bored. At least Kat hadn't shown up yet for the day. She'd been like a sentinel, guarding Megan's hospital room from anyone she deemed a distraction. Unfortunately that was everyone except herself and John. Megan hadn't seen Bri, or Carter, or even Jake for three days.

"Excuse me, sir," she heard a nurse call in the hallway. "You can't go in there. Visiting hours don't start for another thirty minutes."

"I know," his voice was like butter. "But, if I don't see her now," he was already pushing the door open.

"I suppose if you're quiet it'll be fine." The nurse sighed. "Just don't wake her up."

"Thank you," his silhouette filled the door opening.

"Good morning," Megan felt the blood rush to her cheeks.

"Good morning," Carter quietly moved across the floor. "I didn't expect to find you awake."

"Wish I could actually get up and do something," she smiled, grateful to see him. She adjusted her amber hair, consciously pulling it over her cheek, though she knew it was too dark for him to really see much anyway.

He looked at her through the darkness. Deeply. Intently. She wondered what he was thinking.

"I brought you something," he finally spoke. He set a vase on the bedside table. Megan blinked at the bouquet but the room was too dark to make a full accounting of the flowers. Daises, she thought, but didn't ask him to turn the light on. She must've looked horrendous.

"They're beautiful," she nodded at the arrangement.

"How do you know?" He skirted next to her bed. "It's awful dark in here."

"Because they're from you." Her heart danced at his presence. "Here I thought you'd forgotten all about me."

"Never," he bent down to her level and pushed the hair off her forehead. "The swelling has gone down nicely," he said.

She quivered with his touch. "It's still pretty ugly," she twisted her lips in frustration. "You must be blinded by the dark in here."

"There's nothing ugly about you." Holding her gaze, he traced his finger along the contour of her jaw. Her eyes beaded with moisture. "How's the rest of you coming together?" he offered.

"Sore." She wrapped her arms protectively around her torso. Her trembling lips cracked a smile.

He withdrew his touch from her face and reached for her hand. "Well, I think you're looking a lot better."

"You think this ugly scar is an improvement, huh?" she teased him for a compliment.

"Even a scar looks beautiful when it's on you," he took her bate. "But what I meant is that you're healing more and more every day. Noticeably so... even in the dark."

"Thank you," she smiled, basking in his attention.

"I'm glad you're awake today," he sat down on the edge of her bed, "I've had to slip in every morning before your mom gets here. No offense, but that lady's crazy."

"Tell me about it," she said, but her head was stuck back at his other comment. *Had he really come every morning?* "How's Jake?" she finally asked. "Will you bring him to see me later?"

"I'd love to," he grinned, "that is, if your mom lets us in."

"I'm an adult woman. If I want to see my son, she can't stop me."

"I'd like to be a fly on the wall when you tell *her* that," he chuckled, but they both knew it wouldn't be a well-received conversation. "I think she's paid off the nursing staff," he added with a grin.

Megan didn't doubt that he was right. "Does Bri have Jake?" she didn't want to talk about her mother.

"Actually," the rising sun had splintered into the room just enough to softly touch his smile. "Bri had her baby last night."

"What!?" Megan gasped. The excitement was a brutal reminder of the pain in her torso. She took a gentle breath and touched her hand to her ribs. "She had her baby?"

"Little boy. Nine pounds, twenty-two inches long. And definitely cuter than his father."

She wondered how Bri had carried - let alone delivered - such a big boy. "Is she here? In this hospital?"

"Well, there aren't a whole lot of other options around here," he shrugged. "Third floor," he added with a grin.

"Do you think they'll let me see her? Can you take me?" She couldn't wait to see her friend and the new baby.

"Maybe later. I'll talk to the nurse and see what we can work out," he squeezed her hand. "I heard rumor that they may be lettin' you out this afternoon. If that's the case, you can make the trip to the third floor before you head home."

"I'd like that." The rising sun started to splinter through the blinds. Lines of gold painted softly across the room... across Carter's face.

She wondered where home was. She'd had a lot of time to reflect on it as she lay in her hospital bed. And, after days of tolerating Kat's cynicism and bitterness, she was sure her mother wasn't happy. Kat had all the money and comfort and luxury anyone could ask for and she was miserable. Megan wanted more. She wanted to be happy. She wanted to laugh and live... and love. She wanted to feel the way she did when Carter was around. She wanted to be the person she was in his presence. And, if he'd just let her in, she was pretty sure she could make the adjustments needed to live his lifestyle. Fully aware of his hand wrapped around hers, she took hope. "I never thought I'd say this, but I sure do miss that stinky dog of yours," she said.

"Is that so?" he raised his brow and returned a smile.

"Uh, huh," she nodded. *Was she reading too much into his smile?* "I've also been thinking I'd like to try another ride on that redneck machine of yours."

"You don't say," he nodded. "I might just be able to hook you up with that."

"Good," she said, then clarifying the obvious, added, "Not today, of course."

"Of course," he chuckled.

"So, you'll give me a rain check?"

"You can have as many rain checks as you want if it means I get to see you."

"Well," she teased. "Technically, if you're driving and I'm sitting behind you, you won't be able to see me."

"Megan," he scooted in closer then gently ran his finger over her unbandaged brow and down the side of her face. Her cheeks warmed at his touch. "Please don't leave," he whispered.

Her heart leapt, but she was hesitant to fall too quickly. Still unwilling to read too much into his statement, she looked around the sterile room then down at all the tubes attached to her. "I don't think that's an option," she lifted her tethered arm.

"I hope not," he didn't feed into her joke. He leaned in closer and locked eyes with her. She thought she saw a tear. She dismissed the idea. Must've just been a reflection.

"I'm assuming you're still technically married?" His breath was warm on her cheek.

"Technically," she swallowed the newly formed lump in her throat as her eyes met his. Her dad's lawyers had spent the last several days dealing with the technicalities and she hoped to be free soon. The last thing she ever wanted to think about again was Matt.

"Then," he sighed, "what I'm about to do could be my quick ticket to hell," he took another exaggerated breath. "But," he continued softly, "I think it's worth the risk." With more caress than she imagined his strong hands were capable of, he traced his fingers along her jaw. His touch warmed her earlobe then settled at the base of her neck. "I think I'm ready to kiss you now." The words barely left his lips before Megan was pressing hers into them.

He pulled away long enough to smile at her then touched his lips gently into hers again. Her heart did a full series of somersaults. Her hands gripped his shoulders tightly.

"Does this mean the farmhouse is still available?" she smirked when their lips finally parted.

"Well, ma'am... I mean Bob... a pretty young lady happens to have a lease on it." He draped his arm over her shoulder. "And I'm kinda partial to her son," he shrugged, "but we may be able to work something out."

"Like what?" She traced her trembling fingers up the nape of his neck.

"Another one of those kisses will probably do the trick," his eyes sparkled as he grinned.

"You drive a hard bargain, Cowboy." She closed her eyes and melted into the tenderness of his kiss.

"Daisies, huh?" Kat paraded into the room. "Wow, someone really out did themselves," she chided with a huff. "I assume *those* are from you, Cardwell?"

"How nice to see you, Mrs. Williams." Carter touched Megan's cheek one last time then scooted back.

Megan missed his touch instantly. Her mother's boorish stab was just salt on the wound. She wished Kat would just head back home. Surely the country club ladies missed her. She shook her head. Carter softly touched her hand then encircled his fingers around hers. She looked at him, then at her mother, then over at the flower arrangement. There was just enough light in the room to set the daisies aglow. Dozens of white blooms burst from the simple vase. But one was different. She stretched her neck for a better view. Right in the center of the daisies stood a single, perfect, unassuming red rose.

"Is that what I think it is?" she ignored her mom and turned to Carter.

"Simple. Plain. Beautiful," he smiled.

She glared at her mom through the corner of her eye. "Do you mean it?" she whispered to the man she'd grown to love more deeply than she ever imagined possible.

"One-hundred and ten percent," he whispered.

"You know she's married," Kat interrupted.

The wheels of the nurse's cart rolled noisily through the door and across the white tile floor before coming to a stop beside Megan's bed.

Megan bit back the words she had reserved for her mother. Kat was not going to ruin her day.

"Sorry," the young nurse smiled at Carter. "I didn't mean to interrupt anything." She situated her clipboard on the cart then grasped Megan's arm to check her vitals.

"It's okay," Carter smiled back. "I probably ought to be on my way anyway."

"Do you really have to go already?" Megan grasped his hand tightly.

"It's probably best for your bouncer and me to keep our distance right now," he smirked at the lady gawking over his shoulder.

Megan didn't care what Kat thought. "Please stay. I'd really like you to stay." She also didn't care if she sounded desperate.

"Wish I could, but I really should get home. I left Sam and Sarah in charge of Jake. Not that I don't trust them, but I'd feel a whole lot better if I were there to supervise."

"Thank you." Tears welled up in her eyes. She didn't care what her mother saw or thought. "My purse..." She paused to think about it for a moment. "Have you seen my purse around? I think I set it on my bed before..." she trailed off. *Before Matt showed up*, she finished in her head.

"I saw it," Carter stopped her from retrieving the awful memory. "Do you want me to bring it to you?"

"No," she shook her head gently. "My car keys are buried in it somewhere. I don't think I can make it up into your truck, so when you come to take me home, bring *my* car."

"Done," he winked at her then waved goodbye. The nurse scribbled notes onto her clipboard, but Megan hardly noticed. Her focus was on her heart as it disappeared with Carter into the hall.

Chapter Forty

Carter strode past the nurses' station, consciously calculating his gait as he and Jake stepped through the door to Megan's hospital room. Eagerly, he drank in every inch of her radiance. Her face, in stark contrast to the sterile room, bore the bronze kiss of summer. Her lips beckoned the red of a thousand rubies. He couldn't believe it'd taken him so long to kiss her and, as he walked into the room, he couldn't wait to do it again.

She eyed him with a grin.

He smiled back, catching a hint of the medicated glaze in her eyes. Still screening his emotion, he nonchalantly approached her bed. "Aren't you supposed to be taking it easy?" She'd ditched the hospital gown in favor of her red summer dress. It was one of his personal favorites.

"Probably," she tittered on the edge of the bed, "But I'm kind of tired of this place. I feel like I'm in prison." Her eyes rolled toward her mother still holding vigil in the corner of the room.

"Well, here's a little something to brighten your day," he pulled an envelope from his pocket and handed it to her.

"What is it?" she asked, not waiting for an answer before tearing the flap. She guarded the contents from Kat's view and stared at the small check in her hands. "You weren't kidding when you said little," she laughed.

The check was a humble confession that her website had actually made a drop of money. Over time he hoped they'd gain more advertisers, but for now, he grinned at the nominal amount. "It's not much," he set a wiggly Jake on the foot of the bed, "but it's a start."

"What is it?" Kat nosed her way in.

"Nothing," Megan slid the check back into its envelope and tucked it along her side.

"Just a little income from her website," Carter tried to sooth the tension between the two ladies.

"Website?" Kat muttered.

"Yep," Carter beamed because he knew Megan wouldn't do it herself. "A cooking one."

"You've got to be kidding me." Kat clasped her hands behind her back and shuffled her designer shoes across the tile. "Cooking? *You?* This just gets better and better, doesn't it?"

"Let it go, Kat," John grasped his wife's arm. She glared at him, opened her mouth to continue then clamped her jaw closed again.

"Kat," Megan's face cringed with pain as she inhaled deeply. "Thank you for standing by me these last few days."

Literally, Carter thought. *Thanks for literally standing by.* He stifled the urge to laugh out loud.

"Carter has come to take me home," the room lit up with Megan's smile. "Which means you are free to go home now, too."

Carter watched Kat's jaw tighten. He braced himself for the rant he thought was coming. Despite the fire in her cheeks, she didn't blow a gasket. Instead, she mumbled a string of incoherencies under her breath and picked her purse up off the end table.

"We're not going to go the rounds about this again, Kat!" John raised a cautionary brow.

Kat muttered something so quietly nobody could hear her.

"Thank you," Megan nodded. "All afternoon was plenty."

"Just so we're clear, Megan," Kat huffed towards the door with John right behind her. "If I walk out that door without you, you can consider yourself disowned." She tucked her purse tightly under her arm. "Alone," she added through clenched teeth.

"Kat!" John snapped.

"Okay," Megan smiled smugly.

John didn't follow Kat's lead as her heals clicked their way out the door and into the hall. "I got you something," he pointed to a box in the window seal. "I'm sure your mother would think they're ridiculous, but I hope you like them." He flashed a quick, smile, then followed his storming wife with his eyes. "I probably ought to go catch her," he shook his head and stepped towards the door. "And, for the record, I hope you know you aren't alone."

Uncomfortable silence hung in the air. "That was unexpected," Carter finally said. "Are you going to be okay? Do you want me to go bring her back so you can smooth things over?"

"She'll get over it," Megan shrugged. "Daddy will make sure of it."

"Okay," Carter said. He wondered what else her daddy had been able to take care of, specifically anything pertaining to Matt. He wanted to ask about the charges, the divorce, the *situation*, but Grandma Beth's voice hollered to mind his own business. *When does this become my business?*

"Are you ready to go?" a nurse asked as she pushed a wheel chair into the room.

"Yes," Megan about bounced off the bed. "And I don't need that," she pointed to the wheel chair. "I think I'm okay to walk," she said, dangling her feet towards the floor.

"Maybe you are," the nurse said with a smile, "but hospital policy says you've gotta be in this chair until you leave the building."

"Ugh," Megan sighed. "Can I roll out the front door then walk back in? My friend is in the maternity ward and I want to see her before I go home."

"I'll bet this handsome young man would be happy to wheel you up to the third floor before you leave." The nurse winked at Carter.

"Absolutely," Carter quickly answered.

While the nurse took care of the discharge paperwork, Carter loaded up his arms with the personal effects and flowers from Megan's hospital room and delivered them to her car. At her request, he handed her the box from her dad before walking out the door. When he returned, she was happily sitting in the wheel chair with Jake securely in her arms.

"Ready to roll," she grinned.

His attention was drawn to her legs. Red leather swathed half way up her delicate calves. "Where in the world did those come from?" he asked.

"My boots?" She raised a foot in front of her. "Do you like them? Daddy bought them for me."

"What?" he hedged at the idea. They didn't seem like the typical gift of a well-moneyed city-slicker. "I love them, but they don't seem like *your* typical fare," he smiled.

"You wouldn't think so," she explained, "but it seems that daddy did some asking around town - you know, trying to get a feel for the place - and someone mentioned that I needed more appropriate shoes if I was going to stick around."

"So," Carter wondered out loud, "does this mean he supports you in your decision to stay?"

"It means that he wants me to be happy," she smiled.

"Ah, and he thinks the boots will do that?"

"No," she giggled. "He thinks you will."

Even with a swollen eye and battered face, she was radiant. *Don't get your hopes up*, he thought. Then, *maybe it's time to get your hopes up!*

"I'm willing to give it a shot," he said.

"Me too," she sighed.

He bent down for a kiss. "Red was a good choice. It is definitely your color," he glanced at her boots, then kissed her again.

Chapter Forty-One

The screen door floated to a close without a sound, causing Carter to smile at his handiwork. Megan had been back in the farmhouse for barely two weeks but they'd already settled into a routine. Being on bed rest meant Megan rarely left the confines of her tiny room, which worked out well since the living room was barren of furniture and Carter had commandeered the kitchen table to set up a temporary office so he could be near if she needed him.

"What am I supposed to do with all this stuff?" Carter called. He followed the sound of women's chatter to Megan's bedroom.

"It's here already?" Megan asked as Carter scooped Jake into his arms. Her own arms were filled with Bri's peacefully sleeping, curly-headed baby boy. "That was a lot faster than I thought," she barely took her eyes off the tiny bundle snuggled peacefully to her bosom.

"And a lot *more* than I expected." Carter slid past the bed and over to the window. He opened the curtains and pointed at the moving truck in the front yard. Between taking care of Megan and Jake, and the whole Sam and Sarah situation, he'd had a lot on his plate lately. Assault charges against Matt were still pending. Of course nothing was final or easy, but he hoped the appearance of all of Megan's penthouse furniture meant that Matt was getting closer to signing the divorce papers.

"What are you going to do with it all?" Bri peered out the window. "Surely all that stuff can't fit in this little house," she added.

"Honestly?" Megan coddled the baby gently, "I don't think I want any of it except the big, soft rug. I think it'd look nice over the wood in the front room. That, and maybe the bed." She looked around the room apprehensively before adding, "But, you're right Bri, I don't think it will fit."

"We can try," Carter offered. "Maybe if we rearrange things a bit it will work." He wanted her to be comfortable, even if it meant having Matt's bed in his grandma's house. He tensed at the thought. "What about everything else?" he asked.

"How about we give it away to someone who needs it?" she smiled up at him.

"Like who?" he asked.

"Bri, will you take the bed? It's really nice and I'd hate to see it go to just anyone." Her face was aglow with the offer. "And the crib. Take the crib."

"I can't take the crib," Bri shook her head. "Jake's still in a crib and, even if he wasn't, you might need it again someday."

"I'm not going to hold on to it and let it collect dust for a distant *someday*. Besides, I think I like Carter's better," she said.

The glint in her eye as she held the precious new baby wasn't lost on Carter. Neither was the way she accentuated the word *someday*. First things first, he reminded himself. They'd only had a couple of weeks to explore this whole relationship thing, plus there was still that tiny detail that she was still married.

"Take the couches and the coffee table to Doc Stone's office. They'd look ridiculous in here, but they'll be perfect there." She disappeared into her thoughts for a moment then added, "He'll have to paint though. The black leather will look hideous with mauve walls."

"Actually," Bri smiled, "pretty much anything looks hideous with mauve walls."

Megan gently guarded her ribs as she laughed. Despite her smile, the pain was evident on her face. She tilted her head back and took a weak, wheezy breath.

"Okay, ladies," it was time for Carter to play the bad guy. "I think you've had enough fun for one day. It's probably time to get some rest." He grinned at Megan then used his eyes to gesture at Bri to leave.

"Not until you tell us about your day," Bri softly protested as she took her sleeping babe from Megan's arms.

"Yeah. How'd it go?" Megan asked. Regardless of any pain she might have been suffering, she was determined to hear his news.

"What'd the judge have to say?" Bri asked.

"All things considered," Carter nodded, "it went pretty okay."

"What exactly does that mean?" Megan asked. "Just okay?"

He checked his watch and picked up Megan's bottle of pain pills form the nightstand before answering. "It means that Nadine is going to get some help," he paused, still absorbing the details himself, "... and as of about an hour ago, custody of both Sam and Sarah has been reassigned." Pretending to be unfazed by the court proceedings, he handed her a pill.

"To who?" Megan let the pill rest in the palm of her hand.

Carter stalled. As much as he was happy to have some help for Nadine, he wished the court date had been to settle Megan's case.

"Who's going to take care of the kids?" she asked again, pulling him from his thoughts.

"Well," he smirked, letting on for the first time that the judge's rule had been more than just okay. "It's a little complicated." He grinned at the anticipating ladies. "An anonymous donor has offered to subsidize some of the expenses for their care."

"An *anonymous* donor?" Megan wondered out loud. "As in the same *anonymous* donor who offered to buy you a new truck the other day?"

"No," Carter answered, though he wasn't surprised that she'd jumped so quickly to the assumption that her dad was going to help. He'd turned down the generous offer for a much needed new vehicle, but that hadn't stopped John's gracious offers and gratitude for taking care of his daughter from generously rolling in all week.

"Which means what?" Bri asked again. "Why do you have to be so cryptic? Just spit out the details already." She capped the good-humored demand with a smile.

He grinned at her persistence. "The wife of Sam's birth father wants to contribute to their financial care. She's already been doing it for years anyway - ever since her husband passed away - but for whatever reason, she's decided that it's time to make it official."

Megan's face softened, he assumed it was because it meant her dad was off the hook.

"But," Bri tried to decipher the information. "No one helps them out but you and..." her eyes grew in their sockets as she trailed off.

Carter nodded. "Me and who, Bri?"

She shook her head in disbelief. "No. It can't be."

"Who?" Megan asked.

Bri furrowed her brow. "Ruth?" The doubt trembled off her tongue. "How have I never put that together?"

Carter validated Bri's deduction with a huge smile.

Megan met his grin with one of her own. "That's fantastic. You were assigned custody! When do they move in? Officially, I mean."

"They're having dinner with their mom before she checks in to the facility, then I'm supposed to meet them back at their house and help them pack up the rest of their stuff." He gave Jake an excited squeeze then checked his watch. "In fact," he grinned excitedly, "I probably ought to be heading over there soon." He gently set Jake on the floor.

"Can I come with you?" Megan rustled her blankets.

"I'm sure they'd like that," Carter considered the idea. "But only if you promise not to do anything but watch."

"I promise," she said, flashing a grin full of dazzling white teeth. "You'll have to drive my car though," she twisted her lips thoughtfully. "We don't all fit in your truck and I just took one of those pain pills that says I shouldn't operate machinery."

Chapter Forty-Two

Doctor Matthew R. Hamilton walked slowly down the office hall, his eyes fixed to the floor. If ever he thought he'd be leaving his practice at such a young age, he'd have chided himself, but the small box of personal affects under his arm didn't lie. As much as he didn't want to admit it, he'd gotten in over his head and he understood now, perhaps better than anyone ever should, that John Williams knew how to play hard ball.

Before he'd even made bail and been granted release from the county jail, the local press had printed their version of the story: "Successful Plastic Surgeon Makes Attempt at Wife's Life." They didn't know anything. The first paragraph of the piece had Megan holding on to her life by a mere thread. Hardly accurate or believable.

...Yet everyone believed it. In the court of public opinion, Doctor Hamilton was guilty. In a matter of weeks his practice lost most of its clients. And, without any money coming in, he had no hope of paying off his gambling debts, let alone floating the payroll. It didn't help much that John Williams had used every connection he had to persuade the District Attorney to file criminal charges.

Ronda was the only staff member present to say her goodbyes, though he sensed it was more of superficial show than anything. The only loyalties his personnel had were to their paychecks, the last of which he'd posted that day. Maybe when his lawyers found a buyer for the practice, she'd get her job back. Maybe the whole staff would. Frankly, he didn't care.

"Don't forget this," Ronda pulled the name plaque off the office door and set it on the top of his box.

He didn't say thank you or even wait to watch her lock up before stepping into the elevator. He was in no mood to make pleasantries. Gratefully it was a Sunday and the office complex was empty.

As the elevator doors closed he pulled the framed picture of Megan out of his box. Cursing out loud, he threw it back into the box and dug around until he found the smooth, familiar contours of his pewter flask.

"I had a feeling I'd find you here," Carl Hudson offered his stumpy hand to Matt as soon as the elevator door opened to the lobby.

Matt slid the flask into his pocket then gripped his box more firmly. "Did you find a buyer?" he snarled at the squat little man.

"Maybe," Carl shrugged, "but that's not why I'm here."

Matt hated his new dependency on his attorney. He raised his brow and kept walking.

"Matt, this is a big deal. We really need to talk."

"I don't see what there is to talk about. Do your job and get me out of this mess so I can move on." He pulled his car keys from his suit coat. The Jaguar was the only possession that Megan hadn't cost him.

"Mr. Williams has filed suit." He tried to keep up with Matt's swift pace.

"Didn't he already do that?" Matt grimaced. "Isn't that why I had to sell the penthouse and give Megan everything else I ever owned? That man's got so much money of his own, yet he won't stop until he's got every last drop of mine!" He kicked the office complex door. The tempered glass did little but dance under the pressure.

"I'm afraid this time he's going for more than gold." The stumpy man stopped his pursuit. "Matt," he stuffed his sausage hands into his trouser pockets, "as soon as Megan's abuse charges are done playing out, he's going to file a malpractice suit."

Matt stopped dead in his tracks. *John couldn't... he wouldn't!* He dropped the box to the sidewalk. John really was going to ruin him. He pulled the flask from his pocket then, removing the lid, sat down on the curb.

"It'll take a couple of years to work through it all," Carl sidled up to his side. "In the meantime," he took the flask from Matt's hand, "I suggest you work on getting sober."

Epilogue

"Where are we going?" Megan questioned as she snuggled into Carter's back. The late autumn sun was far behind the mountain, leaving only the four wheeler's headlights and the faint light of the moon to guide their way.

Carter pulled the machine to a stop at the top of the mountain and, dimming his headlights into the trees, turned with a smile. "Stay put for just a second." He squeezed her hand. "I'll be right back."

"But," her question was cut short as his black jacket disappeared into the darkness.

Her eyes adjusted to the night as she followed Carter's shadow across the rocky terrain. He hovered in the darkness for a moment before a small flame flickered to life. Between the four wheeler and the sparkling lights in the valley sat a finely set, candle-lit table for two.

Still smiling at his cleverness, Carter assisted Megan off the machine. Her red boots moved capably across the dirt to the beautifully decorated table. Tucking her jacket against the mountain's unpredictable wind, she waited for Carter to situate himself on the opposite side of the table. "This is very nice," she smiled at his obvious effort.

"I had to do some homework," he admitted, looking down at the array of silverware that adorned the white tablecloth. "Not sure why anyone would need so many," he touched the line of forks playfully. "I only have one mouth."

"Four forks would indicate four different courses," she released a laugh into the quiet night.

"But why can't I use the same fork for all of them?" He shook his head then nodded at a shadow in the trees.

"You've got to be kidding," she smiled as Sam and Jamison emerged from the thicket in black suits and bow ties. They each carried a silver domed plate. "So many formalities," she grinned. "You really did do some homework," she teased.

"Every now and then my serious bone starts aching for a little attention." His eyes sparkled as their young waiters approached.

"Your hors d'oeuvres, ma'am," Carter nodded as the boys revealed the contents of their delivery. "Marinated Artichoke Hearts Venezia."

She eyed the little plates with suspicion. "No offense," she laid her napkin across her lap, "But I hope the boys didn't make these."

"No worries," he ensured, giving the boys a parting wink as they disappeared back into the shadows.

"To what do I owe this great pleasure?" she asked, savoring the delicacy of the artichokes. The candle light flickered in the breeze.

"The pleasure is all mine."

"Well, thank you. It's lovely." She touched his hand across the table. "I hope you know that I don't like you just for your money and fancy stuff."

"I've got a little secret for you." He leaned across the table and whispered. "I don't have any money. But," his eyes twinkled with anticipation, "I do have a little something else you might like." Still leaning across the table, he pressed his lips to hers.

"Eww," the boys belted in unison from the darkness.

"You were right," Megan smiled. "I do like that."

"Good," he sat back down. "But that wasn't the little something I was referring to." He produced an envelope from somewhere under the table.

"What's this?" she asked as he handed her the large cardboard envelope. "What've you been up to?" She looked first at Carter then to the thicket she knew the boys were hiding in.

"I don't know," he shrugged.

She glared at him.

"No, really," he confessed. "I don't know. It came today while you were gone today. I had to sign for it."

She turned the package around looking for some indication as to the sender. There wasn't so much as a return address. "What could it be?" she wondered out loud as she tore the seal and groped for the papers inside.

"I have no idea," Carter anticipated.

"*Really?*" Megan stared at him questioningly as she read the letterhead out loud. "*What's Cooking Cali?*"

Carter raised an eager brow. "Well, what does it say?" he impatiently asked as she skimmed over the document.

"It's from the network. They're starting a new local segment called *What's Cooking Cali?* And they've..." She traced her finger over the text, rereading the words in disbelief. "It says that they'd like to offer me a monthly feature spot." Wide eyed, she looked up at Carter. "Did you have something to do with this?"

"I might have pulled a few marketing strings." He couldn't tell if she was excited or upset about the offer. Her eyes glazed over. "I'm sorry, Megan, I should've asked you first, but your website's been getting a lot of hits and..."

"And what?" she scowled.

"And I think you have the potential to take this thing big." He still couldn't read her features. "That is, if you want to," he cowered his enthusiasm to her stare.

"Thank you," she finally smiled.

His chest released the bubble of air it'd been holding. "You can always say no," he shrugged.

"Can I think about it?" Moisture rolled down her cheek and hitched itself on the top of her turned up lips. "I'm not sure I want to go big time," she tittered. "I think I'm kind of getting accustomed to this low-frills kind of life."

"Oh," Carter raised his brow. "Then I probably shouldn't give you this," he pulled another, bigger package from under the table and nestled it into his chest.

"Wow, you're full of surprises tonight aren't you?"

"On second thought," he tucked the package under his chair. "I probably ought to hold on to this one. I don't think you're going to like it after all."

"Ooh, you're a tease." She leaned across the table and planted a kiss firmly on his eager lips. "But, I love you anyway."

"Well, in that case," he pulled the gift back up to the table.

She reached across the table and pulled the ribbon. "What do you have up your sleeve?"

She nestled her manicured fingers under the side seam of the wrapping paper as he looked down the cuff of his jacket. "Nothin' but an arm," he grinned, showing her the contents of his sleeve.

"You spend far too much time with twelve year olds," she shook her head.

He pretended to be offended by the quip. "And all this time I thought this was a very grown up kind of gift."

Her brows lifted. "Grown up, huh?" she tore greedily into the package.

"So – Was I right?" He finally asked after she'd discarded the wrapping paper and stared breathlessly into the box.

"How?" Her eyes boggled. "What?" She exchanged glances between him and the red fabric. "Why?"

"Do you like it?" he asked.

She pulled the luxurious fabric from the box and touched it to her face. "I thought you said you sold it," she whispered.

"I did," he offered. "To a love-struck, backwoods carpenter and his stinky dog."

"Carter –"

"You know," he grinned facetiously, "Vera Wang – or at least the idea of it – has got to be extraordinary on you."

"But – "

He pressed his finger gently to her lips. She coddled the fabric in her fingers. "Megan," the sound of her name rolled smoothly off his tongue.

"I don't deserve this." She felt her cheeks flush as tears glazed down them. "And you can't afford it either."

"I can't afford not to."

"You're too much, Ammon Carter," she gently blotted her napkin at the tears leaking from her eyes.

"And you're beautiful," his deep voice rumbled softly under the stars.

Self-consciously she glazed her hand along the line of her newest scar.

"You know what else I think?" He pulled her hand from her face and held it softly in his.

"I'm not sure I want to," she swallowed back the unsolicited emotion.

"Well, I'm going to tell you anyway." He tilted his head tenaciously. "I think you're more radiant than any one of those stars. And it has nothing to do with the brand name on your jeans, or the color of your hair, or even those awesome red boots- although those are nice touches. It's just you. Your smile. Your laugh. Your propensity for four forked dinners." He winked his quirky, enticing smirk then continued. "I know this isn't a lot, but it means a lot to me." He pulled a small velvet box from inside his breast coat pocket and held it out across the table.

"I thought you didn't have anything up your sleeve," Megan's heart fluttered. Her cheeks warmed. She clenched her hand in his. Anxiously, she bit at her lower lip and stifled back yet another tear in her eye.

"This was my grandma's," he said cracking the box open under the candlelight.

Her hands went limp. Her heart did a double take. A tear slipped down her cheek.

"You don't like it?" The color drained from his face.

"No," she rescued her breath. "It's..." *not what I was expecting,* she wanted to say, but the look on his face told her not to. "It's beautiful."

"Let me put it on you," Ammon excitedly pulled the diamond pendant from the satin lined box and fumbled its chain nervously in his hand. She swooped her hair up and allowed him to fasten the clasp at the back of her neck.

"It's amazing," she said, touching the pendant to her chest. "Thank you."

"You're welcome," he leaned around and kissed her cheek before returning to his seat. "My grandma gave it to me before she died. She told me to save it for someone special." He smiled so proudly it melted her disappointment.

Sam and Jamison silently delivered the next round of dinner then disappeared into the trees. Megan fondled the beautiful pendant at her neck. Two fantastic courses later, the crickets serenaded as the boys brought out a couple of beautifully plated desserts. As they edged closer to the candle light, however, Megan smirked. The heart shaped cakes were definitely prettier from a distance.

"They collapsed in the oven," Carter defended.

"Good," she smirked, "I was starting to feel like my cooking abilities weren't really needed."

"I'd be lying if I told you that I prepared everything." He scraped at the clumpy frosting with his fork. "In fact," he shrugged, "other than these beautiful cakes, Ruth put everything else together."

She took a hesitant bite of the haphazard looking dessert then immediately spat it into her napkin. "Thank heavens for Ruth." She set her fork down and pushed the cake away. "You cannot do cake ever again. I forbid it."

"Okay," he agreed easily as he pushed his untouched cake away. "I think you should know that there's something else I can't do," he offered somberly.

"Oh, really? And what's that?"

He locked his eyes with hers and took her hand into his. "I can't live without you." He pulled her hand to his mouth and gently pressed his lips to it. Then, seamlessly, he slid his knee to the dirt and pulled a second velvet box out of his pocket. "Didn't pull it from my sleeve," he teasingly shook his coat sleeve.

Megan shook her head.

"Megan," he presented the box in front of her, "as much as I'd love to, I can't give you all the finer things..."

"You already have," she whispered as she threw herself into his arms. She didn't care about the tears on her face, the subsequent mascara on her cheeks, or the boys gawking somewhere in the shadows.

"You didn't let me finish," he grinned after her long kiss abated.

"Shut up," she pressed her hand to his lips.

"You don't want me to finish?" He pretended to stand.

"That's just the problem, Ammon Carter. You have so much self-control and patience – and, honestly, I don't."

He pulled her into him and silenced her rambling with the warmth of his lips. She held on tight, melting into his touch.

"I suppose I can take that as a yes," he whispered.

"Yes," she answered. "Absolutely, yes."

~   ~   ~

Megan had her dream one last time that night. But this time it was different. At the summit of her upward jump, a pair of arms reached out to her. They were large and bronze and, despite their strength, she didn't fear them. Instead, she found herself drawn to them. And them to her. She twisted her head for a peek back over her shoulder, awaiting the evil hands that in subsequent series had always stopped her progress. She was greeted only with darkness – a mass void encroaching onto itself, self-consuming, and moving away from her. She turned away from the empty space and refocused on the light. The arms reached for her again and as she fell into them she realized that she was home. Safe. Loved. Whole.

About the Author

Stephanie Connelley Worlton lives in the shadow of the Rocky Mountains where she enjoys frequent opportunities to observe nature and feed her creative spirit. Aside from the busy schedule she keeps as a wife and mother of four, she enjoys interior design, gardening, painting, carpentry, photography, and being involved with the youth of our rising generation. She has her own collection of power tools, a plethora of camera equipment, and a passion for shoes.

You can learn more about Stephanie's writing, tag-along (virtually, of course) on her family adventures, see some of her photography, and enjoy her random musings at www.stephanieworlton.com or on her blog http://stephanieworlton.blogspot.com/

www.ingramcontent.com/pod-product-compliance
Lightning Source LLC
Chambersburg PA
CBHW070859180626
46817CB00003B/841